The Labyrinth of Dreaming Books

A Novel from Zamonia by

Optimus Yarnspinner

Translated from the Zamonian
and Illustrated by

Walter Moers

*whose German text was
translated into English by*
John Brownjohn

The Overlook Press
New York, NY

This edition first published in hardcover in the United States in 2012 by

The Overlook Press, Peter Mayer Publishers, Inc.
141 Wooster Street
New York, NY 10012
www.overlookpress.com
For bulk and special sales, please contact sales@overlookny.com

First published with the title *Das Labyrinth der Träumenden Bücher* in 2011
by Albrecht Knaus Verlag, Munich

First published in Great Britain in 2012 by
HARVILL SECKER, Random House

Cataloging-in-Publication Data is available from the Library of Congress

Manufactured in the United States of America
FIRST EDITION
ISBN 978-1-4683-0126-7
1 3 5 7 9 10 8 6 4 2

Once Upon a Time

The Darkman once in olden days
did set fair Bookholm town ablaze.
The crackling flames to heaven rose
unquenchable by any hose.
Book after book to fire fell prey
until the town in ruins lay.
And yet, as year succeeded year,
Bookholm began to reappear.

Bookholmian Nursery Rhyme

A Surprise

ere the story continues. It
tells how I returned to Bookholm and descended for a second time
into the catacombs beneath the City of Dreaming Books. It tells of old
friends and new enemies, new comrades-in-arms and old adversaries.
But above all, incredible as it may sound, it tells of the Shadow King.

And of books. Books of the most diverse kinds: good and bad, live
and dead, dreaming and awake, worthless and precious, harmless
and dangerous. Books, too, whose hidden contents cannot even be
guessed at. Books which, when you read them, can spring a surprise
on you at any moment – especially when you're least expecting it.

Books like the one you are holding in your hands right now, gentle
reader. For I must, alas, inform you that this is a toxic book. Its poison
began to penetrate your fingertips the instant you opened it – tiny,
microscopically small particles of venom compared to which the
pores in your skin are as big as barn doors that permit unrestricted
access to your bloodstream. Already on their way into your arteries,
these harbingers of death are heading straight for your heart.

Listen to yourself! Do you hear your accelerated heartbeat? Do you feel your fingers tingling slightly? Do you detect the chill creeping slowly up the veins in your arms? The tightening of your chest? The breathlessness? No? Not yet? Be patient, it will soon begin. Very soon.

What will this poison do to you when it reaches your heart? To be blunt, it will kill you – end your life here and now. The merciless toxin will paralyse your cardiac valves and check the flow of your blood once and for all. The medical term for this is *infarction*, but I find *cardiac buffoonery* more amusing. You will, perhaps, have time to clutch your chest in a histrionic manner and utter a bewildered cry before collapsing, but that's all. Please don't take this personally, though. You aren't the carefully selected victim of a conspiracy. No, your murder by poisoning fulfils no purpose; it's just as pointless as your imminent death. There's no motive, either. You simply picked up the wrong book. Fate, chance, bad luck – call it what you will. You're going to die, that's all, so resign yourself!

Unless . . .

Yes, there's still a chance – *if* you follow my instructions without hesitation. This poison is a very rare contact poison whose effect is lethal only if a certain amount of it is absorbed. It all depends on how long you hold the book in your hands. The dose has been so precisely calculated that it will kill you only if you *read on to the next paragraph*! So lay this book aside at once if you consider it important to go on living! You'll experience an accelerated heartbeat for only a while. Cold sweat will break out on your brow, your slight feeling of faintness will soon subside and then you can continue your barren, miserable existence for as many hours as fate still has in store for you. Goodbye for ever!

Well, my courageous friends, we're on our own at last, for my blood is flowing in the veins of all whose hands are still holding this book. I, Optimus Yarnspinner, your true friend and companion, bid you welcome!

Yes, it was just a bluff. This book *isn't* poisonous, of course. If I really want to kill my readers, I bore them to death with 260,000 pages of interminable dialogue about double-entry bookkeeping, as I did in my series of novels entitled *The House of the Norselanders*. I find that a subtler method.

First, however, I must sort the chaff from the wheat. Why? Because we can't afford to take any ballast – any milksop readers who would tremble and lay the book aside at the very mention of danger – to the place we are bound for.

You've already guessed it, haven't you, my intrepid brothers and sisters in spirit? Yes, it's true, we're going back to Bookholm. What's that, you say? The *City of Dreaming Books* was burnt to the ground? Yes, it was indeed. It was devastated long ago by a pitiless inferno – of that, no one is more painfully aware than I. For I was there at the time. I saw with my own eyes how Homuncolossus, the Shadow King, set fire to himself and ignited the biggest conflagration Bookholm has ever undergone. I saw him descend into the catacombs like a living torch, there to unleash a firestorm that not only burnt down the buildings on the surface but ate deep into the bowels of the city. I heard the tocsins ring and saw the *Dreaming Books* reduced to sparks that danced among the stars. That was two hundred years ago.

Bookholm has been rebuilt since then. More splendidly than before, so it's said, and furnished with even richer antiquarian treasures. These are reputed to have come from areas of the catacombs inaccessible until the fire opened them up. The city is now a vibrant metropolis dedicated to Zamonian booklore, a magnetically attractive place of pilgrimage frequented by literati, publishers and printers, and one compared to which the old Bookholm would seem like a second-rate, second-hand bookshop compared to a national library. Nowadays, as if it were a completely different place, the inhabitants self-confidently refer to the city as 'Greater Bookholm'. How many fanatical bibliophiles would not be tempted to see for themselves the true grandeur and splendour of the new City of Dreaming Books that has arisen from the ashes?

11

But I myself am motivated by something considerably more compelling than mere touristic or bibliophilic curiosity. And you, my inquisitive and dauntless friends, would like to know what that is, wouldn't you? Rightly so, for from now on we shall be sharing everything: joys and sorrows, perils and secrets, adventures and vicissitudes. We're an exclusive band of brothers and sisters, you and I. Very well, I'll tell you my reason, but I'd better admit right away that what sent me off on my life's greatest adventure was nothing particularly original: merely a mysterious letter. Yes, just like before, on my first trip to Bookholm, it was a handwritten missive that started the ball rolling.

Return to
Lindworm Castle

You're welcome to pronounce me a megalomaniac for claiming that, at the time this story began, I had already become Zamonia's greatest writer. What else can one call an author whose books were being trundled into bookshops by the cartload? Who was the youngest Zamonian artist ever to have been awarded the Order of the Golden Quill? Who had had a fire-gilt cast-iron statue of himself erected outside the Grailsundian Academy of Zamonian Literature?

There was a street named after me in every sizeable Zamonian town. There were bookshops that stocked my works exclusively – plus all the reference books devoted to them. My fans had founded associations whose members addressed one another by the names of characters in my novels. 'Doing a Yarnspinner' was a vernacular expression for triumphing in some artistic discipline. I couldn't walk down a busy street without attracting a crowd, enter a bookshop without causing female members of the staff to swoon, or write a book that wasn't promptly declared a classic.

In short, I had become a conceited popinjay pampered with literary prizes and public esteem. One who had lost all capacity for self-criticism and almost all his natural artistic instincts – one who quoted only himself and copied his own works without realising it. Like an insidious mental disease of which the patient himself is unaware, success had overtaken and infected me completely. I was so busy wallowing in my own fame, I didn't even notice that the Orm had long since ceased to suffuse me.

Did I write anything of importance during this period? I don't know when I could have done so. I wasted most of my time reading from my own works in a self-infatuated sing-song, whether in bookshops and theatres or at literary seminars, after which I would get drunk on applause, condescendingly chat with admirers and sign copies of my books for hours. Alas, my faithful friends, what I then considered the zenith of my career was really its absolute nadir. Long gone were the days when I could anonymously roam a town and undertake research without being pestered. I was instantly surrounded by crowds of admirers begging for autographs, professional advice, or simply my blessing. Even on country roads I was dogged by hordes of fanatical readers eager to be there when the Orm overcame me. This happened more and more rarely at first and then not at all – and I didn't even notice because, to be honest, I could hardly distinguish between the Orm's trancelike state and a wine-induced stupor.

It was to escape my monstrous accretion of popularity, my bizarre success and my demented admirers, that I decided, after many years of restless wandering and sundry adventures, to return for a while to Lindworm Castle and rest on my laurels there. I moved back into the small house bequeathed me by my godfather, Dancelot Wordwright. I did this also – let us look the facts in the face, dear friends – in order to pretend to the public and my peers at the castle that I was returning to my roots. 'At the zenith of his career, the prodigal son returns home to augment his titanic oeuvre, humbly and unpretentiously, in the cramped little cottage that had once belonged to his beloved godfather.'

Nothing could have been further from the truth. At this period, no one in the whole of Zamonia was less root-bound than I, and no one led a more decadent, aimless existence without a care for his cultural mission and artistic discipline. Lindworm Castle was quite simply the only place that offered me perfect protection from my own popularity. Lindworms were still the sole life form permitted to dwell there. Only there could I be an artist among artists, and only Lindworms

15

observed the perfect etiquette that guaranteed each individual his privacy. Solitude was accounted a precious commodity at Lindworm Castle. All were so busy with their own literary work that no one noticed how inexcusably I neglected mine.

All that worried me, apart from the usual attacks of hypochondria, was my weight. Thanks to a leisurely lifestyle, chronic lack of exercise and hearty Lindworm fare, I had soon put on several pounds around the hips. This sometimes depressed me, but never so much that my spirits couldn't be restored by a few jam omelettes or a haunch of roast Marsh Hog. I might perhaps have ended as Lindworm Castle's fattest and loneliest writer had I not been jolted out of my lethargy by a mysterious letter.

It was on an otherwise unexceptional summer morning that my life received this jolt. As on any other day, I was sitting over an inordinately protracted breakfast in the little kitchen of my inherited

house, engaged in my customary hours-long perusal of the latest fan mail, munching chocolate-encased coffee beans and a dozen croissants filled with apricot purée. Now and again I would reach into one of the mailbags delivered every few days by the sullen postman, take out a letter, open it and impatiently scan it for the most flattering passages. I was faintly disappointed as a rule, because I always imagined such letters would be a trifle more laudatory than they already were. And so, while reading them, I would mentally replace their 'excellents' with 'historic' or 'sublime' or 'unsurpassable', then clasp them to my bosom and, with a sigh, toss them into the fire. Although I burnt my fan mail with a heavy heart, its sheer bulk would soon have driven me from house and home had I not disposed of it at regular intervals. Thus the ashes of Yarnspinner panegyrics belched from my chimney all morning, enriching Lindworm Castle's air with the perfume of my success. After breakfast I often devoted an hour or so to my new amateur hobby, playing the Clavichorgan.* I had recently taken to tinkling my own modest renditions of works by Evubeth van Goldwine, Crederif Pincho, Odion la Vivanti and other great exponents of Zamonian music. That, however, was the full extent of artistic activity in my normal daily round.

One brief moment, sometimes no longer than the bat of an eyelash, can often determine one's destiny. In my case it was the time required to read a sentence of eight syllables. My claws plucked an envelope at random from the bulging mailbag while my other paw dunked a croissant in hot chocolate and whipped cream. Ah, little letter, I thought, you'll hold no surprises for me either! I know precisely what you contain. What's the betting? An ardent declaration

---

*Clavichorgan: primitive keyboard instrument manufactured exclusively for the inhabitants of Lindworm Castle. The clavichorgan's keyboard has only twenty-four keys. Unusually wide and robust, the latter were specially designed for the Lindworm's three-fingered paw. Music of true refinement cannot be played on the clavichorgan. (Tr.)

of love for my poetry or a servile obeisance to my audacious prose style? An enthusiastic encomium on one of my stage plays or a genuflection to the Yarnspinner oeuvre as a whole. Yes, yes . . . On the one hand, this never-ending torrent of adulation bored me stiff; on the other, I'd become addicted to it, perhaps as a substitute for the Orm that had deserted me for so long.

I effortlessly succeeded in tearing open the envelope with my left-hand claws, removing the letter and unfolding it while simultaneously dunking another croissant in hot chocolate, for I had often tried this. Submitting the letter to my blasé gaze, I unhinged my lower jaw and tossed the croissant into my mouth without raising my elbow from the table. This I did with the intention of reading the first few flattering lines of my admirer's missive and simultaneously gorging myself on delicious flaky pastry. That's how low I had sunk!

'*This*', I read as the croissant disappeared between my jaws, '*is where the story begins.*'

I suppose I must have stopped swallowing at the same time as I gasped in surprise. The only certainty is that the croissant had not been sufficiently moistened, so it lodged in my gullet. The latter tightened convulsively, squeezing the hot chocolate and cream out of the pastry and pumping them upwards. My windpipe became so flooded with them, I made noises like a frog being strangled under-water. Crumpling up the letter in one paw, I waved the other futilely in the air.

Unable either to swallow or to breathe, I abruptly leapt to my feet in the hope that an erect posture would remedy the situation. It didn't, though. I merely gargled with cream.

'Aaarghle,' I went.

The blood shot into my head and my eyes bulged from their sockets. I dashed to the open window in the vain expectation of getting more air there, but I only succeeded in making more gurgling noises as I leant out. Two Lindworms who were just then strolling down the street glanced over at me.

'Aaargh!' I went, waving frantically and staring at them with bulging, bloodshot eyes. They must have assumed that this was a jocular form of salutation, because they reciprocated it by imitating my gurgling noises.

'Aaargh!' they called gaily, opening their eyes wide and waving back. 'And a very good aaargh to you, Master Optimus!'

And then they laughed.

I had become such a darling of the gods that my fellow Lindworms had taken to imitating my quirks for fear of missing out on some up-to-the-minute trend I was in the process of setting. Gurgling and laughing, they walked off down the street without paying me any further heed. The new Yarnspinnerish greeting would be bound to catch on.

Cream was trickling from my nostrils. Leaving the window and tottering back into the kitchen, I tripped over a stool, fell headlong and pulled myself up by the edge of the table. All I could now make were the sort of sounds emitted by blocked drains or trombophones. In search of assistance, my tear-filled eyes lighted upon an ancient portrait in oils of my godfather Dancelot. It stared down at me uncomprehendingly. During his lifetime Dancelot had enjoined me to eat steamed vegetables and warned me never to bolt my food. Now I was only moments from following him into the world hereafter – far too soon for my taste. My eyes bulged still further from their sockets and my senses were bemused by an irrepressible feeling of exhaustion. A strange, contradictory mixture of panic and total indifference overcame me: I wanted to live and die at the same time.

It was in this of all situations, dear friends, when I was no longer capable of rational thought, that a fundamental realisation dawned on me: my success, my meteoric career, my life and ambitions, my existing oeuvre, my literary prizes and multitudinous editions – all were outweighed in importance by a breakfast croissant. For me, the arbiter between life and death was a cheap confection of flaky pastry, a mixture of common flour, sugar, yeast and butter.

And that, despite my dramatic predicament, made me laugh. Mine wasn't a joyous, optimistic laugh, as you can imagine, merely a short, embittered 'Hah!'. It did, however, suffice to remedy the disastrous situation in my oesophagus.

For, thanks to my laughter, the croissant leapt in my throat, as it were, and headed for my stomach with renewed momentum. This time it slid down with ease and disappeared into my alimentary tract in the regulation manner. The cream flowed after it, almost clearing my airways. Having coughed and trumpeted the remainder through my nostrils, I was able to breathe once more.

'Bwaaah!' I gasped like a drowning man who has just made it to the surface. Oxygen! The best things in life are free! At once exhausted and relieved, I flopped down on a kitchen chair and clutched my chest. My heart was beating like a corps of drums. Heavens alive, I had escaped a totally ridiculous demise by a hair's breadth! That confounded croissant had very nearly ruined my biography:

'Yarnspinner chokes to death on a croissant!'

'Zamonia's greatest writer carried off by puff pastry!'

'Obese Golden Quill Prizewinner found dead in a pool of cream!'

'Heavyweight among Zamonian writers succumbs to a featherweight specimen of the baker's art.'

I could picture the headlines as easily as I could the critic Laptantidel Laptuda's spiteful obituary in the *Grailsundian Gazette*. They would have engraved a croissant on my tombstone!

It wasn't until I went to mop my perspiring brow that I realised I was still clutching the letter in my paw, claws buried deep in the paper. Curse the thing! Into the fire with it! I got up to hurl it into the fire, then stopped short. Just a moment! What were the words that had disconcerted me so? Sheer agitation had driven them from my mind. I took another look.

This is where the story begins.

I had to sit down again. I knew that sentence and so, my faithful friends and companions, do you! You also know what it meant to me, my life and my work to date. Who had written this letter? No, I couldn't afford simply to burn it, even though it had nearly killed me. I read on.

I read the letter from beginning to end, every last word of its ten closely written pages. What was in it apart from that riveting opening sentence? Well, my friends, that can easily be summarised in two words: almost nothing. Those ten pages contained almost nothing significant, important or profound.

Almost nothing, mark you.

For there was one other short sentence of note: the one that formed a postscript to the whole rigmarole. Only four words, but they were destined to turn my life completely upside down.

First things first, though. The letter dealt with a writer confronted by a blank sheet of paper and suffering from *horror vacui*. An unknown author paralysed by writer's block? What a cliché! How many letters on this subject had I received? Too many, for sure, but I had never read one that handled the basic idea with such a lack of originality and inspiration or was so plaintive and self-pitying, depressing and disconsolate. Even bleak pieces of writing can attain artistic greatness, but this one resembled the twaddle talked by a self-centred patient who happens to sit next to you in a doctor's waiting room and bores you with his trivial aches and pains. The writer's remarks revolved exclusively around himself and his physical and mental condition, his absurd problems and stupid phobias. As if they were incurable and terminal diseases, he complained of matters such as raw gums, of cutting his finger on a piece of paper, of hiccups, callouses and feelings of repletion. He railed against critical reviews of his writings, even when well-intentioned, and whinged about the weather and migraines. The letter contained not a single sentence of value, just banalities unworthy of being committed to paper. While reading it I grunted and groaned like someone toiling up a steep mountain path on a sultry midsummer's day with a rucksack full of paving stones on his back. I had never before burdened myself with – or felt so annoyed by – such reading matter. It was as if the author were clinging to my leg and being dragged across a barren, lifeless, stony desert. Words like desiccated cacti, sentences like dried-up ponds. This writer wasn't suffering from writer's block! On the contrary, he couldn't hold his pen in check although he truly had nothing whatever to say. In short, it was the worst piece of writing I'd ever read.

And then something struck me like a kick from a skittish horse: I had written this myself! I smote my brow. Of course! These were *my* style and *my* choice of words. These long, convoluted, tapewormlike sentences were *mine*. No one other than myself had written like this since I'd scaled the pinnacle of success. Here, a sentence containing seventeen commas: my syntactical trademark! There, a self-indulgent Yarnspinnerish digression on 'The Perfect Breaded Escalope of Veal'! Here, a vituperative attack on literary critics in general and their doyen, Laptantidel Laptuda, in particular! There it was, the unmistakable song of my noble pen. At that moment I realised that it was years since I'd read my texts after writing them down. Indeed, I often gave them to the printer with the ink still wet, so uninhibited was I by self-criticism. It was a long time since I'd tolerated any editing beyond underlines beneath particular sentences and marginal notes such as 'Brilliant!' or 'Inimitable!'.

And yet . . . This wasn't my handwriting. I'd never actually written anything of the kind, I felt sure. Puzzled, I read on. No, dear friends, this letter certainly wasn't my handiwork, but it could well have been, *stylistically* speaking. It clearly exemplified all my weaknesses. It even embodied the characteristic flights of hypochondriacal fancy in which I imagined myself to be suffering from diseases I alone could have devised: cerebral whooping cough and pulmonary migraine, fistulisation of the liver and cyrrhosis of the middle ear, et cetera. By the Orm, its authenticity extended even to meticulous records of body temperature and pulse rate! If it was intended to be a parody of my style, I had to concede that it was embarrassingly successful. The letter maintained its mixture of megalomania and petulance to the very end, where it abruptly broke off as if the writer had simply lost interest. And indeed, in recent times I myself had more and more often taken to ending my works in this slipshod manner.

I looked up from the letter with a groan. As a reader I felt betrayed and robbed of precious time; as a victim of parody, thoroughly seen through and humiliated. Reading the missive had taken me perhaps fifteen minutes, but it felt like a week. Did I really write such frightful, Ormless stuff? When I finally saw the signature at the end I felt like someone who, after years of imprisonment, looks in a mirror for the first time and sees his face disfigured by old age. It read:

Optimus Yarnspinner

Even my signature had been perfectly forged. I had to check several times to convince myself how well it had been imitated down to the last detail, the last flourish.

I was shocked. Could I have I written the letter after all, in a disguised hand but with a genuine signature, and sent it to myself in a fit of mental derangement? Had my authorial self detached itself and become autonomous? Had I become a victim of schizophrenia, a psychosis triggered by inordinate creativity? The possible side effects of the Orm had never been researched. Perla la Gadeon, whom the Orm had inspired more often than any other writer, had died in a delirium. Dölerich Hirnfiedler, too, was carried off by dementia and expired in his ivory tower. Eiderich Fischnertz was said to have conversed with a horse shortly before dying insane.

Was that the tribute I had to pay to my fame? Had I not shown symptoms of a split personality in my youth? I'd written a whole volume of letters entitled *To Myself*, but I'd never gone so far as to actually send them off. Heavens, my hypochondriacal fantasies were running away with me again! I definitely needed to calm down. To distract myself, I cast a final glance at the letter. Only then did I catch sight of a postscript written in microscopically small letters at the foot of the last page. It read:

PS The Shadow King has returned.

I stared at the words as if they were a ghostly apparition.

PS The Shadow King has returned.

Cold sweat beaded my brow and the letter in my paw started to tremble. Five words, twenty-four tiny characters on paper, were enough to disconcert me utterly.

PS The Shadow King has returned.

Was it a practical joke? What cruel prankster had sent me this rubbish? One of my innumerable envious rivals? A resentful colleague? One of the many spurned publishers who bombarded me with offers? A demented admirer? With trembling claws I reached for the envelope so as to read the sender's name and address. I raised the torn paper cover, turned it over, and spelt out the words like a schoolchild:

Optimus Yarnspinner
The Leather Grotto
Central Catacombs
Bookholm, Zamonia

Then I burst into sobs, and those tears at last brought me the solace my agitated mind so badly needed.

The
Bloody Book

At dawn the next morning I stole out of Lindworm Castle like a thief. I saw no one, supplied no explanations, provoked no farewell scenes – among Lindworms that was considered a courtesy, not an act of cowardice. If I say that I thoroughly appreciate sentimental scenes in literature but firmly reject them in reality, that applies to all my kind. It may be because we Lindworms can for the most part express our emotions through our literary work. In society and in interpersonal relations we're exceptionally cool, composed and courteous – indeed, almost formal. Saying goodbye, especially for a considerable period, is one of the least pleasant things a Lindworm can conceive of. I feel sure, therefore, that my friends and relations were subsequently grateful to me for sparing them the embarrassment of a farewell scene.

I walked unaccosted along the deserted, dew-damp main street that spirals down from the castle's summit to its base, passing shuttered shops in which unsuspecting Lindworms lay peacefully snoring. Having composed a brief, hexametrical letter of farewell during the night, I addressed it to the entire community by tossing it into the gutter. In so doing I was observing an ancient custom whereby departures from Lindworm Castle are poetically governed. The risk that the wind might blow my verses over the battlements of my place of birth unread, or that the ink might be obliterated by a shower of rain, was one aspect of this custom. We Lindworms may be an emotionally crippled species, but we don't lack a sense of the dramatic.

It was getting light although the sun had not yet risen. When had I last seen a sunrise? No idea! I had slept away real life for far too long already. I felt almost as I had the first time I set off for Bookholm: overweight, worn out, world-weary, and in the worst mental and physical condition imaginable, but almost childishly excited about the events and adventures ahead. Isn't that the definition of a fresh start?

Having left Lindworm Castle behind me, I traversed the barren, stony desert that surrounds it on all sides. I made my way through dense swaths of mist that looked like rain clouds fallen to earth. The sun had risen now, but it didn't warm me. Again and again I had to resist the cowardly impulse to retrace my steps and return to the safety of my native mountain, which radiated an agreeable warmth because of its volcanic innards, even in winter, and exerted the same attraction on a Lindworm as a warm stove does on a cat.

Why on earth was I going to Bookholm? The city had almost killed me once already. I was a trifle overweight, true, but I could have remedied that by dieting. I was no longer a young, twenty-seven-year-old Lindworm capable of overcoming all his existential fears with juvenile optimism. I was far too sensible for such a venture. Or should I have said, far too *old*? Over two hundred years had elapsed since my first visit to Bookholm. Two whole centuries! The very thought made me shiver even more violently.

Is there a word for the kind of mixed feelings that overcome you when you're on the verge of a long expedition but could still abandon it? Your mind seems to be split into two halves: a daring, youthful, inquisitive half, eager to break out of its wonted environment; and a mature, comfortable, risk-averse half, anxious to cling timidly to its accustomed surroundings. Shortly after I had resolved to christen this cross between excitement and loss of itchy feet *excitrepidation*, it evaporated into the fresh air with every step I took, almost like a mild headache. Had the spell of Lindworm Castle lost its hold over me at last?

But . . . Had I brought the indispensable earplugs without which I couldn't get to sleep, least of all in a strange environment pervaded by unfamiliar noises? My tablets against the acidity that assailed me whenever I drank too much coffee? Enough money? A notebook? A map, a thermometer, an address book, some throat pastilles? My monocle, some pencils, a clasp-knife, eye drops, attar of roses, burn ointment, dental floss, flavoured whiting powder for oral hygiene? When I rummaged in the numerous pockets of my cloak and my travelling bag, I found some matches, three candles, a pipe and tobacco, migraine powder, needle and thread, a tin of skin cream, some bicarbonate of soda and charcoal tablets. Ah, there were my earplugs! I also unearthed *Ringdudler's Miniature Encyclopaedia of Ancient Zamonian Literature*, some powdered ink, claw clippers, sealing wax, two erasers, postage stamps, cough drops, valerian pills, corn plasters and bandages, a pair of tweezers . . . Heavens, why would I need a pair of tweezers on a trip to Bookholm? Oh yes, at the last minute I'd fantasised about being afflicted with tiny splinters or bee stings that only a precision instrument could remove before they caused fatal blood poisoning. While rummaging I also came across a ball of crumpled paper: the letter that had prompted me to undertake this journey.

At last I came to a halt and endeavoured to calm my nerves. Yes, there was a reason for this journey: this letter, whose pages I smoothed out before refolding it. Had it come from the catacombs of Bookholm? Did it really hail from the Leather Grotto, the home of the Booklings, and did I really want to learn the truth? Nonsense! Not for anything in the world would I ever again set foot in that subterranean world. There were dozens of more compelling reasons for my journey! World-weariness, itchy feet, boredom, altitude sickness, obesity. Besides, I didn't have a single reason to return to Lindworm Castle apart from love of comfort. This wasn't a youngster's headlong flight into the unknown, as it had been once upon a time. By the Orm, I was Optimus Yarnspinner, an established author with a solid career, and I'd thoroughly reconnoitred my destination once before. What could go wrong? I had taken far greater risks under considerably less favourable circumstances. This was just a walk in the park, a biographical footnote. A voyage of exploration. A minor research trip. A change of air. A piece of fun. And this time I would substitute experience and maturity for youthful high spirits, not blunder into any old trap like the greenhorn of two hundred years ago. And what traps would await me, pray? Nobody knew I was coming and, as long as I kept the cowl of my cloak over my head, even Zamonia's most popular author could roam the City of Dreaming Books incognito and undisturbed for as long as he pleased.

Perceptibly reassured by these considerations, I stuffed the letter back in my cloak, tidied the contents of my pockets and suddenly came across *The Bloody Book*. Yes, in obedience to a sudden impulse I had packed that too. Why? Well, in the first place I wanted to take it back to the city where it really belonged. Although the terrible tome had been in my possession for two centuries, I'd never felt that it truly belonged to me. I had plucked it from

the flames and saved it from certain destruction, but did that act make *The Bloody Book* my property? I had no more claim to it than a looter who pillages someone else's house during a disaster. I hadn't even read the book, I simply couldn't! Every time I ventured to open it, the most I could do was to read one sentence – I'd read three in all – before shutting it again in horror and leaving it untouched for years.

I wanted to get rid of the accursed thing at last, but I naturally couldn't just throw it away. Immensely valuable, it came high up on the *Golden List*, Bookholm's hierarchy of precious antiquarian volumes – indeed, it was one of the most coveted antiquarian books in existence. Perhaps I would find a buyer for it in the City of Dreaming Books. If not, I would donate it to Bookholm's municipal library. Yes, that's what I would do: I would add a good deed to the other reasons for my journey. Feeling suddenly relieved, I stowed the terrible tome away once more.

The last of the mist evaporated in the midday sun, whose rays were warming my face at last, and I strode on more confidently. Travelling is no different from writing. You have to get into your stride, but once you've overcome the first few obstacles, further progress is usually automatic. Not long after Lindworm Castle had disappeared from view, my mind was inundated with ideas for short stories and poems – even whole novels. This went on all day long and I kept having to stop to jot down the essentials in my notebook. It was as if literary brainwaves had been lurking beside the route from Lindworm Castle to Bookholm, ready to pounce on a burnt-out writer and inspire him. I was soon loudly declaiming verses I had composed extempore. Alas for the poor Zamonian countryside compelled to listen to them; I must have sounded like a fugitive from a madhouse! I didn't care, though. I had made the right decision. A completely new phase of my existence was opening up ahead. Optimus Yarnspinner was rediscovering himself anew!

Even my scales were falling off! Indeed, the start of my journey had coincided with one of my periodic moulting seasons. Green hitherto, my coat of scales was bidding me farewell and being replaced by one of reddish hue. After the yellowish integument of my childhood and the greenish one of my youth and early adulthood, this was a colour appropriate to my present maturity: a positively majestic red. My new scales glittered nobly in the sunlight. When moulting was complete I would be able to dispense with skin cream for a considerable time; my new skin would gleam like polished armour. The old scales were trickling from under my clothes, only a few at first, but I knew from experience that they would soon fall off in veritable showers. Watching a Lindworm moult isn't a particularly pleasant sight, but Lindworms themselves find it a thoroughly enjoyable process. It itches a little, but in an agreeable way. It's like scratching the scab off a healed wound – all over one's body. I took this as a favourable indication of my body's consent to this journey. 'A moulting Lindworm is a healthy Lindworm,' as my godfather Dancelot used to say. In the immediate future I would be leaving a trail like a fir tree shedding its needles on the move.*

I lay down to sleep in a cool birchwood. It was only with some difficulty that I managed to kindle a small campfire, although it had once been one of the easiest procedures undertaken by an experienced rambler like myself. This was the only precaution I took against wild animals. I had packed all manner of things, but no means

---

*Scaly Lindworms: the species to which Optimus Yarnspinner belongs – moult up to seven times during their lifetime, growing scales of a different colour on each occasion. There exists a special branch of Zamonian literary criticism (dermatological Lindworm etymology), which divides the literary works of these denizens of Lindworm Castle into different periods according to the colour of their scales. If one adheres to this – not uncontroversial – form of categorisation, this marks the beginning of Yarnspinner's Purple Period. See Exegidior Fammstrudel's *The Purple Journey; Yarnspinner's Third Moult and Its Influence on His Biographical Work.* (Tr.)

of self-defence. The most dangerous weapon I had with me was a little clasp-knife. If some beast had emerged from the darkness, the most I could have done was menace it with a pair of tweezers or offer it some cough mixture.

Why wasn't I afraid? I was probably just too tired to feel frightened as well. It was ages since I had taken so much healthy exercise in a single day. I rested my head on my rucksack and eyed the shadows dancing among the trees. My improvised pillow was a trifle hard because of the *Bloody Book* it contained, but I forbore to take it out.

Witches always lurk among birch trees.

That was one of the three mysterious sentences which I'd read in the baneful tome and which kept popping into my head at the most inappropriate moments.

The shadow you cast is not your own.

That was the second.

When you shut your eyes, the Others come.

Thus ran the third.

I had opened *The Bloody Book* on only three occasions and each of these three sentences had etched itself permanently into my memory, but strangely enough, here in these unfamiliar, unprotected and assuredly not undangerous surroundings, they failed to truly frighten me for the first time ever. My enforced companionship with *The Bloody Book* had always made me feel as if I were living with a vicious, dangerous beast that might at any moment pounce on me and tear me limb from limb.

But I was now, in a sense, returning it to the wild in order to release it. That was why it no longer frightened me. Taking a wholemeal biscuit from my rucksack, I consumed it with rapt concentration. I intended to watch my diet from now on and restrict it to what my body really needed. The memories of the croissant incident still chilled me to the marrow.

A cool breeze was blowing through the birchwood. A polyphonous whisper of fallen leaves arose and my campfire blazed up anew.

The wind ruffled the treetops overhead like a child impatiently turning the pages of a big book with no pictures in it. I was reminded of the Shadow King's rustling laughter and of the childish delight in his shining eyes as he went to his fiery death. Since then, there hadn't been a day when I'd failed to think of him at least once, and while writing I'd often felt that he was guiding my paw.

PS The Shadow King has returned.

'Impossible,' I thought drowsily. 'How can someone return who has never left?'

Then I fell asleep.

In the middle of the night I woke up. The fire had almost gone out. Its embers were casting only a faint glow over my sleeping place. I listened. What had woken me?

The leaves were still rustling. Strangely, though, the wind seemed to have dropped completely. I sat up in alarm. No, it wasn't the rustle of the leaves, it was a voice! A whispering voice belonging to a living creature. I was thoroughly awake in an instant.

I peered into the darkness, trying to discern something in the dim light. My eyes accustomed themselves to the gloom agonisingly slowly. I made out some slender tree trunks, a tracery of branches and foliage – and then something that seemed to send ice water coursing through my veins. Standing between two birch trees was a figure.

Witches always lurk among birch trees, I thought.

No, that was no tree! It was a living, breathing being. Tall, thin, and almost imperceptibly swaying to and fro like the body of a huge serpent, it was whispering softly and unintelligibly.

Should I advertise my presence in a loud, self-confident voice, or keep quite still so as not to attract attention? Was it a wild beast or a rational being? A traveller like me? A werewolf? Something quite else? Was it aggressive, or even more frightened than I? Before I could think those questions over sufficiently, I found I could suddenly understand every word the faint voice was saying:

A place accurséd and forlorn
with walls of books piled high,
its windows stare like sightless eyes
and through them phantoms fly.

I knew those verses. I even knew the place they referred to, for I had been there in person. Tears sprang to my eyes. I wanted to jump to my feet and run off, but I couldn't move a muscle, I was so utterly paralysed. Through a veil of tears I dimly saw the figure leave the trees and slowly, silently glide towards me as if it needed no legs to propel it along.

Of leather and of paper built,
worm-eaten through and through,
the castle known as Shadowhall
brings every nightmare true.

The whisper was close beside my ear now and the fearsome shadow was obscuring my view so completely that all I could see was darkness. Out of this terrible, dark void came a smell at once familiar and long forgotten, a sudden smell of ancient books . . . *It was as if I'd opened the door of an antiquarian bookshop and blown the detritus from millions of mouldering volumes straight into my face.*

Only two things in my life hitherto had ever smelt like that: the unmistakable perfume of the City of Dreaming Books, the eternal aroma of Bookholm; and the terrifying exhalations of the Shadow King.

PS The Shadow King has returned.

I may not have screamed because of that alone, because it wouldn't have changed a thing. It was because a wet, glutinous tongue was touching my face and roaming over my lips and nostrils. I woke up with a start.

Dawn was already breaking and the fire had gone out. Standing over me on its slender legs and licking the biscuit crumbs off my face was a snow-white deer. When I sat up it flinched away, gazed at me with wide, reproachful eyes and disappeared among the birch trees with a few graceful, zigzag bounds. I rose from my sleeping place with a groan and shook the drops of dew off my cloak. Dreams like that, dear friends, are due penance for using *The Bloody Book* as a pillow!

The New City

It wasn't until shortly afterwards, when I left the birchwood and emerged into the open, that I saw I'd been sleeping on a hillside overlooking a grassy plain. The clear air afforded a thrillingly panoramic view of a green sea composed of pointed blades of grass waving in the wind, and of the grey expanse of desert beyond it, which stretched away to the horizon. And in the far distance, just on the dividing line between the morning sky and the earth, I could discern the unnaturally multi-coloured speck made up of the buildings of Bookholm.

I could already smell the city. Of course, that was the smell that had occasioned my nightmare! The incessant wind had carried it across the plain and up into the birchwood. I had even dreamed the words in which I'd described that unmistakable smell in my book: *As if you've stirred up a cloud of unadulterated book dust and blown the detritus from millions of mouldering volumes straight into your face.* Was there anything more alluring?

The city seemed not only near enough to smell but near enough to touch. However, I knew from my first visit to Bookholm that it would take me at least one more day's march to get there.

I drank the rest of the water in my flask at a single gulp. Unwise though this may sound, it was meant to encourage me to stride along as fast as possible all day long, for there would be nothing more to drink until I reached my destination. I was a few years older this time; if I wanted to cover the distance in the same time as before, I needed to provide myself with an incentive.

I shall spare you a tedious description of this uneventful trek, dear readers. Suffice it to say that I reached the outskirts of Bookholm just as exhausted, footsore, hungry and parched as I had been on the previous occasion. However, the prospect of obtaining something to drink there had accelerated my pace, particularly in the last few hours, with the result that I reached my destination by late afternoon.

Even from a distance I was able to marvel at the way the city had grown. It had expanded in one or two places (like me) and had also gained height. Hours before I reached the outskirts I could detect a hum like that of a gigantic beehive. It grew louder and more heterogeneous with every step I took. I could make out the hammering and sawing from carpenters' shops, the tolling of bells, the neighing of horses and the never-ending clatter of printing presses. And vibrating beneath it all was the unmistakable acoustic substratum, the hubbub characteristic of any major city, which is produced by thousands of intermingled voices and resembles the ceaseless murmur of an audience or a sluggish stream.

The buildings, of which there were two or even three times as many, were on a more generous vertical scale. Few had boasted more than two floors in the old days, whereas I could now see from afar that some had three, four, or even five storeys. Tall, slender minarets of sheet iron, chimneys as tall as trees, stone towers – none of these would have been tolerated in the Bookholm of old. No longer was this a romantic little place frequented by a surfeit of tourists, nor the antiquarian township of my nostalgic recollection, but an entirely new place with different inhabitants, visitors and destinies. I came to a crossroads where my route intersected with others. From there I proceeded down numerous little streets along which hundreds of people were streaming into the city. I now realised that, if I actually ventured into Bookholm, mine would be no sentimental journey into the past but a foray into an unforeseeable and unplanned phase of my existence. Involuntarily, I stopped short.

Was this another fit of *excitrepidation*? It was foolish to persuade myself that I could still turn back. Impossible! I was hungry, thirsty and utterly exhausted, so I would have to enter the city at least once to refresh myself and rest. I couldn't avoid spending at least one night there. In any case, why was I hesitating? I hadn't tramped this far, only to turn on my heel. Nonsense! What was making me hesitate? Was it instinct? The memory of all I'd been through after crossing the city's magic frontier once before? Undoubtedly. But it was mainly fear of the certainty that time was irrecoverable. Anyone who has entered a building he hasn't seen since his childhood or adolescence – his birthplace, school, or something of the kind – will understand that. It's a painful, melancholy experience that seems to bring you nearer the grave. On such occasions, however, things usually appear much smaller than you remember, don't they? In Bookholm, by contrast, dear friends, my memories could do more than stand the test of time: the city had actually increased in size.

'In or out?' demanded a shrill, disagreeable voice. Jolted out of my reverie, I looked round in surprise and saw that I was obstructing one of the many approaches to Bookholm, a narrow alleyway. People were squeezing past me, all intent on gaining access to the city. The voice belonged to an importunate, unpleasant-looking dwarf carrying a hawker's tray of minuscule books. I was clearly in his way.

'Oh . . . ' I said without moving.

'Well, shift yourself, Fatso!' snarled the uncouth gnome. 'This isn't the provincial dump you come from, this is Bookholm! Time is money here and money rules the book world! Shift your fat . . . '

While he was saying this, various things happened that owed more to my reflexes than to mature consideration. The gnome pushed rudely past me and prepared to storm the city ahead of us with his ridiculous tray, impatient to embark on business transactions that brooked no delay. However, my brain had not only absorbed and analysed the word 'Fatso' in a fraction of a second but devised a suitable response, which was to trip the disrespectful little creature up. He naturally hadn't known that nobody called me that without at once paying the penalty. My sense of humour deserts me on such occasions.

By the time the dwarf uttered the word 'fat' he was already in free fall. He measured his puny length on the ground and the quaint contents of his tray – nothing but books no bigger than matchboxes – went cascading across the dusty alleyway.

'In or out?' I said haughtily. 'What a question! In, of course!' And I stepped over the humiliated dwarf, treading on him with the full force of my fighting weight. Yes, dear friends, I'll even trample on a dwarf if I have to! I swaggered on down the lane without looking back, heedless of the fact that my first crossing of the city limits had coincidentally made me my first bitter enemy in Bookholm.

Noting
Without Notes

The Darkman of Bookholm had left his work undone but made a thorough job of it. That was my rather self-contradictory verdict on the city after surveying the first few streets, which were known as the *Borderlanes*. That legendary figure celebrated in folksongs and fairy tales, the wandering colossus made of blazing straw and pitch whom the more superstitious of the townsfolk still liked to hold responsible for the last conflagration, had allegedly tramped from district to district and set fire to one roof after another before burning up in the inferno himself. That was how I myself might have explained the catastrophe to a child of pre-school age, for the truth was considerably more frightening than that gruesome myth.

It wasn't true that I saw nothing I remembered. Over a third of the city had been spared from the flames and even some of the extremely combustible old buildings, with their bone-dry thatched roofs and half-timbering, had survived. The *Darkman*, who according to legend possessed neither brain nor heart, had performed his task in a correspondingly random manner: he had burned down half a street here but spared a whole district there, devastated the south as far as the city limits but scarcely touched the north, torched a huge municipal library but left the tiny antiquarian bookshop just beside it standing. The *Darkman* had raged and run riot as randomly as skin diseases spread or streams of lava ravage a mountainside. To the clangour of 'brazen bells', as it says in the poem by Perla la Gadeon, he had incinerated everything and everyone unfortunate enough to stand in his path, regardless of status or value, beauty or function.

This could be appreciated only by someone like me, who had known the Bookholm of old. To any newcomer, Bookholm was simply an exciting city filled with architectural antitheses, a curious conglomeration of old and new styles in which Early Zamonian, Dark Age and modern influences of all kinds were closely commingled to an extent found nowhere else. Quite apart from its literary and antiquarian attractions, Bookholm approximated to my personal ideal of a city more closely than ever before. Baroque diversity, creative designs so frivolous as to border on the insane, extravagant ornamentation, lopsided nooks and crannies, omnipresent historical allusions – those were the things that could delight my eye when I surveyed a city, and they were here in superabundance. Nowhere else were Zamonia's past and present crowded together in so small a space.

Even in the *Borderlanes* that enclosed the city I saw buildings composed of the most diverse minerals, metals and other materials; of red, yellow and black brick, of quarried marble, of pebble-dash, of rusty iron, of tin and gleaming brass, of sandstone and soapstone, of basalt, of granite and crushed lava, of shell, slate or fossilised fungi, even of transparent glass or amber brick, of plain mud or shards of china. Every conceivable material had been used, though wood was now extremely rare. Timber I saw on the old buildings, as before, but it had been almost eliminated from modern Bookholmian archi-tecture – one of the consequences of the fearsome inferno. For that very reason I found it all the more surprising how many of the buildings now consisted *of books*. I saw books used for walls and roof tiles, piled up into supporting columns and flights of steps, built into window seats and even serving as paving stones. Books as a building material were omnipresent in the new Bookholm, although they must have been at least as combustible as timber. How did a house built of age-old volumes fare when it rained? Didn't the paper swell? Didn't the cardboard covers disintegrate sooner or later? Were the books impregnated and hardened in some way, rendered fireproof and

45

waterproof? Well, I had neither the time nor the leisure to go into that now. The day was drawing to a close, so I deferred the solution of this mystery and hurried restlessly onwards.

I wanted to see everything at once, as if the city might once more go up in flames or sink into the ground at any moment. *Walk, pause, look* – that had always been my proven motto when travelling and in Bookholm it applied in the fullest measure. Wherever I walked or paused, there was something large or small to marvel at.

I will now, dear brothers and sisters, let you into a secret and reveal a literary technique which I call *noting without notes*. It could also, to put it rather more academically, be termed *Yarnspinnerish mental painting*. It works like this: whenever, while travelling, I get into situations in which incidents or sights threaten to overwhelm me and the normal author would automatically fish out his notebook in order to record as much about them as possible in writing, I quite deliberately refrain from making any notes or sketches. This compels my memory to perform an astonishing feat: my brain paints one *mental painting* after another. I discovered that I possessed this ability a considerable time ago, namely, when I began to write *The City of Dreaming Books*. I had no notes at my disposal because the dramatic events in Bookholm and the catacombs had given me absolutely no opportunity to make any. When I started to write, however, my mind's eye conjured up images and scenes so vivid and detailed that I might have been experiencing them all over again.

Anyone who has seen a panoramic painting – a view of a famous city or landscape reproduced with the utmost possible accuracy by a talented artist – will have some inkling of what I mean. One sector of my brain can be likened to a miniature museum in which products of *Yarnspinnerish mental painting* are displayed. They are details of landscapes and cityscapes so accurate and realistic that they are in no way inferior to the masterpieces of *Florinthian Canalism*.* Indeed, they even surpass them in one vital respect: moving objects do not remain still as they would in a painting on canvas, but are just as much in motion as the scenes that etched themselves into my retinas. I see passers-by walking past, light dancing on water, wind stirring the leaves in the trees, smoke rising, flags fluttering . . . How can this be? I don't know, dear friends. I can only construe it as a side effect of the Orm. It's a gift that I myself find rather uncanny, for sometimes, when my mind's eye contemplates the products of *Yarnspinnerish mental painting*, I feel as if I'm seeing only the surface of a gift beneath which much more may lurk – indeed, even a dark secret of some kind. It's as if I'm looking into a magic mirror that reflects a perfect likeness of my world in order to disguise the fact that a mysterious world of its own lies hidden behind it.

But now, dear friends, I shall conduct you around this imaginary museum and give you an exclusive guided tour through some of the mental pictures of Bookholm that my feverish brain produced on my first reconnaissance, for I could not, with the best will in the world, make any notes.

Mental Picture No. 1
The Borderlanes

The first curiosity that struck me in the new Bookholm was its *Gigabooks*. These monstrous replicas of ancient tomes were erected a century ago at every entrance to the city – one of the architectural luxuries it could afford thanks to its new-found wealth, I later discovered. Designed and painted by various artists, these colossal books in stone or metal leant against the walls of buildings or lay on

---

*Florinthian Canalism: an ultra-realistic style of painting traditionally practised by artists from the city of Florinth. Canalism's favourite motifs are views of the Florinthian canals and the surrounding countryside and architecture in which, as one critic jocularly remarked, 'one can make out the snot in a gondolier's nostril'. (Tr.)

the pavement, immediately suggesting to visitors that they were entering a city in which special importance was attached to the printed word and bound paper.

Ostentatious and pretentious though this may seem to some, I took to it at once because the books were very well made and conveyed a magical impression. Resembling the lost property of well-read but absent-minded giants, they attracted the attention of children in particular. One passed through them into a fairy-tale realm where different orders of magnitude prevailed – even different laws of nature, perhaps – and where things were possible of which one could only dream. What could be wrong with a city that credited the book with such importance?

The Borderlanes were the city's outer ring, a thin network of narrow alleyways that enclosed Bookholm like a porous wall. This was where one gained an initial impression of the city's architectural diversity. There was nothing of importance to be seen in other respects, however, because most of the buildings were occupied by civil servants, who also had their offices there. The Borderlanes contained no taverns or antiquarian bookshops; you went there only when you needed a new rubber stamp, a publican's licence, or a notary.

Mental Picture No. 2
The Outer Ring Road

If one compared the city to a book, the Borderlanes were the jacket and the *Outer Ring Road*, which encircled modern Bookholm inside the Borderlanes like an additional belt, could be the hard cover. Seeming at first sight to represent all that the city centre had to offer, it held the whole thing together. But here, too, the old saying holds true: *Never judge a book by its cover!*

Everything in the Outer Ring Road was new. The fire had raged here too, I discovered later, but all the streets had been levelled and rebuilt from scratch. The buildings, the shops and hotels, the smooth roadway and the well-swept pavements with their splendid mosaics depicting scenes from Zamonian literature – all looked as if they had been constructed yesterday and freshly painted today: neat, clean and displaying no trace of Bookholm's catastrophic past. This street was designed for the visitor desirous of a superficial look at the city, the merchant needing a bed for the night, or the bird of passage in search of a simple meal in an inexpensive restaurant.

The ring road housed some nice but unpretentious bookshops, very few of which sold antiquarian items, or only those that had been done up to lend them a semblance of age. It pulsated with visitors on day trips to Bookholm, tourists travelling in groups, and hawkers specialising in quick sales. The hotels and restaurants bore names like *The Silver Pen, The Empty Inkwell, The Hexameter Rooms*, or *The Old Printing House*. Most of the shops between them sold cheap souvenirs such as snowstorm paperweights containing little old Bookemistic buildings or modern books such as could be bought in any sizeable Zamonian town. You were well catered for here if you wanted a warm rug for the journey or some saddlery, a coffee or a chemist. Anyone in search of an interesting antiquarian book would have looked in vain.

The ring road was devoid of charm and bore no resemblance to the Bookholm of old, but I cannot say that my expectations were really dashed. It was practical. I quickly found a cheap hotel – *The Gilt Edge*, 'breakfast included' – in which to spend my first night, dumped my modest baggage, had a wash and hurried on. I would look around for better accommodation next day, but it was quite good enough for one night. And so, having deposited my belongings and freshened up a bit, I plunged back into the urban bustle. My fatigue and thirst I assuaged with some coffee and water from a stall, my hunger with a wholemeal biscuit and ascetic self-restraint. I was anxious to lose weight, after all.

Mental Picture No. 3
The Antique Arcades

I then turned off the ring road in the hope of soon entering the true, authentic Bookholm. I was rather disorientated, not having a street map or any other form of guide, so my route chanced to take me down some narrow alleyways and into a large square known, according to a street sign, as the **Antique Arcades**. I saw at once that it was an improvement on the Outer Ring Road. Anyone who went there was somewhat more interested in the Bookholm of old (and in books) than a hurried commercial traveller. In the centre was a marketplace with numerous stalls and booths surrounded by an oval arcade containing one shop after another. The size of a small city district, the Antique Arcades were teeming with busy people. The market sold food, basketware and pottery for the most part, but dotted here and there were tables bearing antiquarian books, ancient parchments, and tubs containing carved quill pens, ex-libris and coloured inks. There were also stallholders selling carved glove puppets and marionettes with the heads of famous authors (mine wasn't among them, fortunately!). One could buy edible insects such as the Bookholm crickets very popular with dwarfs, which were caught on the grassy plain outside the city and offered for sale live in wickerwork baskets. The desperate chirping that issued from their cages was as omnipresent and nerve-racking as the noise pollution created by the yodelling street musicians who roamed among the stalls. There were roast bookworms of various sizes strewn with curry powder or paprika, which one could nibble from paper bags, likewise poems on edible paper of various flavours and bookmarks of plaited liquorice. All in all, my feeling that I had truly arrived in *The City of Dreaming Books* was gradually gaining ground.

The maddening smells of food soon drove me out of the marketplace and into the arcades, where I scanned the little shop windows. There in the medieval vaulted gallery, which had many-branched chandeliers suspended from its ceiling, one could stroll dry-shod even in bad weather. There were a number of serious antiquarian books for sale. I spotted a misprinted edition of Yahudir Odenvather's *Out Alone*, the immortal fictional biography *The Salt Giant* by Pharlik Milpiprotz, the self-illustrated, hallucinatory poems of Wilma Kleballi, Wolberg Void's polyhistorical world history, long out of print, and right beside it a signed complete edition of Frautebus Galtev's novels – true rarities and all in immaculate condition. Here too there were shops selling carved marionettes, though of superior craftsmanship and price, also collectibles connected with printing in the most diverse ways: old spectacles and magnifying glasses, prints cut out of books and framed, bookmarks, some gilt and others of gossamer-thin ivory, expensive Bookemical preparations for treating antique leather bindings, ornately carved bookends, discarded type of boxwood and lead, ancient compositor's trays (allegedly of Nurnwood), and even complete ancient printing presses made of cast iron and brass. Anyone entering one of these shops needed to bring a somewhat fatter purse with him. But let us be honest: all these pretty things could just as well have been found in the antique shops of other big cities such as Grailsund or Florinth; there was truly no reason to travel to Bookholm for them. I was overcome by a vague feeling of disappointment. Was this the price of Bookholm's new popularity: that it would sooner or later become a city like any other, with miles of strollers' boulevards identical to others elsewhere? Was that all the progress it had made in two centuries? Covered walkways for up-market souvenir shops? Where was the old, wild, adventurous Bookholm? Preoccupied with such thoughts, I allowed myself to be swept along until I paused in front of a shop window. I couldn't immediately recognise the items displayed in it. Then I realised that they were books.

Are there really books unrecognisable as such at first sight? Clearly so in this shop, which actually specialised in them. I saw objects reminiscent at first glance of all manner of things: pyramids, sausages or accordions, but not books, my friends! Then I noticed that all these curious objects were composed of leather and paper, had printed pages, and were provided with titles and bookmarks. They *had* to be books! I even made out booklets tiny enough to fit into little glass bottles or matchboxes.

'Looking for anything in particular?' demanded a thin, bearded Druid in a linen smock, who was standing in the shop entrance and eyeing me superciliously.

'Are all of these books?' I asked stupidly, at once regretting it.

'Certainly not!' snorted the gaunt individual. 'Ordinary books are on sale everywhere. These are *Unbooks!*' He pointed to the shop sign above him.

A wise Lindworm would have terminated the conversation at that point, but I couldn't restrain myself. 'You sell books in sausage form?' I asked.

'Sausage books from a Melusinian versery in the Impic Alps,' the beanpole said haughtily. 'They're illuminated volumes of a very special kind. Air-dried for five years by Dumbdruids, they contain aphorisms by Deograzia Dottentrott. You can also buy them by the slice.'

'No thanks,' I said hurriedly. I wanted to beat a retreat, but it was already too late, the Druid had grabbed my cloak and was holding me fast. 'Do come in! I'll show you the pyramidal novels by Humidius von Quackenschlamm. They're all set in a triangular dimension.' His eyes glittered with desperation.

I suddenly got the picture: this bookseller was the victim of an imbecilic business plan, whether his own or someone else's. He was a captive in this shop filled with idiotic, unsaleable Unbooks and had only been waiting, like a starving spider in its web, for someone of my kind to come along.

'The traditional book format is doomed,' he hissed at me and I saw beads of sweat collecting on his brow. 'We deal in Unbooks of avant-garde design, circular books that can be opened like a fan! I hold the exclusive dealership for Ligoretto Loyola's accordion books!'

I felt genuinely sorry for him. He might as well have tried to sell square wheels or screws without threads and wickless candles. Why invent something completely new? These were by far the most ludicrous aberrations of the book trade I had ever seen. They would moulder away for ever in the Antique Arcades, he realised that only too well.

'The print in our Minibooks is guaranteed so small as to be illegible!' he croaked after me when I freed myself with a jerk. 'Even the editions are tiny!'

'No thanks, really not!' I called back and plunged into the stream of passers-by. I felt relieved as I was borne along, but not only because I'd escaped that pathetic dealer in crackpot editions. The thing was, I suddenly felt I had truly reached Bookholm at last. An Unbookshop for Unbooks? Nowhere else in the world could such an establishment exist! This was the Bookholm of old – or at least a pale reflection of it. All I needed to do was go on looking and I would find the real thing. I was still in the city's outer districts, after all. My hopes revived.

I strolled on, shoved and jostled by the passers-by. Thronging the Antique Arcades were hordes of visitors, groups on package tours, classes on school outings, and parents with children who seldom ventured into the more expensive shops and merely clamped their inquisitive noses to the windows. Meanwhile, the proprietors sat inside in solitary state, gazing wearily out like mournful fish in an aquarium. This was Bookholm for beginners, I told myself. I was already looking for a way out of this tourist trap when my attention was suddenly captured – and how! – by one of the figures in the crowd surging towards me. It was wearing a strange suit of armour composed of bones and a death's-head mask adorned with semi-precious stones. There was a huge gold axe hanging from its belt and a crossbow on its shoulder. Letting the crowd flow past me, I stared at it. Time seemed to stand still.

Surely it was . . . a Bookhunter! Yes! No! Yes! Impossible! My legs turned to jelly. There weren't any Bookhunters left in Bookholm, they were all dead! Bookhunting had been legally prohibited in the city since the Great Conflagration. And yet . . . That martial attire, those weapons, that frightful mask – only a Bookhunter went around like that. And the strangest thing was, he inspired no form of terror, or even respect, in anyone but me. Nobody was avoiding him and anyone who watched him go by did so with a smile or a positively benevolent expression. Indeed, even children seemed to seek his company. I saw one little girl go up to the mail-clad figure and ask him something, whereupon he paused and gently stroked her head while her parents laughed happily. Then he strode on and disappeared into the crowd. Was this a bad dream?

Jostled by someone, I lurched onwards. And then at last I grasped the truth. It was an actor! A street artist! A performer dressed up as Bookhunter! Possibly even employed by the municipal authorities to entertain visitors. Of course, that was the only possible explanation! I heaved a sigh of relief. My goodness! My knees were still trembling, my paws fluttering like dragonfly wings and my heart was still in my mouth. I extricated myself from the stream of pedestrians and paused in front of a shop window to calm down a little.

When I examined the goods on display to distract myself, I involuntarily shrank back as if I'd seen an aggressive scorpion or a huge, fat spider about to pounce. The truth was far more alarming, however, for in the middle of the display sat an *Animatome*, a live book! A creature of the catacombs! What was more, it was one of the most dangerous kind. It had just captured a rat and was pleasurably engaged in biting off its head!

I had instinctively retreated several paces from the window, so my view was now obstructed by pedestrians. Was it possible? Had my eyes deceived me? Had it happened at last? Had they caught some Animatomes in the catacombs and brought them to the surface? Were they actually being sold as domestic pets like the poisonous snakes or biting toads that were kept in vivaria by many an animal lover with curious tastes? What other explanation could there be for what I'd just seen? Or were my nerves playing a trick on me? I was still traumatised by my encounter with the Bookhunter. Cautiously, I approached the shop window once more and ventured a second look.

There was no further doubt: it was an Animatome, and it had caught a rat with its bookmarks and strangled it. Now it was proceeding to devour its prey; a pool of blood was clearly visible beneath the horrific scene.

Although the victim's head had already been bitten off, the rat's tail was still lashing around in a violent reflex. I noticed only now that the window dressing was a fairly accurate reproduction of conditions in certain areas of the catacombs, with a mossy granite floor on which ancient volumes and scattered parchments were mouldering away and bookworms crawling around. On closer inspection, however, didn't the movements of the Animatome and the rat look somehow unnatural? There, the rat's tail was swishing exactly as it had a moment ago. And the way the book swayed around on its spindly legs – wasn't it always the same? Like . . . yes, like a mechanical toy? It was then that I read one of the signs stuck to the shop window:

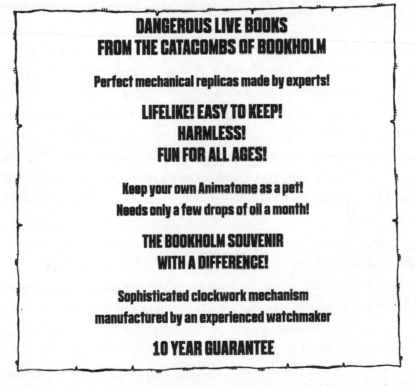

DANGEROUS LIVE BOOKS
FROM THE CATACOMBS OF BOOKHOLM

Perfect mechanical replicas made by experts!

LIFELIKE! EASY TO KEEP!
HARMLESS!
FUN FOR ALL AGES!

Keep your own Animatome as a pet!
Needs only a few drops of oil a month!

THE BOOKHOLM SOUVENIR
WITH A DIFFERENCE!

Sophisticated clockwork mechanism
manufactured by an experienced watchmaker

10 YEAR GUARANTEE

I peered into the interior of the shop. On a shelf against the wall stood dozens of little cages, each containing an Animatome. They weren't moving, though. They were waiting for a key to wind them up and bring them to temporary life like the example in the window.

They were toys! Models! Joke articles for tourists who wanted to throw a scare into their friends back home.

I subsided. By the Orm, how embarrassing! First the fake Bookhunter and now this! I'd been taken in by tourist hokum twice in quick succession. That usually happened only to village idiots from the Graveyard Marshes, I felt sure! Life at Lindworm Castle had sissified and stupefied me considerably more than I'd thought.

I leant against a pillar. I needed to compose myself, that was all. I was tired after my trek, had been subjected to a massive culture shock, and my morbid imagination had made its usual contribution. Having faced up to my colossal fears, I couldn't expect them to disperse like flatulence after a short walk. My return to Bookholm – how often had I been visited by that scenario in my dreams over the years! What nightmare scenes complete with a horrific cast of characters had my sleeping brain not conjured up! A city of blazing pitch and sulphur populated by a hundred incarnations of Pfistomel Smyke chasing me through its streets. Paper buildings printed with poems of my own that went up in smoke when touched by a ray of sunlight. Hordes of underworld insects crawling through the streets while the *Darkman* tore roofs off the houses and devoured their occupants. An inescapable labyrinth of streets with mobile walls like the passages in Shadowhall Castle and filled with bloodthirsty Bookhunters unmercifully pursuing me. I once dreamt that the city was an interminable, charred book graveyard in which I roamed in solitude as I had across the mouldering sea of paper in Unholm, the catacombs' rubbish dump. In my dreams I waded through brittle, age-old paper, forever breaking through it and sinking in. Gigantic bookcases toppled over on me and buried me beneath them, bookworms devoured me alive. My restless brain devised new tortures and ways of dying every night. Why, actually? Why isn't one master of one's own brain? Why can't one rest when asleep? Why is one so constantly tormented by absurd fears when reality tends to be peaceful and innocuous? Just imagine if real life were like our nightmares. Then teeth would suddenly sprout from our noses, we would come face to face with our dead grandmothers and the voice of our long-dead maths teacher would issue from our lips. Volcanic eruptions would be a daily occurrence and our homes would be deep in water inhabited by sharks made of bricks. That's what sometimes happens in my dreams, anyway. But real life isn't (thank goodness) as interesting and dangerous as that. Compared to our nightmares, it's safe and uneventful. There were no sharks in our living room and no more Pfistomel Smyke in Bookholm. No *Darkman* either! All that real-life Bookholm had so far had to offer in the way of threats was a mechanical toy in a shop window, an actor dressed up as a Bookhunter, and an antipathetic dwarf. I needed to relax at last.

I left the Antique Arcades and headed deeper into the city. In order to do so, I had only to get my bearings from the location of the setting sun and head north.

Mental Picture No. 4
The Ugor Vochti Shaft

The only noteworthy feature of the side streets running off the Antique Arcades was the number of shops selling marionettes and other wooden puppets. They all had literary associations and represented authors or the characters in novels. This appeared to be a new line of business in Bookholm. I came eventually to a wide, busy street, which I remembered from my first stay and which looked almost unchanged. It used to be the centre for mass bookshops that sold books cheaper by the dozen and by weight – and it still was, to judge by the hoardings. Horse-drawn carts fully laden with books trundled along the street, and hawkers and extempore poets abounded. Although this district had repelled me in the old days, it now encouraged me to hope I would yet find something of the Bookholm of old, for at least it hadn't been burnt to the ground. I continued to proceed in a northerly direction and was nearing a crossroads when I noticed that the pavement had given way to a boardwalk that creaked and groaned beneath my feet. This was an unusual sight in modern Bookholm. Combustible building materials like timber were only sparingly employed and looked positively old-fashioned when used for pavements. On reaching the crossroads I still saw pedestrians but no vehicles of any kind. In the middle of the intersection was a deep, balustraded pit with the boardwalk running round it. A huge pit in the middle of a crossroads? A surprising sight, my friends! I joined the spectators who were crowding up against the balustrade. Sure enough, there was a crater at least fifty or sixty feet across, lined with timber and so deep that the bottom was out of sight. There were even several flights of steps – many of timber, others of iron – leading down into it. People were climbing up and down them as if this were a thoroughly everyday activity, but to me it resembled one of the absurd scenes in my nightmares.

'What on earth is *that*?' I blurted out.

'It's the Ugor Vochti Shaft, you stupid clot,' said a passer-by. 'Use your eyes.'

I looked up and saw a sign inscribed in handsome calligraphic script. It read:

The Ugor Vochti Shaft

This was really something new, my friends! I was naturally familiar with Ugor Vochti's name. He was a classical exponent of Zamonian literature and had written several genuinely good novels. But why 'shaft'? I had never heard of any 'shaft' in Bookholm. I felt so stupid and provincial, I didn't dare ask any more questions.

I looked down once more. A timber-lined shaft leading down into the ground? What, pray, could its purpose be? Where did it lead to?

Nearly all the descending or ascending figures had lanterns, candles or torches with them. Right at the bottom I could make out tiny specks of light dancing around. What were those people doing down there? Was there something worth seeing? Leaning further over the balustrade, I was suddenly smitten by a gust of air coming straight from the bottom of the shaft. I recoiled as if struck by a fist, staggered backwards into a group of passers-by and apologised, then stood there, swaying, and pulled myself together. It was the smell of the catacombs that had so unexpectedly assailed me with all its might: microscopically fine book dust, the exhalations of algae and fungi, stagnant water and decay. That was how it smelt in the darkness beneath Bookholm! I felt dizzy, but my nausea luckily subsided as quickly as the smell evaporated.

A few pedestrians tittered at my behaviour and I earned the sort of pitying glances usually reserved for drunks. Heavens, I was once more behaving like a country bumpkin on his first visit to the big city! I debated with myself, but only for a moment. Some inner voice sternly forbade me to take another look down the hole. I could discover what it was in due course. Get out of here, I told myself. I took the next turning and strode swiftly along the boardwalk until I felt solid paving stones under my feet once more.

This is where our visit to the museum of *Yarnspinnerish Mental Painting* ends, dear friends, and another – probably more objective – form of Bookholmian reportage begins. I hope, however, that our brief tour has helped to make the state of acute bewilderment provoked in me by such a barrage of new impressions a little more comprehensible. One thing, at least, was clear: I couldn't go on like this. I was running around like a headless chicken. What I badly needed was some reliable information, possibly a well-written tourist guide or something of the kind. Without more ado I went over to the nearest bookshop and peered through the window. Did they sell tourist guides? Street maps? Bookholm regionalia? A list of hotels wouldn't come amiss either, because it was time I worked out where to stay for the next few days.

There was a loud rustling sound behind me and something plucked at my cloak. 'Hello?' said a piping voice. 'Hellolioli? Care for a Live Historical Newspaper?'

All in Gothic

I turned to look. Standing behind me in the dusty street and rudely tweaking my cloak was a dwarfish figure entirely encased in strips of newsprint – indeed, he looked like a newspaper on legs that had been run over and reduced to tatters.

Curious sight though this was, it took me aback for only a moment because I well remembered the so-called Live Newspapers from my first visit to Bookholm. They were smart, nimble little gnomes – journalistic errand boys, so to speak – who professionally disseminated the tittle-tattle of the cultural scene. I recalled that you could, for a small fee, tear the strips of newsprint off the gnomes and read them. They carried items such as:

Shock in the summerhouse! Mimolette van Bimmel swoons after completing her novel 'The Yawned-Away Year'! Will she ever be able to write again?

Or:

Radiolarius Runk in punch-up with Vartok Smetterling at the 'Golden Quill'! Rival authors accuse each other of plagiarism and alcohol abuse, then celebrate a liquid reconciliation!

Or:

Relief in the summerhouse! Mimolette van Bimmel able to write once more! Having recovered from her fainting fit after two days, she has embarked on her new bodice-ripper, 'A Candle Underwater'!

Recalling this, I said to the gnome:

'No thanks, gossip doesn't interest me.'

He glared at me indignantly.

'Me not gossip!' he said in a trembling voice. 'Me *Live Historical Newspaper*! Tested by Bookholm Tourist Association! All in Gothic!'

All in Gothic? I noticed only now that several tourists in this street were being followed around by similar little fellows attired in newsprint. The gnomes were reading aloud from their strips of paper.

'Live Historical Newspaper?' I demanded suspiciously. 'What does that mean?'

'Aah!' The little creature's eyes lit up and he abruptly dropped his affronted tone of voice. 'New in city? All clear! You want me explain?'

'Yes please,' I said, nodding. 'I want you explain.'

'Live Historical Newspaper new service in Bookholm!' he said eagerly. 'We walk along together. You ask, I read answer from old newspaper. One street one pyra, six streets five pyras, twelve streets nine pyras. Not satisfied, money back.' He handed me a sample strip torn off his paper costume. It was tomorrow's weather forecast, duly printed in Gothic script. Rain was predicted in the afternoon.

'We walk?' asked the gnome, rustling his sheets encouragingly. I thought for a moment. Not a bad deal, actually. A smart idea for conveying information at an acceptable price. Or would it be too embarrassing to walk the streets with a gabbling dwarf in tow? Would I be branding myself an idiotic provincial tourist like the people who made spectacles of themselves in Florinth by being chauffeured around in bridal carriages or gondolas? On the other hand, I could see any number of tourists accompanied by Live Newspapers and no one looked twice at them. The alternative would be to wander around for days engaged in guesswork, studying expensive tourist guides and pumping local inhabitants.

'All in Gothic!' the dwarf said again, almost pleadingly. Silly as it may sound, my friends, that statement somehow clinched it for me! Gothic is to typography what half-timbering is to architecture, so to speak. Both convey a certain antiquity coupled with sound crafts-manship and timeless durability. Gothic inspires confidence. What the hell, I said to myself, it's worth trying.

'Very well,' I said graciously. 'I'll try a *Live Historical Newspaper* for once. Do I pay now or later?'

'Later, please,' the dwarf cried happily. 'Not compulsory, but tips accepted. If satisfied!'

'I understand,' I said. 'Payment in arrears, but for that you expect a bit more, eh?' Well, that wasn't a bad business principle. If he meant to take me for a ride he'd have pocketed the money in advance. Good for modern Bookholm! Even the tricksters were more trustworthy than of old. Or smarter, at least.

'Live Historical Newspapers steadily gaining popularity!'

the dwarf suddenly proclaimed, reading aloud from one of his strips of paper with a surprising absence of regional accent and grammatical errors. '"The new form of tourist guide is becoming more and more widespread in Bookholm. Its curious mixture of local and historical information and lively conversation is going down well with visitors, says UNKO VAN PAPPEL, the Tourist Board spokesman. For a small charge the visitor not only receives factual information purveyed by respectable journalists but is also guided safely through the city with no risk of being swindled. The number of Live Historical Newspapers has risen by seventy-five per cent within the space of a year."'

All right, first a little self-promotion. That was permissible, but now I wanted to put my vertically challenged guide through his paces. Looking around for some notable feature in the vicinity, my eye lighted on a remarkable building distinguished not only by its size but by a truly noteworthy architectural peculiarity: one section of it projected high into the sky on metal stilts. I had already been struck that day by several buildings of similar construction.

'What's that?' I asked, pointing to the curious edifice. 'Can you explain?'

The dwarf rummaged self-importantly among his galleys. Then he found what he was looking for.

'"Bookholm's First Aerial Library Inaugurated!"'

He read out the headline very loudly, then lowered his voice a little. '"Barely a year after the Great Conflagration, the first house to be equipped with a so-called aerial library has been inaugurated in Urinoscopic Avenue."'

Urinoscopic Avenue? I had just read that name on a street sign. It felt strange somehow, suddenly finding myself in the midst of a newspaper article.

The dwarf read on: '"Speaking at the ceremony, the proud architect, SULIBRAT UHU, stated that 'aerial library' is a misleading description. 'That part of the building in which a valuable library is housed can, in the event of fire, be cranked into the air by means of a cable mechanism which, despite its complexity, even a child could operate with the aid of a simple flywheel. The precious volumes are thus so far from the ground that even the most disastrous conflagration cannot reach them. The stilts are made of fireproof steel."'

The gnome held up another strip of paper.

'"Aerial Libraries – Bookholm's Latest Fashion!"'

he read. '"Houses on stilts are the latest architectural fad in our city – but only, of course, for people who can afford them, because those who acquire a crankable library must have deep pockets! This is why architect SULIBAR UHU, who specialises in this form of construction, has a clientele currently restricted to wealthy book collectors, successful authors and big-time publishers. It's said that Uhu has just been commissioned to design aerial libraries for the popular cookbook author GLUTTONIUS GLOD ('Fine Dining on Labyrinthine Algae' – 'Dishes that Glow in the Dark') and his agent and publisher COUNT MAXIMILIAN PELTRADO. Whether these fireproof buildings actually enhance the appearance of our city is another matter. Neighbours complain that the owners of aerial libraries crank them into the air at every opportunity, even when there's no risk of fire, and thereby obstruct their view – purely to show off."'

'Thanks, that'll do,' I called over my shoulder. 'I get the picture.'

My Live Historical Newspaper stowed his article away as we continued to stroll along the street. I noticed that the dwarf seemed to be imitating the way I walked. He was following me like a little shadow – like a shrunken caricature of myself. If I walked slowly, he slowed down too. If I speeded up, so did he. Eagerly, I looked around for some other sights to question him about, because this business was beginning to amuse me. Being unable to discern any particularly noteworthy building at that moment, however, I asked my guide about something else that had aroused my curiosity.

'Why have all these books been used as building materials? One building in five seems put together partly out of books. How can that work? They're only paper and cardboard and a bit of leather at most.'

The gnome came to a halt, raised one hand and rummaged in his chaotic archives with the other. Then he brought out a piece of paper.

'"Immense Deposit of Petrified Books Discovered in the Optimus Yarnspinner Shaft!"'

he cried.

I was surprised for three reasons. First, because these books consisted of stone. Second, because there appeared to be another of these mysterious 'shafts' in Bookholm. And finally because I was naturally amazed that one of them bore *my* name.

'What?' I broke in. 'You mean there's a—'

The gnome stopped short. 'Me read on?' he asked. 'Or another question?'

'No, no,' I said. He was right. First things first. 'Read on by all means!'

He cleared his throat. '"**City Hall announced yesterday that a copious**

71

deposit of fossilised books had been discovered during clearing-up operations in the Optimus Yarnspinner Shaft. Ancient tomes of immense age and hitherto unknown provenance, they are presumed to have been exposed to a rare petrological process that has also been observed in trees and whole forests.

'"PROFESSOR FERRUGINUS SCREE, a geologist at Bookholm University, explained this phenomenon to your correspondent as follows: 'When books are embedded in mud by subterranean floods, the natural process of decay can be considerably slowed by the removal of oxygen. If silicic acid seeps in through the groundwater, quartz deposits itself in the books' cavities. This, when combined with exposure to great pressure, can result in the formation of quartz books resembling marble or similar minerals in texture and appearance.'

'"The authorities are as yet unable to reveal what is to be done with this deposit of quartz books."'

The dwarf produced another galley.

'"Quartz Book Deposit Released for Use as Building Material!"'

he declaimed. '"After intensive research by the geological department of Bookholm University, the mayor's office has decided that the rich deposit of quartz books found in a lateral branch of the Optimus Yarnspinner Shaft (as we reported) shall now be released for use as a building material free of charge. 'The universal shortage of building materials occasioned by the Great Conflagration,' Mayor HEMATITUS HEMO personally announced, 'coupled with the scientific discovery that the process of petrification has deprived the fossilised books of all their ability to transmit information – and thus their status as antiquarian treasures – allowed of only this conclusion. The petrified books make excellent ashlars and roof tiles. They also look extremely handsome and are quite in keeping with the general character of Bookholmian architecture.'"'

The gnome unearthed yet another galley.

"'Quartz Books Used as Building Material Promote the City's Architectural Development!'"

he crowed. "'The official release of excavated quartz books for use as a building material has led to record building activity, particularly in districts surrounding the Optimus Yarnspinner Shaft. The local builders' association has announced that the use of quartz books, especially for libraries—'"

'All right!' I broke in. 'So the things are fireproof, I get it. Waterproof, too. That's all I wanted to know.'

My Live Historical Newspaper obediently fell silent and stowed his galleys away. Quartz books, well, well. So the catacombs were still full of undiscovered marvels and treasures. Any other city would have made a big song and dance out of this find, which was one of nature's miracles, whereas here it was disposed of as a building material!

We walked on in silence for a while, then turned down an alleyway and eventually reached a small square where the dwarf came to a sudden halt and solemnly announced: 'We come now to older districts. Here Revolution Square. Here Naborik Bigosu burnt to death.'

I looked around. The little square made an inconspicuous impression and contained no shops. Some of the buildings surrounding it were Buchting Brick Gothic, others in the rusty Ironvillean Heavy Industry style or in frivolous Florinthian Baroque – the usual picturesque architectural farrago, in other words, and interspersed with quartz-book brick, which I was beginning to like more and more.

'Narobik Bigosu?' I asked my guide. 'Never heard of him. Was there a revolution in Bookholm? Really? What kind?'

He rummaged among his papers and held a galley up to the light.

"'From Prohibition to Revolution.
A Historical Summary to Mark the
Two-Hundredth Anniversary of
the Bookholm Fire Revolution,
by HEMLO DRUDEL.'"

The gnome looked at me with his head on one side. 'Read you?'

'By all means,' I replied. 'Sounds interesting.'

'"The prohibition of fire is one of the darkest chapters in recent Bookholmian history,"' he began. '"In hindsight it seems almost inconceivable that a genuine attempt was made to ban the lighting and use of fire in Bookholm, yet it really forms a part of the city's history. That it happened shortly after the last conflagration, and was attributable mainly to the ambition of certain reactionary Bookemists, may render it somewhat more comprehensible, but far from entirely so. Bookholm's population was in a hopeless, aimless state of mind, the political situation anarchic, the city administration completely paralysed. Conditions were so chaotic that a group of fundamentalist Bookemists under the leadership of the charismatic antiquarian, astronomer and alchemistic charlatan NABORIK BIGOSU (an adherent and former adviser of PFISTOMEL SMYKE, incidentally) was able for the space of a year to establish an Ugglian regime in Bookholm that was not only medieval in character but devoid of any legal foundation."'

'This really happened?' I exclaimed. 'Here in Bookholm?'

The dwarf just glanced at me and read on. '"In the course of this short-lived Bookemistic dictatorship it was strictly forbidden (only one of a series of equally bizarre prohibitions) to light any kind of fire within the city limits, whether on an open hearth or inside a stove or even in the form of a candle flame. Quite simply, the Bookemists proclaimed that this natural element was an addictive drug whose use led ultimately to destruction – a contention for which the recent conflagration naturally provided a convincing argument. The city's inhabitants were still so traumatised by the event that they gratefully accepted anything that promised them protection from another inferno, so what could be more obvious than simply to ban fire itself?

'"After the fire ban had come into force in the spring of that year, Bookholm swiftly reverted to a condition of almost Stone Age barbarism. Without light there was little protection from wild beasts at night, and it was, of course, impossible to boil water and kill bacteria in foodstuffs. Wolves and bats descended on the city in the darkness, rats and other vermin crawled out of the catacombs, and diseases of all kinds proliferated on an epidemic scale. The unsterile conditions had a disastrous effect on public health."'

The gnome turned over the sheet and read the rest of the article on the back.

"'The totalitarian Bookemists suffered least of all,'" he went on, "'because they had claimed the best and safest of the surviving houses for themselves and controlled the city's food supplies, which they allegedly had to submit to alchemistic spells. Many a Bookholmer reported on the quiet that he had often noticed smoke rising from the Bookemists' chimneys, seen candlelight in their windows and smelt burnt fat. When the winter of this darkest of all years finally arrived, the Bookholmers' endurance was put to the hardest test in their history. Notwithstanding, some of them had to perish of cold before even the most obtuse of the city's inhabitants grasped that civilisation without fire was a lethal misconception that had to be ended at once. And that was how the Fire Revolution of Bookholm, whose centennial we celebrate today, eventually came about."'

The dwarf drew a deep breath.

"'If an individual lights a prohibited fire, he is easily identified and punished, but if everyone lights a fire at once, punishment is impossible. The basic idea underlying any revolution is that the oppressed must rebel collectively, not individually. That was what happened on that memorable winter's night in Bookholm. Fire after fire was lit until the whole city was bathed in a flickering glow that was eerily reminiscent of the Great Conflagration. This time, however, the flames served to cure the city, not destroy it. In the end the townsfolk built a bonfire on which they cooked their first hot meals for a long time. For reasons of journalistic accuracy it should be noted that the fuel with which they stoked this bonfire included their temporary overlord, Naborik Bigosu. Having mentioned his name, however, let us strike it from our records for ever. That was the end of traditional Bookemism in Bookholm. We do not know where the surviving Bookemists disappeared to because the city's inhabitants preserve a stubborn silence on the subject. It is, however, reported that many hot meals of fresh meat were cooked over campfires that night – and this although meat was in extremely short supply . . . "'

The gnome ended his reading, folded up the article, stowed it away and looked at me expectantly like a dog waiting for another stick to be thrown.

This was all entirely new to me, dear friends, but it naturally wasn't the kind of story the city's Tourist Board could have used as an advertisement for the warm-heartedness of its inhabitants. So we strolled on, my Live Historical Newspaper mutely rustling along at my heels and I myself lost in dark thoughts about the account I'd just heard. What other events in Bookholm had escaped me thanks to my mulish ignorance? Such gaps in my knowledge were thoroughly embarrassing. After all, I'd written a book about the city!

Hearing a series of creaks and groans underfoot, I glanced down to find myself treading on planks again. It wasn't until I looked along the street we were traversing that I saw its pavement had given way to the same sort of boardwalk I'd seen running around the mysterious Ugor Vochti Shaft.

'What's that?' I asked.

'Oh,' said my guide, 'that just the Optimus Yarnspinner Shaft. Over there by crossroads.'

'Really?' I replied, startled but wary. I couldn't afford to let the cat out of the bag if I wanted to preserve my incognito. 'The, er . . . Yarnspinner Shaft?'

'You know who Optimus Yarnspinner?' asked the dwarf.

'Er . . . no,' I lied.

'Not important,' the dwarf said dismissively. 'Not any more. Silly ass now. Was good, now bad – no more Orm. You want me read lousy review of Yarnspinner novel?' He rummaged in his archives.

'Er, no thanks!' I said quickly.

'But is *good* lousy review! Is by Laptantidel Laptuda.' Disappointedly, he put the galley away.

'I'd sooner hear about these so-called shafts,' I said in an effort to change the subject. We had now reached the crossroads. There, going down into the ground like the Ugor Vochti Shaft but considerably smaller, being only a few metres in diameter, was a timber-lined shaft equipped with flights of steps. There, too, the aperture was encircled by a balustraded boardwalk with numerous people walking around it, among them many tourists accompanied by Live Newspapers.

'Shafts?' asked the gnome. 'You want me explain?'

I nodded. 'Yes, I want you explain.'

'In that case,' the gnome muttered, 'I go further back.'

He burrowed deep into his strips of newsprint. 'Here! Very old article! Just after fire!'

"Mysterious Shafts Yield up Their Secrets!"'

he cried dramatically. '"With preliminary clearing-up operations after the recent disastrous fire still in full swing, mysterious finds beneath the smoking rubble are giving rise to speculation. There is talk of shafts in the ground, some only a few feet across but others considerably larger and capacious enough to swallow a whole city block. According to eyewitness reports, these shafts lead deep into the Labyrinth but cannot yet be explored because they are either ablaze or at least smouldering dangerously. Experts assume that they are parts of the catacombs broken open and laid bare by the fire."'

He produced another galley.

"The First Shafts Explored. Captain of Bookholm Fire Brigade Missing!

'"Now that the last fires have been extinguished, the mysterious shafts created by the conflagration (as we reported) can be examined more closely.

Preliminary research has revealed that they probably resulted from a series of physical phenomena. When burning buildings on the surface of the city collapsed, some of the rubble pierced the ground and created new entrances to the Labyrinth. Oxygen and gases escaped from these entrances – or air and fire were sucked into them – with the result that tunnel fires of immense destructive power broke out and bored into the earth's interior like fiery spears of enormous length. Once the flames had penetrated the Labyrinth they found plenty of fuel there. The chain-reaction fires that resulted ate deep into the catacombs for many miles.

'"In the course of a preliminary exploration of one such shaft in Editorial Street, which is totally gutted, a young and audacious fire chief ventured into it for several feet and has (as we reported) disappeared without trace. Sundry attempts to bring him to the surface by lowering ropes and chains proved fruitless, nor did he respond to persistent calling and knocking. He is now assumed to be a tragic fatality."'

I signed to the dwarf to pause for a moment. I needed to digest this information first! So there were a whole series of these so-called 'shafts' in Bookholm. How many in all? And why was my shaft smaller than Ugor Vochti's?

'Please go on,' I said.

He went on:

'"Locals have given the new phenomena a name. The 'Bookholm Shafts' are born!

'"The burnt-out tunnels that have created new entrances to the Labyrinth have at last acquired a name. Having quickly become known in the vernacular as 'Bookholm Shafts' (on account of their shaftlike conformation), this somewhat unscientific but popular neologism has been added to its geological vocabulary by Bookholm University and is thus in common parlance."'

'Oh, me got many articles on shafts . . . Many . . .' muttered the gnome, foraging for more information. He held up another galley. 'Me fast-forward!

'"The 'Bookholm Shafts' are stabilised!"'

he cried. '"The 'Bookholm Shafts', so often a current topic of conversation, have in recent days (as we reported) been more thoroughly explored and stabilised. Buttresses have been installed and concrete foundations poured, steps and ladders erected and the areas around the entrances secured with balustraded walk-in platforms. Entering these shafts no longer presents any real danger, though few people have so far been permitted access. The official long-term aim is to render the 'Bookholm Shafts' accessible to all."'

I raised my paw. 'You mean you never even tried to fill these things in? You actually *developed* them for opening to the public?' I was horrified.

The dwarf merely glared at me. Interjections clearly displeased him.

'"Bookholm Shafts Given Individual Names!"'

he read on defiantly. '"The Bookholm Shafts have been officially declared urban thoroughfares ~ in administrative terms, streets. This, in turn, has confronted the local government authorities with the task of giving them names. They have resolved, as in the case of many of our streets, to name them after well-known authors. But which shaft will get which author's name? This is still undecided and is bound to cause fierce controversy in the immediate future. We can hardly wait to hear which authors are assigned a Bookholm Shaft. The issue will certainly give rise to heated arguments."'

It certainly would! I really couldn't see why the Optimus Yarnspinner Shaft was smaller than the Ugor Vochti Shaft. Vochti had written a few reasonable poems, but his entire prose output consisted of dusty old, deservedly forgotten novels. However, I kept these thoughts to myself so as not to confuse my guide. He was performing his task extremely well, though I could only shake my head at what had been done about those holes in the ground. To me they still seemed like gates of hell from which the apocalyptic hordes of darkness might burst forth and ravage the city, but the sole concern of Bookholm's inhabitants seemed to have been whether to name one shaft after Orca de Wils or another after Balono de Zacher. That was pretty casual of them.

'"Aleisha Wimpersleake Shaft Ceremonially Inaugurated!"'

declaimed the dwarf as if he'd read my thoughts.

'"The first Bookholm Shaft has at last been given its official name! It was no great surprise to learn that the chosen name was that of Aleisha Wimpersleake, the classic of classics, the bedrock of Zamonian literature. Nor was it any surprise that the largest of the new entrances to the Labyrinth has been named after him."'

In the old days most of the entrances to the catacombs had been anxiously walled up and access to them left to Bookhunters, adventurers, lunatics and suicides, whereas entering them today appeared to have become a kind of popular, happy-go-lucky sport. Here, too, I saw cheerful folk armed with torches and picnic baskets descending the steps into the Labyrinth as if they were going down into a wine cellar. They would once have prefaced such a descent by making their wills and embracing their nearest and dearest.

'And have there never been any problems with these, er . . . holes over the years?' I asked my gnome mistrustfully. 'No unpleasant incidents?'

'Oh, yes!' he said. 'Sometimes. Shafts always good for headlines. Here . . .' He brought out another galley.

'"Kackertratt Invasion from the Perla la Gadeon Shaft Controlled!

'"Kackertratts, some the size of loaves of bread, have in recent months been discovered in bookshops around the Perla la Gadeon Shaft, often by horrified customers and to the chagrin of the proprietors. Experts assume the cause to be so-called 'Wandering Fires', or mobile subterranean hot spots where embers have continued to smoulder since Bookholm's Great Conflagration and periodically burst into flames once more. 'Driven from their natural habitat, the Kackertratts reach the surface,' explained catacomb entomologist **PROFESSOR GOBORIAN CHITIN** of Bookholm University. 'They then instinctively seek out conditions like those in their subterranean home – and these are often found in bookshops.'

'"The Kackertratt traps installed in bookshops tended to frighten their customers even more, however, as anyone can confirm who has seen a Kackertratt the length of his arm uttering shrill sawing sounds as it dies in agony. What was more, small domestic animals such as cats and dogs also wound up in those barbaric contraptions.

'"Help was eventually provided by the Bookholm Fire Brigade, which, in cooperation with experienced pest controllers, sprayed the floor and walls with an effective insecticide. Since then there have apparently been no further complaints about huge insects – not, at least, outside the Toxic Zone.'"

Bookholm Shafts! Wandering Fires! Toxic Zone! I was beginning to grasp the *Live Historical Newspapers'* subtle business principle: one answer always led to the next question and one article to another, so we could have gone on like that to all eternity. Meantime, however, I had been overcome by travel lag. How long had I been on my feet? It was getting dark. Lights were coming on in houses, candles being placed in shop windows. Rather than listen to any more articles on the history of Bookholm, I felt like repairing to a tavern for a short rest.

'You interested in Toxic Zone?' enquired the gnome. 'Me not got much in archives, but colleague over there! He specialist in Toxic Zone! He authority! All in Gothic!'

Before I could do anything, he had beckoned his colleague over. In a trice, more Live Newspapers had converged from all directions and surrounded us. I felt like one of those idiots in Florinth's celebrated Pigeon Square who scatter some birdseed and are then surprised to be almost eaten alive by the creatures.

'Wandering Fires?' cried one of them, rustling his paper attire. 'Me got all about Wandering Fires! You need info? What date? What shaft?'

'Toxic Zone?' cried another. 'You need info? Me got five hundred articles about Toxic Zone! All in chronological order! All in Gothic!'

A babble of voices ensued.

'Bookholmian Puppetism? You interested Bookholmian Puppetism?'

'Influence of Ironvillean Heavy Metal architecture on Bookholm townscape? Me expert! Three hundred articles! All in Gothic!'

'Like hear articles on Biblionauts? Need information? Me got everything on Biblionauts!'

'Want lousy Yarnspinner reviews? Me got all lousy Yarnspinner reviews in order of titles!'

I hurriedly paid my gnome the agreed sum, added a generous tip and bade him farewell. Then I tried to shake off the other Live Newspapers by walking away fast. When they finally grasped that they wouldn't get anything out of me, they all came to a halt but continued to cry their specialised wares.

'Questions about Magmass? Need info? Everything about Magmass!'

'Pfistomel Smyke – legend or reality! All articles! Everything about Smyke!'

'Ugglyism in Bookholm – curse or blessing? Everything about Ugglies!'

I dived into the crowd and let myself be carried along. At that moment my 'need for info', whether in Gothic or some other type-face, was more than satisfied. The only unanswered question that still exercised me, dear friends, was what a Live Historical Newspaper looked like under its paper clothing.

Ovídios

Reaching a street corner, I paused to ponder on an important decision. I had come to Bookholm to change my life, including various bad habits of which I wanted to rid myself: lack of exercise, for example, which I had already tackled by undertaking this trip; an unhealthy diet, which I was combating with the aid of abstinence and wholemeal biscuits; and the social isolation of Lindworm Castle, which I was exchanging for a sojourn in a vibrant city. Even though my social contacts were still limited, I had at least trampled on a dwarf! I was on the right path.

Now I wanted to combat another vice. The fact was, I had for hours felt an urgent and familiar desire to smoke a nice, big pipe of tobacco. I was going to yield to it once more. Yes, dear friends, this was a historic moment: I had decided that it would be the last pipe of my life! Being a hypochondriac who had always derived more anxiety than pleasure from that bad habit, I had steadily reduced my tobacco consumption over the years. I now proposed to give up the weed for good, and what more suitable place to do this than Bookholm, a city in which smoking was more frowned on than in any other?

That was just the problem, though. Where could I smoke in peace? Smoking in public was strictly prohibited – there were signs to that effect all over the place. Nevertheless, I had spotted a few little tobacco shops here and there and had definitely caught a whiff of pipe and cigar smoke, although I'd seen no one smoking anywhere in town. So where could one yield to the vice in peace? It was a mystery. Should I simply ask? *Tell me something, madam: Where can one have a quiet smoke?* That sort of thing? I would have felt uncomfortable, like a drug addict enquiring the way to the nearest illegal pharmacy, whereas all I wanted to do was *stop*!

I roamed around aimlessly for a while until the craving became too much for me, as it usually did when I was obsessed with something I oughtn't to do. I wanted to smoke! At once! Here! Definitely for the very last time but right away! Eventually I looked for a quiet corner. I sneaked into a courtyard and sheltered from the wind in the rear entrance of a print shop that had gone out of business. I looked around. No one nearby. I felt in my pockets for a pipe and tobacco. Found them both. Filled the pipe. Looked around again. I was alone. Good! In that case . . . I was just about to strike a match when I felt something heavy and powerful descend on my shoulder.

Startled, I spun round and found myself confronted by the bared teeth of a full-grown Wolperting. I recoiled a step and shook off his paw. Where had *he* sprung from? Thin air? Had he simply materialised? I knew that superstitious folk credited Wolpertings with such abilities.

'Smoking in public is prohibited in Bookholm, my friend,' he said quietly in a deep, calm voice. He was around a head and a half taller than me and resembled a bulldog in appearance. His clothing was all of brown buckskin, down to the jaunty cap on his head. I had enough experience of life to know that when a total stranger addresses you as 'my friend', it conveys a latent threat. My brain offered me a choice between three kinds of answers:

Cheeky-belligerent-risky

Submissive-ingratiating-cowardly

or

Diplomatic-courteous-circumspect.

'Yes, I know,' I said. 'To be honest, I just couldn't stand it any longer. You can smell tobacco everywhere but not see a soul smoking anywhere. I'm new in the city.'

'Smoking itself is still very much permitted,' the Wolperting said slowly, crossing his muscular arms. 'But only in designated places. What you smelt was the smoke from a Fumoir.'

'A, er . . . Fumoir?' The word sounded somehow disreputable, but I relaxed a little. Something in the Wolperting's voice told me that he was *not* going to beat me up and dump me in a rubbish bin. I would temporarily keep my teeth and might even be able to have a pleasant conversation. Three cheers for diplomacy!

'Fumoirs are public conveniences for smokers,' the huge animal explained, baring his impressive incisors in a smile. 'There's one in nearly every district. You can smoke whatever and however much you want in them. Bookholm is a tolerant city, my friend. We don't want it burning down again, that's all! Fumoirs provide free matches, ashtrays and leaflets on the dangers of smoking. Tea and wine as well, but there's a small charge for those. Shall I show you one?'

We left the inner courtyard and paused on the pavement. My new friend pointed to a windowless building of rough-hewn stone at the end of the street. It was distinguished by its lack of ornamentation and had a grotesquely large chimney. The walls were plastered with posters old and new, and hanging above the entrance was a wooden sign depicting a tobacco pipe.

'That's a Fumoir,' said the Wolperting. He replaced his paw on my shoulder, this time in an almost affectionate, friendly way. 'But just between the two of us, smoking really is terribly unhealthy, quite apart from being the cause of at least ten per cent of all fires.'

'Yes,' I said meekly. Why was my conscience pricking me? After all, I wanted to give up smoking!

'Have an enjoyable stay in our beautiful city,' said the Wolperting. 'I recommend a visit to the Puppetocircus Maximus. It's worth seeing.' Handing me a leaflet, he waved and walked off.

For a moment I stood there like a bewildered child who has lost his mother in the crowd. I would really have liked to prolong my conversation with the Wolperting. He was nice. I'd heard that these battle-hardened individuals were employed as private security personnel – as janitors, bouncers and bodyguards. That they also went in for fire prevention was news to me. And what was that about the . . . what did he call it? The Puppet Circus? I glanced at the handbill. The Puppetocircus Maximus. Funny name. Suggested a puppet theatre. Uninteresting. I threw the leaflet away and strode resolutely towards the Fumoir. I wanted to smoke my last pipe, nothing more.

I needed both arms to push the heavy wooden door of the establishment open. A dense white fog bank of tobacco smoke came billowing towards me accompanied by the hum of many voices. I could smell cumin, ranunculus leaves, sesame canaster, dried zimpinel – good heavens, what *didn't* they smoke in there! Never mind, this would be the historic site of my very last nicotine fix.

It was a big, bare room with a low ceiling and a huge central chimney that collected the rising smoke and conveyed it into the open air. Some two dozen customers were sitting on crude wooden chairs around eight long tables, most of them engaged in filling or smoking pipes or rolling cigarettes. There was no daylight, the only form of illumination being a few candles. Along the wall on the left was an unmanned bar on which stood several jugs of water, cheap wine and cold tea, also glasses, cups and a bowl full of coins in which one was supposed to deposit money for the drinks – voluntarily and at one's own discretion, so a notice said. Very charming. So this was a Fumoir. One lives and learns.

I poured myself some cold peppermint tea from a jug, tossed a coin into the bowl and carried my mug through the nicotinic fog to the back of the Fumoir, where fewer people were sitting, visible only as dim shapes. Seated by himself at one table was an impressive figure who at once caught my eye. No doubt about it, he was a Lindworm! One of my own kind from back home.

My first impulse was to turn and look for somewhere else to sit. Lindworms never impose their company on each other, whether at the castle or far from home. It's instinct and etiquette that guide us, for we aren't a particularly sociable species, so I wanted to sit as far from him as possible. But then I thought, 'You know him, don't you?!'

Of course I knew him, my friends, that was obvious. Every living Lindworm knows nearly every other living Lindworm. That's nothing to write home about, given our relatively small numbers. But this Lindworm I'd almost forgotten because it was such a long time since we'd seen each other. It was . . . yes, it was Ovidios Versewhetter!

Good heavens! Ovidios was a fellow Lindworm who had left the castle when I was still a youngster with yellow scales. He had emigrated to Bookholm after announcing, rather grandiloquently, that he would become a famous author there – something he had sadly failed to do right away. When I met him in this city some years later, he was professionally at rock bottom, vegetating in one of the pits in the *Graveyard of Forgotten Writers*, where he composed off-the-cuff poems for tourists. A Lindworm could sink no lower. I hadn't even spoken to him – indeed, I'd cravenly fled from the sight of his literary downfall instead of offering my help. I now recalled this, filled with shame. I had never thought I would see him again in the land of the living.

Now, however, as far as I could tell in the prevailing visibility, Ovidios made a splendid impression. Instead of the rags he had been wearing then, he was attired in a fashionable robe of expensive material, and his long reptilian neck and claws were bedecked with chains and rings that looked as if they were of high-carat gold set with genuine diamonds. He epitomised one's idea of a successful Lindworm. What had happened?

He hadn't yet noticed me, so I lingered behind a column and hesitated. Should I speak to him? I felt guilty somehow. He had seen me that time in the *Graveyard of Forgotten Writers*. We had exchanged a glance and he must have been quite aware that I'd abandoned him in his wretchedness for unworthy reasons. What else could I have done, though? I was almost penniless myself at that time and I'd gained the impression that he wasn't too anxious to be accosted in his embarrassing position by another of his kind. Many years had gone by since then and I was terribly curious to discover how he had been faring. I pulled myself together and went over to his table. At least I could make a belated apology.

'Is anyone sitting here?' My voice was shaking, I noticed. 'I apologise for disturbing you, but . . . I also come from Lindworm Castle.'

Two diminutive gnomes seated facing each other across the next table were sharing a pipe at which they puffed in turn. Their tobacco smelt pungently of forest herbs. They paid me no attention.

Ovidios gave me a long look. Then, very slowly and in the stand-offish tone of someone who often gets pestered, he said: 'Anyone who goes around muffled up like you could say as much.'

89

'I'm, er . . . travelling incognito,' I replied, abashed. Leaning towards him, I folded back my cowl far enough for him, but no one else in the room, to see my face.

'Ye . . . Yu . . . Yarnsp . . .' he stammered, utterly taken aback, but I raised my paw in entreaty and he promptly fell silent.

'May I join you?' I asked.

'But of course, certainly! I insist!' Ovidios replied. He stood up and sat down several times. 'Heavens alive . . . what a . . . surprise.' Nervously, he brushed a few tobacco crumbs off the table.

The two little gnomes were giggling stupidly, but not on our account. Obviously wrapped up in themselves, they were whispering together in Gnomian, which no one but they understood.

'I'm afraid I have to wear this wretched cowl,' I said apologetically, sitting down opposite Ovidios. 'It makes me feel like one of those silly Dumbdruids, but without it I'd never have a quiet moment in this city.'

'Of course not,' he said. 'Everyone here knows you. Your likeness is reproduced on all your book jackets. Many antique shops and bookshops adorn their windows with your portrait. There's even a statue of you in the municipal park, but on that you still have green scales all over. Are you moulting at present?'

Strangely enough, a Lindworm always finds it somewhat embarrassing to be questioned about his moults, even by another Lindworm. My reply was correspondingly curt.

'Yes,' was all I said.

'Heavens alive,' Ovidios sighed. 'When did we see each other last? It must have been . . . it was . . .'

'In the *Graveyard of Forgotten Writers*,' I blurted out and instantly regretted it.

But he only roared with laughter. 'Hahaha! Yes, that's right! In that goddamned graveyard!' He didn't seem to resent being reminded of it at all. 'You even describe our encounter in your book,' he said.

'You've read it?' I asked.

'But of course! Are you joking? *Everyone* in Bookholm has read it. What brings you here again? The last I heard, you'd gone back to Lindworm Castle. Back to your roots and so on.' Ovidios was treating me like a long-lost friend, which quickly made me relax. I thought for a moment. Should I show him the letter? Lay my cards on the table right away? He was a Lindworm, so I had no doubts about his loyalty, but hadn't I sworn to be far more cautious this time? On my first trip to Bookholm, most of my difficulties had arisen because I'd blithely stuck the manuscript that had occasioned my visit under the noses of friend and foe alike. This time I wanted to proceed less hastily and naively.

'Ah, yes, Lindworm Castle . . .' I said. 'You know how it is. For anyone in search of peace and quiet, plenty of sleep and hearty Lindworm fare, it's the best place in Zamonia. I needed a break from the rat race – needed to instil some order into my life. Or so I thought, at least. In the end, though, the healthy air up there started to make my ears buzz. I developed an urge to knock the stupid helmet off some Lindworm's head after encountering him in the street for the twelfth time in a day. Know what I mean? I could hear my toenails growing in the night.'

'I get the picture,' Ovidios said with a grin. 'Lindwormitis! Is the *Fossilised Brachiosaurus* still the only restaurant in the place?'

'You bet your life it is! And the main course is *Pebbles in their Jackets* every damned night.'

'Yes,' said Ovidios, 'those sound like the reasons why I myself fled from Lindworm Castle. There came a day when the fresh air merely gave me nausea and I got vertigo whenever I looked over the battlements.'

I smiled. 'I hope you won't take it amiss if I ask you something. Why didn't you simply go back to the castle when you were in such a bad way? I've often wondered that since. I mean, it would have been preferable to the *Graveyard of Forgotten Writers*.'

'Depends on your point of view,' he said with a sigh. 'Youngsters are stubborn. I was too proud, too stupid. I'd rather have died than return to that old dragon's rock. I see it in a somewhat different light today, but then . . . I was a completely different Lindworm and my life would have taken an entirely different turn had I not ended up in the *Graveyard of Forgotten Writers*. More boring, certainly, and ultimately not as, er . . . agreeable.'

He clinked mugs.

I grinned. 'You're doing well for yourself now, that's obvious. What happened?'

Ovidios gave me a lingering look.

'The Orm,' he said gravely. 'The Orm happened to me.'

'The . . . Orm?' I whispered.

'Hm, yes . . . It was a while after we saw each other. To be honest, our brief encounter made a pretty deep impression on me.'

'Really?'

'Yes indeed. I became far more depressed after that.' He stared at me sombrely.

I broke out in a sweat. 'Oh . . .' was all I said. The conversation was taking an unpleasant turn after all.

'The look in your eyes that time, Optimus – I shall never forget it. Never! It conveyed sheer terror, naked fear. I saw the full horror of my situation reflected in it – in the eyes of one of my own kind, you understand? I've never felt lonelier or more humiliated in my life!' Were his eyes filled with tears of sorrow, or was it just the smoke?

I sank deeper into my chair. How idiotic of me to have sat down here! Now I was belatedly paying for my past sins.

'But what am I saying!' he sighed. 'How much lower can you sink when you're already at the bottom of a grave? Hm? I even stopped attending to my basic needs. I gave up washing and eating, and drank only rainwater. I composed no more poems for those confounded tourists. I didn't even trouble to pick up the small change they tossed into my hole out of pity. I wanted to die.'

So did I! Die and sink, complete with chair, through the floor of this accursed Fumoir, which I should *never* have set foot in. Why couldn't that stupid, interfering Wolperting have simply allowed me to smoke my harmless last pipe in peace? Why did people always have to make things so complicated for each other? And why couldn't I have a heart attack when I really needed one?

But Ovidios implacably continued his shaming story. 'I simply lay curled up in my grave. For days. Weeks. I didn't know, nor did I care. My will to live had been extinguished. I wanted to decay, to dissolve into the mud.'

He fell silent, leaving the last words to linger in the air. The most embarrassing conversational hiatus in my life ensued.

'And then,' he said at last, 'I heard the bells.'

'The, er . . . death knell?' I asked stupidly.

'No, the tocsin.'

'The tocsin?'

'The fire alarm! Bookholm's Great Conflagration! The one started by the Shadow King. The last chapter in your book was the first in my new existence.'

'What?' I sat up again. Had I detected a reconciliatory note in his voice? I was feeling quite different, anyway. Different in a strange but agreeable manner. Was it the peppermint tea?'

'So I was lying down there in my pit, wanting to die, d'you see?' Ovidios went on. 'It had rained heavily the day before the Great Conflagration and most of our holes in the ground were knee-deep in water in spite of the tarpaulins we'd suspended over them. I was floating more than lying. I could hear the tolling of the tocsin, the panic-stricken cries of the townsfolk and the crackle of the flames, but I couldn't have cared less because I was done with life. I would burn to death, but so what?'

Ovidios lit a match and studied the flame.

'And then came the heat. I don't know if you've ever experienced a gigantic wall of heat fuelled by millions of burning books, but I can tell you this: nothing in life prepares you for it! I dived below the surface of the muddy brew in which I was lying and it instantly began to simmer! I now know how someone must feel who's being boiled to death.'

I leant across the table. He was a pretty good storyteller. 'How?' I asked in a low voice.

'He wants to *live*, damn it!' cried Ovidios. 'He develops an instinct for survival more intense than he could ever have dreamt! Every fibre of his body feels more alive than ever before! And then . . .'

'Yes?' I said breathlessly.

'Then he dies.' Ovidios blew out the match.

I sat back again. I'd become so light-headed, I felt as if my head might at any moment detach itself from my body and float away like a balloon.

'Mind you,' he went on, 'I said the water began to *simmer*, not *boil*. It could only have been a degree at most, a hair's breadth on the thermometer, a single millilitre of mercury, that preserved me from what may well be the most terrible of all deaths! It became so hot, I thought my teeth would melt. Although I'd shut my eyes, the glare was so dazzling I could see the veins in my eyelids throb in time to my racing heartbeat. And I heard an ear-splitting roar, even under-water! In your book you used a very apt metaphor for the Great Conflagration: *The Dreaming Books had awakened!* Yes, that's just how it was. It sounded as if a thousandfold herd of frenzied beasts were thundering overhead, but it was the merciless Fire Moloch devouring the oxygen above me!'

Ovidios drummed on the table with both claw-tipped paws to imitate the hoofbeats of a thousand animals, and one or two heads in the Fumoir turned in our direction. The two little gnomes were undisguisedly staring at us with glassy, red-rimmed eyes.

'And then, quite suddenly, it was over,' Ovidios went on in a low voice. 'From one moment to the next. I couldn't have held my breath a second longer. I rose from the simmering brew, steaming in the cooling aftermath of the wall of fire. I groaned and yelled and flailed my arms like a lunatic who has split his straitjacket. Aaarh! I was incapable of any form of civilised linguistic utterance. I had survived a conflagration of apocalyptic dimensions. Had been nearly boiled alive. Had almost died and resurrected myself. Not a bad outcome for an otherwise uneventful afternoon, my friend! But that was nothing. My real experience of that day was still to come.'

Ovidios sat back and grinned. His eyes had begun to sparkle and a brief sidelong glance told me that the gnomes at the next table were pricking up their long ears in an attempt to overhear the story.

'I wiped the mud from my eyes and looked up. Framed by the elongated, rectangular mouth of my grave I saw the sky. It was dark, though whether with smoke or the advent of night I didn't know, nor could I tell whether what twinkled in it were stars or the sparks from burning books. I only knew that I had never seen a sky like it. I was looking at the *Alphabet of the Stars*, a firmament filled with sparkling symbols, an illegible but wonderful luminous script as old as the universe itself.'

'You saw it too?' I said. 'The Alphabet?'

Ovidios stared at me for a while. Had he lost his thread? Was he even aware of my presence? At length he went on.

'And then I was struck by an invisible thunderbolt – a beam, a blow, a billow, an electric shock, whatever – coming straight from the cosmos. It nearly knocked me back into the mud – it cleft me down the middle like an axe splitting a block of wood. It didn't hurt or frighten me. I almost laughed. It was as if I had been charged with an energy I'd never known before, a creative power that nearly burst my brain. Were flames coming from my nostrils? I didn't know. I knew only this: that suddenly there were two of me standing down there in the pit. The old Ovidios in his tattered rags and the new Ovidios you see before you. I had only to decide which one I wanted to be from then on.'

Ovidios grinned and flung out his arms. His new clothes really suited him. He lowered his voice.

'I know this sounds like the documentary record of a lunatic describing the onset of his dementia. I don't tell this story to everyone, but I'm sure you've experienced something similar. *For at that moment I was overcome by the Orm.*'

His eyes filled more and more with tears until they were streaming down his face. Either he didn't appear to notice or he didn't care. Stretching out his arm, he pointed at the fog of tobacco smoke above my head.

'I could see right into the future! I could see what would happen if I seized this moment and exploited it. I could begin all over again and change everything for the better, because symbols – sparkling characters from the Alphabet of the Stars – were trickling through my brain. Although disorganised and hard to interpret at first, they quickly sorted themselves out into groups, and here and there made glorious sense. Something unique and imperishable was taking shape in my head, an ingenious structure of words and sentences that not only materialised there like a strangely beautiful, extraterrestrial creature but spoke to me in immaculate verse! It was a poem. Quite unconnected with my own thought processes, it consisted of ideas from space: a gift from the stars!'

Ovidios looked at me with sudden severity. He leant over and gripped my arm so hard that it hurt.

'Believe me, Optimus, I'm not mad, nor am I one of those lazy-minded esotericists who believe in inexplicable phenomena, tea leaves, or the voice of their dead grandmother. I'm guided by a strictly scientific view of the world. I put all my faith in the measurability of Zamonian natural phenomena. I'm not a spiritualist. I believe in nothing that can only be grasped with the aid of blind faith. For *that* thing, the power we call the Orm, is more concrete than anything else in existence. It's *real*, even though we can't see it and few have experienced it.'

He let go of my arm and sat back. Then he adjusted his clothing and seemed to grow calmer.

'But what am I saying?' he added with a laugh. 'No writer has ever been more thoroughly suffused with the Orm than you yourself!'

I slumped in my chair again. Fortunately, Ovidios went on at once.

'Well,' he said, 'that was the cosmic prelude, the overture. Now comes the real story. I slowly recovered my senses. I now knew that if I succeeded in capturing and organising these fleeting symbols in my brain – if I wrote them down in the correct order – they would yield an Orm-inspired work. It was as simple as that. The problem was, I was still standing at the bottom of a muddy pit, soaked to the skin, and a catastrophic fire was raging outside. Night had fallen, and people were screaming and sobbing. Hardly ideal conditions in which to commit an important literary work to paper, were they?'

The gnome at the next table was now leaning so obtrusively in our direction, I feared he would fall off his chair at any moment. Ovidios produced a notebook and flourished it under my nose.

'Paper!' he cried. 'I badly needed some paper. I found a pencil in my rags, but the paper in my pockets was completely sodden. I had to get out of that accursed pit, but the rain of recent days had rendered the steps leading down into it so soft that they gave way beneath my feet. It was like a nightmare! My brain was shaping a historic poem, a ballad about the Great Conflagration fit to endure for millennia, and the steps were giving way beneath my feet.'

Ovidios slammed his notebook down on the table and at that moment one of the gnomes really did fall off his chair. His companion rocked with unsympathetic laughter as he promptly scrambled to his feet.

'Then, all at once, a rope was lowered into the pit,' Ovidios went on, unmoved. 'I grasped it at once with both paws and was hauled aloft. It was my friends and companions in misfortune, my neighbours in the *Graveyard of Forgotten Writers*! Submerged in their muddy holes, they had survived the conflagration like me. We fell into each other's arms and exchanged mutual congratulations. But I hastened on. I had to find some paper! The poem, the great, immortal epic on the burning of Bookholm, was now clearly legible before my inner eye in twenty-four immaculate strophes suffused with the purest Orm! I had only to write them down. Paper, paper! I roamed the smoking ruins. Everything was burning and smouldering, and the ground was as hot as a hotplate. Having found paper in my pockets that was too wet to write on, all I found in the vicinity of the graveyard was some so charred or desiccated that it crumbled away between my claws. And the verses in my head were already beginning to fade. I was on the verge of despair. Of giving up. Of sinking to the ground and letting the poem die in my brain, unheard by anyone but me. But then something occurred to me. Do you like choral music?'

'Eh?' I said, puzzled by the sudden question. 'Er, yes. No. Well, I don't know. Er, *choral music?*'

'It isn't to everyone's taste, I know,' said Ovidios. 'But I love chorales. And that was the solution to my predicament. I needed a choir.'

The two gnomes stared at him uncomprehendingly and I too felt that he'd somehow lost the thread.

'I hurried back to my pit,' Ovidios continued resolutely, 'and gathered my fellow sufferers around me – all the residents of the *Graveyard of Forgotten Writers*. And then I delivered a speech.

'"Listen!" I cried. "I've just been pervaded by the Orm!"

'"Oh, sure," someone said mockingly.

'"Happens to me all the time!" cried another.

'Laughter and giggles on all sides, then silence fell. Raising both arms, I began again from the beginning: "I know it sounds rather odd, my friends, especially under present circumstances. Believe it or not, though, the fact is that my inner eye has conceived a revolutionary epic poem which, unless it is recorded in some way, will soon be lost for ever because there's no paper anywhere and it's already fading from my memory. It came to me when the fire engulfed us and I'm convinced that it's an Orm-given gift. I also know, however, that many of you don't even believe in the Orm, so why should you believe such a fantastic story? For that reason, I simply want to ask you all for an act of friendship, whether or not you think I've lost my wits. Please just do as I say. It isn't very difficult.'

'"All right," said someone. "What are we to do?"

'"It's quite simple. I shall now recite the poem aloud, strophe by strophe, and I'd like you to memorise one each. I shall station myself in front of you and very slowly declaim each strophe loud and clear. Please retain it in your memory until you get an opportunity to write it down. That's all."'

Ovidios's gaze became transfigured as he recalled these events. He was positively looking through me now.

'And that was the origin of *The Miracle of the Graveyard of Forgotten Writers*, as it later became known in Bookholm. It was anything but a miracle, of course; it was simply a form of choir practice, but of that we were just as unaware as we were of the fact that this was the moment when all our lives took a turn for the better. It would never have occurred to us in our current state, soaked to the skin and plastered with mud from head to toe.'

I sat back feeling thoroughly relieved, my friends. His story also seemed to be taking a favourable turn and I was feeling in a better, almost silly mood. I kept having to stifle an urge to laugh aloud, even though there was no real reason for it. The two gnomes lit another pipe.

'The laughter and the stupid remarks died away after the first few lines I recited,' Ovidios went on. 'I saw looks of amazement being exchanged, for although we were all failed writers, we did know exceptionally fine literature when we heard it. Even those of us who didn't really believe in the Orm grasped that they were sharing in something quite out of the ordinary. Tears started flowing after only a few strophes and on many faces I saw sheer rapture, undisguised envy or pure delight as their owners memorised the lines. Their eyes glowed with the fire of the Orm and it wouldn't have surprised me to see sparks flying between us. I went from poet to poet, and when I'd finally recited every strophe I heard some of my listeners sob and saw many sink to the ground because their legs had given way. Others laughed aloud, but for joy. My poem had poured what all of us had experienced during the inferno into timeless verse. It had come from the heart. At once a paean to life and a hymn to death and resurrection, it left no one unmoved. I sank to the ground in exhaustion, like a balloon from which all the air has escaped. And that is just what I felt like: the poem had left me, all of it with the exception of one strophe, which I memorised myself. It now lived on in the collective memory of us all.'

Ovidios smiled. 'Do you know what they christened us in Bookholm later on?' he asked. '*The Forgotten Writers' Choir.* We were a more united community than before, except that what united us was the will to live, not thoughts of suicide. We appeared in the streets of Bookholm and recited the poem together. Just like that, without special intent and exactly in the way we'd practised it, one strophe apiece. We had, of course, written it down in the interim, but it gave us the greatest satisfaction to recite it from memory like actors upon a stage. We performed in markets, at weddings and topping-out ceremonies, and we attracted steadily growing audiences. The choir became locally celebrated, an institution. By expressing what all of us had been through, my ballad brought consolation, so it helped the Bookholmers to rediscover their instinct for survival. Dramatic though this may sound, it's true. It was the best thing I'd ever written. I didn't know then that it would remain so, but I've come to terms with that.'

Ovidios sighed.

'I don't want to exaggerate the choir's importance to the rebuilding of Bookholm, but it would be false modesty to deny it. We were a living symbol that a vibrant culture and a strong community can survive the worst of crises and catastrophes.'

'Still,' I ventured to put in, 'that doesn't explain why you've become so prosperous.' I indicated his jewellery.

'Not so fast! The story isn't over yet. Now comes the commercial part.' Ovidios grinned self-confidently. 'Well, after a while the *Forgotten Writers* went their separate ways. A few of them married and moved away. A few died in the nature of things. When the first of us announced that he was leaving Bookholm, we resolved never to recite the poem in public again. That was to remain the privilege of our old closed community. I hadn't until then thought of publishing it in book form, believe me, but when word got around that the *Forgotten Writers* would never perform again, a publisher convinced me that this piece of literature must definitely be preserved for posterity in print. Well, how could I quarrel with that? We made a contract under which all surviving members of the choir would share equally in the proceeds. We were reckoning on sales of a few hundred at most – I mean, who was going to buy a slim volume containing only one poem? That's that, I thought. We had a good time and we're alive, what more could anyone want? But then things really took off.' Ovidios grinned again.

'The book became a bestseller. Only within the narrow confines of Bookholm, admittedly, but with a vengeance! To begin with it was bought by every Bookholmer who had survived the fire. Then it became required reading in schools. Tourists started to take an interest in the book. It became a souvenir, the number-one souvenir from Bookholm. And today, two centuries later? If anyone buys a keepsake from this city, it's my Orm poem. All new and second-hand bookshops display it right beside the till. There's a children's version complete with pop-up illustrations – blazing buildings and paper flames and all! Can you imagine what the royalties have amounted to over the years? It has guaranteed us all a life free from care. The editions are still mounting up from year to year. I've even been able to establish a home for destitute writers.' Ovidios spread his paws wide, a contented and successful Lindworm expatriate.

I subsided in relief, tacitly congratulating myself on having joined his table. A long-standing weight had lifted from my shoulders.

Ovidios reached into his cloak, brought out a small booklet and slid it across the table to me.

'A signed edition,' he said. 'I happened to have one on me.' He grinned. 'Perhaps you'll run your eye over it some time.'

I picked up the little book.

'Well,' said Ovidios, who had clearly got the bit between his teeth and was filling another pipe. 'That was only my little, personal story – just a footnote in the city's development after the fire. Which, in turn, is a big story on its own. Would you care to hear a bit of it? Bookholmology for advanced students?'

'I insist,' I heard myself say. My voice seemed to come from a long way off, but I didn't care. I wanted to hear more, much more! The two little gnomes beside us had dozed off with their heads on the table and were laughing softly in their sleep.

Biblio-this,
biblio-that

The Fumoir had filled up with smokers in the meantime. They were now sitting crowded together at the tables and some had even sat down at ours. Here and there wine bottles were circulating as well as pipes. As far as I could tell in the blue haze, most of the newcomers were a motley assortment of Bookholm residents. I could deduce this from their clothing, for many were in professional dress: the book dealers in their famous brown linen habits with patch pockets for holding books (and the knotted cords round their waists with which they measured a volume's dimensions); the printers with their washable leather aprons and inky fingers; the editors with reading glasses round their necks; the blasé-looking Norselander notaries in their sleeve protectors; the Florinthian chefs in their stupid hats (why did you need a hat to cook in?); and, of course, the young poets whose attire conveyed their militant individualism: jaunty headgear and scarfs carelessly wound round their necks, shoulder bags containing notebooks and the inevitable volume of their own poems peeping casually out of a pocket.

The fumes and the babble of voices steadily intensified. Although we were being smoked like dried cod, I found the place more and more congenial. I felt fine without knowing why. I'd had no idea that the smoke of so many kinds of dried stimulants could be drawn into one's lungs. Plain tobacco was probably the least of it! Herbs, coloured powders, dried fruit, dried roots – even colourful petals or ground-up nuts were being stuffed into pipes or rolled in cigarette paper. I caught the soapy perfume of lilac, the resinous aroma of hemp, the heavy scent of nutmeg, and mingled with them the pungent fumes of phogars. Many pipes emitted tall, thin flames as soon as they were lit. A Froglet was smoking a pipe with three bowls from which threads of different-coloured smoke were rising. Only hardened inhalers with lungs of cast iron could take that for any length of time. It struck me then that I still hadn't produced my own pipe, I'd been too fascinated by Ovidios's account of the Orm, so I felt in my pockets. Unlike me, the loquacious Lindworm had refilled and lit his own smoking utensil, and was resuming his narrative. If I wanted to smoke in here, I had only to breathe in and out.

'From one day to the next, many Bookholmers were no better off than us residents of the *Graveyard of Forgotten Books*,' he began, puffing away. 'In actual fact, we were the lucky ones. Not having owned anything, we'd lost nothing. Half the city's inhabitants were homeless. People were living in book crates and charred ruins, regardless of whether they wore gold chains and rings set with precious stones. Anyone who had survived was a winner.

'Everything had gone back to zero. In the old days people would simply have ignored another's plight, but now they helped each other. Acts of friendship were the universally valid currency of the time. One person might design a house, another lay the foundations, yet another mix cement, and five former neighbours would collaborate in raising the roof. Bookholm arose from the ashes, restored from the bottom up, and grew at breathtaking speed. You walked along a street that had been nothing but soot-blackened ruins yesterday and today a new house – or more than one – would be standing there, built overnight by torchlight and by people who once wouldn't have given each other the time of day. The city never rested for the length of a heartbeat and work went on continuously: stones were knapped, ruins cleared, charred beams sawn up, soup kitchens provided for labourers, burnt earth turned over. The air was filled day and night with the sound of hammering and sawing and the ringing of anvils, with shouts and

laughter and cries and oaths. Nobody really slept at this period. *You can sleep in your funeral urn; sleepers get eaten by Nurns! –* that was a favourite saying. There have been no legally prescribed closing times in Bookholm since then and many bookshops still stay open all night, even today.'

Laughter could always be heard somewhere in the Fumoir. Sometimes it was the resonant bass of a giant printer with a handlebar moustache, sometimes the hoarse giggle of a dwarf, and sometimes an abrupt peal of laughter from a whole group. The good mood seemed to be infectious.

'But the most surprising thing,' Ovidios went on, 'was that hardly anyone moved away. Only a few disheartened individuals turned their backs on the city even during the darkest chapter in its history, the ban on fire. You've heard of that, I suppose?'

'Yes,' I said, nodding.

'Perhaps it was because everyone knew that, although the devastation was terrible, the city still possessed a unique substructure comparable to a huge diamond mine, an inexhaustible treasure chamber: the Labyrinth, with its catacombs and vast store of precious books. It was paradoxical. The evil realm down below, of which many are more afraid than of death itself – the darkness from which destruction arose in the shape of the vengeful Shadow King – was at the same time the glue that bound us all together. It was as if we were reoccupying a volcano that had recently erupted. No, no one ran away, in fact, the opposite occurred. The Great Conflagration occasioned no exodus; it led to an influx of immigrants such as the city had never known before. Adventurers, bibliophiles, authors and would-be authors, publishers with no premises, unemployed editors, translators without commissions, printers, glue boilers, masons, bookbinders, roofers, book dealers – in short, intellectuals and craftsmen of all kinds were magnetically attracted to the half-devastated but newly flourishing city. Nowhere but in Bookholm could people make such a fundamentally fresh start, whether with the pen or the bricklayer's trowel. Only in this crazy city could they participate in a collective renaissance and nowhere else, if fortune smiled on them, could they become so stinking rich!'

The ashtrays danced, Ovidios thumped the table so hard, but no one took any notice. One of the gnomes raised his head briefly, blinked in a bewildered way, then slept on.

'The influx of people in search of fresh opportunities simply didn't dry up. Once the adventurous pioneers and the old inhabitants had relaid the foundations, more circumspect individuals – those who had cautiously observed the phenomenon from afar – also moved in. They had capital and business acumen to offer as well as physical strength and the will to work. Experienced chefs opened restaurants, leading publishers opened branch offices and established authors from other cities moved to Bookholm, all eager to share in this fresh start. Only here, it was believed, did *true* literary creativity flourish. At night the taverns teemed with young and still unknown but boundlessly garrulous and ambitious writers, with financiers, scouts and agents eager to discuss their ideas for new business models and publishing houses. They all wanted to reinvent Bookholm, to make it bigger, more beautiful and even more lucrative. Simultaneously naive and greedy, and sometimes even laughable, their efforts were also touching and inspiring. It was impossible to escape the new city's positive energy; it swept you along as soon as you set foot in its streets. Viewing the matter quite objectively, one could say that we owed it all to the Shadow King.'

I pricked up my ears. 'How do you mean?'

'Let's face the facts. He purified the city with his avenging fire, preserved it from impending decline, and halted the insidious process of decay initiated by Pfistomel Smyke and his henchmen. We're in his debt. Indeed we are, even though the vengeful bastard burnt down half the city! The Shadow King nearly killed me, damn it! He was responsible for nearly boiling me to death in my pit like a lobster!'

Ovidios roared with laughter.

'But to me he's Bookholm's greatest hero, the true ruler of this city and our secret king. We ought to put up monuments to him, one in every street! That's my opinion, anyway, and I'm certainly not alone.'

And then, my beloved brothers and sisters, something truly remarkable happened. At the mention of the Shadow King and Pfistomel Smyke, the fumes around Ovidios began to dance. At first I thought this was caused by a gust of air from the flue above our heads, but it was something different.

The smoke assumed ever more concrete forms. The swaths and clouds of vapour became bodies and faces. I rubbed my eyes and the apparitions disappeared. I breathed a sigh of relief, sat back, looked again – and there they were once more, the billowing clouds. And this time they actually resolved themselves into familiar figures!

'Something wrong?' asked Ovidios.

'No, no,' I said evasively. 'The smoke's stinging my eyes a bit, that's all.'

It was as if the ghosts of my past were dancing around Ovidios's head. Were those some Booklings peering over his left shoulder? Was that Ahmed ben Kibitzer winking at me over his right shoulder?

I rubbed my eyes again, opened them wide, closed them again, reopened them – and they were still there, those phantoms, more distinct than ever! That was Pfistomel Smyke who had materialised behind Ovidios with his arms folded, grinning impudently at me! Some Animatomes emerged from the fog, fluttered around my fellow Lindworm's head and disappeared into it once more. Were those speaking death's heads beside him and, if so, was I losing my mind? Before I could say anything to the disturbing apparitions, the door of the Fumoir opened and a noisy group of newcomers entered, creating a draught. The smoke swirled and dispersed, and the phantoms danced up the chimney with it.

I heaved a sigh of relief. What diabolical herbs were being smoked in here? Did they accord with legal regulations?

'Go on,' I urged Ovidios. He gave me a worried look but complied.

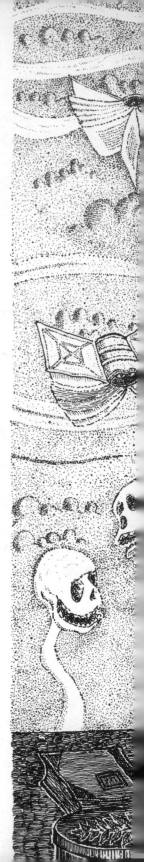

'It was the fire,' he said, 'that turned medieval Bookholm into a modern city and replaced outmoded Bookemistic hocus-pocus with up-to-date Biblionism.'

'Biblionism?' I said. 'Sounds like a disease you can catch in public libraries.'

'My, it really is a long time since your last visit! You've missed out on a few important things, Optimus. All that antiquarian book alchemy is old hat. Biblionism is *the* new thing. Everything's biblio these days. Biblio-this, biblio-that!'

'I may rather have lost touch,' I conceded, 'but I can learn. I'm sure you'll bring me up to date.'

'It isn't complicated. Complex, though. Ours is a city governed by books. *Biblionism* is the umbrella term covering all book-related scientific disciplines, professions and social phenomena – plus one or two other things. Simply imagine the whole of daily life lumped together in a paper bag: that's Biblionism. Look around you. What do you see?'

I complied with his injunction. 'A bunch of total strangers smoking too much,' I replied, rather disconcerted by the question. The truth was, I could still see a few Animatomes fluttering beneath the ceiling, but I preferred not to mention that.

'Exactly,' said Ovidios. 'And they all look different in their own ways, right? There are gnomes, Moomies, Demigiants, Froglets, Norselanders, Viridians, Moories and Midgard Midgets – not forgetting Lindworms, eh? How can one keep one's perspective? I'll tell you: through Biblionism, because what unites us all is our close relationship to books. It's like a sentence in print: it consists of different-looking letters seemingly jumbled up at random, but you can read it all the same. And it makes sense! You can even laugh at it if it's funny. That's how Bookholm works. That's Biblionism.'

'Bookholm makes sense?' I said.

'Now don't be pedantic! Biblionism isn't a religion or association or political party, nor is it a really exact science with fixed rules. It's the

110

ethos of modern Bookholm. Not a sinister alchemistic spirit like old-time Bookemism, but a spirit in the sense of understanding and enlightenment. Would you like a few examples?'

I nodded. What was he talking about?

'Then I hope you've got some time to spare. No one Biblionist is like another,' said Ovidios, looking around him enquiringly. 'That's why it's important to know what differentiates us, so we get along better together. Let's see . . . You see that Vulphead over there in the long raincoat?'

'Yes.'

'He's no Bookholmer. He's got a shopping bag from *Leafwood Antiques*. No local inhabitant would buy anything there, it's only for tourists. On the other hand, few tourists ever stray into a Fumoir. That means he's a Bibliomaniac.'

'Really?'

Ovidios drew a deep breath, which in this room was the equivalent of a lungful of smoke from a well-filled hookah. 'The Bibliomaniac', he went on, 'embodies one of the most popular types of visitors to Bookholm. He's animated by a desire to buy as many books as possible and take them home with him. An average book collector, in other words. As long as he does this within the limits imposed by law and refrains from shoplifting, the Bibliomaniac is the city's most welcome visitor. We all live off him. Bibliomaniacs are a very sizeable group.'

I could do this myself now, I thought. Recognising someone as a Bibliomaniac by a shopping bag full of books wasn't particularly hard.

'But that was no feat of deduction,' said Ovidios. 'Nearly everyone in Bookholm is a Bibliomaniac of some kind. From now on it gets harder. Let me see . . .'

He scanned the smoky Fumoir, craning his neck in an impressive manner so as to peer into every corner. 'Well now,' he muttered, 'in this room at present are . . . a Bibliophrene . . . two Bibliots . . . a Biblioclast . . . a Bibliopath . . . a Bibliophobe – no two Bibliophobes!

Three Bibliomancers—they're unmistakable. And, er . . . yes, a Biblioscope, over there by the bar! And that's only at first glance. Visibility is pretty limited in here. No Biblionnaires today? No, not one. They tend to be rare.'

Quite apart from the fact that I didn't know the meaning of those terms – except that they were obviously Biblionistic subcategories – I hadn't the slightest idea how Ovidios managed to distinguish so eloquently between the Fumoir's various occupants. What were Bibliots? What were Bibliomancers? Was he pulling my leg in some subtle fashion?

'Well, well,' I said cautiously, sounding faintly sarcastic.

'Don't you trust my Biblionistic powers of discernment?' Ovidios demanded, raising his eyebrows. 'You ought to, I'm pretty good at it. I'm a Lindworm of private means and a professional idler, so I've plenty of time and leisure for people-watching. What's more, I've read all Doylan Cone's *Hermes Olshlock* novels umpteen times. They're a great aid to training one's eye and powers of deduction. Listen, I'll prove it to you. Look at that Demidwarf in the green loden coat two tables further on.' He indicated where he meant with an almost imperceptible jerk of the head.

'The one with four books parcelled up beside him?' I asked.

'Exactly. You see the cloth bag at his side with the neck of a bottle protruding from it? That fellow is a Biblioclast, ten to one.'

'A Biblioclast?'

Ovidios nodded gravely. 'You bet your life he is! The books are relatively inexpensive second editions, probably unsigned – not top-notch, in other words, but certainly the most expensive he could afford. The bottle may contain some paper-dissolving chemical, possibly hydrochloric acid. You can tell that from the wax-sealed glass stopper with the death's head on it – Bookholm pharmacies are legally obliged to use those. You see his unhealthy-looking, yellow-tinged eyes? The tremor in his hands? The yellow eyes indicate liver damage caused by regularly inhaling toxic fumes. So does the tremor, but that's also a sign of anticipation. He can hardly wait, the swine.'

'Hardly wait for what?' I asked.

'To go home and *kill* those books lying beside him.'

'What!' I couldn't suppress a puzzled laugh.

Ovidios sighed. 'Biblioclasts are obsessed with a compulsion to destroy books. You can bet that individual will go up to his room, open a good bottle of wine, toss the books into a bathtub and pour the hydrochloric acid over them. That's his idea of heaven.'

'Are you sure?'

'He may set light to them, put them through the mincer or tear them into little pieces by hand, and *then* pour acid over them. One thing's for sure: *I* wouldn't like to be one of those four books of his.'

I was shocked. 'Is this really true?' I said.

Ovidios leant across the table and lowered his voice.

'Biblioclasts' behaviour can have many causes. The most frequent is a disease that any good psychiatrist could cure completely. Another is more ideological. Biblioclasts of that type don't hate books as such, just certain books selected for their contents. Many of them are political crackpots or members of religious sects. Then there are also some inspired by purely personal motives. We have a well-known Biblioclast here in Bookholm who only hates a certain book and tries to destroy whole editions of it. The book is his own *unauthorised* biography.'

Ovidios sat back with a grin. I took another look at the fellow in the green raincoat, but this time with different eyes. I felt sorry for the books at his side.

'Don't look now,' whispered Ovidios, 'but there's a Bibliomat sitting right beside us. Three chairs further along.' He rolled his eyes in the relevant direction.

The person sitting there appeared to hail from Watervale, to judge by his translucent skin and greenish hair. He had a great stack of books beside him, as well as several publisher's catalogues, probably free of charge. He was feverishly leafing through one of one of the latter.

'Bibliomats', Ovidios said softly, 'are mechanical readers. 'It doesn't matter to them *what* they read, they couldn't care less. They read while walking around or standing still, sitting or lying down. They read while eating or having a coffee, while shopping or standing in a queue; they simply read all the time. They lead an obsessive, joyless, futile existence and display no noticeable emotional reaction to what they read. Ants would read that way, I imagine! Ask a Bibliomat what he's just been reading and he'll be terribly embarrassed because he's instantly forgotten it. Hardly surprising, if a person can't tell the difference between a sonnet by Aleisha Wimpersleake and a list of chlorinated cleaning fluids.'

I gave a start. The mere mention of Wimpersleake's name was a painful reminder of the Booklings – and of the manuscript I had with me. But Ovidios was already continuing his exposition. 'And that couple two tables away – they're Bibliots. You can easily recognise them by their identical clothes.'

They were two Yellowlings in orange habits, both of whom had shaved their skulls. I'd seen some of their kind in the streets and wondered if they belonged to a sect.

'If it were up to me, I'd drive the whole bunch out of the city!' Ovidios's voice had taken on a note of uncompromising indignation. 'Bookholm needs those parasites like it needs Kackertratts! Bibliocy is the worst form of ignorance about books. Bibliots not only read no books on principle, they flatly deny their existence – and that while actually standing on a pile of them.' He directed a fiery glance at the Yellowlings.

'You'd have thought they could propagate their pathological ideology more plausibly anywhere other than Bookholm, where it's constantly reduced to absurdity by the visible presence of so many books, but far from it, my friend! It only spurs them on. Bookholm has the highest concentration of Bibliots anywhere in Zamonia. Imagine that! There's a fanatical, wild-eyed, loud-mouthed Bibliot on every other street corner in the city, indefatigably denying the existence of the millions of books around him. And it's all at the expense of the honest taxpayer. Why? Because those morons are so busy preaching their idiotic, misguided doctrine, they don't have the time to do a respectable job. Oh no! At night they queue up outside the free soup kitchens and clog the hostels for the homeless. Toleration has its limits, my friend!'

Ovidios was visibly infuriated. I found it both amusing and gratifying that a Lindworm who had once occupied the lowest rung on the Bookholm ladder should now conceive of himself as an honest taxpayer defending the rights of the homeless. To calm him down a little I pointed at random to another smoker. 'What about him over there?' I asked. 'What sort of Biblio is he?'

'Eh?' said Ovidios, following the direction of my paw. He subsided only reluctantly. 'Him? Erm . . . He's a Biblioklept.'

I peered more closely for the first time. A little old gnome with brown, leathery skin, the Biblioklept was defiantly smoking a gnarled pipe carved from a root and emitting clouds of greenish smoke. It made me cough just to look at him.

'Biblioklepts evolved from common book thieves and ultimately did away with themselves, so to speak.' Ovidios laughed. 'It's an interesting chapter in Bookholm's legal history – Bibliojuristics, in other words. It happened like this. When book thieves were caught, some of them tried to justify their theft by pleading a pathological compulsion. They even made that stick – if they had a good lawyer. They were quickly released or given extremely lenient sentences by judges who had probably sat their law exams at Crook University. That opened the door wide to book theft, because nearly *every* defendant charged with shoplifting books pleaded diminished responsibility and cited precedents. I'm sure you can imagine what that meant for a city like Bookholm. The authorities had to think of something quickly.'

'They changed the law?' I hazarded.

'Exactly. Someone hit on the simple idea of forbidding Biblioklepts

115

to enter the city. It was as simple as that. Since then, every entrance to Bookholm has had a sign hanging above it. The gist of it is: "𝕿𝖗𝖆𝖛𝖊𝖑𝖑𝖊𝖗𝖘 𝖘𝖚𝖋𝖋𝖊𝖗𝖎𝖓𝖌 𝖋𝖗𝖔𝖒 𝖆 𝖕𝖆𝖙𝖍𝖔𝖑𝖔𝖌𝖎𝖈𝖆𝖑 𝖆𝖉𝖉𝖎𝖈𝖙𝖎𝖔𝖓 𝖙𝖔 𝖇𝖔𝖔𝖐 𝖙𝖍𝖊𝖋𝖙 (𝕭𝖎𝖇𝖑𝖎𝖔𝖐𝖑𝖊𝖕𝖘𝖎𝖆) 𝖆𝖗𝖊 𝖕𝖗𝖔𝖍𝖎𝖇𝖎𝖙𝖊𝖉 𝖋𝖗𝖔𝖒 𝖊𝖓𝖙𝖊𝖗𝖎𝖓𝖌 𝕭𝖔𝖔𝖐𝖍𝖔𝖑𝖒 𝖆𝖓𝖉 𝖆𝖉𝖛𝖎𝖘𝖊𝖉 𝖙𝖔 𝖙𝖚𝖗𝖓 𝖇𝖆𝖈𝖐 𝖆𝖙 𝖔𝖓𝖈𝖊. 𝕴𝖓 𝖙𝖍𝖊 𝖊𝖛𝖊𝖓𝖙 𝖙𝖍𝖆𝖙 𝖙𝖍𝖊𝖞 𝖎𝖓𝖋𝖗𝖎𝖓𝖌𝖊 𝖙𝖍𝖎𝖘 𝖔𝖗𝖉𝖎𝖓𝖆𝖓𝖈𝖊 𝖆𝖓𝖉 𝖘𝖙𝖊𝖆𝖑 𝖆 𝖇𝖔𝖔𝖐 𝖔𝖗 𝖇𝖔𝖔𝖐𝖘, 𝖙𝖍𝖊𝖞 𝖜𝖎𝖑𝖑 𝖇𝖊 𝖘𝖚𝖇𝖏𝖊𝖈𝖙 𝖙𝖔 𝖉𝖗𝖆𝖈𝖔𝖓𝖎𝖆𝖓 𝖕𝖚𝖓𝖎𝖘𝖍𝖒𝖊𝖓𝖙, 𝖓𝖔𝖙 𝖔𝖓𝖑𝖞 𝖋𝖔𝖗 𝖙𝖍𝖊𝖎𝖗 𝖙𝖍𝖊𝖋𝖙, 𝖇𝖚𝖙 𝖋𝖔𝖗 𝖈𝖔𝖓𝖙𝖗𝖆𝖛𝖊𝖓𝖎𝖓𝖌 𝖙𝖍𝖎𝖘 𝖕𝖗𝖔𝖍𝖎𝖇𝖎𝖙𝖎𝖔𝖓. 𝕿𝖚𝖗𝖓 𝖇𝖆𝖈𝖐, 𝕭𝖎𝖇𝖑𝖎𝖔𝖐𝖑𝖊𝖕𝖙, 𝖜𝖍𝖎𝖑𝖊 𝖞𝖔𝖚 𝖘𝖙𝖎𝖑𝖑 𝖈𝖆𝖓." Or words to that effect. Understand?'

I nodded. I had seen such a sign on entering the city.

'A Biblioklept isn't all that easy to recognise, of course, but anyone charged with stealing books and stupid enough to try to blame the theft on Biblioklepsia is punished twice over – for theft *and* for entering the city illegally. The result has been a dramatic decline in Biblioklepsia, but that doesn't mean there are no Biblioklepts left in Bookholm. They've simply become ordinary book thieves.'

Ovidios smiled.

'Just a minute,' I said. 'That old man looks completely harmless, surely? He doesn't even have a book with him. How do you know he steals them?'

'Because I've spotted him at it on three occasions,' Ovidios replied.

'Oh, I see,' I said. Then something occurred to me. 'But . . . how could you tell he was just a normal shoplifter, not a compulsive book thief?'

Ovidios's smile grew even broader. 'Because he was stealing books written by *you*!' he said. 'They're published in such huge editions, they're worth almost nothing on the black market. No professional thief would steal that sort of thing. Only a Biblioklept would.'

Touché! That elegant sideswipe at my reputation as a prolific commercial author hit home. Only a Lindworm could have insulted me so charmingly.

The door opened and two Wolpertings came in. One of them I recognised as the one who had shown me the way to the Fumoir. Their manner was ostentatiously inconspicuous, as if they were loath to attract attention but at pains to ensure that everyone was aware of their presence.

'Bibliofficers,' Ovidios hissed between his teeth in an unmistakably contemptuous undertone. Conversation at the tables didn't cease but became more subdued. It was as if a teacher had entered a noisy classroom.

'Are the Wolpertings Bookholm's new police force?' I asked.

'No, peace and good order are still maintained by the municipal constabulary. The Bibliofficers are exclusively responsible for fire. They're a preventive fire brigade, so to speak.' The Wolperting with a face like a bulldog gave me a friendly nod as he and his companion passed our table.

'They seem respectable enough to me,' I said when they had gone past. 'They do make a rather intimidating impression, but—'

'Oh, one can't really say a word against them,' Ovidios growled. 'Minor outbreaks of fire have drastically decreased in number since they've been responsible for safety. They set up the Fumoirs and installed hydrants everywhere. Nothing wrong with that, but even safety has its price. They manage to give me a bad conscience whenever they show up. You feel you're a dangerous pyromaniac when they look you in the eye. They're like walking admonitory forefingers, if you ask me.'

'Who pays them?'

'We all do. From taxes. That's another consequence of Bookholm's new-found prosperity. The local authorities have a problem envied by every other municipality in Zamonia: we've got too much money. That's how we can afford a luxury like our own fire police.'

The Bibliofficers left the Fumoir after their brief tour just as ostentatiously and inconspicuously as they had come. I thought I heard a collective sigh of relief when the door closed behind them. Conversation and laughter promptly recommenced at full volume.

'We're turning into a Bibliocracy,' said Ovidios. 'See those three Norselanders over there, the ones smoking long cigarettes?'

I nodded.

'Only Bibliocrats can afford to take such long cigarette breaks,' he growled. 'But what's the alternative? A Biblionistic city needs administrators. I strongly advise you never to cross swords with those pen-pushers – by failing to pay a library fine, for instance. They're even more cold-blooded and vindictive than the old-time Bookhunters. There's nothing worse than getting mixed up in the toils of the Bibliocracy.'

I was gradually acquiring a better grasp of prevailing conditions, my friends. The old-time Bookholm I'd known had been a medieval city in which most things were left to chance. That was how Bookemism had been able to flourish in such poisonous profusion. That was how professional murderers like the Bookhunters had been able to go about their criminal business in the streets undisturbed. That, too, was how someone like Pfistomel Smyke had almost succeeded in gaining absolute power. For in those days sheer anarchy had reigned in Bookholm. In hindsight, that state of affairs may sound exciting and adventurous, but it was unsustainable in the long run. Biblionism had turned Bookholm into a modern city, with all the advantages and disadvantages that entailed. Everything – from culture to daily life and commerce – was based on books, but in a more open and rational way, not in the secretive fashion dear to Bookemists and upmarket second-hand booksellers. This was a trifle disenchanting, sadly, but you could now walk down dark alleyways without having to fear that some Bookhunter would chop off your paws and sell them on the black market as literary memorabilia from Lindworm Castle. From my own point of view, dear friends, that was a definite sign of progress!

My eye had been caught by two Druids seated at a nearby table. They were poring over an open blueprint, jabbing it with compasses and arguing fiercely. I caught exotic terms such as *joist elasticity*, *substructive statics* and *procedural triangulation*. What really fascinated me, however, was that they both wore similar hats composed of printed and skilfully folded paper that made them look sensationally ridiculous. I just managed to suppress a grin. Ovidios noticed my inquisitive glances and protruding eyes.

'Those are Bibliotects,' he explained. 'There are Bibliotects *and* architects in Bookholm, but there are marked differences between the two. Architects build houses such as you can see in any other city, whereas Bibliotects have subordinated their profession to Biblionism. Their buildings are distinguished by elaborate book ornamentation, for example, or they use fossilised books as building materials. Their roofs often resemble open books upside down and their symmetrical proportions are sometimes based on poetic metre. There's a law in Bookholm that twenty per cent of all new houses must be built in accordance with the rules of Bibliotecture. The silly hats are part of their guild uniform. They consist of pages from second-hand books on architecture. The Bibliotects may know a lot about statics, but they don't have a clue about fashion.'

'Sounds sensible, that law,' I put in. 'There are enough buildings constructed of ordinary brick. I took to those book buildings on sight.'

'You're right, it was a good law. Petrified books make a handsome building material. Vast quantities of them were discovered in the upper catacombs after the fire, though their origin is still a mystery. They're inexpensive too, being local, but one can also overdo all this goddamned bookery! Imagine you're a professional bookseller or bookbinder. Would you really like to come home after work to a house built of fossilised books with a roof that looks like an open volume of poetry? I wouldn't. I like looking at Bibliotect-designed houses but I wouldn't care to live in one. We can count ourselves lucky that our city isn't based on the butcher's trade, say. The Tourist Board would probably insist on our living in houses built of petrified cutlets. Think of it: The City of Dreaming Sausages!'

The Fumoir was gradually emptying. Pipes were being knocked out, smoking utensils stowed away, people leaving. The various scents had condensed into a vaporous broth that was only very slowly flowing up the chimney and out into the open air.

'Pay attention,' cried Ovidios. 'We'll play a game to make it a bit more difficult for me. I won't single people out, you will. That's so you won't think I only pick the easy ones.'

'All right,' I said and looked around. My curiosity was aroused by a trio of youngsters dressed in black, who were sitting two tables away. 'Them. The ones in black gear. What sort of Biblios are they?'

Ovidios's face suddenly assumed a melancholy expression I couldn't at first interpret.

'Them? That's easy.' He sighed. 'They're Biblionecromancers, all three of them.'

They were young Demidwarfs from Ironville. One could easily tell that from their rust-coloured hair and pale-grey complexions, but these three were more than usually pale. Their clothing, which was black from headgear to shoes, seemed to suggest that they'd just come from a funeral. They were listlessly passing a tiny pipe from hand to hand and puffing at it in turn.

'They look unhealthy somehow,' I said. 'Are they ill?'

'No, appearances are deceptive. "Never judge a book by its cover" – you know the old saying? Most Bibilionecromancers, or Necros, as they're also called for simplicity's sake, are remarkably fit, believe me.' Ovidios heaved a sigh. 'The pale complexion and the rings round the eyes are largely make-up. Most of them take great care of their health. Many are vegetarians.'

One of them, as I myself could see from a distance, was reading aloud to the others from a book of short stories by Perla la Gadeon.

'Their style of dress mightn't appeal to some,' I remarked, 'but their taste in literature is beyond reproach. They're reading La Gadeon.'

'Once again, my friend, I'd beware of jumping to conclusions. La Gadeon is certainly one of the Necros' favourite authors, but not so much because of his literary qualities, more on account of his stories' morbid and other-worldly orientation. And of his personality. In that respect, Perla la Gadeon can undoubtedly be regarded as the progenitor of the Biblionecromancers. They also read a lot of trash, though, take it from me. The Necros' preferred reading must deal with the Undead, the half-dead and, of course, the dead, or they won't so much as touch a book. A kidney clinic full of incurable invalids and situated beside a graveyard in an unhealthy mangrove swamp – that would make an ideal setting. The absence of athletic, well-tanned principal characters in bright, colourful clothes would also be an asset. And if the patients are attacked by a horde of bloodthirsty Moorwood Vampires or a brain-devouring fog from another dimension – preferably both at once – you can assume that the book will prove a bestseller with the Necros. But only, of course, if the jacket bears an illustration of a tattoo in the form of a secret Bookemistic symbol, still oozing blood.'

'You certainly know your stuff,' I said.

Ovidios sighed yet again, this time particularly heavily.

'Hardly surprising. Both my children are Necros. They hold a Black Mass in our cellar every other Wednesday.'

'You're married?' I said, startled. The loquacious reptile was full of surprises.

'Why not? Female Lindworms also leave the castle and travel afar, my friend. My wife is Cecilia Dactyl, a third cousin. She came to Bookholm shortly after the fire. You must know her.'

'Cecilia? Of course. She used to water my godfather's vegetable garden when he was away on lecture tours.' Heavens, what a small place Zamonia was! I now understood Ovidios's intimate knowledge of Biblionecrophily. He had two of these walking cadavers living at home with him! That figured, somehow. I couldn't help grinning at the thought of teenage necrophilic Lindworms.

He made a dismissive gesture. 'It's not so bad. What annoys me is not the artificial blood in the bathtub or the splashes of black wax on the carpet that never come out. No, it's the eternal nagging about my eating habits. They want to convert me to vegetarianism and wean me off smoking, the little philistines! Why do you think I have to smoke my pipe in a Fumoir although I own a nice house in the best district in Bookholm?'

'They hold Black Masses?' I put in smugly.

'Not really. Biblionecromancy isn't a religion, more the opposite. They've got a morbid relationship with books, that's all. No book can be old and fragile enough for them.'

'Many people think the same. Antiquarian booksellers, for instance.'

'Yes, but they're interested in a book's monetary value. The older, the more valuable. To Necros, antiquarian status is completely immaterial. On the contrary, they prefer books that were utter flops – ones that never got beyond a first edition. Dormant stock, unsuccessful debut novels brought out by small, specialist publishers and written by utterly unrecognised authors who not only never wrote another line thereafter but, if possible, committed suicide soon after publication for lack of sales. The sort of books that are found behind an empty bookcase in a bankrupt bookshop. Titles like *Journal of a Bubonic Plague* or *The Attractions of Piecework*. Or *Bulimic Odes*. Books that no one will ever read apart from the author. That's the ideal stuff for a Necros' ritual.'

'So they do hold Black Masses!' I whispered. These Necros were beginning to interest me.

'Not really, as I said. I'd prefer to call them lugubrious wakes. The Necros love literary *corpses*. After acquiring the mildewed volumes they lay them out at home in a darkened room, the way people do for a few days when paying their last respects to the dear departed. The coffins, which they make themselves, are naturally far smaller. They light joss-sticks and play the Horrophone. They even deliver funeral orations.'

'And then they attack the neighbours and drink their blood?'
I persisted.

'No, no,' Ovidios said with a dismissive laugh. 'Biblionecromancers can't hurt anyone, not even themselves, despite their eternal flirtation with murder and self-extinction. They're interested solely in the ritual of *literary mourning*, which is possibly the most poetic form of suicidal yearning. And the most innocuous! I'd sooner that than see my children pine to ride an avalanche in Devil's Gulch, I can tell you! But enough of my offspring. We've forgotten about our game.'

I took another look around. The Fumoir was becoming more and more deserted. I would have to hurry, or the last interesting specimens for our game would be gone.

There was one corner of the establishment where the tobacco smoke seemed to be swirling with special intensity, as if different laws of nature prevailed there. I put this down to my befuddled condition. Until now, I had only been able to make out a silhouette that vaguely reminded me of someone, but who? At last the fog cleared. Just a little at first, then more and more. I gave a start. Was that . . . ?

Yes, a robe embroidered with invocative Bookemistic poetry . . . a hat such as only a scarecrow would wear, with little animal bones and insect fetishes dangling from the brim . . . a face like something out of a nightmare, and on it the self-infatuated grin of someone who can not only endure such a spectacle in the mirror but can't get enough of it. It was an Uggly! Heavens alive! Could it be Inazia Anazazi, the Ugglian bookseller who, together with Ahmed ben Kibitzer, had been largely instrumental in rescuing me from the catacombs?

I rubbed my eyes and looked again. Yes, it was an Uggly. But no, it wasn't Inazia.

She didn't even resemble her closely. Three things were responsible for my brief spell of confusion:

First, that Ugglies favour an extraordinary but almost uniform style of dress. This makes it easy to mistake one for another.

123

Second, that I hadn't set eyes on an Uggly for an eternity and on Inazia for at least two eternities. What must she look like today?

And third, that all Ugglies seem to possess a common aura. This renders them a collective organism that goes around in many individual incarnations, so to speak. If you see one Uggly, you always see them all.

So this was *an* Uggly, but not *the* most important Uggly in my life. Why did I feel so relieved? I ought really to be feeling disappointed that it wasn't Inazia. My memories of her were predominantly good, for I owed it at least partly to her that I was back in Bookholm safe and sound. All the same, dear friends, there's something about Ugglies. No matter how friendly your relations with them, a certain uneasiness always persists. Imagine being married to a scorpion! There's an old Zamonian proverb that very aptly summarises the problem in a single sentence: *I need that like an Uggly in my bed.*

'She's an Ugglian Bibliomancer.' Ovidios's whispered remark roused me from my reverie. 'Stop staring at her like that, or she'll be all over you!'

'Eh?' I said absently, turning to him. My visit to the Fumoir had unexpectedly become a veritable journey into the past.

'Bibliomancers foretell the future from books,' Ovidios explained. 'Elsewhere, the future is foretold from playing cards or the entrails of dead cats; in Bookholm from books. Bibliomancy is sometimes regarded as a science, but it's hocus-pocus. It has as much to do with science as astrology does with astronomy. Total humbug, but sadly as widespread as warts on a warthog. Bibliomancers claim to be able to take any newly acquired book and foretell the buyer's future from it.'

'A brilliant business concept!' I said. 'The streets of Bookholm are teeming with such customers. Every other person has a newly acquired book under his arm.'

'Exactly. And with practice any books can be made to yield a few fragmentary oracular pronouncements. There are Ugglian soothsayers, Hellrazorish stichomancers, oracular rhymesters from the Impic Alps, Watervalian syllaboprophets . . . There are Moomy women in Bookholm market who'll tell your fortune from boiled spaghetti letters of three different flavours. Any old Turniphead can come along, call himself a qualified Bibliomancer and prophesy the money out of pea-brained tourists' pockets. That's how things are these days. Toleration also has its price. We can't fence the city off.'

I cast another covert glance at the Uggly, who was now completely wreathed in smoke again. I wondered where Inazia was now. Still in Bookholm?

Ovidios sighed. 'Ugglies are still reputed to make the most accurate predictions and be thoroughly respectable and reliable. But why should I be interested in things to come? It's enough of a burden to cope with the present and past. I don't have to know what awaits me in the future.'

I nodded. 'I've had my own experience of Ugglian prophecies,' I said. 'They can be surprisingly accurate, but I've no need for a second helping.'

I glanced over at the Uggly for the last time, but there was nothing in the place where she'd been sitting a moment ago save swirling tobacco smoke. She had disappeared.

'Well,' said Ovidios, 'I'm afraid we'll have to call it a day soon. We're running out of Biblios.'

'Hang on,' I protested. 'Not now, just when it's getting interesting.'

'But we could go on for ever,' Ovidios said with a laugh. 'There are as many Biblios as there are Bookholmers. Biblionists, Bibliodromes, Biblionnaires, Biblioclasts, Bibliologists, Bibliodonts, Bibliogoths, Bibliospasts, Bibliots, Biblioklepts, Bibliometrists, Bibliogants, Bibliomants, Bibliophasts, Bibliophants, Bibliogomes, Bibliobiles, Bibliophages, Bibliogames, Biblio—'

'All right,' I exclaimed, 'I'm shameless. I've taken up enough of your time. I doubt if two Lindworm expats have ever spent so long talking.'

'You could well be right. You know, it's important to discover what Biblionism means to one – what sort of Biblio one is oneself. You should use your stay in Bookholm to find that out.'

I adjusted my cloak in readiness to get up and take my leave. Only one question was still on the tip of my tongue.

'Tell me something, Ovidios: What sort of Biblio are *you*?'

He gave me a long look of mingled bafflement and perplexity.

'No idea,' he said with a laugh. 'I've never given it any thought.'

I made to get up, but before doing so I scanned the Fumoir for the last time. It was largely deserted now, but a few scattered figures were continuing to smoke in peace. My survey ended in the furthest corner of the room. Someone was still sitting there. I hadn't spotted him before, doubtless because he'd been obscured by another smoker who had since left. He might also have escaped my notice because he looked more like an inanimate object than a living creature. This was probably also due to his clothing, which was better described as a suit of armour. He sat at his table, motionless as a discarded doll. I was overcome by an old and very familiar fear inspired mainly by the helmet he was wearing. It served him as a mask and resembled a gun turret in miniature. All in all, the sinister fellow looked like a walking fortress.

And now at last he moved. With slow, mechanical movements he picked up a manuscript lying on the table in front of him, rolled it up and stowed it beneath his cloak. Rising to his feet with an effort, he stiffly strode out.

'That looked like a Bookhunter,' I said in a tremulous voice. 'It can't have been, though. Bookhunting was prohibited here after the fire. I've seen similar figures in the city. What are they, a stupid stunt to put the wind up tourists?' It was my turn to become agitated. Bookhunters are no joke to me.

'That was a Biblionaut,' said Ovidios. I could tell he felt rather uneasy about the subject. 'And that one over there,' he went on hurriedly, 'is a—'

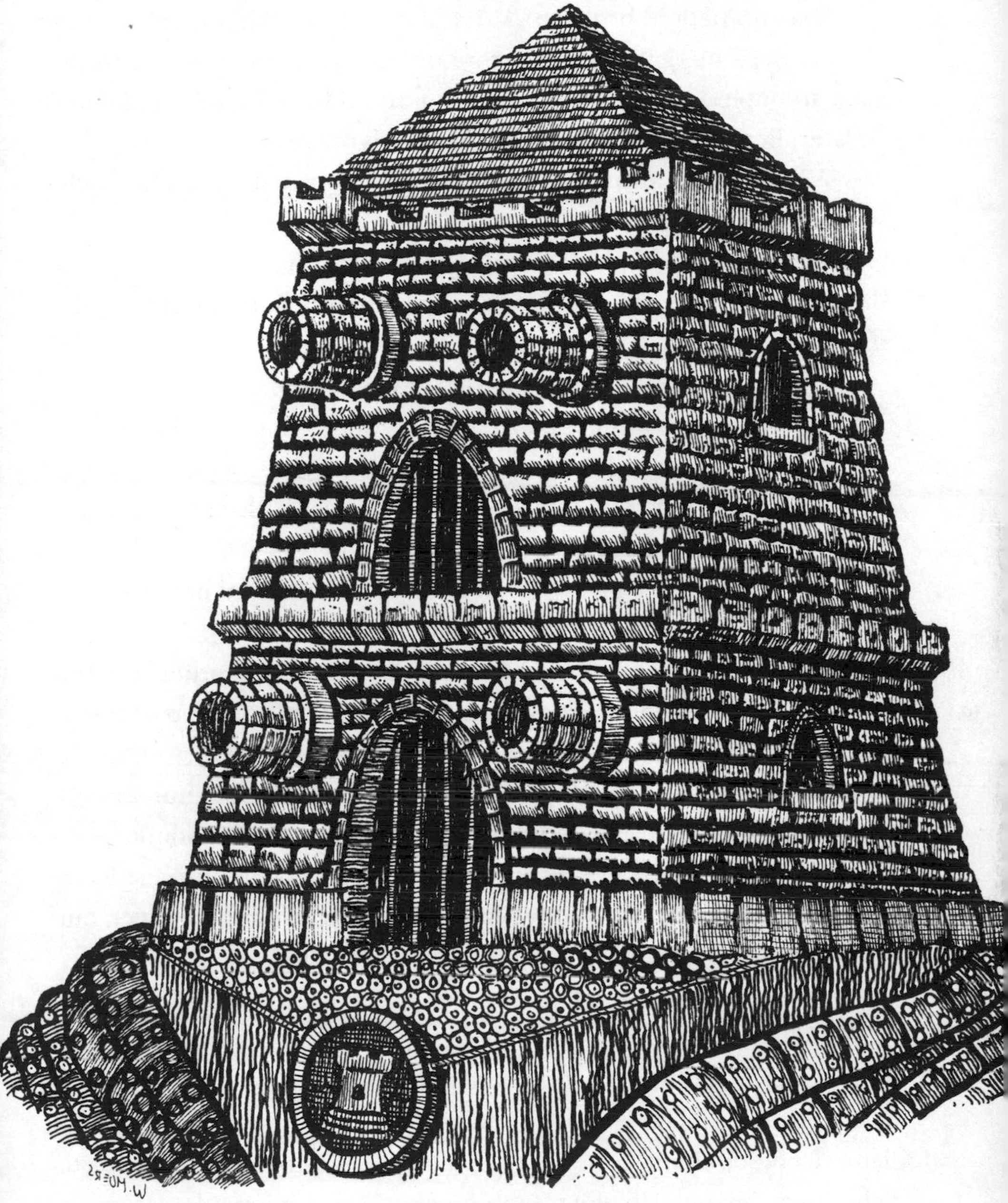

'One moment,' I broke in. 'What the devil is a Biblionaut?'

'He eyed me gravely. 'A shame our conversation has to end on such an unpleasant note,' he said. 'But you'd have found out sooner or later. Besides, I can relieve you of your worst fears.'

'What does that mean? What fears? Are you telling me he really was a Bookhunter?'

'Yes and no. Well, I'd best give you the bad news first. Around a dozen years ago, the authorities permitted Bookhunting once more.'

'What?' I said dully. That was bad news indeed.

'They didn't publicise the fact, and they don't call it Bookhunting any more. It's termed Biblionautics, as if it were a literary method of trawling for fish, and today's Bookhunters are now called Biblionauts.'

'But why? Everyone was so relieved when Bookhunting was abolished! Nobody missed those fellows.'

'I must go back a bit further,' said Ovidios. 'It's rather like the Bibliocists or the Bibliocrats. People aren't particularly fond of them, but sometimes they're glad they exist. Like dentists.'

'Who on earth welcomes the presence of Bookhunters?' I growled. I was more agitated than I would have cared to admit.

'I told you, they're called Biblionauts these days. You must learn to make the distinction. I know you can't accept the situation yet, but look at it this way: Biblionauts are a necessary evil.'

'That's what people used to say about the Bookhunters.'

'Well? Wasn't it true? The city made money out of them. The authorities keep quiet about that today because it smacks of complicity. You'll have to say goodbye to your former fears sooner or later. The Bookhunters are dead – have been for two hundred years. They live on only in your nightmares. The Biblionauts are quite another kettle of fish.'

'Bookhunters, Biblionauts – what's the difference?' I insisted. 'They look just as martial and menacing as those criminals of old.'

Ovidios sighed. 'But they aren't dangerous any more. Not to us, at any rate. They're an entirely new generation – they operate in accordance with a strict code of conduct and the methods espoused by Colophonius Regenschein. They don't bump each other off down below. They don't kill or injure anyone except the dangerous creatures they have to deal with in the catacombs. They've retained the martial attire because it's essential in the Labyrinth, as a deterrent and for personal protection. They venture far deeper into the catacombs these days. Areas are being explored in which no one ever set foot in the old days. Those who are bold enough to enter them need more than just audacity. They need the heart of a Bookhunter.'

'Bookhunters have no heart,' I said coldly. Ovidios had no idea what he was talking about.

'I meant to say they need the heart of a Biblionaut. I still keep mixing up those terms myself.'

'Perhaps you should simply start again from the beginning,' I suggested. 'Since when have you believed that Bookholm can't get by without Bookhunters – or Biblionauts?'

'It was a gradual process. You never saw it, Optimus, but please try to visualise the streets of Bookholm without any Bookhunters. That might sound a welcome state of affairs from your point of view, but it's also rather boring, isn't it? Something would simply be missing. I experienced it for myself. I didn't know *what* I was missing on my walks until one day it dawned on me: walking through Bookholm after the Bookhunters had disappeared was like visiting a zoo devoid of wild animals. They were as much a part of Bookholm as thunder and lightning are of a storm. They supplied the drama in our city. The kick. The salt in the soup and the sugar in the coffee! At least admit that their costumes were great!'

I naturally understood what Ovidios was getting at and he was right. But he would never persuade me to say a good word about that gang of professional cut-throats. *He* hadn't come up against them in the catacombs. *I* had.

'The municipal authorities thought up a remedy. They engaged clowns from Florinth and mimes from Grailsund. Brass brands, too. Can you imagine it? Ludicrous, made-up buffoons and brass bands as a substitute for Bookhunters! Imagine Florinth without its museums! Ironville without its rivers of mercury! There was a dramatic drop in hotel bookings and sales in the antiquarian bookshops stagnated. Worst of all, however, there were no discoveries of books on the *Golden List*, because these had traditionally been made by the Bookhunters. And without any fresh *Golden List* discoveries the really affluent customers stayed away – people like the book-collecting biblionnaires and industrialists who used to come to Bookholm to bid at *Golden List* auctions and nonchalantly bought up whole bookshops or city blocks. The really big money stopped coming. We suddenly lacked the crowd pullers that had lent the book trade its glamour. And we also, shameful though it was, began to realise how important to us the Bookhunters had been. Bookholm was threatening to become a city like any other. And then a miracle occurred! All at once, from one day to the next, they were back.'

'Who were?' I asked slow-wittedly.

'Why, the accursed Bookhunters! Or the Biblionauts, as they now styled themselves. It was like a dream. As if conjured into being overnight or sprung up like mushrooms, heavily armed, mask-wearing figures in bizarre suits of armour stalked the city's streets once more! Awesome beings from a darker, deeper world, none resembled any other. It was initially assumed that they were a trick on the part of City Hall: that they were simply costumed actors hired to reactivate the tourist trade – and indeed, plans of that kind did exist. But then some *Golden List* books suddenly turned up – in substantial numbers, what's more. Biblionauts would march into up-market antiquarian bookshops and plunk a copy of *The Yellow Almanac* down on the counter, say, or Wimpersleake's long-lost, handwritten diary of his boyhood! Things of that kind! It truly did seem like a miracle and the Biblionauts were hailed as saviours.'

Ovidios leant forward.

'Of course, their new professional name was only a little subterfuge, which the Bibliocrats at City Hall were happy to go along with. Even though Bookhunters had been banished from Bookholm, it wasn't forbidden to go around there in bizarre suits of armour or search the catacombs for rare books. Business picked up again within a few months.'

Ovidios gathered his smoker's paraphernalia together and prepared to leave.

'And that's all there is to the Biblionauts – or the latter-day Bookhunters, if you prefer. Not a very edifying story, I grant you, but I'm afraid you'll have to come to terms with it, because they're still very popular in Bookholm. And now I fear I must take my leave – the family calls, you understand. I enjoyed our conversation – perhaps we can resume it some time soon. Come and see us.'

Having handed me a card bearing his address, he rose and walked out with measured tread.

'Like a king in exile,' I thought as I watched him go. It was nice to have met him again and to see that he was prospering.

Then I myself set off. I was genuinely the last to leave the Fumoir, which was empty apart from me and swaths of toxic fumes. At the door I paused, suddenly aware that I'd forgotten something of great importance. I thought for a moment, then it came to me. I had forgotten the real purpose of my visit: I'd omitted to smoke my very last pipe.

Book Wine
from Bookholm

Anyone who has already visited a tavern or two will know what I mean. You've propped up the bar for hours and indulged in some heavy drinking, but you still feel comparatively sober. Then you emerge into the open air and – wham! – that's when the alcohol utterly unexpectedly takes full effect as it mingles with the oxygen in your blood. You're suddenly as drunk as you deserve to be.

That was more or less what happened to me when I left the Fumoir. Although I'd drunk no alcohol, my lungs had semi-involuntarily absorbed vast quantities of intoxicating substances, some of exotic provenance. All at once, I could hardly keep my feet. I lurched out into the street and came to a brief, swaying halt. The ground tilted first to the left, then to the right, as if I were aboard a ship in rough weather, and the stars were whirling overhead. The stars? Yes, night had fallen during our conversation.

I tottered along unsteadily for a few steps and clung to a wall, feeling sure I was about to pass out. Instead, my circulation and sense of balance stabilised themselves, and I was overcome by a surprising feeling of happiness – indeed, of absolute euphoria. The state of intoxication I'd acquired in the Fumoir was probably unique in its way. Where else could one try out such an unpredictable and experimental cocktail of drugs without – at least in my case – really meaning to? This was probably the secret of the Fumoir's obvious popularity. You didn't go there to smoke at all, but to be surprised by what the others had to offer. The most significant feature of my condition was that I couldn't have described *how* I felt. I didn't even know a word for it.

Once I had more or less regained control of myself, I looked around. The nocturnal streetscape glowed with unreal colours, almost like a painting by Edd van Murch, the great exponent of *Grailsundian Devil-Painting*. The buildings were swaying gently to and fro, and the air was filled with the sound of countless whispers. None of this alarmed me; on the contrary, I found it entertaining. When I tried to catch the ethereal voices in the air, I saw I had ten claws on each paw, but it didn't dismay me, it made me giggle stupidly. The paving stones beneath my feet felt soft and warm, almost hot, which also amused me. I'd never found walking so interesting! I felt I was taking giant strides across an endless feather bed on grotesquely long legs, like a gigantic stork. The people who passed me were transparent, their only response to my humorous remarks being wholly unintelligible quacking sounds. I felt I was in an echo chamber that multiplied every sound: my footsteps on the pavement, the rattle of horse-drawn vehicles, the slamming of doors. Perhaps I'd left the Fumoir by the wrong exit and was walking through another dimension in which everything was more vivid and interesting – and funnier!

Heavens alive, how thirsty I was! My throat was so dry, my tongue was cleaving to my gums. I simply had to have something – anything! – to drink, so I strode on through the darkened streets in search of a tavern, continually shaken by uncontrollable paroxysms of laughter. Was I feverish? Yes, but in a *delectable* way! If this was a symptom of some disease, I never wanted to recover from it! I firmly resolved to visit every Fumoir in Bookholm regularly from now on, one after another.

In these streets there were numerous shops full of souvenirs: cheap tourist trash such as snowstorm paperweights containing city sights, poor copies of books on the *Golden List*, coloured postcards bearing greetings from the *City of Dreaming Books* and the inevitable puppets resembling famous authors in appearance. This junk amused me as immensely as every- thing did at that moment and, although my thirst was urging me on, I paused in front of every other window, sometimes roaring with laughter. I passed one window whose display was hard to make out in the darkness, but I spotted something out of the corner of my eye that struck me as familiar and captured my attention. Looking more closely, I discovered that the window was full of Booklings!

I stood rooted to the spot. A sign hang- ing above the door of the shop announced that it specialised in *Literary Sculptures*, in other words, carved, sculpted or modelled bookends, paperweights, authors' busts, or scale models of printing presses. But the window itself was exclusively devoted to miniature effigies of Booklings of the highest quality. I was amazed. The artist had succeeded in making his miniature figures so incredibly lifelike, he had to be intimately acquainted with the Booklings. This greatly surprised me, because very few people apart from me had ever been privileged to see this subterranean species in the flesh. Or had that, too, changed since my last visit? I found one group sculpture particularly admirable. It represented two Booklings engaged in printing, complete with a scale model of a press and printed pages lying around.

Yes, that was just how the Booklings looked in the bowels of the Labyrinth. I had witnessed such scenes with my own eyes. Then I discovered a small handwritten notice in the window. It read:

> *All portrayals of Booklings based on Optimus Yarnspinner's description in his book 'The City of Dreaming Books'. Accuracy, though striven for, cannot be guaranteed.*

Tears of emotion sprang to my eyes. If an artist who had never seen any Booklings himself could portray them in such a natural, lifelike fashion with the aid of my descriptions alone, those descriptions couldn't be too bad. Well, yes, but at that time the Orm had still been pervading the convolutions of my brain with some intensity! I was reminded of the reason for my trip: I had received a letter from the catacombs – more specifically, from the Leather Grotto, the Booklings' subterranean home! This was now only a few miles away, directly beneath my feet but separated from me by the dark world known as the *Labyrinth of Dreaming Books*.

This realisation made me feel suddenly sentimental, although my extremely fragile condition may also have been responsible. I tottered on in tears, thinking of the little one-eyed friends I hadn't seen for so long. I sobbed to myself until I heard the strains of an old-fashioned hurdy-gurdy such as Bookholmian street musicians often play. This dispelled my tearful mood and I looked up. Standing here and there in the entrances to various buildings were small groups of loudly chatting, laughing people – usually a sign that there are places of liquid refreshment nearby. Excellent! My maudlin state of mind abruptly left me. Having instinctively headed in the right direction, all I needed to do now was settle on a suitable establishment. One particularly numerous group was being entertained by a busker playing an ancient Aerophone – he was no virtuoso – and warbling in a reedy falsetto:

'Traveller, if you go to Bookholm,
don't forget to bring a book home,
bring a book home!
Traveller, if you go to Bookholm,
don't forget to drink some Bookwine,
drink some Bookwine.
But be warned that those who do
will themselves become books too.'

That was meant metaphorically, of course, but it sounded inviting. It also presaged something to drink. At last! I elbowed my way into a taproom chock-full of carousing customers – tourists, as I could tell from their multilingual babble of voices. I heard the low moans of Gloomberg Dwarfs, the froglike croaking of Moss Trolls, the mercurial syllabic sing-song of Camomills and the eerie yodelling of Devil's Gulchers. When a chair chanced to become vacant I promptly flopped down on it and beckoned to a waiter, a squat little Wood Goblin with shaggy hair and a mournful expression. Far from saying good evening, let alone taking my order, he simply plunked a glass and a brimming pitcher of wine on the table in front of me.

'One Bookwine!' he yelled without looking at me and walked off. That was absolutely fine with me. I preferred this uncomplicated mode of service to an arrogant wine waiter. Before I could pour myself a glass, I noticed that the table was strewn with slips of paper. At first I took them for beer mats, but then I saw that something was printed on them. I picked one up and read it.

TURN INTO

Traveller, if you go to Bookholm, don't forget to drink some Bookwine!

Acquire an intimate knowledge of age-old Bookholmian customs!
Sample some of the legendary Bookwine pressed centuries ago
by Bookemists employing an expensive secret process.
A unique fusion of alchemy, vinology
and printer's craftsmanship!

The greatest adventure in Bookholm will take place inside your head!

The grapes used in Bookwine are pressed
with obsolete printing presses!

The wine is stored in subterranean libraries
in barrels made out of antique bookshelves!

While it is maturing, great works of
Zamonian literature are read aloud to the barrels
by genuine authors!

Finally, before being bottled, the wine is blended
with scrapings from mildewed books,
which lend it its unusual colour and luminosity.

I couldn't help laughing. Great! I'd ended up in a tourist trap! It was only now that I spotted the hunchbacked glass engraver in the corner of the tavern adorning cheap glasses with customers' names to order, likewise the trashy oil paintings on the walls from which gilt-edged greats of classical Zamonian literature, from Aleisha Wimpersleake to Bethelzia B. Binngrow, looked down self-importantly at the customers. The wine here was bound to cost three times as much as elsewhere and

A BOOK!!!

Last of all, the wine is submitted to an alchemical process known as metavinoistics, an art and science believed to be extinct since the Great Conflagration.

Only metavinoistics transforms Bookwine into the absolute rarity it is. It will give you a treat you will NEVER forget!

Become part of a mystery!

Discovered in subterranean vaults after the Great Conflagration, Bookwine exists in limited quantities only. Its method of manufacture remains a secret to this day!

Only while stocks last!
Metavinoistic metamorphosis guaranteed!
Money-back guarantee!
FOR ADULTS ONLY!!!

Free after three pitchers of Bookwine: get your own name engraved on your glass – the perfect Bookholm souvenir!

Enjoy!

was probably – what was the betting? – the lousiest plonk to be found anywhere in Bookholm. However, I'd sat down, been served and was tormented by thirst. So I poured myself a glass. The first thing that struck me was the wine's truly exceptional colour. It was green, by the Orm! I held my glass up to the candlelight. It was as vivid a green as woodruff lemonade and slightly luminous. Or was that another after-effect of my Fumoir fix? Everything within me baulked at drinking the stuff. Then I thought, what the hell, I've got to drink *something*, so down the hatch and get it over! Just one glass, then pay and find a quieter, more congenial establishment that serves decent local wine without any alchemical additives. So I gulped the green brew down.

That wine, my friends, was downright sick-making! By that I really mean it was an absolute emetic. It was only with the utmost self-control that I managed to suppress an urge to throw up on the taproom floor. The taste might have been that of an ancient tome simmered for days in cheap grape juice and then cooled to cellar temperature. Either that or a bucket of dishwater with an old blackboard sponge squeezed out in it. It certainly didn't belong in a wine glass!

Pulling myself together, I resisted the impulse to slam down some money on the table, storm out and relieve myself in the open air. I simply remained seated and gave my innards a chance to settle down. My nausea gave way first to a vague sense of foreboding, then to a warmth that suffused my stomach. I was feeling better! I'd been completely parched and in need of some fluid inside me, but that I could have obtained free of charge and more palatably from any municipal fountain. Now I had to get out of there! Wanting to summon the waiter and pay, I looked around and noticed that some of the customers were sitting there as if totally transfixed and entranced, with their eyes shut and empty wine glasses in their hands. I had no idea what uncivilised province they hailed from – perhaps it was the first glass of wine they'd ever drunk in their life. Then again, perhaps they'd drunk a few glasses too many.

Suddenly, everything went black.

For one terrible moment I feared I'd lost consciousness. No wonder, considering all the unpredictable toxic substances I'd involuntarily absorbed in the Fumoir! But then it occurred to me that you can't be worried if you've really lost consciousness.

My next thought was that I might have gone blind from one moment to the next. Such a thing could happen, I'd read. Almost simultaneously, however, my eyesight returned in a puzzling manner: it was as if I were a worm wriggling out into daylight through loose soil. Above me was a dazzlingly blue sky with white clouds sailing across it. But if I was neither unconscious nor blind, surely I must at least have lost my mind? A moment ago I'd been sitting in a noisy tavern full of people and now I was suddenly all on my own. Yes, but where? In a wood, obviously, because I was surrounded by young trees. More than that, I myself was clearly a tree! Or what else grows out of the ground in the middle of a wood and puts out little green tentacles? If this didn't indicate that I'd just been afflicted with some mental illness, what was it?

Very well, so I was a tree. A very small tree, though: just a sapling that had not long broken through the forest floor. But I grew, and I grew very fast. I rose higher and higher as night and day alternated at whirlwind speed overhead. The sun traversed the sky within seconds, rising and setting, rising and setting and giving way to the moon, which waxed and waned with breathtaking rapidity. Months went by in a few moments. I developed little branches, put out roots, grew leaves and proliferated in all directions until, in a trice, I was enclosed by a dense tracery of branches and foliage. I had become a majestic poplar in whose branches birds nested and squirrels clambered around. At times I was surrounded by dark forest floor, at others by brilliant green foliage, at still others by dazzling white snow. The seasons came and went as swiftly and regularly as the pendulum of a metronome. I had almost reconciled myself to my permanent, peaceful existence as a poplar when I suddenly toppled over.

Crash!

I had been felled.

I was carted off and dumped in a river, then drifted downstream with many other tree trunks, slowly at first, then faster and faster. Water eddied and foamed around me, and all at once I wasn't a tree trunk in water any more, I was an idea! Or rather, a concatenation of ideas, a serpentine succession of words. In short, a whole sentence drifting down a mental river through the cerebral convolutions of an author engaged in writing an entire novel. Drifting in this river like people drowning were the novel's principal characters, who were calling out printable sentences such as '*Ah, Hector, my love for you is as futile as a desire for warm glaciers!*' Yes, dear friends, I had clearly become insane.

Or had I? The next moment, foam engulfed me once more. I was again a tree trunk in a river and the stream was slowing. In company with all the other tree trunks I was drifting towards a massive building with tall chimneys, and issuing from it came the demented screech of circular saws. It was a paper mill! That spelled the end of my existence as a poplar, because I was swiftly sawn into ever smaller pieces. At first into thick slices, then into thin planks, then cut up into cubes, shredded into shavings and finally reduced to thin fibres. Having been once more steeped in water and stirred into a pulp, I was sieved by fine-meshed screens and finally air-dried. I had become *paper*!

But not for long, my friends, for scarcely had I been dried and stacked when everything went black again. All at once I was . . . an *anxiety*! Yes, a gnawing anxiety in the agonised mind of a publisher desperately wondering how to put his almost bankrupt firm back on its legs. He paced restlessly up and down his office, yelling at the furniture, kicking over piles of books, and cursing the public's fickle and unpredictable taste in reading matter. And suddenly, from being a gnawing anxiety, I became a *flash of inspiration*! Yes, I became a glorious idea, which was to talk a successful author into writing a novel that, when equipped with the right title, could – nay, had to! – become a bestseller. The publisher promptly proceeded to write a letter. He reached for pen and paper, and . . . yes, I was paper once more! I was inserted in a press, smoothed with a printer's bone and moistened. Then the platen descended on me, pressed me up against the ink-smeared forme and tattooed me with text. I felt what it's like to be *printed*! When it became light again I was being clamped in a vice with lots of other sheets, like a sinner in an inquisitor's torture chamber. We were pierced with fine needles, equipped with a thread binding, well glued and finally stuck into a handsome leather cover. I was now a *book*!

But hardly had I grown used to this idea when I became an anxiety once more. Not, this time, in the publisher's mind but in that of the author who had written the book. And I was only one anxiety among many. He wondered how well his novel would sell; what friends and critics would think of it and write about it; whether the title (*A Desire for Warm Glaciers*) had been a good choice; whether the jacket should have been green rather than yellow; whether the multiplicity of parentheses in the text didn't seem a bit overdone; whether he would ever follow up this masterpiece with anything equally perfect; and many other worries. Then the author got drunk and began to weep. Tears blurred his vision and – bingo! – I turned back into a book: a book in a bookshop picked up by a hand that paid at the cash desk, took me home and opened me. And then I once more found myself in a stream of ideas, of immaculate, perfectly copy-edited sentences that poured themselves out of the book and into the reader's brain. I was being *read*!

But – hey presto! – it was suddenly light again. I was sitting in the taproom with an empty wine glass in my hand, instantaneously hemmed in by people and noise. I was neither comatose nor blind, nor had I gone mad. I had merely got drunk on Bookwine.

By the Orm! *That* was some alcoholic delirium! Not only had I imagined being a book in all the various phases of its existence, but I had written it myself and printed and published it. And, on top of everything else, I had experienced the unique sensation of *being read*! I now knew what it was like to be a book. Incredible!

How much time had elapsed? An hour, three hours, a year? No idea. It seemed highly probable that such a trance had lasted less than a minute, because nothing around me had changed. The same people were sitting in the same places and the house musician, a lutenist whose music filled the taproom, was still playing the same tune.

I promptly poured myself another glass and knocked it back. At once, exactly the same thing happened. The light went out and I became tree, paper, author, publisher and reader in turn. After this swift and fascinating metamorphosis, the light went on and it was over again. I repeated the process another three times until the pitcher was empty, but even on the penultimate occasion I experienced a certain satiety and even nausea, as if I'd spent too long on a merry-go-round. So I left it at one pitcher, beckoned to the waiter, paid him and staggered outside.

I said 'staggered', dear friends, because this Bookwine appeared to pack a powerful punch, not only metamorphically but alcoholically as well. Or was it Fumoir poisoning? Both, of course. Besides, the fact that I'd eaten almost nothing all day was certainly no aid to stability. I simply had to get something solid inside me!

Not far away was an establishment that seemed familiar to me as soon as I crossed the threshold. Of course, it was the nameless little coffee bar in which I'd eaten my first (and hitherto last) slice of bee-bread!* This was where I'd met the scheming literary agent Claudio Harpstick, who had artfully put me in touch with Pfistomel Smyke and was largely responsible for my abduction into the catacombs of Bookholm.

I took an involuntary step backwards, then changed my mind and went inside. The smell of food was too tempting and my hunger too overpowering. Besides, it was only a snack bar like any other, even if it had been the place where my troubles began. Time seemed to have stood still there. The décor was just as it had been two centuries ago: bare brick walls, shelves filled with cheap books one could read while eating at the scrubbed wooden tables. There was also the same old

---

*See *The City of Dreaming Books*, p. 72 ff. (Tr.)

counter surmounted by a big blackboard inscribed with the chef's specials in coloured chalk. They still served the same simple, typically Bookholmian food and drink as they had in days of yore: *Reader's Espresso* and *Balono de Zacher Biscuits*, *Prince Sangfroid Pie* and *Mantho Snam Spaghetti*. Oh yes, and *Bee-Bread*, of course. It was a touching sight. I'd have taken a bet that even the chalk inscriptions hadn't altered in two hundred years.

I fear that all my good resolutions about a sensible diet had been left behind in the Fumoir, together with my wits, because I now threw over the traces. I devoured three bowls of Mantho Snam Spaghetti, two Prince Sangfroid Pies, some thyme-flavoured toast with melted Midgard cheese and four assorted slices of cake, each named after a different author and all topped with whipped cream. This time I passed on the bee-bread for reasons you, my sympathetic friends, will doubtless understand. Having bought myself a big bag of Balono de Zacher biscuits for later on, I emerged into the street once more. The night, my revitalised self decided, was still young. Besides, I was thirsty again.

A Reunion
with Kibitzer

When I awoke the next morning I didn't, for a dismayingly long time, know where I was. Nor did I know *who* I was.

Then both things came back to me: I was Optimus Yarnspinner and I was in my hotel room in Bookholm. In the first instance I was right, in the second utterly wrong. This certainly wasn't *my* hotel room.

I noticed that because of three things: first, the wallpaper; second, the four suitcases beside the bed (I've never owned a suitcase in my life); and third, the Frogling standing beside the window, who was quaking with fear and staring at me round the curtain.

'Please go away!' he said in a hoarse voice. 'Just go!'

To cut a very embarrassing story short, I'd spent the night not only in the wrong hotel room but in the wrong hotel as well. In my inebriated condition I had simply staggered into the nearest one, marched into some room or other, barricaded the door behind me with a wardrobe, flopped down on the bed and fallen into a swoonlike sleep.

The Frogling, whose room this was, had been so startled and intimidated by my behaviour that he hadn't even tried to remove the wardrobe or cry for help. He had simply waited for me to wake up. He didn't want to hear any explanations or excuses for my uncivilised conduct; he just asked me to leave. So I did him that favour, having seldom felt so ashamed in my life. My hotel was three streets further on.

As I was laboriously and remorsefully piecing together last night's mosaic of incidents, a thoroughly ridiculous book title – *A Desire for Warm Glaciers* – kept going through my head. What I could still remember quite well was that, immediately after my orgy of gluttony, I had lurched into a nearby wine bar to keep my promise to myself, which was to drink something other than hallucinogenic Bookwine. I sampled – rather over-liberally – some grape juice from the Bookholm area. From that point onward my powers of recall developed fine cracks at first and then lacunae of steadily increasing size. I could still remember having a fierce argument with a gigantic Turniphead, but I'd forgotten what it was about. Then we came to blows and I had to change locations. I discovered a basement dive situated in a seedy side street and patronised exclusively by famous authors of whom I'd never heard. The last thing I recalled was that the wine there, although not particularly good, was sensationally cheap and served in rusty little buckets. Then my thread of recollection snapped.

Suffering from fierce self-reproach and an even fiercer headache, I returned to my hotel, where I had a wash, settled my bill and set off with my modest baggage, intending to find some better and more central accommodation during the day. In the course of a long walk that took me to the city centre, I endeavoured to clear my head and straighten myself out. When you're approaching your three-hundredth birthday, as I was, you have to admit it takes longer to recover from such a binge. I was through with intoxicants of all kinds – that I solemnly swore to myself while walking! The only kind of intoxication to which I still aspired was an Ormic trance.

The Bookholmers had always been fond of self-confident and inventive forms of advertising. For their own trades, for books, for publishing houses, for artistic projects, for readings and poetry evenings, for cultural functions of all kinds, for cures for writer's block, for delicious cakes and hot coffee. Painted hoardings, posters, the sides of buildings, fliers stuck to lamp-posts, banners suspended across streets, stentorian-voiced barkers reading aloud from books, importunate touts attired in printed galleys – even 'walking books' on legs – were among the city's omnipresent features. But the propensity for barefaced selling of all kinds of things had inexorably increased during my absence. I found this far more noticeable on my midday stroll than I had the previous day.

My thick head precluded me from deciding whether or not I liked this: whether I found it amusing, intrusive, ingenious, embarrassing, original, or simply brash. It certainly added to the city's entertainment value. When in Bookholm, I had always felt as if I were roaming through the pages of an illustrated book in which the pictures moved. But where one sign had hung in the old days, three were now hanging, and where a wall had borne one poster, it now bore ten. If I looked up while walking along a street, the sky was filled with promises in the form of billboards advertising cheap or expensive books, hot coffee or pastries fresh from the oven, the best eyeglasses in the city, or a refreshing neck massage administered by muscular Peat Midgets.

Many of them I could decipher with ease, for instance advertisements for alternative book manufacture using hempen paper or Bibliognostic health check-ups, an Ugglian publisher or a dwarfs' printworks. Others meant nothing to me. I was lucky if I could even identify the languages on many of the billboards by referring to the script, but what they were advertising I couldn't say. Ovidios and the Wolperting had emphasised what a tolerant and cosmopolitan city Bookholm had become since the overthrow of Bookemism. I now realised how far that process had gone. Ornian cuneiform, Demonistic ligatures, Dullsgardian hieroglyphs, Midgardian knot writing or archaistic Troll runes – I could usually only guess at the products or services they offered. Sometimes the addition of drawings, coats of arms or symbols were an aid to deciphering them. But what did a gold death's head with snakes wriggling out of its eye sockets signify? What about a seashell with a spider sitting on a pearl?

What could one buy in a shop whose sign displayed a fully bandaged chicken? No thanks, I didn't want to know that, so I kept to the middle of the street and left it to my imagination to visualise what these shops actually sold.

The district in which I had now been for some time was quite familiar to me because it had largely escaped the fire and I'd formerly roamed around there. I was surrounded by a reassuringly nostalgic maze of old half-timbered buildings, some of which housed the most delightful antique shops. Not snobbish luxury establishments selling prohibitively expensive items from the *Golden List*. No, what still predominated here was the traditional spirit of old Bookholm. I at last saw shop windows displaying the kind of books for which the true bibliophile came here. After only a short spell of window-gazing I discovered rare first editions like *The Third Side of the Coin* by Elmura Voddnik, *Gingivitis Salad* by Tomok Zebulon, *Pain in My Wooden Leg* by Hugobart Cramella and *No Coffin for Mother* by Count Petroso di Gadusti – Zamonian literary jewels such as one would seek in vain elsewhere. Here, however, they occupied their due place: right at the front of the display but affordably priced. In the next window I was overjoyed to see collected editions of Orphetu Harnschauer, Clas Reischdenk and Avegeus Luftbart, together with the long, character-rich novels of Asdrel Chickens, which one can reread again and again. The trenchantly satirical novels of Slainco Brafesair, six hundred years old but still ultra-modern, in the long-out-of-print woodcut edition. The gigantic tome by Marvin de Lescetuge with illustrations by the immortal Oved Usegart! All the fairy tales by Nartinan Schneidhasser in the much sought-after India-paper edition, signed! A quarto edition, bound in blue bamboo-worm silk, of Abradauch Sellerie's brilliant essay on Perla la Gadeon. All Doylan Cone's *Hermes Olshlock* novels in the legendary collected edition complete with magnifying glass. The collected letters of Volkodir Vanabim – uncensored! A volume of the best humorous sketches by the great Rubert Jashem! The complete first editions of Eglu Wicktid! The youthful reminiscences of

Abradauch Sellerie, unabridged! The unsurpassable jungle tales of Plairdy Kurding with watercolour illustrations. Eri Elfengold's amusing and informative cultural history, which renders it unnecessary to read a whole library of books. The tension-laden novellas by Trebor Sulio Vessenton, which still fill me with unadulterated envy. And *Cronosso Urbein* by Felino Deeda – the first really good novel in Zamonian literary history! All these in a single shop window and at prices reasonable enough to bring tears to one's eyes. This was Bookholm at its best!

Well, pleasing though this was, it wasn't my real reason for lingering so stubbornly in this district. For the moment, the acquisition of antiquarian books came very low on my list of priorities. The true reason, dear friends, was that I was in the vicinity of *Colophonius Regenschein Lane*, where Dr Ahmed ben Kibitzer kept his small antiquarian bookshop specialising in Nightingalistics. But going there wasn't quite as simple as it sounds, dear friends. Oh no! It was an extremely tricky undertaking, a regular suicide mission. Clearing the air with Ovidios had been a piece of cake compared to the settlement of accounts that faced me now. Why? Because Kibitzer and I had been at loggerheads for a hundred years or more. A hundred years! Can you imagine it?

I briefly considered disappearing. Perhaps I hadn't found the lane after all. Modern Bookholm was the very devil – nothing was the way it used to be! Yes, that was the answer!

Nonsense, the lane was just round the corner. Whom was I kidding? Myself? No, I had to go there or I wouldn't have a moment's peace. I tossed three peppermint pastilles into my mouth to offset my hangover breath and resolutely headed for Regenschein Lane. It was now or never! Into battle!

Shortly before reaching Kibitzer's shop I came to a halt once more. What on earth would I say to him and in what tone of voice? How to start? A prey to indecision, I paced up and down the lane, repeatedly casting fearful glances at the shop out of the corner of my eye. It looked exactly as I remembered it: the darkest and most inconspicuous shop in the street, with candlelight fitfully flickering inside. To me the entrance looked like the gate of hell with a three-brained monster lurking inside, ready to devour me. By the Orm, was I nervous! I sucked a fourth pastille.

Kibitzer's was another of those fortunate establishments that had escaped the flames and its outward appearance hadn't changed at all since then. It was clear that he still specialised in the curious writings of Professor Abdul Nightingale, the Nocturnomath-in-chief whose abstruse work *Domesticated Darkness* was the only item displayed in the window. From the look of the shop, therefore, Kibitzer hadn't changed a jot. Why was I so scared, then?

How cordial, friendly and productive our relations had been for so many years! After I left the city we had regularly exchanged yards-long missives devoted to passionate debates about literature, art, science and philosophy, though we strictly avoided the subject of Bookholm at my request. I could have filled numerous volumes with this meaty correspondence, in which, after all, four brains had taken part. I had written to Kibitzer from all over Zamonia during my extended travels. It was correspondence of the highest order. Brilliant ideas flew back and forth between us like electric sparks. Arrogant though it may seem to say so, the correspondence between Ojahnn Golgo van Fontheweg and Heidler von Clirrfisch is thoroughly inane by comparison. But then . . . Well, then came success. *My* success. And with it, fame. Good gracious, I was soon too preoccupied with replying to admirers' letters and accepting literary prizes to keep up with an old pen friend. Our letters became sparser, my literary output more and more copious. Then Kibitzer, in his now only sporadic letters, dared several times to express criticism of my work, hesitant at first but ever more outspoken as time went by. In his opinion I wrote far too much and was becoming slipshod. My initial response was to defend myself in mild terms, as if shooing away an importunate fly. Then, when Ahmed repeated and specified his charges, allegedly in the name of friendship, I reacted with undisguised asperity. In the end, when he stubbornly insisted that the Orm had deserted me, my treatment of him was thoroughly condescending. How can I put it? One word led to another, the tone of our correspondence became increasingly offended and offensive, and finally it ceased altogether. I still recall the last sentence I wrote him: 'Looking down on you from the dizzy height of my sales figures, I can only smile at your stylistic bean-counting, you third-class Three-Brain!'

The latter was a mean and not particularly subtle sideswipe at his membership of the Nocturnomath category that possesses only three brains, not five or six like many of his kind, still less seven like his great idol, the celebrated Professor Nightingale.

That must have touched a nerve, because he never wrote to me again. Not a line. Not even a postcard. And what did I do? Nothing. In all that time I failed to summon up even a smidgen of magnanimity and apologise to Ahmed for my crude blow beneath the belt. A whole century had gone by! And now I was standing outside his shop, kneading the hem of my cloak in agitation.

'My *dear* Ahmed,' I experimented in my head, 'didn't you get my latest letters? The Zamonian postal service is becoming more and more unreliable.'

No, no lies, Nocturnomaths can read one's thoughts!

Better to remain icy cold? After all, I didn't really feel guilty, did I? He had no more written to me than I had to him. He had wounded my pride and was just as responsible for the situation as I was, the pigheaded creature! So, quite coolly:

'Good afternoon, Kibitzer. How are you?'

Nonsense. That would be stupid. Not my style. How about the jovial touch, as if nothing had happened?

'Hello there, Ahmed, you old bugger! Long time no see, what, hahaha?'

No, that would be too barefaced. Ours had been a genuine friendship, after all, but still . . . No, better to be really personal right away. Reproachful. Go straight into the attack:

'Ahmed, oh Ahmed, old friend, why have you forgotten me?' Then a long, silent, plaintive look with outstretched arms and tears in my eyes.

Perfect! The melodramatic act! That was it! I rubbed the corner of my eye to start the tears flowing.

At that moment: 'Come on in,' said a very soft, reedy voice in my head.

'What?' I asked, dumbfounded.

'I've been watching you for the last half-hour, Optimus. You've put on a lot of weight around the hips, my dear fellow. All right, come in. And stop strangling your cloak!'

Damn it! Kibitzer had been standing there in the dark, watching me through the window! Nocturnomaths could also read one's thoughts through closed doors, of course. What an idiot I was! I wished the ground would swallow me up.

'You'd like that, wouldn't you? Come on in, my time is precious. In with you!'

I let go of the hem of my cloak and drew a deep breath. Then I turned the door handle and entered the gloomy shop.

A bell jangled in the same discreet manner as it had two centuries ago, of that I felt sure, but didn't it now sound a trifle jarring – almost imperceptibly discordant? I was engulfed by the same musty odour of books, but didn't it smell a trifle more ancient than before? There was the same dim candlelight, but wasn't it a little dimmer than in the old days – dimmer and harder for the eyes to adjust to? There were no curtains or blinds, so how did Kibitzer manage to keep the interior so confoundedly dark when the sun was shining outside? Well, Nocturnomaths loved darkness above all things because it facilitated their brain work, so they were bound to have their ways and means. Perhaps Kibitzer bred a certain kind of book dust that filtered the light. At all events, the air was filled with whirling motes of dust stirred up by my entrance. I was almost blinded for a few moments, but that, too, reminded me vividly of my first visit to this antiquarian bookshop.

'Ahmed?' I said, blinking. 'Are you there?'

The spell was broken. Those opening words had issued from my lips unbidden. They were neither false nor overly cold or brash, but simply spontaneous. I felt relieved.

'Of course I'm here,' came the low-voiced reply. 'We've been expecting you.'

I rubbed my eyes in an attempt to see better. I'd been expected? Who was 'we'? Was he speaking in the royal plural, or was there really someone else there? Where *was* the confounded Nocturnomath, anyway?

Then a candle flared up, just as it had the first time we met. I could almost have believed that someone was staging the whole thing to awaken old memories.

Suddenly, conjured up by the candlelight, Kibitzer was standing in front of me, only a few paces away in the whirling book dust.

'Hello, Optimus,' he said, this time in his proper voice because his lips moved. It sounded even reedier and frailer than his cerebral voice. We exchanged a long look.

Kibitzer had aged in a positively dismaying way. In the many years since our last meeting he had developed a growing resemblance to his desiccated book covers, with their shrunken leather skin and faded colours. Tanned by age, his face would probably have been indistinguishable from the book-lined walls, with their rows of gnarled and mildewed spines, had it not been for his big, shining eyes. I was worried to note, however, that the latter were far less luminous than of old. The light in them was dim and fitful, like that of dying embers. Formerly huge, the orbs in his imposing thinker's head were half obscured by drooping eyelids, which he clearly found it hard to keep open.

'Hello, Ahmed,' I replied. 'So you knew I was coming?'

'Yes and no. I didn't really believe it until half an hour ago, but she has known for weeks.'

His head shook alarmingly as he spoke. It was amazing that his thin, tremulous neck could still support the heavy thing with its three brains. I noticed only now that one of his ears had a tiny hearing aid inserted in it.

'She?' I queried.

'Inazia,' he said. 'Inazia Anazazi.'

He shone the candle on a niche in the shelves beside him. Inazia Anazazi the Uggly was sitting on a chair, staring at me. She loomed up out of the darkness like a ghost, and I only just managed to suppress a cry of horror.

'Hello, Yarnspinner,' she croaked in her unpleasant, grating voice.

'Er . . . Hello, Inazia,' I said haltingly. 'What a surprise! You're looking well.' That blatant lie tripped off my tongue with ease.

'Thanks,' said the Uggly. 'You've grown fat.'

It was nice to be back among friends. There was no need to waste time on pleasantries – a luxury I'd almost forgotten about.

'She knew exactly, to the nearest day and hour, when you would come – has done for weeks. Since I don't believe in Ugglian hocus-pocus, I'm sure it was a trick of some kind. Are the two of you in cahoots?'

That was ridiculous. He must have been joking – Nocturnomath humour! I hadn't set eyes on the Uggly since I'd last seen Kibitzer, nor had I been in contact with her in the meantime. Unlike the old, multicerebral creature, she'd hardly changed at all. She was looking as old and hideous as ever. I think Ugglies are born old. Hideous, anyway.

'To anticipate your question, Optimus,' said Kibitzer, 'yes, your eyes don't deceive you, I'm ill. Very ill. I'm suffering from a rare disease called *senescentia rapida* – also known as Nocturnomathitis.'

'Is it, er . . . catching?' I asked, involuntarily retreating a step. I instantly felt ashamed of my tactless and hysterical reaction.

'Still the inveterate hypochondriac, eh?' Kibitzer grinned. 'No, it isn't infectious. Never fear, only Nocturnomaths can catch the disease. It's accursedly genetic, and it affects only a handful of us. I'm one of the lucky ones – I've hit

the jackpot! There's only one symptom, actually, but it's a tough one. Once the disease manifests itself, you age rapidly, and by rapidly I mean at a really appalling rate. It's to do with my three brains' simultaneous consumption of energy. We think too much! Many Nocturnomaths' physiques can't sustain that in the long run. The cells go into premature retirement, to employ a humorous metaphor. I've aged a century in the last ten years.'

'That's, er . . . most regrettable.' *Regrettable?* Good God, we hadn't seen each other for ages, he'd just revealed that he was terribly sick, and all that occurred to me were tactless platitudes. Could he hear me? I wondered. He was wearing a deaf aid, after all. 'I mean . . . I simply can't cope with diseases,' I said somewhat louder. 'I'm sorry I couldn't think of anything better to say.'

'Know the first thing that tells you you're really old?' Kibitzer demanded in a quavering voice. 'Not forgetfulness, oh no. You notice that people are speaking louder and slower, as if you're an imbecile or a little child. I'm not hard of hearing, damn it!'

'But you *are* hard of hearing!' I insisted. 'You're wearing a deaf aid.'

'But I can hear perfectly well with it – I'm not deaf when I wear the thing. That's the whole point of hearing aids!'

I said nothing. We were heading straight for one of those nit-picking altercations such as can only occur between two very old friends who habitually hold opposing views.

'You've no need to burst into tears over my fate, either,' Kibitzer said stubbornly. 'I came to terms with it long ago. There aren't many advantages to knowing you're going to die more quickly, but there are some. Death loses its terrors, for example. You don't have time to feel afraid.'

The Uggly laughed as if this were a particularly good joke. I seized the chance to change the subject.

'Did you really know I was coming, Inazia?' I asked.

The Uggly coughed and fanned some book dust away. 'It's no hocus-pocus, Kibitzer knows that perfectly well. It's a natural ability.

Stupidly, a lot of Ugglies make a big thing out of it so as to coax money out of tourists' pockets, and that has blighted our reputation. But it isn't right. Time is relative and Ugglies simply have another perception of it. From time to time we can look into the fourth dimension. It's not witchcraft, it's a defect. Yes, I knew you were coming, but not only through my Ugglian senses. We cooked it up between us.'

Now it was Kibitzer's turn to laugh. It sounded like a laborious effort to draw breath.

I felt puzzled. 'Have I got this right?' I asked. 'You mean the two of you engineered my visit to Bookholm?'

'There's a letter in your pocket, isn't there?' asked Kibitzer, tidying some papers on the counter. 'A letter that pretty cogently confirms my personal opinion of your work. Our bone of contention: that you're stuck in an artistic cul-de-sac and have lost the Orm. That is so, isn't it?'

'Now he'll have to come clean!' the Uggly cried triumphantly. 'This is getting exciting!'

It was quite an effort for me to find the right words for a suitable riposte. I could have turned stubborn and picked another quarrel with Kibitzer. I wielded a sharp rapier when verbosely defending my own work and had often pinned many an opponent to the wall with it. I could easily have argued frail old Kibitzer into the ground. I would then have advised the Uggly to take a look in a mirror instead of concerning herself with other people's obesity problems. I would have stalked out with my head held high, torn the stupid letter to shreds and spent a few more pleasurable days in Bookholm. After that I would have returned to Lindworm Castle with a bag full of antiquarian books and continued to live a life of ease, as before.

Could have . . .

Would have . . .

Instead, I said, 'Yes, I've lost the Orm. That's why I came to Bookholm.' And then I burst into tears.

Any other participants in such a scene would now have gone up to each other and exchanged a consoling embrace, but let's be honest: we were a Lindworm, a Nocturnomath and an Uggly, three life forms that had always striven for victory on the battlefield of pathological egoism and emotional atrophy. So Kibitzer simply remained standing and the Uggly sitting where they were while I sobbed without restraint. They shuffled their feet a little and made uneasy noises. When I stopped at last, all Inazia said was, 'Are you through?'

'Yes,' I sniffed. 'Thanks for your sympathy.' I noisily blew my nose and felt better.

'Listen,' said Kibitzer. 'I don't have much time left, as I already mentioned, and I mean that literally, so let's get down to brass tacks. We really did send you that letter.'

'*You* wrote that letter?' Involuntarily, I felt for the letter in my pocket. I'd had no idea that Kibitzer possessed a gift for parody. Or was it the Uggly?

'No, we didn't write it,' Kibitzer gasped asthmatically. 'We only forwarded it. Inazia, you'd better explain . . .'

The Uggly rose from her chair with a loud groan. I'd completely forgotten how tall and thin she was. She topped me by a head.

'Yes,' she began, 'this is my part of the story. It begins one stormy night—'

'Like a pirate yarn by Trebor Sulio Vessenton!' Kibitzer interjected. 'There's even a sort of pirate in it.'

'A pirate?' I pricked up my ears. 'In Bookholm?' It really wasn't necessary to arouse my interest with dramatic details. I *was* interested!

'Not really,' Inazia said with a grin, 'but almost. You'll laugh, because I was reading your latest book and had almost dozed off over it. I'd got to a frightfully boring chapter on bronchial tea and moist throat compresses, and—'

'Get to the point!' Kibitzer commanded her. 'You can tell him the unimportant details . . . ' – he inserted a long pause – ' . . . later.'

'Then don't keep interrupting me! Well, it was a rainy, stormy night,' the Uggly began again. 'I hadn't had a single customer in my bookshop all day and was boring myself to death by reading your latest book, as I already said. So I was in a thoroughly miserable mood. I decided to close early and go and eat somewhere. I was standing outside the shop in the act of locking the door when I heard a tapping sound. Rather like this . . .'

The Uggly tapped a bookshelf with her long fingernails: tap, tap. tap . . .

'Turning round, I saw a terrifying figure standing in the rain. I don't scare easy as you know – I'm an Uggly, people are usually frightened of *me* – but that fellow would have put the fear of God into anyone, believe you me! Especially as the whole scene was stereotypically illuminated by lightning and accentuated by thunder.'

'Trebor Sulio Vessenton!' croaked the Nocturnomath. 'Pure Vessenton of the highest calibre!'

'True,' said the Uggly. 'The fellow really could have been a pirate. He was wearing a kind of armour and a mask of leather patches crudely sewn together. He looked almost like one's idea of the *Darkman of Bookholm* – but the leather version – and he was wearing a jaunty tricorne that would have looked well on a pirate. Although there was a long sabre dangling from his belt, he made a rather frail and harmless impression. He was leaning on a stick, you see, and dragging a small wooden chest behind him on a rope. It resembled a child's coffin. I realised at once that he could only be a Bookhunter.'

'A Biblionaut,' I amended mechanically. 'There aren't any Bookhunters these days.'

'You must forgive me if I still prefer the original term, even if it isn't, er . . . politically correct any more,' Inazia put in. 'I simply can't get used to it. You're right, though, he was a Biblionaut, I could tell that from his civilised manner. But the really bizarre aspect of his appearance was the fact that he wore two eyepatches. Two of them, one over each eye!'

'He was blind?' I asked.

'Exactly. Hence the tapping sound. He was finding his way through the rain with his stick. "Excuse me," he called, "I couldn't help hearing you lock your door. From that I infer that you live here and are acquainted with the district."

'"Maybe,"' I said cautiously. "How can I help you?"

'The dark figure had come to a halt and was leaning on his stick. "I fear I'm lost, madam. I was on my way to sell some old books and got overtaken by the rain. I only know this district in dry weather and now it sounds quite different. I have to find my way by sound, alas." He indicated his eyepatches. "Can you tell me where the nearest antiquarian bookshop is?"'

The Uggly sighed. 'I felt sorry for the blind fellow, no matter what he looked like. The thought that, for someone unable to see anything, the world suddenly undergoes a complete change as soon as it rains – I found that deeply moving despite myself! So I invited him in for a cup of tea and said he could wait in my shop until it stopped raining.'

'Yes, yes,' croaked Kibitzer, 'you can forget about the violins. Get to the point!'

While Inazia was speaking, the Nocturnomath had been busying himself in a way that made me feel rather uneasy. Hobbling back and forth from one bookshelf to another, he tidied their contents, rummaged in drawers, laid out various manuscripts on a desk and pored over them with a sigh.

'In Bookholm,' the Uggly went on, 'there have always been crippled and badly injured adventurers who acquired their injuries in the catacombs. There have also been, in addition to Bookhunters, suicidal individuals who ventured into the Labyrinth to make their fortune. Or their misfortune! There are more of those today than ever, I might add. If they're incapacitated, their only recourse as a rule is to live rough and beg. Although new to me, a blind Biblionaut was really more of the same: just another victim of the catacombs, a sort of war veteran like many others. We second-hand booksellers live largely on the audacity of those daredevils, for without them our businesses would be no more interesting than any other bookshop in Zamonia. I make far more money out of a good antiquarian find from the catacombs than I do out of a dozen ordinary books.'

'Grave robbers!' Kibitzer croaked as he applied a wax seal to a document. 'They're grave robbers, the lot of them! I've no sympathy for them. Half the city makes money out of the dead! Books by the dead and dead books – that's the diseased compost on which this city grows. We're living on top of a graveyard!'

'After I'd given him a cup of tea and a blanket so that he could dry off and warm up, he proved to be a charming companion,' the Uggly continued. 'I'd never conversed with a Biblionaut before. I was struck by his rather hesitant, effortful way of speaking, which I attributed to his injuries. Still, he made a courteous and cultivated impression. His name was Belphegor – Belphegor Bogaras.'

'They're all killers, courteous and cultivated or not,' Kibitzer said angrily. 'Bookhunters or Biblionauts – they're all the same to me, even if they do soft-soap people.'

He was laboriously rearranging a shelf of very old books and muttering to himself. There was something hectic, almost panicky about his demeanour that was entirely new to me. I couldn't imagine why he had chosen this particular moment to tidy up his gloomy shop.

'The Biblionaut told me that he had lost his eyesight in the *Labyrinth of Dreaming Books*,' Inazia went on, 'just as I'd thought. He now scraped a living by selling such second-hand books as he could find in the entrance to the Bookholm Shafts. That was as far into the catacombs as he dared to go, with his disability. Most of them were third-rate and ill-chosen, as he himself frankly admitted. If I cared to, he said, I was welcome to take a look at his wares. Without obligation. At that moment, of course, I realised that he'd hoodwinked me.'

I couldn't help smiling at Inazia's naivety. 'A hoary old huckster's trick,' I said. 'Once you've let them over the doorstep, they've as good as sold you something.'

'Exactly. Who would look at a blind hawker's wares and tell him to his face that they were no use to anyone? But I resigned myself to my fate. Even though this definitely hadn't been my day, I resolved that it would at least end with my one good deed of the week. So I examined the books in his child's coffin.'

'Ah, here it is!' croaked Kibitzer. He held a big sheet of parchment up to the light, then put it down on the desk, smoothed it out and weighed it down with paperweights. 'Vertical Labyrinthine Cartography!' he said. 'An almost forgotten craft. Subterranean longitude and latitude – they exist! Very hard to determine! A form of science, really. Almost an art . . .' I had no idea what he was blathering about. He continued to mutter to himself as he disappeared behind some bookshelves.

'That was when I found the letter,' the Uggly said suddenly and very quickly, with one hurried glance at the spot where the Nocturnomath had vanished. 'And then . . .'

'One moment!' Kibitzer broke in from the gloomy back of beyond. 'Haven't you forgotten something?'

'Damn it!' Inazia hissed almost inaudibly and stamped her foot. 'That comes of your constant interruptions! I thought I was supposed to be brief.'

'Carry on!' called the invisible Kibitzer.

'Must I really?' the Uggly called back in a subdued voice.

'He needs to know the whole story. The important details, Inazia, not the unimportant ones.'

'Very well,' Inazia said with a sigh. She straightened up, seeming to become another head taller, and noisily cleared her throat.

'Well . . . This Biblionaut was a really smart salesman. He even poked fun at himself by emphasising that he'd never seen the books he sold, so he couldn't gauge their value. He honestly had no idea what he was offering for sale, he said, so he left it up to me to pay whatever I wanted for any book that took my fancy.'

'Very shrewd.' I nodded admiringly. 'Who's going to cheat a blind

Biblionaut? So you not only bought a book but voluntarily paid too much for it?'

'I might have done,' said the Uggly, 'but it didn't turn out that way.'

'That's right,' Kibitzer called in the background. 'That's the way! Out with the truth.'

Inazia sighed submissively. 'So I rummaged around in Belphegor's weird little box of books with no great hopes of finding anything worthwhile in it. Just charred, rubbishy paper, as I'd expected. But then, quite suddenly, I found myself holding *The Hammer of the Ugglies*.'

'The *what?*' I asked, dumbfounded. 'You don't mean . . .'

'Yes,' said Inazia. 'I do indeed. One of the most sought-after items on the *Golden List.* Not a copy, not a fake – the original. In excellent condition.'

'My goodness,' I blurted out. The Uggly was talking about one of the most valuable books in the catacombs.

'I had many reasons for becoming an antiquarian bookseller,' said Inazia. 'But the existence of *The Hammer of the Ugglies* was certainly one of them. It was the possibility – extremely remote, I grant you – that entering the profession might enable me to set eyes on the book at least once that prompted me to major in Uggliological Biblionistics at Bookholm University.'

'A far from disreputable branch of learning,' croaked Kibitzer, who had re-emerged and was blowing dust off an ancient volume, which he stowed away in a cupboard. '*If* one discounts all the Bibliognostic nonsense.' He disappeared among the bookshelves once more.

Inazia ignored that remark. 'There's no book more heartily detested by Ugglies,' she went on. 'We consider it the most loathsome work in Zamonian literary history, but that's just what makes it so fascinating! It's filled with malice and has sealed the fate of many of our kind. But we Ugglies have survived its ill-written vituperations and that experience has welded us into the close-knit community we are today. Now it's no more than a vile old book full of medieval stupidity, superstition, and utterly barbarous instructions for torturing and killing Ugglies. Unreadable, if the truth be told! Eventually, after its spell was broken, the book was destroyed whenever possible. That's why there's only one last original extant copy – one that disappeared from view for a very, very long time. And that was the one I was suddenly holding in my hands.'

'Well,' I asked, 'what did you do?'

The Uggly laughed. 'I can tell you that, apart from our joint experiences in the catacombs with the Shadow King, it was the most dramatic and exciting moment in my life. I was holding *The Hammer of the Ugglies* in my hands – one of the most valuable books on the *Golden List*! And facing me sat its finder and lawful owner, a Biblionaut who had no idea what a fortune the book was worth – who had just invited me to buy it for a price I set myself.'

'Don't keep him on tenterhooks!' Kibitzer called in the background. 'Tell him what you did. Get it off your chest!'

'Well,' said the Uggly, shrugging her shoulders, 'there were really only two alternatives. I could have told the blind Biblionaut the truth and enlightened him as to the book's value. He would probably have thanked me nicely and sold the book to whichever Biblionnaire offered him the most. *The Hammer of the Ugglies* would doubtless have disappeared into some private collection and been lost to Uggliology for ever.'

'Quite,' I said. 'That's probable.'

'The second alternative was to cheat him. Pretend I had scant interest in the book. Fail to tell him it was as rare as it was and pay him a small sum for it. He would probably have been satisfied and gone on his way, believing that he had pulled off a nice little deal.'

'And you would have swindled blind Belphegor,' I said.

'True.' Inazia nodded. 'But a third possibility occurred to me. I told him it was a very rare book about Uggliology – which wasn't even a lie. Then I expressed great interest in it. Although a gross under-statement, that was also true. Eventually, I suggested paying him a fair price for it. This, I freely admit, was a blatant lie. Only the Zaan of Florinth could have paid him a fair price for that book. But I went down to my secret Ugglian safe in the cellar, took out all my savings – no small sum! – and gave them to him.'

The Uggly looked relieved. The truth was out at last.

'So you *did* cheat a blind huckster out of his book,' I said coldly.

She gave me a pert stare. 'One can't say that. I gave him some money – a great deal of money by my standards. All I possessed.'

'He could have got more elsewhere. Considerably more.'

'Are you sure?' asked Inazia. 'Why did it occur to him to offer *The Hammer of the Ugglies* to an Uggly, of all people? I might have flown into a fury and hurled the book into the fire, where it belonged. An Uggly would have had every right to do so.'

'But he didn't know it was *The Hammer of the Ugglies*,' I said. 'He was blind. Maybe he didn't even know you were an Uggly.'

'Don't quibble!' Inazia snapped. 'I could have said nothing at all and let him go off with his book. What would have happened then? The next bookseller might have swindled him good and proper. To that extent, he could count himself lucky he bumped into me.'

Kibitzer interrupted our argument by tottering out of the darkness carrying a huge jar. He hefted it on to a table and unscrewed the lid, which was perforated in numerous places. Then he shook the jar and whispered, 'Fly away! Fly away!'

With a buzzing sound, a grey cloud emerged from the mouth of the jar, rose to the ceiling and dispersed into hundreds of little specks that flew off in all directions.

'Fly away!' Kibitzer whispered. 'Fly away! You're free! Free!'

The little specks began to glow in a wide variety of colours. They were will-o'-the-wisps, which he had bred in a jar for reasons probably comprehensible to Nocturnomaths alone. Humming and whirring, they fanned out all over the shop, filling it with a vivid, multicoloured glow that lent the scene a look of dreamlike unreality. Dry-as-dust volumes lit by flickering, magical luminescence! Inazia Anazazi and her crazy story! Kibitzer and his irrational behaviour! Was I really here, or was I lying in my bed in Lindworm Castle and only dreaming this nonsense?

'Go on, then!' urged Kibitzer. 'You can argue . . . ' – he inserted another curious pause – ' . . . later.'

'I presume you then came across the letter in the book,' I said in an attempt to cut the story short. It was making me feel uneasy somehow, like the whole situation. I yearned to be back outside in the sunlit streets of Bookholm.

'Not right away,' said the Uggly. 'Something else happened first. Something that's bound to interest you.'

'Yes,' wheezed Kibitzer, who was once more rummaging in some papers. 'This really ought to interest you.'

'It had stopped raining by now,' Inazia went on, 'and Belphegor Bogaras prepared to leave, believing he'd done the best bit of business in his life. I escorted him to the door, but before I showed him out my nagging curiosity got the better of me. Unable to restrain myself, I tactlessly asked him how he'd lost his eyesight in the catacombs.

'"Oh," the Biblionaut replied casually, "that was down to the Shadow King."'

At that moment, dear friends, I really did grow uneasy. My visit to that bookshop had already been full of surprises, but this turn in Inazia's story was truly unexpected.

'But the Shadow King is dead!' I blurted out.

'That's what I told the Biblionaut myself,' the Uggly replied. 'But he paused in the doorway, turned to me with the last of the lightning flickering behind him and said words to the following effect: "With respect, madam, no one who has spent any length of time in the cata-combs truly believes that the Shadow King is dead. Every Biblionaut has his own tale to tell of the Shadow King, every last one! Some have only heard him rustling, others whispering, yet others laughing. Some

170

claim to have seen him with their own eyes and many allege that they actually felt him when he whispered in their ear in some dark tunnel. There are some whom he led so badly astray in the Labyrinth that they took weeks to find their way out. To the Biblionauts, the Shadow King has long ceased to be a myth and become a commonplace. It's like the dangerous beasts of the wilderness: you can roam the Great Forest for years without ever encountering a werewolf, but werewolves are always on your mind. Always! Is one lurking behind the nearest tree? Or not? If you're lucky you never meet one, but if you're unlucky, one will cross your path some day. That's what happened to me. The last thing my poor eyes saw before they were plucked from their sockets was the Shadow King! Believe me, madam, or believe me not!" So saying, Blind Belphegor doffed his hat, performed a courteous bow and went tapping off into the night.' Inazia heaved a sigh of relief and resumed her seat.

'Nonsense!' I said. 'A catacomb fairy tale! Any number of things could have robbed him of his eyesight. There are creatures down there for which we don't even have names. I know from personal experience that some of them rustle like paper and emit the strangest noises in the dark.'

Inazia shrugged her shoulders. 'I'm only telling you what the blind Biblionaut said. We thought it would interest you.'

'What about the letter?' I asked impatiently. I'd heard enough creepy stories. I wanted to get out into the daylight.

'Well,' said Inazia, 'as soon as the Biblionaut had finally departed, I naturally leafed through *The Hammer of the Ugglies*, my new antiquarian treasure. And I suddenly came across the letter—'

'The letter that's now in your pocket,' Kibitzer broke in. 'A letter from the Leather Grotto. Addressed to you.'

'I brought it here at once,' said Inazia, 'and Kibitzer thoroughly analysed it on the spot.'

'The paper consists of fungal fibres,' **Kibitzer pontificated**, 'and this, because of their minimal saturation with carbonic acid, leads one to the almost inescapable conclusion that they hail from the lower reaches of the catacombs and were processed there. The paper isn't even very old and the ink was obtained from the blood of Grotto Lice, which live only at very low levels. The letter came from the Labyrinth, that's beyond doubt.'

'But who wrote it?' I asked. 'Can you shed any light on that?'

'Well,' growled the Nocturnomath, 'if the authorities requested me for an expert opinion and I had to testify in court under oath, I would then, having meticulously analysed the writer's vocabulary and submitted his handwriting to the most thorough graphological research, submit that only one person can enter into consideration.'

'And that would be . . . ?' I demanded in an agony of suspense.

'You,' Kibitzer replied tersely.

'But that's absurd!' I cried. 'I can't have written the letter.'

'I know,' Kibitzer growled. 'That's the mystery. I like riddles, but I detest riddles I can't solve. This is one such.'

'Is that all?' I asked. 'Can't you say anything more?'

'Only that the writer – since it wasn't you – can brilliantly imitate the style of your Ormless period.' Kibitzer tittered. 'I laughed so much, my hearing aid fell out.'

'The sender's address is given as the Leather Grotto. Could it have been written by a Bookling?'

'Booklings don't write, you should know that better than anyone. They're notorious readers who devote their lives entirely to reading. They're persistent consumers of literature, but they don't produce it. A complex parody such as that letter represents can only have been produced by someone of long experience and great literary ability. And in that connection too, only a certain name comes to mind.'

'Homuncolossus?' I asked. 'The Shadow King?'

'Well, he's the only person that occurred to me who possesses those qualifications and lives deep down in the Labyrinth. He's also the only creature that knows you personally and might take it into his head to write you a letter – for whatever reason! Provided he's still alive, of course. This is circumstantial evidence, not proof, but one can't simply brush it aside.'

'But I saw the Shadow King in flames,' I cried. 'He was absolutely ablaze, how often do I have to repeat that? No one could have survived that, not even he.'

'I'm only weighing up the facts,' said Kibitzer. 'I'm not saying the letter actually came from the Shadow King.'

'We spent a long time wondering whether or not to send you the letter,' the Uggly put in. 'In the end we agreed that there were no two ways about it, the answer went without saying. Kibitzer insisted on sending it without any explanation. I'm sure he was still angry with you.'

Kibitzer nodded. 'I didn't believe you would actually come to Bookholm. I didn't even believe you would read the letter at all. I thought you'd become an incorrigibly arrogant twerp. Well, I was wrong. You *have* become an arrogant twerp, but you may still be curable. I apologise for the first of those assessments.'

Friends are quite something! They tell you to your face you've become fat and arrogant. They think you're a twerp, they scare you with their horrific tales of diseases and catacombs, they send you hurrying halfway across Zamonia because of some mysterious letter, and then they beg your pardon and expect that to put everything right.

'All right,' I said with a sigh. 'Let's bury the hatchet.'

'Excellent!' Kibitzer exclaimed, rubbing his hands. His voice, which had hitherto sounded resigned and quavery, took on an almost energetic note. 'Then we'll now proceed to read the will at last!'

'We'll do what?' I said.

'Read the will,' Inazia echoed sadly. She looked at me and rolled her eyes.

'Why,' I asked, 'has someone died?'

'Not yet,' Kibitzer said cheerfully. 'Not yet!'

The goings-on in this demented bookshop would not have been

out of place in a loony bin for senior citizens. I'd really been hoping to make myself scarce and now I was expected to attend the reading of a will although no one had died! Probably the two oddest booksellers in the whole of Bookholm had become even more eccentric in their twilight years, and that was saying something! Could it be the effect of the dust from the crazy old tomes they dealt in? It was bound to get to their brains via their airways. (I instinctively started breathing a little shallower.) Or did their quirks stem from the curious works in which they specialised? Uggliology and Nightingalistics? How could those who devoted a lifetime to the writings of Professor Abdul Nightingale and militant Uggliologists be expected to preserve their sanity? Moreover, why was I their only customer? Had anyone apart from me ever strayed into their esoteric establishments? I could hardly wait to leave that gloomy hole at last and breathe some fresh air.

Kibitzer had stationed himself at a lectern constructed entirely of books with two candles burning on it. The scene was invested with a look of unreality by the multicoloured will-o'-the-wisps ecstatically whirring around his tremulous head. Was that music I could hear? Yes indeed! Kibitzer was humming a solemn melody in one of his brains and telepathically communicating it to my own. Was that . . . Goldwine? Yes, quite so. It was Evubeth van Goldwine's last, unfinished symphony, the one he wrote shortly before his final brainstorm. Yes, I was absolutely right: nowhere else in this city could one come closer to insanity.

'Last will and testament!' Kibitzer cried dramatically. 'I, Dr Ahmed ben Kibitzer, hereby bequeath—'

'Just a minute!' I exclaimed. 'Is this *your* will you're reading?'

'What did you think?' Kibitzer demanded curtly. 'Can you see anyone else here of testamentary age?'

'But you aren't dead yet,' I protested.

'And you can hardly wait, eh? Patience, my son, I'm doing my best.'

I fell silent. I'm extremely partial to black humour, but I couldn't bring myself to find that funny. The old Nocturnomath had probably lost a good proportion of his wits. If a person's cells die off, those of the brain are surely no exception – in fact, they may even be the first to leave the sinking ship of the intellect. Reading a will prior to death! What on earth had I got myself into?

'I hereby bequeath', Kibitzer declaimed solemnly, 'my entire stock of antiquarian books, together with my shop premises and basement rooms, to Inazia Anazazi the Uggly. This bequest includes all my first editions of works by Professor Abdul Nightingale plus the relevant secondary literature and works on the same subject.'

I looked over at Inazia. A single tear was oozing from her eye. She had clearly been prepared for this bizarre occurrence and was accepting it without demur. I could expect no support from her. Until a few minutes ago I'd attributed the whole thing to a touch of senile dementia, but now it was becoming alarming.

'My financial assets, which are held in a deposit account earning 5.5 per cent at Bookholm's Antiquarian Bank, I likewise bequeath to Inazia Anazazi. They should suffice to offset her expenditure on *The Hammer of the Ugglies* and enable her to make new investments in the antiquarian field.'

The Uggly emitted a loud sob and I yearned to extricate myself from this situation by dissolving into thin air.

'I leave the fruits of my research into Nightingalistics, which are stored in lightproof, waterproof, fireproof containers in the basement of my shop, to Bookholm University. These include various dissertations on a total of 147 subjects, all my working diaries, a Nightingalian logarithmic table with Kibitzerian additions, over 4,000 test tubes plus contents and all the Nightingalian devotional objects I was able to obtain during my lifetime, together with two of Professor Nightingale's eyelashes preserved in amber, complete with a certificate of authenticity. All the Nightingalian scientific instruments in my possession are also to go to the University. The relevant instructions for use can be found in my working diaries.'

Some of the airborne glow-worms went into a spin and crash-landed on Kibitzer's lectern, where they expired beside the candles. I envied the fortunate insects for putting the situation behind them, whereas I, for better or worse, had to attend the ceremony in its entirety.

'I bequeath to Optimus Yarnspinner all the letters I wrote him, but never posted, in the past two hundred years,' said Kibitzer. I found this statement as startling as a full-blooded smack in the face.

What? Letters? To me? Had I heard aright? What letters?

With his fingertips, Kibitzer withdrew a dark cloth from a tall object standing right beside the lectern. What came to light was an immense stack of letters yellow with age and tied up in bundles. There must have been several hundred of them.

'At first I wrote these letters in the hope that our idiotic dispute would one day be settled. By the time it became clear that this was unlikely to happen during my lifetime, writing to him had become a fond habit I couldn't give up. Even if Optimus is uninterested in them, the letters are addressed to him and, thus, his legal property.'

Now it was I whose eyes filled with tears. He must have written to me every few days throughout the years, but he hadn't had the courage to send the letters off because I, in my mulish obstinacy, had ceased to correspond with him.

'I also bequeath to Optimus a masterly example of Vertical Labyrinthine Cartography personally drawn by the great Colophonius Regenschein. This I do in the express hope that he will never need to make practical use of this map.' Kibitzer emitted a dry cough, and I took the opportunity to quickly wipe my tears on my sleeve.

'I further stipulate that Inazia Anazazi has my full authority to make my funeral arrangements and administer my estate, expressing the hope that she will not suffer from the bureaucratic despotism to which Ugglies in Bookholm are still, regrettably, exposed. Finally,

176

I wish that my body be cremated and that no one apart from Inazia attend my funeral. My ashes are to be interred in the Antiquarians' Cemetery in Bookholm.

'Signed, Ahmed ben Kibitzer.'

Kibitzer rolled up the document. 'Well,' he said, 'that's that.'

Goldwine's immortal melody died away in my head.

'What is all this?' I protested angrily. 'You may be ill, but you aren't dead! Why are you disposing of your goods and chattels like this? Are you crazy? You're frightening me, Ahmed!'

Kibitzer merely smiled and tottered over to a mass of books stacked up to form a flat-topped table. Closer inspection revealed them to be, not printed books but leather-bound volumes of the kind used for making notes or bookkeeping.

'These are the handwritten journals of Professor Abdul Nightingale,' he said proudly. 'I can't think of a worthier deathbed.'

I dearly wished that Kibitzer would stop making these tasteless jokes about dying, which were really beginning to get me down, but the old Nocturnomath pursued his macabre conceit even further: he climbed on top of the book table and lay down.

'Ah,' he said. 'Comfortable it isn't, but that's not the point. Do you know my absolutely favourite passage in your books, Optimus?'

'No,' I replied. 'You mean there's a passage you actually like?'

He laughed softly. 'You're still resentful, aren't you? But you're right. Nothing gets deeper under a person's skin than criticism from a friend. I should have expressed myself more diplomatically. It was pretty insensitive of me.'

'All right,' I said. 'Let's bury the subject – er, I mean, let's forget it.' I couldn't think straight. I was still suffering from a monumental hangover and Kibitzer's funereal metaphors were starting to colour my own use of language.

'What are you doing on that table?' I demanded apprehensively. 'Are you tired?'

Kibitzer completely ignored my question. 'My favourite passage occurs in *The City of Dreaming Books*,' he said. 'It's the scene where Colophonius Regenschein dies.'

'Really?' I rejoined. 'Why that one in particular? I've written better.'

'It's not that. Readers of books tend to look for passages with which they identify and I've always considered the way in which Regenschein died to be exemplary.'

It had never occurred to me that a way of dying could be exemplary, but I was at pains not to contradict him at this moment. 'Regenschein died of his own free will,' I said. 'It was . . . impressive.'

'That's just how I've always wanted to go myself!' said Kibitzer. 'Under my own steam! An uninhibited decision! The triumph of mind over matter! Nothing could be greater!'

Tears sprang to my eyes again. I had finally grasped what was going on here. The real reason for our presence.

'You intend to die,' I said quietly. 'Here and now.'

'Yes,' Kibitzer replied with a blissful smile. 'This is my final wish. I'm dying now. So will you, but a bit later on. We all die the whole time because we really start dying at birth, so let's not be melodramatic about it.'

He stretched out, and the last of the will-o'-the-wisps spiralled down and landed beside him, where their light faded and went out.

'I've discovered how Regenschein did it,' said the Nocturnomath. 'I finally found out after years of concentrated cogitation. It's a breathing technique. Or rather, a technique that enables you to avoid breathing. Not to be recommended unless you want to die!'

I glanced helplessly at Inazia, but she was simply standing there in frozen silence, like a statue.

'Listen,' said Kibitzer. 'We both know you didn't come to Bookholm on my account, nor to overcome an existential crisis. Those were only secondary considerations, so let's not pretend otherwise! You've got to look facts in the face. You came because of a few words. Because of five words, to be precise – because of one brief sentence in a letter.'

Kibitzer turned his big eyes on me. Their yellow light flickered like that of a guttering candle.

'That sentence was: *The Shadow King has returned.*'

I started to say something, but he silenced me with a limp gesture.

'I know you can't bring yourself to admit this because you're too afraid, but you want to return to the Labyrinth. That's why you came.'

'Not true!' I dared to contradict him only in a whisper. 'Nothing in the world would persuade me to go back there.'

'I'm glad to hear it,' said Kibitzer, 'because I hope your fear will prevail over your curiosity. You survived the catacombs once. That was more luck than any one person deserves. Don't give the Labyrinth a chance to swallow you up a second time, or it'll make a thorough job of you. Listen to your fear. Fear springs from common sense and courage is the fruit of stupidity! Who said that?'

'No idea,' I replied uncertainly. Mental gymnastics were too much for me at that moment.

'I did!' Kibitzer gasped. 'I said it! I fear I don't have much more in the way of worldly wisdom to bequeath you, but I'd happily have that aphorism carved on my tombstone. Mark it well!'

That was just the kind of advice Kibitzer had always given me. Its gist was that you should trust your reason more than your emotions. Nocturnomaths were renowned for their mental acuity, not for their sentimentality.

'You've no need to worry,' I said, still whispering. 'If anyone's bad personal experience gives him good reason to fear the catacombs, it's me. Even looking down the Bookholm Shafts makes me feel sick. I shall never again set foot in the Labyrinth – never!'

'That's the attitude,' said Kibitzer. 'Your fear fills me with hope. Your terrors are your friends, so foster them. Think of all the frightful experiences you underwent down there. Think of them as often as you can.'

'I dream of them every night,' I said. 'I don't have to call them to mind.'

'Good,' wheezed Kibitzer. 'Very good, but all the same . . . Inazia, please bring him the map.'

The Uggly went over to the table on which Kibitzer had spread out a map shortly before. She came back and handed it to me.

'Take a good look at it,' said Kibitzer. 'It's a *Vertical Labyrinthine Map*. Personally compiled by Colophonius Regenschein in the course of years-long excursions into the catacombs. A masterpiece of speleocartography. It's worth a fortune, but I haven't bequeathed it to you for financial reasons. Its practical value is far greater – inestimable, in fact. Keep it with you all the time. Constantly, wherever you go. Will you promise me that?'

I nodded, even though I wasn't too attracted by the thought of carrying a map of the Labyrinth around with me all the time. My eyes were still so full of tears, I couldn't make out very much. All I vaguely saw was a maze of white and grey zigzag lines. The map meant nothing to me.

'The white lines are the correct routes – insofar as one can talk of correct routes down there. At least they're less dangerous than others. There are no *un*dangerous routes in the catacombs, as you know, but the tunnels, flights of steps and caves marked in white are the ones which, in Regenschein's experience, harbour the fewest unpleasant surprises. The ones marked in pale grey are the dangerous ones. They should be avoided. The dark grey routes are lethal. They are not to be followed at any price, for what awaits one there is certain death of one kind or another. Or something even worse, for in the catacombs there are worse things than death. You see the cross on the map?'

Yes, I could see a big cross on the map. Although nothing could have mattered to me less at that moment, I nodded.

'That wasn't made by Regenschein, but by . . . someone else . . .'

'Someone else? Who?'

Kibitzer was breathing heavily. 'That's immaterial now. What do you think that cross signifies?'

'I don't know,' I said, puzzled. 'Some important spot in the catacombs?'

'The cross means treasure!' Kibitzer exclaimed. 'Don't you ever read pirate romances? Treasure is always marked with a cross.'

'This is a treasure map, you mean?'

'No. That's to say, metaphorically speaking, yes . . .' He raised his head with an effort. 'Now listen carefully and I'll tell you what to do when the time comes.'

'When the time comes for *what*?'

'You'll know . . . if it happens.'

The Nocturnomath was speaking in riddles more and more. His voice had grown fainter, but his breathing was all the more hectic.

'When the time comes, you must scratch the paint off the cross on the map – it's painted on – and then press down on the spot. Have you got that?'

'Yes,' I said uncertainly. I really did have more important concerns than some damned cross on a map I would never use. My friend was dying and he was wasting his precious time on this cryptic nonsense.

'Take the map,' Kibitzer commanded. 'Put it in your pocket. Take it everywhere with you!'

I folded up the map and put it in an inner pocket. At least that disposed of the subject. Kibitzer grasped my paw.

'I'll be there soon . . . I'll be there soon,' he gasped.

Inazia moved closer to us. Looking at her, I was shocked by the despair in her eyes.

'It's time . . .' she whispered.

Kibitzer raised his head once more. 'I'm immensely glad you came,

Optimus. I'm happy to be able to die in the company of the three people who meant most to me in my life.'

Three people? Inazia and I made two. Then I realised that he wasn't delirious. The third person he'd alluded to was Professor Abdul Nightingale, whose works surrounded us on all sides in his shop. To Kibitzer, books had always possessed more personality than living creatures.

'This is all happening too quickly for you, isn't it? You've suddenly thought of so many questions you still wanted to ask me, haven't you?'

He was right in a terrible way, but I didn't want to put him under any pressure, not now.

'No,' I said, 'I've no more questions for you. Don't exert yourself.'

Kibitzer grinned with difficulty. 'Never lie to a Nocturnomath,' he said. 'I can read people's thoughts, had you forgotten that yet again? I will answer one question because it outweighs every other thought in your head.'

He drew three deep breaths.

'You want to know if I believe that the Shadow King has returned.'

What else could I do but nod?

'No,' he whispered, 'I don't believe he has returned, for how can anyone return ...' – he drew another deep breath – '... who has never been away?'

Then he closed his eyes for ever.

Ugglian Mourning

I don't know how long it was before I managed to tear my gaze away from the dead Nocturnomath. You always think that the sight of a dead person whom you've loved must be unbearable, but if you're confronted by the irrevocable fact that you'll never set eyes on that body again, parting from it is harder than you can imagine. That was how I felt about Kibitzer's corpse.

It was only when I awakened from my mournful trance that I noticed the Uggly had left the room. I could hear her moving around somewhere and found her standing in front of a bookcase at the back of the shop, busily rearranging its contents. She had her back to me.

'Everything here needs completely reorganising,' Inazia muttered absently. 'This isn't a bookshop, it's utter chaos. How did he classify them? By colour? By weight? I can't detect any system at all. It was high time the place got sorted out.'

Her callousness horrified me. Kibitzer had only just died – his body was still warm – and she had embarked on a spring-clean.

Then she turned round. Her eyes were filled with tears, and I had never seen anyone look more helpless and hopeless.

'How could he do this to me?' she demanded in a trembling voice. 'He was my only friend in this city. We did everything together in recent years. We shared everything. Joy and sorrow – everything! How could he simply leave me on my own?'

I now realised how unimportant my own sorrow was compared to hers. She had plunged into this bout of activity so as not to succumb to despair or lose her reason. Her whole existence had been suddenly rent asunder.

'I'll have to deal with everything. Reorganise the whole place, everything!' she babbled. 'The books, the estate, the papers, the death duties, the funeral. I must make an inventory! Definitely! I must write everything down, rearrange and catalogue everything. New prices! I'll write new prices in the books and rub out the old ones. Everything'll be tidied up.'

She tottered over to another bookcase. 'Three brains! No wonder the whole place is in such chaos. That screwball! He used to sprinkle sugar on his boiled eggs, put salt in his coffee and brush his teeth with whipped cream. Nothing mattered to him as long as his brains could solve some crazy Nightingalian equation with a hundred unknown quantities. It wasn't like living with a loony. Oh no, it was like living with demented triplets! If he went shopping on his own he'd come back with a sack of birdseed and forty pairs of underpants instead of bread and milk – and he didn't own any birds and never wore underpants!' Inazia chucked a pile of books on the floor and laughed insanely.

'I had to take care of everything. Everything! He would have starved to death at his desk or died of hypothermia because he'd forgotten to stoke the fire. What do I do, now I've got nothing left to take care of? How can I live without Ahmed?' Still babbling to herself, she nonsensically shifted books from one shelf to another. 'I'll make an inventory. Yes, that's what I'll do. An inventory.'

'I'll help you,' I said helplessly. 'I'll help you with the funeral arrangements too, and . . .'

Inazia gave start. She abruptly fell silent and froze for several seconds, as if suddenly turned to stone. At last she very slowly turned and gave me a long, strange look that made my blood run cold. Then, in a cold, crystalline voice, she said, 'No. No thank you, Optimus. He wouldn't have wanted that. I shall take care of everything. That was his last wish. We discussed it at great length.'

'So what would you like me to do?' I asked. I honestly had no idea how to deal with the situation and was feeling completely redundant.

'Please don't misunderstand me,' said the Uggly. 'I genuinely appreciate your sympathy and am grateful for it, but there's nothing you can do to help at the moment. I don't need any help. That isn't the way we Ugglies deal with bereavement. Believe me, you don't want to know what I'll do as soon as you leave me alone with Kibitzer. It's Ugglian mourning, understand?'

I nodded although I naturally failed to understand a thing.

'Kibitzer understood,' she said with a melancholy smile. 'That's why he stipulated that I should handle the funeral and his estate by myself. I'll also take care of the letters he left you and make sure they're posted.'

'As you wish,' I said. If the truth be told, I was rather relieved by Inazia's resolute approach to the situation. She had pulled herself together in a trice. Ugglian mourning, eh? So much the better. I also preferred to be alone at this juncture.

'I suggest', said Inazia, 'that we meet at the same time tomorrow. The worst will be over by then and I'd like to comply with another of Kibitzer's wishes. The thing is, he asked me to take you to the theatre on the day after his death.'

'The theatre?' I was perplexed.

She nodded. 'A very special theatre – the one he liked best of all. He thought you should definitely see it, and since he himself will be unavailable tomorrow—'

'I understand,' I replied quickly. 'Then of course we'll go. Where shall we meet?'

'Do you know Revolution Square? Where they burned Naborik Bigosu to death? The Bookemist?'

'Yes,' I said, 'I know where it is.'

'Good,' said Inazia, 'then let's meet there.' She looked around and rubbed her hands. 'In that case . . .' She proceeded to rearrange some books and behave as if I wasn't there any more.

I stole quietly out of the shop.

Dried Laurel Leaves

After an almost sleepless night I spent the next morning roaming the alleyways of Bookholm in the blackest of moods, unable to summon up any interest in the sights the city had to offer. My thoughts revolved ceaselessly around the events of the previous day and the question of whether I shouldn't simply leave without saying goodbye to Inazia. My whole trip had been a disastrous miscalculation. All it had yielded so far was a series of unpleasant experiences: a Fumoir binge, a spell of mental derangement and a dear friend's death – all in two days. What if this streak of bad luck persisted or even got worse? There was no escaping my present emotional nadir, so why should I spend a distressing evening with the Uggly on top of everything else? I dared not imagine what 'Ugglian mourning' really signified and how long it lasted. Moreover, why should I continue to beat my brains about a mysterious letter whose meaning not even a three-brained Nocturnomath had been able to decipher? My sojourn in Bookholm had become utterly pointless.

Pulling my cowl down lower over my face, I entered a small but well-patronised café in the hope that a strong coffee would raise my spirits. A sign announced that the establishment sold hot drinks in takeaway mugs made of compressed book pages that could be discarded once you'd drunk their contents. This was a Bookholm novelty and I was eager to try it once.

When I finally reached the counter and placed my order after standing in a long queue, the pretty Elfin waitress asked, '*Dwarf, Voltigork* or *Turniphead?*'

'Er,' I replied, thoroughly perplexed. 'I'm not any of those, I'm a . . .' I stopped short. Should I really tell her I was a Lindworm? What business was it of hers?

'They're mug sizes,' she said in a slightly irritable tone of voice. '*Dwarf* is small, *Voltigork* medium and *Turniphead* large.'

'Oh, in that case, er . . . a *Voltigork*, please,' I said.

'*Chocked, shugged, mulked* or *moggled*?'

'What?'

The Elf cast her eyes up to heaven.

'With chocolate, with sugar, with milk, or with everything?'

'Oh, I see. Er, just black please. I'm on a diet.'

'Black?' she said. 'Then you'll miss out on the moggle discount. This is our grand moggle week. There's a fifty per cent reduction on coffee with everything.' She pointed to a sign above the counter. It read: *Grand Moggle Week! Moggled Coffees Half Price. Have a Moggle with us!*

'I don't care,' I snapped. 'I want my coffee black – and some time this century, please!'

'Suit yourself. Would you care for a Balono de Zacher biscuit with your coffee?'

'No!' I shouted the word so loudly, the crockery on the shelves rattled. 'I just want a coffee!'

Instantly, a graveyard hush descended on the café. Everyone stared at me and a child began to cry.

When my coffee finally appeared I snatched it up and walked out in a hurry. I had to be more careful! I was the best-known author in Zamonia, and if anyone recognised me this excursion might turn into a nightmare. It then transpired that someone had put sugar in my coffee, probably to pay me back for my behaviour.

To take my mind off this I went at once into the bookshop next door. Clearly not an antiquarian establishment, it stocked a range of modern books. The sight of my own works always brightened my mood provided they were well-arranged, piled high and displayed with due prominence. Besides, I was curious to know what methods

Bookholmian booksellers employed to market them. I scanned the shop window first, then the tables and finally the shelves, but I failed to spot a single book of mine. There had to be some mistake! Didn't this bookseller want to make any money, or had he completely sold out again? I saw the latest novels by Freechy Jarfer and Proojy Licel, Joghan Rimsh and Maisky Cleniple, but not even my longtime bestsellers were represented. The walls were hung with portraits of young authors like Humido le Quakenschwamm, Yohi Scala and Goriam Zepp – but none of me. I left the shop and looked at it again from the outside. *Modern Zamonian Fiction* read a notice over the entrance and beneath it in somewhat smaller lettering was an impudent announcement I'd failed to spot when going inside: *Definitely No Lindworm Castle Literature!*

As if I needed another damper! My spirits couldn't have been lower as I stomped off down the street, distastefully swigging my sweetened coffee. So that's what I'd come to! I was a decrepit old classic, not a modern Zamonian author any more! I was already being excluded from current displays. My works were on the way into second-hand bookshops, there to share the fate of other *Dreaming Books*. I was yesterday's news, junk, waste paper, and I'd never even noticed. That came of my insistence in recent years on restricting my signings to bookshops that sold only my own books and the relevant secondary literature. That was the price of our cosy isolation in Lindworm Castle, our ivory tower in a no-man's-land far from the cities. We had lost contact with the modern market, and I myself, as my success waned, had actually become a symbol of this arrogant classicism. I was an old fart – young booksellers considered it chic *not* to include me in their stock! I couldn't even order a coffee without running foul of everyday language. My books were being transferred to the upper shelves in living rooms, where they languished beside other old rubbish which no one ventured to throw away but no one ever read either. You had to climb on a chair to reach them, but only in order to dust them every few years.

These and other, even more depressing thoughts were going through my mind when I suddenly sighted a puppet in a shop window that was definitely meant to be me. 'Definitely' doesn't mean that it was a good likeness – quite the contrary! – but attached to it was a slip of paper bearing my name – misspelt YARNSPINER – and the additional words SPECIAL OFFER!

That was the limit! A mere trifle that would normally have amused me at most, in my current state of mind it aroused my primeval, predatorial instincts. A chance to let off steam at last! Snorting with fury, I strode into the little puppet shop to call the owner to account and demand to know why he abused people's reputations for profit by selling ill-made dolls. Rage had overcome me. In situations like this I can develop an attribute not commonly associated with an author weakened by soft living, namely, immense physical strength. I was in what was, by my standards, a very exceptional mood: I was quite prepared to engage in physical violence.

The shop was deserted, so I promptly strode to the window and snatched the puppet bearing my name out of the display. 'Shop!' I called impatiently.

No one appeared, so I surveyed my surroundings. There were puppets everywhere, either suspended from the ceiling, from beams and washing lines, or seated on chairs and shelves. Although intended to resemble well-known writers, most were identifiable only by the name cards pinned to them. They swayed to and fro, clattering eerily in the draught from the open door. It looked like a medieval mass execution of authors whose only crime was to have achieved a certain degree of popularity. Dangling there were Hermatius Mino the Younger and Munkel van Klopstein, Stiggma Hokk and Walgord Wurstwermer, Mandragora Xanax and Notoria Notstrumpf, Histrix Lhama and Volko Lukkenlos, Degura de Boken, Count Edwald von Knozze and Delvatio Winterkrauth – all of them young and not so young contemporary novelists who regularly competed for the foremost places on bookshops' bestseller lists. I never read any of that

modern stuff because I was kept busy enough reading the great, late authors of the past and my own galleys, but I was quite familiar with their names and faces. Having their miserable likenesses strung up here in the shop of a fifth-rate puppet-maker was a fate they no more deserved than I did. It cried out for vengeance! Someone had to put a stop to this parasite's dirty game.

'Shop, damn it!' I called even louder, thumping the counter with my fist.

At last a gaunt, bald-headed Yellowling in a dirty smock appeared in the doorway at the rear of the shop. Eyeing me with hostility, he folded his scrawny arms on his chest and said, 'What do you want?'

'What do I want?' I retorted sharply. 'For a start, I want an explanation for this thing here! Who made this Yarnspinner puppet?' So saying, I held up the lousy puppet by its strings.

'I did,' the cadaverous creature said with ill-concealed pride. 'Kindly put it back where you found it. Handling the puppets is forbidden.'

Instead of complying with his request, I slammed the puppet down on the counter. He gave a start. I took a step closer.

'Really?' I snorted. 'Forbidden, is it? But the exploitation of literary fame *is* permitted, I infer from the look of your merchandise!' I made a sweeping gesture that – ostensibly by accident – swept a whole row of puppets off a shelf with my claws. 'Ooops!' I said.

The Yellowling winced. 'Who are you?' he asked, a trifle less self-assured now. 'What do you want?'

'Who am I?' I replied quietly. 'I'm someone who has just had a very bad day. Someone who has just looked death in the face and lost a very good friend. Someone who looked in your shop window and was displeased by what he saw there. Someone who believes that vultures, hyenas and carrion of all kinds belong in the wilds and shouldn't open shops in Bookholm.'

'But they're all famous authors,' the puppet-maker protested in an uncertain voice. 'They're public figures. It's legally permissible to portray them.'

'I realise that,' I said. 'But do you know what *isn't* permissible? It isn't permissible to be so untalented!' I took the Yarnspinner puppet from the counter. 'And d'you know *why* it isn't permissible? Because *I* don't permit it!' On that note, I hurled the puppet straight at him. The physical violence bit could come now, as far as I was concerned. My wild, dinosaurian genes were running riot.

He instinctively caught the puppet, hugged it to him and stared at me in utter dismay. I almost felt sorry for him.

'But it's a Yarnspinner puppet,' he said plaintively. 'I made it as lifelike as I could.'

'Lifelike?' I laughed. 'Call that lifelike, you amateur? It isn't even a bad caricature.'

'How do you know?' the Yellowling had the audacity to ask. 'What makes you think you can judge the quality of a Yarnspinner puppet? Are you a puppet-maker?'

'No!' I thundered. 'I'm not a puppet-maker, *I'm Optimus Yarnspinner*!' So saying, I threw back my cowl.

The Yellowling retreated a step. His face turned pale and he dropped the puppet. I really enjoyed that moment, I have to admit. Being able at last to profit from my popularity directly was an entirely new experience: a sense of power! It was better than a punch, better than kicking that exploitative creature in the backside. I had traumatised him merely by revealing my face! He would never forget this moment, never! He would probably relive it on his deathbed. I felt great.

'Yarnspinner . . .' the Yellowling said in a low voice.

'Yes,' I replied with head erect. 'That is my name.'

'Yarnspinner . . .' he murmured again, making for the door. 'Yarnspinner . . .'

Perhaps the shock had robbed him of his few wits. From now on, all he'd be able to do was babble my name in a soundproof cell in Bookholm Asylum. I couldn't help grinning at the thought.

Standing in the doorway, the puppet-maker yelled, 'Yarnspinner! Optimus Yarnspinner is in my shop!'

I froze. My euphoria instantly evaporated. This was the last thing I'd expected. The creature ran out into the street and shouted at the top of his voice, 'Yarnspinner's in my shop! Yarnspinner, the famous author! He assaulted me!'

Looking through the window, I saw people hurriedly converging from all directions. Damn it! I had to get away! I pulled the cowl over my head and went out into the street.

'Yarnspinner!' the Yellowling kept shouting. He pointed to me. 'That's him! Optimus Yarnspinner! He hit me!'

I took to my heels at once and sprinted down the street, but the fellow didn't give up. 'That's Yarnspinner!' he called after me. 'The one in the cowl! Optimus Yarnspinner! The author! He bust up my shop!'

Glancing over my shoulder, I saw that a whole gang of Live Newspapers had clustered around the yelling puppet-maker. The newsprint-clad gnomes listened to him for a moment. Then, as though in response to a word of command, they came scampering after me.

This wasn't good! I put on speed. On reaching the next intersection, I looked back once more. Heavens, those gnomes were quick off the mark! A moment later they'd overhauled me.

'𝕺𝖕𝖙𝖎𝖒𝖚𝖘 𝖄𝖆𝖗𝖓𝖘𝖕𝖎𝖓𝖓𝖊𝖗 𝖘𝖎𝖌𝖍𝖙𝖊𝖉 𝖎𝖓 𝕭𝖔𝖔𝖐𝖍𝖔𝖑𝖒!' cried the first of them. '𝖄𝖆𝖗𝖓𝖘𝖕𝖎𝖓𝖓𝖊𝖗 𝖇𝖆𝖈𝖐 𝖎𝖓 𝖙𝖔𝖜𝖓!' yelled the next. '𝕳𝖎𝖘 𝖋𝖎𝖗𝖘𝖙 𝖆𝖕𝖕𝖊𝖆𝖗𝖆𝖓𝖈𝖊 𝖎𝖓 𝖙𝖜𝖔 𝖈𝖊𝖓𝖙𝖚𝖗𝖎𝖊𝖘!'

I pulled my cowl down even lower and hugged the wall, but the little creatures simply ran past me.

'𝖄𝖆𝖗𝖓𝖘𝖕𝖎𝖓𝖓𝖊𝖗 𝖇𝖊𝖆𝖙𝖘 𝖚𝖕 𝖉𝖊𝖋𝖊𝖓𝖈𝖊𝖑𝖊𝖘𝖘 𝖕𝖚𝖕𝖕𝖊𝖙-𝖒𝖆𝖐𝖊𝖗!' cried one. '𝕭𝖊𝖘𝖙𝖘𝖊𝖑𝖑𝖎𝖓𝖌 𝖆𝖚𝖙𝖍𝖔𝖗 𝖜𝖗𝖊𝖈𝖐𝖘 𝖘𝖍𝖔𝖕!'

I crossed over, ran down the nearest side street and turned off yet again, but even in this narrow alleyway other Live Newspapers came hurrying towards me.

'𝖄𝖆𝖗𝖓𝖘𝖕𝖎𝖓𝖓𝖊𝖗 𝖜𝖗𝖊𝖈𝖐𝖘 𝖕𝖚𝖕𝖕𝖊𝖙 𝖘𝖍𝖔𝖕 𝖋𝖔𝖗 𝖓𝖔 𝖗𝖊𝖆𝖘𝖔𝖓!' cried one of them. '𝕴𝖓𝖏𝖚𝖗𝖊𝖉 𝖔𝖜𝖓𝖊𝖗 𝖕𝖊𝖗𝖒𝖆𝖓𝖊𝖓𝖙𝖑𝖞 𝖙𝖗𝖆𝖚𝖒𝖆𝖙𝖎𝖘𝖊𝖉?'

Incredible how quickly false reports could spread here! I tried to kick the newspaper gnome when our paths crossed, but I missed.

'**Yarnspinner flips!**' another Live Newspaper cried from a safe distance. '**Golden Quill Prizewinner beats up puppeteer and threatens Live Newspapers in the street!**'

I hastily turned down yet another alleyway. There were no Live Newspapers in sight, but I could hear them shouting in the distance.

'**Yarnspinner runs amok in Bookholm! Is the famous author suffering from some mysterious mental illness?**'

The Magmass

I sneaked back to my hotel, where I'd checked in under a false name, by way of the most deserted side streets I could find, intending to wait there until the rumours going the rounds (in the most literal sense!) had died down. I lay slumped on my bed, a prey to the most depressing thoughts, until I finally fell asleep in a state of mental exhaustion. It was late afternoon when I awoke feeling rested and refreshed. I debated whether to take my baggage and return to Lindworm Castle, but only briefly. Leave the city without having raided a single antiquarian bookshop? That was unthinkable! Besides, I would have felt mean, leaving the Uggly alone with her grief. My eventual plan was as follows: I would spend tonight and tomorrow in Bookholm. Today I could do my duty as a friend; tomorrow, preserving the strictest incognito, I would make an extended tour of the antiquarian bookshops. After that I would turn my back on Bookholm for ever. I was done with the *City of Dreaming Books*.

Having fortified myself with tea and pastries at a stall near the hotel that still provided genuine cups, not mugs made of waste paper, I set off for my rendezvous with the Uggly. Hordes of Live Newspapers were roaming the streets, but none of them was spreading reports about me. It seemed that news in Bookholm reached its sell-by date pretty quickly. A hectic and objectionable business, this sensational journalism! By tomorrow, everyone would probably have forgotten the incident altogether.

Inazia Anazazi was waiting for me in Revolution Square, as agreed. The festive garb she was wearing was in glaring contrast to her usual attire and at odds with the fact that she was in mourning and had just come from a funeral. From her appearance, she might have been going to a ball or a wedding. If the occasion hadn't been so sad, I would almost have laughed at the idea that she had stood over Kibitzer's grave in such a get-up. An Uggly's taste could never be questioned, though. That would have been as pointless as criticising the laws of nature prevailing in another dimension.

'Must I now beware of you?' she asked with a grin. 'You're back in town and beating up defenceless Bookholmers – the Live Newspapers are already crying it from the rooftops.'

I shrugged. 'A combination of unfortunate circumstances,' I said darkly. 'I can't say this city has ever brought me luck, but this time I really seem to have got out of bed the wrong side. What's all this latest puppet business? The damned things are everywhere.'

'Puppetism!' the Uggly said mysteriously. 'It isn't all that recent, but I'll explain later. Tell me something: until we go to the theatre and while it's still light, how would a small detour appeal to you? What if I show you a part of Bookholm I'm sure you've never seen before? A sight few people tend to be interested in?'

'Sounds like a contradiction in terms,' I said with a laugh. 'But if *you* think it's worth seeing,' I added politely, 'there must be something about it.'

'It isn't far,' said Inazia, 'and we've still got plenty of time before the performance.'

We began by walking along a few streets reasonably familiar to me from the old days. Inazia told me of the depressing circumstances surrounding Kibitzer's cremation and the bureaucratic problems entailed by settling an estate. Ugglies, she said, were always subjected to particular harassment by the Bookholm authorities, even in such a reverential matter. My own share of the estate, the big packet of letters, she had sent off to my address in Lindworm Castle. We then came to a district which I didn't know at all but was pretty uninteresting because it consisted almost entirely of warehouses containing paper and newly printed books, and was almost deserted. I proceeded

197

to enlighten Inazia about the incident in the puppet shop, so we were both up to date with each other's doings.

I cannot say that this stroll was calculated to raise my spirits. To describe the buildings in the next district we came to as run-down would be a charitable understatement. Windows were smashed and doorways devoid of doors, nettles sprouted from letterboxes, wild ivy was creeping up the walls, and the roofs, which had partly collapsed, were thickly covered with putrid moss. Silence had fallen and the eerie hush was broken only by the croaking of some ravens. For no apparent reason, the buildings had been abandoned to dilapidation. This was exceptional in a city like Bookholm, where every square foot of living space was utilised and every vacant lot coveted by predatory property developers. A strange miasma of desolation hung over the area.

'These used to be good houses,' I said as we paused halfway along one of the deserted streets. 'Why have they been left to decay?'

'Nobody lives here any more,' the Uggly replied. 'This part of Bookholm belongs to the Magmass.'

'The Magmass? Who's that, a property speculator?'

She laughed. 'No. The Magmass is a river.'

Was she pulling my leg? There weren't any rivers in Bookholm.

'Smell that?' Inazia went on. 'That's the smell of the Magmass. That alone was enough to drive people away.'

Yes thanks, I'd already noticed the local aroma. It was a weird, wholly unfamiliar smell that seemed to indicate one was entering an exceptionally hazardous part of the world. The crater of a volcano, perhaps, or a bat cave. I felt uneasy – claustrophobic too, although we were out in the open.

The Uggly raised her head and listened. 'Can you hear that?' she asked in a low voice.

'Yes, if I listen hard . . . A sort of gurgling, liquid sound. A distant roar. Is that what you mean?'

'Come with me,' she commanded.

How many times had I obeyed her brusque injunctions in the past? Although I felt more like a lapdog going walkies than a visitor on a guided tour, I obediently followed Inazia down an alleyway in which weeds and thistles were sprouting from the cobblestones. It certainly wasn't a popular tourist route.

'A city destroyed by fire can be rebuilt,' said Inazia as she briskly forged a path through the weeds. 'Rubble can be removed and ash buried, but some fire damage can never be obliterated. There are wounds that never heal. In such cases, Nature is best left to itself.'

I was beginning to enjoy the Uggly's enigmatic blather. It was like going for a walk with a crossword puzzle or an oracle. Every problem solved posed another. That kept the conversation going without rendering it irrelevant.

'Magmass . . . River, seven letters . . .' I said to myself. I'd heard the name before somewhere. Or had I read it? I couldn't recall.

'Ever thought of becoming a professional tourist guide?' I enquired with a grin. '*Inazia Anazazi's Cryptic Mystery Tour*, perhaps? *Every question answered with another? Flagellation with stinging nettles thrown in?*'

The burnt-smelling scrub grew waist-high here. We had left the eerie buildings behind us and were now wading across a broad plain covered with the kind of scrub and weeds that proliferate on uncultivated land. There was no one around but us, and for good reason. What did she want to show me, her secret herb garden?

'Stop!' the Uggly cried abruptly. She came to a sudden halt and thumped me on the chest with her arm. If she hadn't, I would have strode smartly on – and the next moment plunged into an abyss. Yawning ahead of us was a massive crater.

'Phew!' I said, shrinking back. 'What's *that*?'

'That', Inazia said with a smile, 'is the Magmass.'

The crater was some hundred metres long and fifty wide, so it was more of a rift or fissure than the circular mouth of a crater. It did, however, possess a quality which I, for want of a correct geological term, would simply call *volcanic*, so crater seems to me to be a suitable description. Geologists are welcome to pour scorn on me, but I don't, alas, have a copy of Meridius Pyroclastian's *Glossarium Geologicum* to hand. The sides of the chasm, which went straight down for about twenty metres, were pitch-black like congealed lava and flowing along below, in a perfectly visible ravine, was a river.

'By the Orm,' I exclaimed, 'that really is a surprise. A river in Bookholm! There wasn't one in the old days.'

'There isn't one now, strictly speaking,' said Inazia, 'because that isn't a river.'

'What is it, then?'

'Something else – something whose exact definition is still fiercely debated by the scientists of Bookholm. As long as the question remains unresolved, we call it a river.'

Cautiously, I peered down. What I saw did, in fact, bear little resemblance to a river. It reminded me more of an animal, a gigantic serpent, a monstrous insect, a gargantuan millipede or worm that was sluggishly writhing along the ravine. It was dark, almost black, and viscous as molasses. Boulders were floating along on its surface. I shrank back again. One push from the Uggly, one false step, one moment of inattention, and the Magmass would carry me along and sluice me into the depths. I had never wanted to venture as close to the catacombs of Bookholm again.

'The Magmass looks different every day,' said Inazia, whose fingertips were now holding a handkerchief over her nose. 'Today it's black as ink, probably because shortly before emerging from the ground it flowed through a seam of coal or an oil well. Tomorrow, having devoured and dissolved a few old libraries, it may consist of leaden grey papyrus pulp. The day after tomorrow it'll be filled with hissing, smoking, incandescent lumps of lava. Ugly, angry and dangerous it may be, but it's never boring.'

'So it sometimes contains lava?'

'Of course. It carries along anything that can be washed away below ground. Soil, coal – and, of course, books. More and more books from the catacombs. Sometimes half-liquid, half-cooled magma drifts along in it. Hence a part of its name.'

The Uggly indicated the vast chasm with a theatrical gesture. 'The biggest factory in Bookholm used to stand here: the *Timbertime Paperworks*. "No paper burns for longer than Bookholm paper!" – you know the old slogan? That came into being after the fire. It must have been thought up by someone who saw the *Timbertime Paperworks* ablaze. Immense quantities of inflammable material were stored here. Huge vaults filled with paper. Stacked timber, whole trees, half a forest. Also combustible chemicals, glues, alcohol. Some blaze *that* was, I can tell you! It burned for months, in fact we thought it would never stop. By the time it finally *did* go out, it had eaten deep into the Labyrinth – and exposed one arm of the Magmass.'

The Magmass . . . *Now* I remembered! I'd read about it many years ago. The Magmass was the legendary subterranean river referred to by Colophonius Regenschein in his book *The Catacombs of Bookholm*, the mysterious labyrinthine stream of which the Bookhunters used to talk. Regenschein had mentioned it only in passing, though, which was why I'd almost forgotten the name.

'Many people used to think that the Magmass was a myth, a Bookhunters' tall story. No one would have believed that one arm of it flowed just beneath the surface of Bookholm.' The Uggly gazed down at the foul stream in disgust. 'And no one wanted such a thing in the city. It smells sometimes of sulphur, sometimes of oil, sometimes of camphor or animals' cadavers, depending on what it happens to be transporting. The stench causes headaches, bouts of depression and panic attacks – sometimes all of them at once. An attempt was made to bury it beneath the rubble and detritus of the gutted city, and it looked at first as if that would work. One day, however, the Magmass was back. It had simply swept away the rubble on top of it and sluiced this down into the catacombs, layer by layer, until it was exposed once more. A second attempt was made with the same result. Then everyone gave up. The Magmass had the last laugh! It's a suppurating sore that never heals.'

Inazia made her way along the edge of the ravine with me following cautiously behind.

'This area went steadily downhill,' she said. 'The first to move out were those who could afford to, followed by those who *couldn't* really afford to. It then became a rent-free district for the homeless, but even they couldn't stand it. Better to sleep rough under the stars than in a house near the Magmass! Finally, underworld types moved in and the place became *genuinely* dangerous. But the polluted stream proved too much even for the most hardened criminals. Not even they stayed. Now it's a no-man's-land, almost like the Toxic Zone.'

'The Toxic Zone?'

'All in good time.' The Uggly laughed. 'You'll become acquainted with it soon enough. It's another of the city's *not*-to-be-seen new attractions – worse even than this one.'

I was now feeling really nauseous. My head ached like that of a migraine sufferer and my knees had turned to jelly. All I wanted was to get away from this stench, which awakened the most dreadful memories. Fortunately, the Uggly was now heading away from the crater and back across the field towards the city proper.

'No one has lived here since,' she called over her shoulder. 'And because no one had to see or smell the Magmass unless they wanted to, legends became rife – glorified old wives' tales. That the Magmass is a living creature. That it can *think*. That it influences the thoughts of those who venture too close to it. That it tries to lure incautious souls into its depths. You know, prophylactic myths for children, to keep them from going too near it. Not that anyone is crazy enough to do so, not even children.'

'Apart from us,' I said hoarsely. The foul air had dried my throat.

'I only wanted to give you an uncensored view of the new city. Unless you'd prefer the tourist version? Shall I show you the side streets where the souvenir shops are?'

'All right, all right,' I said. 'I appreciate your efforts. It's just that I'm feeling a bit queasy.'

Inazia made a dismissive gesture. 'It'll soon pass. The effect of the Magmass wears off fast, fortunately.'

We tacitly agreed to adopt a brisk goosestep and quickly left behind the bleak, deserted streets around the Magmass, together with its cloying odour and the croaking of ravens. We soon heard voices, saw people strolling along and lights in windows. I breathed easier and felt better. Every additional step that separated me from that dark, subterranean river took me further away from the Labyrinth. And that, dear friends, came as a genuine relief to your harassed narrator, physically as well as mentally. It would be a long time before anyone else took me so close to the catacombs, that I promised myself.

We now entered a city district where the fire must have raged with special destructive intensity, because although I'd been there before, I saw nothing I recognised. This had once been the site of *Editorial Lane*, which constantly resounded to the despairing sighs of overworked copy-editors, and also, just beyond, of the *Graveyard of Forgotten Writers*. There wasn't a trace left of either. Their place had been taken by a modern quarter with brand-new, very plain and unadorned buildings and a completely different street layout.

'This district is inhabited almost entirely by theatre staff,' said the Uggly. 'And their families. It's like a city within a city. It doesn't have an official name, but the Bookholmers call it *Slengvort*.'

'Slengvort?'

'The Puppetists have a professional language, which is passed on only by word of mouth, a jargon composed of various languages and dialects – still completely unresearched. They call this language *Sleng*. It has words for things of no interest to a non-Puppetist but of great importance to themselves.'

'For instance?'

Inazia didn't have to think for long. 'Well, for bursting a costume at the seams just before a performance: that's called *splooching*. If a puppet's strings get tangled up in the middle of a scene, that's a *noodlemesh*. If a puppet makes a clumsy, inappropriate movement onstage, that's an *unskroot*. If it's made to bat its eyelids, that's an *okku*. A member of the audience who gets up and goes to the toilet during a performance is a *pissot*. Too little applause after a show is *krakki*.'

I laughed hoarsely.

'One very important word in this language is *slengvo*. *Slengvo* means the state of affairs when a puppet comes alive – when it takes the stage and entertains the audience. When it moves. If it's not in use and merely hangs on the wall by its strings, it's *niartslengvo* or *unalive*. Dead, in other words.'

'I see.'

'At some point, *Slengvort* was adopted as the name of this district. It could be freely translated as *Place Where Puppets Come Alive*. Or *Puppets' Birthplace*.'

'Aha, interesting,' I said.

Somewhat more attentive now, I looked around. The effects of the Magmass had worn off completely. This vibrant district was considerably more to my taste than the ghostly streets beside that dreadful river.

'Not only puppeteers live here. The residents also include stage designers and costumiers, scene painters and technicians, directors and musicians, writers and usherettes, lighting engineers and puppet-makers, prompters, cleaners and bouncers. They come from all classes of society: Dwarfs, Demidwarfs, Vulpheads, Trolls, Midgardians, Watervalians, Gnomelets – you name it. This is a pretty lunatic part of town. Imagine a few hundred highly gifted children whose bodies have developed but not their brains: that's the population of *Slengvort*. It's a big asylum full of harmless nutters. I wouldn't like to live here. I need my beauty sleep!'

Issuing from the open windows of the unpretentious apartment houses came loud sounds of activity. I could hear the chatter of sewing machines, the screech of a circular saw, a soprano practising her scales. Someone was playing the cello, someone else the kettle drum. Two laughing Demidwarfs were wheeling a mobile clothes rack into an entrance. Visible through a basement window, an actor wearing a death's-head mask delivering a monologue from a play by Aleisha Wimpersleake. Children were rampaging around in the backyards, puppets hanging like washing on lines suspended between buildings. Some scenery painted to resemble a surreal, dreamlike landscape was propped against a wall. In front of it, two dogs were tussling over a broken puppet. Someone, somewhere, was ruthlessly trying out a thunder sheet. The activities that went on here were quite different from those that prevailed in other parts of the city. The place smelt of wet paint, turpentine and wood preservative, not coffee and books.

'These are the earliest buildings in modern Bookholm,' said Inazia. 'That's why they're so plain and unadorned. Some of them were built of smoking rubble while fires were still burning elsewhere. They're occupied exclusively by people used to seizing the initiative, improvising, giving each other a helping hand. There's always something going on here. The theatre operates round the clock – it has never closed. Never! Six day-and-night performances in twenty-four hours and every one sold out.'

I was becoming curious.

If this to me wholly unfamiliar cultural attraction was such a success, it must have something truly exceptional to offer. It even boasted a district of its own!

We strolled along a street lined with buildings nearly all of which incorporated small shop windows. Most of the objects standing or lying in these were timepieces. Pocket watches, wristwatches, wall clocks, clocks under glass domes, dismantled movements, cogwheels, metal springs, tiny screws – every window displayed the same jumble of little parts. I thought I could detect a faint, thousandfold ticking sound.

'A street full of clockmakers?' I said.

'A street full of *former* clockmakers,' Inazia amended, raising her forefinger. 'An important distinction, my friend! The theatre is always engaging clockmakers to construct and service its puppets. Who better suited?'

'They must be very fine mechanics,' I said jokingly.

'The finest!' she agreed. 'The very finest!'

Turning a corner, we came upon a choral ensemble of eight Gnomelets in leather habits. They were practising a strange, melancholy song in a language unknown to me. All of them were holding up small glove puppets dressed like potatoes.

I was wholly unprepared for my first sight of the theatre, which loomed above the row of buildings like a ghost, and a pretty massive ghost at that. All one could see through the mist was a grey silhouette resembling a circus tent, but it was the largest building I'd ever seen in Bookholm.

'Good heavens,' I exclaimed, 'is that . . . ?' I was so astonished, I omitted to complete the question.

'Yes,' said the Uggly. 'That's the Puppetocircus Maximus.'

'Well I never! It's huge.' I had instinctively come to a halt.

'It's so big, it needs several names.' She giggled. 'Puppetocircus Maximus is the official designation, but who wants to keep saying all that? It's a silly name – far too long and cumbersome. The townsfolk of Bookholm call it simply "The Tent", although it isn't a tent at all. The residents of Slengvort call it "Puppetholm", but people of romantic bent refer to it as the "Theatre of Dreaming Puppets".'

I looked at Inazia enquiringly.

'Well,' she said, 'there really is a distant relationship between the theatre's puppets and the city's antiquarian books. Both are wrapped in a kind of enchanted slumber when not in use, aren't they? They don't awaken from it until they're touched by a living hand. In one case it's the hand of the reader, in the other that of the puppeteer. They don't come to life until they're perceived by an audience.'

'And become *slengvo*, you mean?' I grinned. 'Sounds more like a clever advertising campaign on the part of the theatre management. A cute fairy tale for tourists. Bookholm kitsch. Nice, though.'

'I'll forgive your lack of respect for the moment,' the Uggly said magnanimously, 'because you still don't have the first idea about Puppetism. That'll change very soon.'

'Why aren't I allowed to know the name of the goddamned play?' I complained as we walked on, making straight for the circus tent in the mist. 'I hate not knowing what to expect.'

'It's meant to be a surprise.'

'I don't like surprises either.'

'Then you're in for a tiring evening, my friend.' Inazia laughed and took my arm. 'A very tiring evening.' She smelt of buttermilk.

The Theatre of
Dreaming Puppets

We came out into a big, cobblestoned square and there it was in front of us at last: the Puppetocircus Maximus. Even from this distance it still resembled an enormous circus tent with three peaked roofs, a big one in the middle and two smaller ones to left and right. On coming closer, however, I quickly realised that it was anything but a tent composed of thin canvas; it was a solid stone building.

'Even the theatre's outward appearance is programmatic,' Inazia said eagerly. 'Nothing is what one thinks it is. Cloth is stone and circus is an art. There are no certainties.'

The Uggly's enthusiasm reminded me that I didn't really like circuses. They always smelt so strongly of large animals in need of house-training. There were also the awful clowns of whom most children were scared. Circus folk did idiotic, daredevil things and compelled animals to perform unnatural tricks to roars of applause from the audience. My heart sank lower and lower. How dearly I would have preferred to roam Bookholm's twilit streets, which offered the kind of sensations which *I* craved! Romantically secluded bookshops filled with rare editions. Poetry readings, interesting people, lively literary activity. Instead of that I was going to the circus. Worse still, to a puppet circus. I sighed.

'The stone for the building was specially imported from Florinth,' the Uggly said proudly, as if she had designed the confounded theatre herself. For my part, I rather doubted the architect's sanity. What was the point of reproducing an itinerant circus tent in solid masonry? The latter was a combination of red marble and yellow sandstone laid in alternate courses so as to convey the appearance of striped canvas. When just in front of it, however, I could detect the veins in the marble and the fissures in the sandstone, the joins between the blocks and the mortar that held everything together. This building was no more suited to travelling around than a mountain; it was an edifice intended to occupy this site for years to come.

'Look down now!' the Uggly commanded. 'You mustn't read the sign over the entrance or it won't be a surprise.'

I reluctantly lowered my gaze as we climbed the steps – an alternation of red and yellow slabs – that led to the entrance. We were surrounded by streams of people converging from all over the square.

'Would you mind pulling your cowl down lower over your eyes?' asked Inazia and promptly did this for me. 'You don't want to be recognised, do you?' She presented the tickets and steered me into the foyer.

The entrance hall, which was very spacious, resounded to the chatter of the theatregoers streaming in. The prevailing atmosphere was boisterous – more suited to a public festival than a cultural function. The laughter was as loud as the conversation, coffee and mulled ale were served, children purchased nibbles and sweets. Suspended from the lofty ceiling were hundreds of small, wooden, articulated puppets devoid of costumes. They all looked similar in an abstract way, like those that painters and sculptors use for anatomical purposes. They were the only form of decoration in this part of the theatre. The foyer was festively but discreetly lit by candles flickering everywhere in big chandeliers. The Uggly pushed me vigorously through the throng.

'This way,' she commanded.

We passed a long wooden bench on which sat a group of puppets whose curious appearance attracted my attention. They displayed noticeably fine craftsmanship and looked valuable despite their obvious age and decrepitude. They were not traditional children's toys, being far too carefully finished and detailed. Carved from fine woods or made of precious porcelain, elaborately painted and equipped with complicated eye and mouth mechanisms, they were attired in gorgeous costumes. They did, however, reveal definite signs of wear, were scuffed in many places or displayed cracks, fissures, tears in their costumes and other traces of use. They were unique – genuine theatrical puppets and much in demand. We paused in front of the bench.

'Are these the puppets we'll be seeing tonight?' I asked.

Inazia laughed a trifle superciliously. 'No, they're in retirement. They used to be the principal characters in plays that are no longer performed. That one is Professor Bimbam from *The Legendary Professor Bimbam*, and there's King Carbuncle from *King Carbuncle's Lost Weekend*. Those two are Veliro and Dyhard from *Snails Have Many Teeth*. Genuine classics. An impressive collection, isn't it? Worth a fortune, too.'

Her enumeration of titles and protagonists made me squirm a little. It reminded me that the puppet theatre was really an outmoded, positively ancient – indeed, almost archaic – art form aimed mainly at

a juvenile audience. Something to which adults were sometimes compelled to go in order to keep their children quiet for a while. But I didn't have any children! I feared for the rest of the evening. A combination of circus and puppet theatre? It couldn't get much worse, but I didn't show anything.

'Do they just lie around like this?' I said in surprise. 'Anyone could steal them.'

'It happens sometimes,' said the Uggly. 'A puppet disappears under someone's cloak from time to time, but they always return it after the show.'

'Stolen puppets are returned?' I said as we walked on. 'How come?'

'Because people have a totally different idea of puppets after the performance,' Inazia replied, giving me a mysterious smile. She paused in front of a wallpapered wall and took a key from her cloak. 'In here,' she commanded, opening a concealed door and slipping through it. Both curious and surprised, I followed her. Inside, a short

spiral staircase led upwards. The Uggly climbed it briskly. 'Our private box,' she announced as we came out on a little balcony at the top of the steps. There was a hint of pride in her voice.

I went to the parapet of the balcony and surveyed the auditorium. My initial impression was that it looked bigger than I'd expected. Far bigger.

'It's the same with everyone,' Inazia remarked, not that I'd said anything. 'No idea how it's done. There are bigger auditoriums in Zamonia, but none that *looks* even half this size. These people really know something about creating illusions. Wait and see.'

We sat down in the comfortable armchairs, which were upholstered in black velvet. Two pairs of opera glasses were lying ready on a little table between us. The fact that one of them must surely have belonged to Kibitzer made me feel a trifle uncomfortable for a moment. To distract myself from that unpleasant thought, I leant over the parapet and surveyed the scene below. The stalls were rapidly filling up with theatregoers.

This was no normal theatre – that much could be said without exaggeration. There wasn't just one big curtain, but seven of various sizes disposed in a semicircle. One was all of red velvet, another pitch-black, another of gold silk and four were embroidered with fairy-tale figures, musical notes or abstract patterns – not a particularly tasteful-looking feature. All around the auditorium, the walls were lined with tall mirrors that visually doubled the rows of seats and contributed to the false impression of size. The obligatory fire buckets of sand and water stood everywhere.

What was genuinely impressive was the design of the dozen boxes encircling the auditorium, which were skilfully modelled on the skulls of mythical creatures. It looked rather as if huge dragons, horned sea serpents and gigantic gryphons were thrusting their heads through the walls of the theatre. Each box was individually designed and lined with black velvet, the balconies being richly adorned with ornamentation and gold leaf. The other boxes were quickly filling up too, I noticed.

The ceiling of the auditorium was unusually high for a theatre. It could hardly be seen in the gloom because it tapered to a point like a circus tent. Plain but many-branched chandeliers hung down on long cords, casting only a dim light because few of the candles were lit.

'The interior designer must have worked on a trapeze,' I remarked with a grin.

'Hm . . .' said Inazia, giving me a sidelong look. 'People here still attach great importance to the origins of Puppetism. Most of those employed here used to be in street theatre. Far from rejecting that provenance, they're proud of not belonging to the established, highbrow theatre. Does that worry a successful winner of the Golden Quill like you?'

'No, no,' I said with a laugh, 'I enjoy light entertainment. What's it to be tonight, *King Carbuncle's Lost Weekend*? Spit it out, I can't escape now.'

'You'll see soon enough. You'll be captivated.'

The Uggly fished out a paper bag of wholemeal biscuits and proceeded to crunch them without offering me one. I spent the rest of the time leaning over the balcony and inspecting the audience.

They were a motley crew. Many different species of the Zamonian population were represented. Dwarfs and Moomies, Norselanders and Voltigorks, Druids and Hellrazors, locals and tourists, adults and children – the auditorium was packed down to the last spare seat. I saw some masked Biblionauts sitting here and there – an alarming sight. The barbarous old-time Bookhunters would never have attended a cultural function – it would have caused a certain amount of trepidation if they had – whereas these Biblionauts seemed to be attracting little attention, far less disapproval. On the contrary, some of them were chatting animatedly with their immediate neighbours – one of them even with a child who was happily laughing up at him in spite of his horrific insect mask. Most of the theatregoers were festively attired and conversing in polite whispers.

I felt rather ashamed that all those people down there were

familiar with the evening's cultural highlight, whereas I didn't even know the title of the play. Indeed, I was probably the only philistine who had been dragged here against his will and hadn't bought a ticket. That suddenly reminded me whose seat I was currently occupying. I rose to my feet with the uneasy feeling that I'd been sitting on a ghost.

'Going already?' Inazia said with her mouth full. She was strewn with biscuit crumbs. 'You'll miss out if you do, my friend. Why? Because the play is about *you!*'

I flopped down on my chair again. 'About me?' I exclaimed in astonishment.

'Whoops!' she said, blowing some crumbs in my direction. 'It slipped out! I'm not giving away anything more, though.'

A play about *me*? Was the old scarecrow pulling my leg, or just coaxing me to stay? Just a minute! Were they staging a satire that made an idiot out of me and did she think I'd find that amusing? I had to be prepared for anything. Ugglies have a strange and sometimes inconsiderate sense of humour.

Becoming restless, I strove to disguise my nerves and concentrate once more on the auditorium, more particularly on the area above the stage. In an ordinary theatre the gridiron was usually concealed, whereas here the area above the curtains was open to view, though the dim lighting bathed it in mysterious gloom. One could catch only sporadic glimpses of sections of stairway and suspended platforms, ropes and wires, sandbag counterweights and cables, sometimes also of dark figures clambering around on scaffolding. The stage machinery seemed to play an important role and clearly required a large number of technicians who had to remain for the most part invisible.

At long last the signal for the start of the performance rang out and the hubbub in the auditorium died away. A resonant gong, it was struck a second time soon afterwards, whereupon the Uggly stowed away the paper bag containing the rest of her biscuits and brushed the crumbs off her cloak. 'It's starting!' she trilled, her eyes shining like those of a child opening a birthday present.

A lively tune struck up and one of the smaller curtains – the one embroidered with musical notes – slowly rose to reveal an orchestra behind it – or, at least, what passed for an orchestra in a theatre of this kind. It consisted solely of musical instruments. Musicians had been dispensed with, because all the violins, oboes, flutes and so forth were clearly quite capable of playing themselves. I saw a string bass with mechanical arms and legs plucking away at itself, a drum beating itself,

a violin bowing itself, a tuba blowing itself. The instruments were equipped not only with limbs but with mechanical eyes that rolled dramatically while they were playing, thereby reinforcing the illusion that they were alive.

'The *Doremifasolatidosian Music Puppets* from Doodleton,' Inazia whispered with a knowing air. She sat back contentedly as if she had supplied me with a thoroughly enlightening explanation.

I counted up to thirty instruments in this extraordinary orchestra and each of them looked so convincing onstage that I couldn't tell whether the crazy contraptions were really producing the music themselves or whether there was a genuine orchestra hidden somewhere in the building. Dancing above them were funny little puppets in note form, likewise equipped with mechanical eyes, and wriggling wildly between them on strings were snakes made of music paper, which the children in the audience found particularly amusing. Before I could pay due attention to this absurd piece of musical theatre, I was distracted by the next sensation.

A gigantic copper chandelier with hundreds of candles burning in it was lowered from the gridiron. It was flanked by two large spheres covered with little facets of red, green, yellow and blue mirror glass. These now began to revolve, suddenly showering the whole auditorium with bright, multicoloured will-o'-the-wisps of light. But that, of course, *wasn't* the true sensation, nor were the two trapezes lowered at a considerable distance from each other. It was the three monkeys who occupied them.

But – of this, dear friends, I was thoroughly convinced – they weren't real monkeys. Never! Their faces were far too grotesque – more like caricatures of monkey faces – and no wild animal would have let anyone squeeze it into the fancy dress they were wearing. They had to be puppets!

When the trapezes came to rest above the heads of the audience and I was able to examine the creatures' faces more closely through my opera glasses, I thought, 'No, it's impossible! No mechanical creature could have such a lifelike physiognomy.'

For the monkeys were grimacing wildly, opening their eyes wide, pursing their lips and putting out their tongues at people the way only living creatures could have done. Moreover, they now began to move restlessly, clamber around on the trapezes, do chin-ups on the bars and hang from them upside down. No puppet could have done that, it was impossible!

Then I had an idea.

'Oh, I get it!' I whispered to Inazia, feeling reassured. 'They're actors in costume. Dwarf artistes dressed up to look like primates, right?'

'No, wrong,' hissed the Uggly.

'Not dwarfs? Not gnomes?'

'No.'

I stared at her stupidly.

'No? What are they, then?'

'They're puppets.'

I looked more closely. 'Oh, nonsense!' I laughed. 'They aren't puppets. I see no strings. How can they be operated without strings? In mid-air, too? Puppets need puppeteers.'

She didn't answer. I grinned at her.

'You don't know either!' I said triumphantly. 'Ha! You've seen this umpteen times and you still don't know how it's done.'

Inazia preserved a stubborn silence, so I redevoted my attention to the monkeys. Like professional circus artistes, they had set their trapezes in motion and were now, to the accompaniment of a dramatic orchestral crescendo, swinging to and fro above the heads of the audience. Then, at the end of one wide arc, one of them let go of the bar. To a roll on the drums and piercing screams from the audience, it soared through the air, described a neat somersault, and was safely caught with both paws by the monkey hanging upside down from the other trapeze. Ta-daaa!

Thunderous applause.

'Well I'm damned!' I exclaimed, joining in the ovation. Inazia gave me another sidelong look.

'They're dwarfs,' I said firmly. 'Dwarf artistes dressed up, undoubtedly, and very well trained. A feat of athleticism, especially in costumes like those. Very impressive.'

The Uggly merely uttered a bark of derision.

The monkey acting as catcher released its partner in mid-air again.

The latter soared back to its trapeze, pirouetting like an ice skater on the way, and clung to it nonchalantly with one paw. There was a brief pause during which the trapeze just swung to and fro. Then the two trapeze artistes regained their momentum, let go of the bar, turned a synchronised double somersault and were caught by the catcher, one with each paw.

The audience clapped and stamped their feet. This was trapeze artistry of the highest order. I was impressed.

Now suspended from the same trapeze, the trio swung back and forth. Then the catcher released the other two monkeys, which sailed through the air in the flying-angel position and landed safely back on their own trapeze, screeching merrily.

More applause, louder still.

This proved it. No puppets could have been made to do that. There wasn't even a gridiron above them in which a puppeteer could have concealed himself. And even if there had been, manoeuvres and body movements of that kind were far too complex for any marionette to have performed them convincingly.

The next turn was heralded by another drum roll, this time backed by a long trill on the violins. Now one of the monkeys started swinging on its own, hanging from the bar while its partner remained seated above it. Letting go of the bar, it sailed over the heads of the audience, turning one pirouette after another, and caught the catcher's paws with practised precision. The pair swung back and forth a few times in this position while the third monkey set the other trapeze in motion, hanging from it upside down in a catcher's position.

The drum roll swelled. As the two trapezes swung towards each other, the monkey in the middle caught the paws of the second catcher – this time with its feet – and the whole scene froze in mid-air. The three monkeys were clinging to each other like links in a living chain suspended above the heads of the audience. The drum roll ceased and total silence reigned. Everyone was staring upwards.

But now the monkey in the middle started screaming. It wasn't a joyful, exuberant scream of the kind those creatures sometimes utter, but a cry of pain. This wasn't entertainment, it was agony! Being held by the other two and pulled in two directions at once was obviously hurting the animal badly. The audience grew restless and I gripped the parapet. Was this genuine or part of the show? No, it had to be genuine! A slip-up! Suddenly, I wasn't so sure the monkeys were artistes in costume. But could they be real animals trained in some inexplicable manner to perform such unnatural feats? The screams sounded convincingly animal, anyway. All my enthusiasm had evaporated.

But neither of the other two monkeys let go. They continued to cling grimly to their fellow primate in spite of its spine-chilling screams. Their insensate cruelty enraged me. One of them simply needed to let go, couldn't they get that into their little simian brains? Or were they smarter than I thought? Were they afraid of releasing their partner simultaneously and sending him plummeting head first into the audience?

The monkey's screams had now given way to heart-rending whimpers and some of the audience had risen to their feet. I stood up too and would have yelled at the accursed animals, had not something happened a moment later, dear friends, which I shall never forget to my dying day.

The monkey split in half before our eyes – yes, it was literally rent apart by members of its own kind! The two halves of its body burst asunder with a frightful sound and blood showered down on the audience – big red drops of blood that seemed to me, at that horrific moment, to descend on the theatregoers in a strangely slow and unreal manner. I shrank away from the parapet, gasping for breath, but couldn't tear my eyes away from the horrific spectacle. The other two monkeys swung apart, each holding one half of their partner's body in their paws. Horrible enough though that would have been, dear friends, what I found almost more shocking at that moment was the fact that the Uggly had remained seated and utterly unmoved.

Smiling happily, she seemed to be positively enjoying the incident. Was she out of her mind?

The monkeys swung back, laden with their frightful burdens. Then, swinging forward again, they converged on the point where the terrible incident had occurred – and the two body parts were reunited! With an audible metallic click they snapped together like the components of a constructional toy and all at once the dismembered monkey was whole once more! It even emitted a bleating chimpanzee laugh. A buzz of astonishment ran round the auditorium.

For a few moments the three artistes remained suspended in the air, a curious garland of monkeys and trapezes outlined against the big top and backed by another roll on the drums. Then the catcher monkey let go, the other two swung back, then forward, and the miraculously reconstituted trapeze artiste, having performed an immaculate triple somersault, soared into the catcher's grasp.

Breathless silence in the auditorium.

I tottered back to the parapet, weak at the knees. I was still convinced that I had witnessed an inexplicable marvel until one of the drops of blood came floating very slowly down in front of me and landed on the edge of the box. It was a red rose petal.

Inazia was grinning broadly at me. 'Dwarfs, eh?' she said.

A triple fanfare, deafening applause, enthusiastic cries from the audience.

I was utterly overwhelmed, dear friends!

'A conjuring trick!' I exclaimed in relief. 'The best I've ever seen and the best trapeze act as well!' I applauded wildly and whistled through my teeth. The spectators were chattering like a flock of startled geese, but isolated guffaws could also be heard.

The puppet orchestra had now launched into a reprise of the lively tune it had played at the beginning, probably in order to pacify a few sobbing children and indignant mothers in the audience. To more loud applause, the monkeys and their trapezes were hauled upwards. As they ascended, one of the animals removed his head and handed it to his partner, who stared at it briefly and uncomprehendingly. Before he could give it back, they disappeared into the darkness beneath the big top.

'Incredible,' I gasped as I resumed my seat. 'So they really are puppets beyond a doubt! But they aren't ordinary marionettes. There aren't any strings – they aren't operated by invisible, airborne puppeteers. They move by themselves! How can that be?'

'Puppetism!' the Uggly said proudly.

'Just a minute,' I protested. 'Is that your only explanation? Puppetism? *One* word? How, pray, can a puppet . . .'

There was another resounding gong note and the Uggly said 'Ssh!' I fell silent perforce and redirected my attention to what was happening in the auditorium.

Several Doubles

The music struck up again and the largest curtain slowly rose while the curtain above the puppet orchestra was lowered, doubtless so as not to divert attention from the main attraction. The murmurs in the auditorium died away, to be replaced by a sound of lively birdsong.

The stage set represented a street of picturesquely weatherworn old houses above which a prettily painted sun was rising from the mist. The transition from semi-darkness to light, combined with the music, which resembled a suite by Gravid Greed, conveyed the awakening of a new day. It was, therefore, a morning scene. Some of the buildings were clearly bookshops or antiquarian bookshops with piles of books outside them. One moment, though, I actually knew this street! I had immediately been struck by its architectural peculiarities, all of which had some connection with antiquarian printed matter: a roof resembling an upturned open book, bricks in book form and so on. It was surely . . . yes, exactly: the street in which Ahmed ben Kibitzer had had his shop! It was Colophonius Regenschein Lane, site of some of the most popular antiquarian bookshops and one of the city's classic attractions that had luckily survived the Great Conflagration unscathed. Well, well, so the play was set in Bookholm. The street had indeed been well conveyed – or, to put it somewhat more aptly: it had been perfectly reproduced down to the smallest detail. Every window frame, every roof tile, every doorknob seemed to have been accurately copied. An extraordinarily elaborate set for a puppet theatre.

Suddenly, a first-floor window in one of the houses was flung open and a puppet with dishevelled hair – it closely resembled an Uggly – looked out. To a few guffaws from the audience, it proceeded to sing in a hoarse voice:

225

'Bookholm, city of dreaming books!
Bookholm, city of starving writers!
Bookholm, city of coloured lights!'

A second window burst open and a Demidwarf
puppet leant out and bawled:

'Bookholm, in thee alone the Orm
still burns in uncorrupted form.
Bookholm, the one and only pure
and perfect source of lit'rature!'

A third, fourth and fifth window opened. More puppets appeared and sang at the top of their voices:

> 'Bookholm, where books still dream of days
> when they were naught but swaying trees,
> Bookholm, where poets dream of times
> when every line they think of rhymes!'

I squirmed in my armchair. What awful lyrics and why were they singing them? This was a *singeretta*, of all things! Also known, derogatively, as a *yodeletta* or *moron's opera*, in other words, a piece of popular literature set to trivial music and adapted for the stage – certainly not one of my own favourite art forms, dear friends! Most singerettas were churned out by mass producers who brutalised the original literary material and mercilessly boiled it down to a handful of ill-rhymed little songs designed to be inflicted on crowds of easily impressed pleasure seekers who had strayed into a singeretta tourist trap – just as I had! Damn it! I should have known there was a snag to the evening! I would now be bawled at for two hours by singing puppets that mangled some unfortunate author's work three times over. Great! That came of trusting the cultural taste of a Bookemistic Uggly. Someone who foretold the future from toad shit! Who drank her own urine by the light of the full moon! Ugglies did that sort of thing! And to think I'd allowed such an esoteric poison pill to spoil my evening in a city brimming with interesting cultural offerings! I mechanically chewed my thumbnail (as I always do when something annoys me – I simply can't help it). Curses! I was stuck there for the first act, but I might be able to decamp during the interval – to feign some indisposition or something. Lying was my profession, after all.

More and more multifarious puppets were assembling onstage. Glove puppets were singing in windows and doorways, and appearing from behind handcarts and piles of books. They strutted around in the street as marionettes or toured the set in the form of full-length puppets – in other words, puppeteers themselves dressed up as puppets. Within a very short space of time the stage was teeming with grotesque figures that presented a picturesque spectrum very like the real hurly-burly prevailing in the streets of Bookholm. I saw down-at-heel poets with unsaleable manuscripts under their arms, ruthlessly jostling Hoggling agents, hunchbacked booksellers toting stacks of antiquarian tomes from shop to shop, marvelling tourists bumping into lamp-posts, hawkers with handcarts full of books, roaming book advertisements, scurrying

Live Newspapers, and here and there a masked Biblionaut in full armour. There were even a chimneysweep dancing on a roof and rats singing at the entrance to a sewer. It was all very meticulously done, I had to admit, and I might almost have been mollified – had the lyrics not been so frightful. The puppets had launched into a reprise of the refrain:

'*Bookholm, where books still dream of days*
when they were naught but swaying trees,
Bookholm, where poets dream of times
when every line they think of rhymes!'

One moment! It hadn't occurred to me before, but the words were mine! They were ill-abridged and garbled Yarnspinner!

'*Where books still dream of days when they were naught but swaying trees . . .*'

Yes, that was my intellectual property, it came from . . . I gave a terrible start that derailed my train of thought. Why? Because of a monstrous development onstage: I myself had just rounded the corner of a building!

This subject – an encounter with one's own doppelgänger – had already been tackled several times in Zamonian literature, dear friends, and it was usually a metaphor for the onset of insanity. I only hope, therefore, that the following remark will not be construed as metaphorical, for what came round the corner onstage really did look *exactly* like the person I sometimes regarded, not without a certain satisfaction, in the mirror: my own likeness! If you encounter your own likeness *elsewhere* than in a mirror, you're surely entitled to doubt your sanity a little, aren't you? For one long, terrible moment, the two monkeys from the trapeze act seemed to be tearing at my brain and ripping it asunder like their fellow simian. I had an urge to jump up, run off, sink into my chair, awaken from this nightmare, cry out, dissolve into thin air, and laugh and weep at the same time. Insanity must truly feel like that! In the event, I merely leant even further over the parapet, staring helplessly at the apparition onstage until my trance was dispelled by a dig in the ribs from Inazia.

'Surprised?' she croaked in a triumphant voice. 'I almost gave the game away – I really had to bite my tongue! What do you think of the Yarnspinner puppet, eh? It's fantastic – go on, admit it! You jumped as if you'd seen a ghost!' She cackled heartlessly.

I had broken out in an ice-cold sweat. It was a puppet, of course, and the words were mine. They were putting on something from my oeuvre. I *hadn't* lost my mind! My brain *wasn't* being torn in half. I *wouldn't* have to spend the rest of my life in a padded cell. That much was reassuring. I slumped back in my chair, fighting for breath.

'*The City of Dreaming Books*!' Inazia whispered, wagging a bony finger at me. 'Your book about Bookholm – *that's* what they're doing tonight!'

The music was now reminiscent of Sweng Ohrgeiger's spirited *Atlantis Symphony*, which had first lent artistic expression to the hectic hurly-burly prevailing in modern Zamonian cities. The orchestra at least imitated its unusual concept, which was to reproduce the sounds and motifs of urban bustle by musical means. Rhythmically plucked violins, clattering castanets and blaring brass underpinned the impression made by the shoving and jostling puppets that hustled gawping Yarnspinner (I had still to get used to the idea that *I* was the figure onstage) along the busy streets of Bookholm. Buildings sprouted from the floor of the stage or glided down from above as the Yarnspinner puppet tottered through this hive of activity, vainly trying to take in as much of it as possible. Inazia grinned at me, and I strove to relax by sitting back and concentrating on developments onstage.

Some Bookhunters came striding across the stage – life-size marionettes operated from above by thick wires and accompanied by terrifying blasts on the trombophone and thunderous drumbeats. Their get-up – from martial armour to fearsome helmets and murderous weapons – was extremely realistic. This was truly how they had looked in the old days, as I shuddered to remember. The marionettes' robotic movements were well suited to those heartless fighting machines.

'Now comes the olfactory solo,' the Uggly announced casually. 'Better blow your nose first!' She produced a handkerchief and did so herself. I noticed that several members of the audience were doing likewise. The whole auditorium suddenly rang with trumpeting and sniffing.

'Why?' I asked. 'I don't have a cold.'

'Can't you smell anything?' Inazia retorted.

It was true! It occurred to me only now that I'd smelt quite a lot of things since the play began. The scent of freshly baked bread, for example. Coffee being brewed. Crispy breakfast bacon. I'd assumed that these odours emanated from the theatre café and just happened to suit the morning atmosphere onstage. Was that what the Uggly had meant? Before I could ask, applause rang out. One of the smaller curtains rose while the scene on the main stage was still in full swing. It presented a view of a remarkable set almost the size of a single-storeyed house.

Was it a set at all? Or a machine? It could also have been part of the theatre's heating system – I didn't have a clue, dear friends. If it was a machine, its builder had a sense of humour, because I'd never seen such a peculiar apparatus. It consisted largely of glass and metal, flasks and pipes, test tubes and balloons, spirals and pistons, cylinders, retorts and condensers, funnels and countless receptacles interconnected in a complicated manner with tubes and hoses. Some of the containers were filled with liquids of the most diverse colours, others with steam and fumes in different stages of aggregation: sometimes light and thin like mist, sometimes black and thick as ink, sometimes pink and flickering, sometimes yellow and luminous. The liquids, gases and vapours were being pumped through the maze of tubes in so many different ways that this alone would have been a sight worth seeing. But the really sensational sight on this secondary stage did not reside within the crazy contraption's system of tubes. Oh no, it was situated just in front of it: a Murkholmer was standing at a complicated console and operating the machine.

Yes, dear friends, your ears did not deceive you: a Murkholmer! You remember, don't you?* It was as impossible for a genuine Murkholmer to mount the stage of a Bookholm theatre as for a Bookhunter to be seen in the city's streets, for both were illegal. The Murkholmers had played such an inglorious part in the machinations of Pfistomel Smyke† that they were all banished from Bookholm after the Great Conflagration. This fellow on the stage could not be real.

'Is that . . . a puppet?' I asked Inazia uncertainly.

'No,' she hissed, 'he's the real thing.'

'A live Murkholmer? Here? I thought they were banned.'

'It really is a long time since your last visit,' the Uggly whispered. 'There have been a few changes, my friend. Bookholm is a tolerant city. We can't afford to outlaw a whole species just because a few of its members overstepped the mark.'

'Overstepped the mark?' I expostulated. 'The Murkholmers helped Pfistomel to brainwash half the population of this city! You experienced that yourself – personally! They—'

'Calm down!' the Uggly said soothingly. 'That fellow on the stage wasn't one of them – he wasn't even born then! Relax! One has to be able to forget sometimes.'

I saw a few heads in the audience turn in our direction and heard someone shush us indignantly. There's only one thing worse than someone talking during a cultural event and that's being the talker yourself, so I fell silent.

But the Murkholmer on the stage continued to unnerve me. Erect and immovable as a lamp-post, he stood there in the midst of a bewildering maze of pipes equipped with countless armatures, valves and cocks, pressure gauges and thermometers. In conformity with the

---

*See The City of Dreaming Books, p. 112. (Tr.)

†See The City of Dreaming Books, p. 114 ff., the trombophone concert. (Tr.)

unchanging dress sense prevalent among those weird inhabitants of
Zamonia's north-west coast, he was wearing a black suit which, like
his flat hat, was in sharp contrast to his milk-white complexion.
Fanning out behind him was a multiplicity of long brass pipes, all of
which ran upwards and ended in butterfly valves that constantly
opened and closed without a sound. Immediately in front of the
Murkholmer was a stepped console from which jutted at least two
hundred stops with porcelain knobs. These he operated incessantly,
now and then using a foot to depress some wooden pedals in the floor.
A Murkholmer! I still couldn't take it in.

'You're in luck,' whispered the Uggly, clutching my forearm.
'That isn't just *any* old Murkholmer, it's Oktobir van Krakenbeyn,
Bookholm's finest performer on the scent organ.'

'Organ?' I whispered back. 'Is that supposed to be a musical
instrument? What's, er . . . a scent organist?'

The Uggly gave me the look she reserved for provincial tourists who had strayed into her shop and stupidly asked for directions.

'A scent organ is designed to set the scene olfactorily,' she explained in a whisper. 'It's unique to Bookholm – unique to this theatre! Together with the music, it contributes an olfactory dimension to the production. Sight, hearing, smell! Even a blind member of the audience knows what's happening onstage when the scent organ gets going. Playing the thing is an art in itself. There are seven scent organists in Bookholm, but Krakenbeyn is by far the greatest virtuoso. He designed and built that instrument himself. A grand master of nasal scene-setting! His compositions smell the best. Pay attention, the solo is beginning!'

While the street scene on the main stage continued with music but no singing, the Murkholmer did little more than pull and push the stops on his console and depress the occasional pedal. This he did with dignified stolidity, never once abandoning his grave demeanour, as if operating the furnace in a crematorium. The fluids and vapours in the organ reacted with remarkable rapidity: they came to the boil, condensed and evaporated, glowed and incandesced, hissed and bubbled. The valves on the organ pipes opened and closed too fast for the eye to follow.

Meanwhile, on the main stage, the Yarnspinner puppet continued to roam the streets of Bookholm, which was represented by the series of sets across which it trudged. Buildings, towers and walls sprouted from the floor or floated down from above, only to disappear in ever quicker succession. The drumbeats accelerated, the oboes and clarinets tooted more and more frenetically.

I raised my head and sniffed the air. It smelt just as Bookholm had smelt the first time I wandered its streets. It was redolent of the freshly roasted coffee beans which many Bookholmers liked to nibble from paper bags while reading; of steaming yeast cakes with lemon curd; of burnt toast and vanilla-flavoured tea; of freshly processed printer's ink. Nothing remembers better than the nose! A whiff of lemon balm or tar or the scent of strawberries or new-mown grass are enough to catapult me back over the decades and into the past. But there was more in the air, much more! If asked whether I'd seen a tannery onstage, or a glue works or a carpenter's shop, I would unhesitatingly have answered in the affirmative. I would also have felt convinced that the stage had held a soap factory, a waffle bakery and a barbershop, yet no such sets existed! The scent organ had only bamboozled me into thinking I could smell tanned leather, bookbinder's glue and fresh wood shavings, also perfumed soap, baked waffles and aftershave. That was enough for my brain to imagine whole streets lined with shop windows and billboards that weren't there at all. Olfactory scene-setting! Nasal architecture! I now grasped what the Uggly had meant.

I saw the Murkholmer direct a long, expressionless gaze at the audience, then turn back to his labyrinthine apparatus and very calmly pull out one stop after another. I was just wondering what sort of curious mélange of smells this would produce when an olfactory tsunami swept over me and the audience. It was simply overwhelming! We could smell chimney soot and eau de cologne, fried eggs and sweaty armpits, boiled milk and machine oil, cat's piss and horseshit, camomile tea, burnt fat, the intoxicating scent of a florist's roses, stale dregs of beer from the cellar of an inn, camphor and ether fumes from a pharmacy, toadstool tea and henbane soup from an Ugglian herbalist's, pigs' blood from a butcher's, fresh newsprint, warm rolls. We smelt all the smells a person can detect in a city awakening to a new day. But there was also an unmistakable odour that existed in no other Zamonian city: the smell of *Dreaming Books* arising from the Bookholm Shafts. Inazia nudged me in the ribs and grinned. I was speechless.

Then there were the sounds! I mustn't, dear friends, forget to mention the skilful contribution made to this synthesis of the arts by the theatre's talented sound-painters. I deliberately call their activities sound-painting rather than background noises or acoustic scenery to indicate the level of artistry attained by its practitioners at the Puppetocircus Maximus. Hammerblows and pealing bells, cocks crowing and dogs barking, wagon wheels crunching on gravel or rumbling over cobblestones, birds twittering, children yelling, voices mingling – all these combined to form melodies and rhythms of their own that were in no way inferior in precision and harmony to the orchestra's musical accompaniment. I was inside a huge, well-oiled, perfectly functioning theatrical machine in which everything, from the smallest prop to the last trill on the flute, was in its proper place.

'What you're looking at', the Uggly informed me as quietly as she could, 'is really only a fraction of the instrument – the tip of the iceberg, so to speak. The entire theatre is, in fact, threaded with a maze of pipes connected to the organ. It's like the circulation of the blood or the nervous system. Concealed in the floor, the walls, and even in this box are very fine jets that spray us with invisible odoriferous substances. Kibitzer believed that they probably acted in conjunction with an additional gas capable of temporarily neutralising those substances and breaking them down. Otherwise, all that this organ-playing produced would be a portmanteau of a stench and probably unbearable.'

'Kibitzer had a point,' I whispered back. 'He's . . .' – I stopped short – 'I mean, he *was* a smart fellow.'

'There's even a rumour', Inazia went on in a low voice, 'that the instrument on the stage down there isn't a real organ but only for show – a glamorous fake – and that the real organ is somewhere else and doesn't look in the least spectacular. Furthermore, that the organist down there is an ingenious puppet, not a Murkholmer at all.'

'What did I tell you!' I said triumphantly.

'It isn't true, though,' she retorted. 'That's nonsense.'

'How do you know?'

'An Uggly can sense these things.'

The Ugglies' traditional killer blow! When they ran out of rational arguments, they came out with their mysterious sensory perceptions, their feelings and presentiments, their esoteric knowledge! There was no point in arguing, you always came off worst. At all events, I felt slightly reassured by the thought that the organist might not be a Murkholmer after all.

Meantime, the onstage action continued. My first sojourn in Bookholm was conveyed with due dramatic brevity, whole chapters of my book being boiled down into short scenes with no dialogue. For instance, the stage version of my encounter with Ovidios in the *Graveyard of Forgotten Writers* lasted only a few seconds. So did my reading of Colophonius Regenschein's book, which had really taken me a whole night. The Yarnspinner puppet was shown buying Regenschein's account of the catacombs from an itinerant hawker and perusing it in the street, whereas I had actually purchased the book from a shop and read it in a café. In this scene an immense backdrop the size of a house was lowered. It was painted with something vaguely reminiscent of the treasure map Kibitzer had bequeathed me. The resemblance consisted mainly in the fact that it was a vertical representation of the catacombs. In contrast to Regenschein's precise cartography, however, it depicted them in medieval style. We were shown cross-sections of caves and tunnels in which fearsome monsters such as dragons, trolls and giant spiders crouched over precious books and devoured Bookhunters, or similar horrific motifs portrayed in the naive manner of early book illuminators, with false perspectives and a great deal of gold leaf. Very pretty! Meanwhile, to some plaintive music, a voice (probably meant to be that of Colophonius Regenschein) sang a ballad describing the adventurous conditions prevailing below ground and recapitulated the history of the catacombs in a very truncated form:

'In days of old the Bookemists
concealed their books from sight.
They stowed them all in oaken chests
deprived of air and light,

then hid the books down in the depths
where still they dream today.
Their resting place is hard to find
oft seek it though you may.'

The recurring refrain was the same each time:

'Hail, ye suicidal creatures
eager precious books to see!
Leather, ink and age-old paper,
long-forgotten library!'

That, of course, was plagiarised from Evubeth van Goldwine's immortal last symphony, from which the melody for the ballad had also been borrowed. Although cheeky, it was well-stolen. If you're going to steal, steal only from the best, that's my motto too.

Then, on the main stage, the puppet finally reached Kibitzer's bookshop. The music died away, the big curtain closed and that of a smaller stage rose almost simultaneously. And there I – or rather, my puppet double – was again! All alone now and only dimly illuminated in a sea of darkness. At once, piles of books sprouted from the floor and bookcases fraught with ancient tomes trundled forward out of the background. It grew lighter, but only a little. Clouds of fine yellow dust swirled into the air and then I smelt it: the unmistakable Nocturnomathian book dust that only the works of Professor Abdul Nightingale could produce.

'This is incredible!' I gasped. 'It smells just like Kibitzer's shop!'

Mutely, Inazia laid a hand on my arm. A candle ignited itself as though lit by a ghostly hand, then a curious figure with huge, luminous eyes emerged from the darkness: Ahmed ben Kibitzer, almost as lifelike as in real life! I would have been little less startled had his ghost appeared in our box. I almost uttered a shrill cry, once more aware of whose chair I was occupying. Tears sprang to my eyes. I made to jump up, but the Uggly soothingly gripped my arm and prevented me from doing so.

The Kibitzer puppet was really spooky, especially when one knew it personified the dead. It was operated by black-clad puppeteers equipped with rods, but they were scarcely visible in the gloom and one forgot them as soon as the puppet moved. It was a mystery to me how they illuminated its eyes from within and imitated Kibitzer's quavering voice so perfectly, likewise how that voice could be heard in every last corner of the theatre as clearly as if it were whispering in one's ear. It was as if he had returned from the hereafter to enact his role on the stage. One could hear woodworms munching away at the shelves and the humming of Kibitzer's brains, smell mouldy paper and ancient leather. The theatregoers were quiet as mice.

What ensued, however, wasn't a dramatic scene but some snappy, humorous dialogue between me and the Nocturnomath that had never taken place in real life or in my book. But that didn't matter at all, because it not only epitomised the disputatious relationship between us but made the audience laugh. Its culmination was that Kibitzer threw me out of his shop. Even I couldn't help grinning.

'That was Kibitzer's favourite scene,' Inazia whispered beside me and tears welled up in my eyes once more. Before I could completely surrender to emotion, however, there was an abrupt change of lighting and scenery. Curtains rose and fell, and the Yarnspinner puppet roamed the darkened streets to music whose pounding chords on the piano reminded me of Igöri Iglegty's disturbing compositions, with their notes like dagger thrusts. In a ballet-like scene, I encountered Bookhunters and other shady characters from the Bookholmian underworld and was marooned in the most obscure corners of the city, the latter being conveyed by grandiose sets that seemed to have been borrowed from nightmare paintings by Chicorigi de Gorio. Eventually, my puppet left the menacing shades of night behind and came to a brightly lit inn. The sinister music died away.

A curtain descended on that set and another immediately beside it rose. We were now inside the inn, which was occupied by numerous puppets playing walk-on roles. This was the passage from my book in which I met the scheming literary agent Claudio Harpstick and had a conversation with him that would later propel me into the clutches of Pfistomel Smyke. The actual course of events had been quite different, chronologically speaking, but that no longer mattered because I was now being carried along unresistingly by the dramatic flow.

Harpstick was played by a life-size puppet seated at table so that his body was visible from the waist up only. The scent organ was disseminating appetising smells of grilled sausages and bacon, roast garlic and pea soup, hot cocoa, and sage in melted butter. The illusion of a well-patronised eating place was completed by the clatter of dishes and the tinkle of glasses, lively chatter and boisterous laughter. A dwarf marionette even mounted a table and recited an extremely bad poem in a nasal voice – an almost exact reproduction of what had actually happened.

In addition to all the smells of food, the air was also unmistakably redolent of field and forest, resin, pine needles and wet wild boar's bristles. This was quite subtle, because Harpstick had been a Hoggling and really did smell like that. Even as a puppet he radiated an impressive, almost intimidating aura combined, however, with boyish charm. I was struck by the convincing way in which his appearance and character had been captured. The Harpstick puppet sang his lines in a fine baritone voice, which I found a little bit silly and inappropriate for such a malign and scheming rogue, but the music was excellent and reminded me of Ossigichio Ronani's comic opera *The Confectioner of Ironville*, so I graciously overlooked this. The libretto dealt in a humorous way with Harpstick's dubious trade as a literary agent:

'You use a pen but I use my nous,
I know when something'll be successful,
I am the cat and you are my mouse,
reading itself I find too stressful.

'I'm just an agent and you are a writer,
you are inspired but I go with hunches.
My fees make your pockets very much lighter,
You like renown, I prefer business lunches.'

That was how Harpstick loudly and confidently summed up his conception of the agent/author relationship. Not necessarily the best scene in the play, but it amused the audience and drove the action along. Harpstick ended by advising Yarnspinner to call on the literary scholar Pfistomel Smyke and gave him his address. Then the curtain fell. The embarrassing bee-bread incident had been omitted completely. Although quite all right with me, this was hard to understand; it would certainly have raised a few laughs.

A moment later I saw myself wandering through the city's narrow alleyways on another stage. Would I ever, I wondered, get used to seeing myself onstage? I gave a violent start whenever 'I' reappeared. My puppet suddenly paused outside the wonderfully painted representation of a crooked old building. I could read the sign above the door even without opera glasses:

And this is *my* favourite scene!' Inazia trilled in my ear. She had laid a hand on my arm and was gazing spellbound at the stage. Her eyes were shining with ill-concealed pride.

The curtain rose and we found ourselves in the Uggly's antiquarian bookshop. Inazia Anazazi, who was in reality sitting beside me, was revealed standing in the midst of her Ugglian paraphernalia. I was enchanted! Her shop had been reproduced with such attention to detail, one might have believed that the whole place had simply been winched on to the stage. The scent organ was diffusing such a stupefying miasma of age-old book dust, wild garlic tisane, musky perfume and Ugglian herbal soup, it made me itch to bury my nose in a perfumed handkerchief. But that was exactly how Ugglian bookshops smelt!

'The actress who's imitating my voice spent a whole week in my bookshop,' Inazia whispered proudly, 'purely in order to study its modulations.'

That actress's research must have been no enviable task, my friends, but it had certainly paid off. She had clearly been at pains not only to imitate Inazia's voice as closely as possible but to reproduce the Ugglian *concert pitch* – that appalling form of vocalisation which is common to all Ugglies and sounds like the product of centuries of cigar-smoking, acute suppuration of the frontal sinus and a badly healed tracheotomy. She had succeeded admirably.

Wisely, this scene had dispensed with song and was accompanied only – if I'd identified the musical quotation correctly – by a few motifs from Gynasok Strivir's ballet *Devil Dance*. At all events, the almost subliminal drum rolls and hectic xylophone-playing were admirably suited to the puppet representing Inazia, whose gaunt upper body loomed over the counter and was skilfully operated by concealed puppeteers. Its physiognomy had been only slightly exaggerated, for how can a caricature be caricatured? Indeed, it might even be said that this slight exaggeration flattered Inazia, because in this case a good caricature was more flattering than the reality. She delivered a brief but informative monologue that dealt with the superstitions of traditional Bookemism and not only cast a dramatic shadow over coming events but highlighted the Uggly's prophetic abilities. Although this, too, had not occurred either in reality or in my book, it strategically paved the way for Pfistomel Smyke's appearance on the scene and inserted a little breathing space between the musical numbers. I could see out of the corner of my eye that Inazia was fervently mouthing every syllable of her lines. She knew them all by heart.

The whole theatre went dark again. Although the orchestra could still be heard, it sounded as if the musicians were only tuning their instruments – a chaotic hubbub of scraping strings and blaring brass. Then, cavorting through the darkness like hallucinations, came some almost invisible objects. At first they seemed to me like the fleeting shapes and abstract patterns you can sometimes see with your eyes shut, but I gradually identified them as symbols: letters, runes and hieroglyphs that flitted through the air in the form of marionettes on strings and were lit from within. The puppets flew right over the heads of the audience, performing graceful pirouettes or daring nosedives that evoked excited cries and laughter, especially from the younger spectators. But the ballet of the cryptic symbols ended as abruptly as it had begun: they disappeared into the darkness, whispering and giggling. The unmelodious tooting and scraping died away and the lights came up very slowly. Like a mirage, the scenery and props of Pfistomel Smyke's ill-famed typographical laboratory came into view on the main stage – not just a room, but a whole realm with a topography of its own. My blood ran cold.

The typographical laboratory and Smyke's house had been burnt to the ground, as had the whole of Darkman Street and the surrounding Bookemists' district, but my book contains a detailed description of them. The stage designers seemed not only to have kept to this but even surpassed it in a certain manner. Their version of the typographical laboratory looked considerably more decorative than the real thing. Smyke's hexagonal workroom devoted to applied codicology had been picturesque but chaotic, whereas every object here appeared to be in its proper place and perfectly illuminated by candlelight. Looking at this set, one wanted to move into it at once, become a scribe and dedicate a lifetime to graphological analyses or calligraphic calibrations with the aid of the Bookemistic equipment ready to hand. I knew enough of this profession to be able to assert that the props were not dummies but carefully assembled Bookemistic implements such as Smyke himself might have used:

243

microscopes and magnifying glasses, letter counters and alphabetic spectrographs, ink thermometers and versometers, poetological tabulators and silver-plated septants. There was even an antiquated novel-writing machine and, of course, shelves filled with ancient tomes, mountains of manuscripts, bottles filled with inks of many colours, and armies of quill pens. Interspersed with these were flasks containing *Leyden Manikins*.* I couldn't tell whether the latter were real or puppets themselves, but they were certainly in motion.

I found it very alarming to see myself in this laboratory, if only as a puppet, especially as the orchestra – if my musical memory didn't deceive me – greeted Pfistomel Smyke's entrance with a rendition of the shattering fanfare from Smygort Messodusk's *Night in the*

Gloomberg Mountains. On that note, the biggest villain in my book entered the room in the flesh – and 'in the flesh' is really no exaggeration, my friends. The puppet representing the diabolical literary scholar onstage was so lifelike and realistic, I broke out in a cold sweat at the sight of it.

'Pfistomel!' I whispered the name so loudly that the Uggly beside me gave a start and several members of the audience turned to look. Smyke glided across the stage like a gluttonous slug across a lettuce leaf, humming and buzzing and cooing and purring his lines as beguilingly and ingratiatingly as he had in real life. The movements of his massive form, as soon as he began to speak, were accompanied by some gradually swelling music reminiscent of Uvera Miracel's

famous, light-footed *Elfin Ballet*, which was remarkably appropriate because it sounded a little like the hypnotic melodies employed by snake charmers. For what else was Smyke but a huge, dangerous constrictor, and a hypnotist into the bargain!

By operating his stops, the player of the scent organ unleashed a series of smells whose individual components would have been familiar only to an experienced literary scholar – or to someone who, like me, had himself been in Smyke's laboratory. For who else would have been acquainted with the unique smell of the fibrous pulp from which deckle-edged Nurn Forest paper is manufactured? Of the ancient chemical substances used to bleach book paper in the Late Middle Ages? Of calcium sulphide solution? Who still had any notion of how papyrus smelt? There were also the countless subtle olfactory nuances of perfumed letter paper, of Bookemistic tinctures or the resinous scent of the sandarac powder which only eccentrics still use to dry ink, not to mention the stupefying vapour given off by fresh book glue, the animal exhalations of untanned bookbinder's leather and the aroma of centuries-old sealing wax.

But these strange smells made a vital contribution to the menacing atmosphere of the scene and its unfamiliar, mysterious aura. If one could tear one's eyes away from the sight of the main stage, one saw the Murkholmer organist on the side stage rapturously manipulating the stops of his bizarre instrument. He swayed back and forth in time to the orchestral crescendi like a sapling in the wind while his olfactory notes went fluttering through the auditorium. Now that I knew its purpose, the organ and its luminous liquids looked to me like the pipe dream of some megalomaniac alchemist with musical ambitions. An instrument of that kind really belonged in the recreation room of a lunatic asylum.

I took an apprehensive look through the opera glasses. The Smyke puppet not only withstood closer inspection but actually intensified my fear – and my respect for the puppet-maker! I had no idea what material it was made of, it all looked so authentic. The skin made a firm but spongy impression, like maggot flesh. It was slightly translucent, and one could even see blue capillaries in it. The fourteen little arms gesticulated in such a lifelike fashion, one could believe they were natural excrescences. Someone had to be concealed inside that flabby figure and operating it, but I didn't know what kind of creature it was. Nor did I know *how many* of them there were, for a single puppeteer couldn't possibly have managed on his own. I could detect neither wires hanging down from above nor rods supporting the massive contraption from below. A theatrical device of the latest type, it defied all the laws of nature and was a masterpiece of Puppetism, but I had no idea how it worked. Anxiously, I laid the opera glasses aside. I preferred to marvel at the miraculous puppet's brilliant entrance from afar.

Fortunately, they didn't spoil Smyke's performance by making him sing, which would have ruined the scene and robbed the treacherous scholar's character of its menacing quality. The silent horror inherent in his person was, therefore, able to develop as sluggishly as Smyke himself moved. I saw theatregoers fidgeting in their seats, simultaneously revolted and fascinated, as if uncertain whether to applaud or take to their heels. I felt just the same. It was like watching a spider spinning its web. You knew it was at work on a lethal weapon, yet you couldn't help admiring its dexterity and precision. Villains are always the most interesting characters and Smyke was no exception. My own character paled into insignificance beside the charismatic scoundrel, and his skilfully made puppet outacted my own so effortlessly that I felt positively envious of a creature composed of inanimate materials, of wood and rubber, wire and glue. I degenerated into a mere cue for Smyke's grandiose monologues, which constituted the literary highlight of the play to date. His insane desire to destroy everything beyond his control by means of murder, intrigue and machination, and his burning hatred for everything of no use to art and himself – all these were conveyed by every word of his hypnotic pontifications. This was theatre of the calibre of Wimpersleake's historical dramas! Dialogue and puppetry, music and olfactory dramaturgy became welded into an artistic synthesis such as I had never before seen or heard, let alone smelt, on the stage.

The two puppets performed what resembled a very slow, old-fashioned, formal dance to the ballet music. Meanwhile, I was manoeuvred ever closer to the trapdoor in the centre of the stage until everyone in the audience must have realised that Smyke meant to entice his visitor to go down into the cellar with him. Down into the catacombs!

And here I noticed for the first time, and with some displeasure, that it hadn't been like this at all. Large parts of my book were missing. They had boiled down my two visits to Smyke into a single encounter and simply omitted the whole of the trombophone concert I'd attended in the interim. That was a bold and brutal cut. In retrospect, though, it strikes me as quite understandable because it would not only have created a hiatus in the dramatic flow but would probably have proved too much for the audience, who couldn't wait for the scene of the action to be transferred to the Labyrinth at last. This cut didn't worry me for long, however, because an artistic representation of what was doubtless the most momentous decision in my life was now being shown onstage: the two puppets disappeared through the trapdoor without a word and the music ended. It seemed remarkably undramatic, but the actual course of events had been no more spectacular. Then the curtain fell and the auditorium was once more wrapped in total darkness and silence. But only for a few moments, dear friends, for the ensuing applause was louder than I'd ever heard in any theatre. To say that the play really took off thereafter would be a gross understatement.

A Dream Within
a Dream

Once the storm of applause had died down, darkness and silence fell once more. All that could be heard were the murmurs of the audience and sounds of activity from the stage area. Before long, however, my attention was sufficiently aroused by the appearance of something on the edge of the main stage for me to resort to my opera glasses again. It was a metal-framed glass receptacle with a flickering object inside it – a so-called jellyfish lamp. This was a lantern such as people often used when exploring the Labyrinth. Although the phosphorescent jellyfish inside it gave off only a meagre and fitful light, it lasted for as long as the jellyfish survived – which, if the creature was kept well-nourished, could be a good few years.

Soon afterwards, another prop appeared onstage in the ghostly light of this jellyfish lamp. I initially thought it was an untidy stack of books – until it started to speak unaccented, stageworthy Zamonian in a deep and resonant voice:

> 'A place accursèd and forlorn
> with walls of books piled high,
> its windows stare like sightless eyes
> and through them phantoms fly.
> Of leather and of paper built,
> worm-eaten through and through,
> the castle known as Shadowhall
> brings every nightmare true . . .'

It was a puppet! A book puppet in the most literal sense, reciting the verses with which I had prefaced the second part of my book. On closer examination I saw that it was composed of publications of my own: a volume of early poems, two volumes of essays, my works on the Orm theory, a collection of fairy tales and several novels. My own oeuvre in puppet form! I was entranced. Then grey dust billowed into the air and the speaking head, bowing in all directions to subdued applause from the audience, sank through the floor of the stage.

Music struck up again and with it came noises. All one heard at first was the whisper of the curtains opening – one could hardly see them in the gloom. I cannot find words to describe the sound that then came wafting through the theatre, but I must try nonetheless. It was a mournful, high-pitched sound such as might have been made by some creature in terrible pain. If ghosts existed, they would probably attract attention in that way. Although I was firmly seated in my armchair, I had a frightful feeling that beneath me yawned a miles-deep shaft in which this creature was imprisoned. I turned cold as ice, and I noticed that Inazia was drawing her cloak more tightly around her. There came a low, soughing sound, as of wind that had strayed inside the walls of a ruined castle and was seeking a way out. The music was no less ghostly and eerie: now and then, isolated notes on the piano were struck or harp strings plucked like raindrops landing in puddles. At the same time, something in the middle of the stage slowly took shape in the gloom. It looked like a bundle of cloth or a heap of old blankets – until it suddenly stirred. Then a scaly, saurian head emerged from it. It was *me*! Once again, I started at the sight of myself. The Yarnspinner puppet was just waking up in the catacombs, crawling out from under its cloak and slowly struggling to its feet.

So they'd cut several more passages out of my book, dear friends! The scene in Pfistomel Smyke's gigantic subterranean library was entirely missing. My being anaesthetised by the poisonous book had also been left out, likewise my waking up in the catacombs in the company of Smyke and Claudio Harpstick.

The Uggly leant over to me. 'The treasures found in Smyke's underground library made a sizeable contribution to Bookholm's reconstruction and new-found prosperity,' she whispered. 'People are loath to remember that chapter in your book. That's probably why the playwright left it out.'

251

I brushed this aside. Although the cut verged on censorship, it didn't bother me at all. I wanted to know how the play went on, everything else was secondary. While Yarnspinner was patting the dust off his cloak, his surroundings became a little lighter. We could now make out earth walls, beams, worm-eaten bookshelves with mouldering volumes on them, cobwebs, sheaves of age-old paper on the ground. Glow-worms drew calligraphic curlicues of light in the air. We could also hear disturbing noises: a dull, throbbing sound, subterranean gurgles, a persistent hiss. The music had become something that no longer merited the description. It was more of a noise, a menacing *basso continuo* produced by the orchestra's organ. In the darkest corners of the stage, behind the bookshelves and between the books, movement could be discerned here and there: sometimes a groping tentacle, sometimes the glossy chitin of an insect, sometimes a monstrous, multicoloured, faceted eye – but they withdrew as quickly as they had emerged.

I suddenly felt as short of breath as I did during my bouts of asthma, which my doctor attributes to hypochondria. In my growing enthusiasm, I had almost forgotten that the bulk of my book was set in the catacombs of Bookholm and, thus, that the rest of the play would be so too. Things could yet turn very unpleasant, my friends, but I'd resolved to overcome my fears.

I smelt worms. I smelt coal. I smelt mildew, wet rat's fur and the nutty effluvium of the Papyrus Cockroach, which, as Colophonius Regenschein states, lives only in the upper reaches of the catacombs. I smelt petroleum, the fishy exhalations of phosphorescent jellyfish, the liquorice tang of black seaweed. I also, of course, smelt books in such diverse states of decay as I had never smelt since the old days. There it was again, the alluring and unmistakable perfume of the *Dreaming Books* – not that which pervades the streets of Bookholm, however, but the exclusively subterranean scent of the huge, dark repository of antiquarian books that extended beneath the city. It was only now that I took another look at the Murkholmer organist, whose subtle olfactory musicianship I now took so much for granted that I'd almost forgotten about him. He was impassively manipulating the stops with his fingertips.

'Incredible,' I said in an awestruck voice. 'This is just how the upper reaches of the catacombs smell.'

'That's not quite right,' the Ugly whispered back. 'It's how the catacombs *used to* smell. Today they smell of burning.'

The melancholy background music that now struck up consisted only of some soft but endlessly repeated piano notes with rhythmical string accompaniment. Wasn't this the moving *Andante con moto* by Zach Brestrunf? At all events, it was admirably suited to this phase of the drama, for now began the less felicitious part of my first visit to Bookholm – one that marked the all-time low of my life hitherto, dear friends! Betrayed and hijacked, a helpless victim buried alive in the catacombs of Bookholm – even a death march would have suited the context pretty well. The set was simple but realistic. Dark, earth-brown colours occasionally interspersed with grey granite: that's what the walls down there really looked like. All that broke the monotony were some old books picturesquely mouldering away on rotting shelves. My character now launched into a rather silly sung mono-logue that somewhat detracted from the scene, which was perfect in other respects.

> *'Alas, a prisoner am I,*
> *far from the sight of open sky.*
> *I can no hope at all discern,*
> *and do not know which way to turn.*
> *Accurséd be that poisoned book*
> *which me so far from daylight took!*
> *Why has that monster Pfistomel*
> *entrapped me in the bowels of hell?'*

. . . and so on and so forth in the same appalling style. I myself had never written such doggerel, even in the depths of despair over writer's block. Still less had I sung it, dear brothers and sisters in spirit, especially as in this case the music had obviously been composed off the peg by some singerettist and was in sharp qualitative contrast to the classical quotations hitherto. I cast a sceptical glance at Inazia, who responded with a resigned shrug. At least she shared my opinion that this was the low point of the production to date. The scene soon ended, however, and its dramatic sledgehammer tactics had made it clear, even to the most dull-witted member of the audience, what had happened to the hero. Enough said!

The very next scene delighted me so much that I soon forgot about the embarrassing warbling that had preceded it. The curtain mercifully fell and another rose to reveal a wonderful model of the catacombs. Or rather, of a part of them. It looked like the cross-section of an anthill, the difference being that roaming its passages were no creepy-crawlies but a tiny Yarnspinner no bigger than my paw! The little puppet made its way ever deeper down serpentine tunnels until it came out in a cave at the foot of the model. This gave the audience a very good idea of the ramifications of the Labyrinth, which were conveyed with great structural and dramaturgical skill. The curtain fell, another rose and Yarnspinner, a full-sized puppet once more, was discovered standing in a wonderful dripstone cave that occupied the entire stage.

'It gets a bit silly now,' Inazia warned me with a grin, stuffing a biscuit into her mouth at lightning speed, 'but I like it.'

Eerie but beautiful, the dripstone cave was bristling with stalagmites and stalactites. The stage designers had striven to recreate the subterranean light of phosphorescent algae, so the dripstones, some of which were three-dimensional and some painted, glowed in a variety of colours like the late, demented oil paintings by Vochtigang Venn. In the centre stood a big, dark bookcase adorned with a wealth of carving and filled with ancient tomes – around a hundred of them. As soon as Yarnspinner entered the cave, these books came to life. Their spines started to wobble and jostle, but they didn't stir from the spot.

Enlisting the aid of my opera glasses, I examined the curious old volumes more closely. In truth, the ribs on the leather spines were opening up into blithely chattering mouths and expressively rolling eyes. The whole bookcase was, in fact, a colossal puppet. A puppet composed of numerous little puppets!

'What passage in my book is this supposed to represent?' I whispered. 'The Animatomes didn't appear until later, in Shadowhall Castle. And they couldn't speak, either!'

'It's a symbolic synopsis of the chapters in which you roam through the catacombs,' Inazia explained with her mouth full of biscuit. 'You try to get your bearings from the old books in the Labyrinth. That bookcase represents the whole of Zamonian literature, which is showing you the way like the omniscient chorus in the tragedies of old. Delightful, isn't it? An oracle in book form. It seems a trifle pretentious at first, but one gets used to it.'

One of the fat old tomes cleared its throat audibly and spoke in a rumbling bass voice:

'Down from the sunlit Overworld
a visitor to us was sent.
By fate into the Labyrinth hurled,
he does his tragic lot lament.
He has no compass him to guide,
no tentacles and no antennae.
It's certain that, whate'er betide,
the dangers facing him are many!'

A smaller book on the shelf above continued
in a much higher-pitched voice:

> 'He must the catacombs defy
> sans drink or even a bone to pick,
> That's quite enough, one can't deny,
> to make a famous author . . .'

Before the final word could be uttered, two ancient volumes hurriedly
sang a duet:

> 'Alas, alas, how sad to be
> abandoned in the depths of night.
> Poor Yarnspinner will ne'er be free
> unless he can escape his plight.
> The Reaper Grim his scythe prepares,
> the jaws of Death are open wide,
> wild beasts are lurking in their lairs.
> The books his only hope provide,
> but soon he'll curse their bad advice,
> for him to stray they will entice.'

Wherepon a whole shelf full of books sang the following words in unison:

'Go left, no better to the right!
Or better still, go straight ahead
and jump into a yawning pit,
for then you will be good and dead!
Die fast, and count yourself in luck
because you don't a slow death merit.
No Harpyr* then your blood will suck
and maggots will your corpse inherit.'

***Harpyrs**: unpleasant inhabitants of the catacombs of Bookholm. See *The City of Dreaming Books*, p. 295 ff. (Tr.)

The speaking books continued to declaim in this loquacious manner. I thought I could occasionally recognise the style and vocabulary of one or another heavyweight from the higher echelons of Zamonian literature: Ojahnn Golgo van Fontheweg, for example, with his know-it-all sentences and winged words, but also verses by Dölerich Hirnfiedler, the megalomaniac effusions of Eiderich Fischnertz, the preachifying tone of Akud Ödreimer and the sometimes involuntarily comical sing-song intonation of Ali Aria Ekmirrner. They all painted my forthcoming sojourn in the catacombs in the darkest colours and were unstinting in their textbook maxims and pieces of advice. So as to retain the audience's attention, a glowing will-o'-the-wisp flitted from book to book, illuminating the volume that was currently declaiming and changing colour each time. How the director managed this was a mystery to me. The jabbering classics then resorted to recommendations – nay, injunctions – regarding my literary work. In so doing, they became more and more vehement and eventually bombarded me with conflicting commands:

'Turn out novels long and thick!
Books with lots of personnel!
Prose alone has timeless chic!
Only novels cast a spell!'

'No! Write poetry sublime!
Put your verses into rhyme
and they'll stand the test of time!'

'Write novellas, medium length,
then you'll go from strength to strength!
Nothing's better than novellas
if you want to write bestsellers!'

'Nonsense! Write plays that last for days
and the public you'll amaze!'

'You crave literary status?
Write an essay with afflatus!'

'No! Write axioms profound!
They're the best things to expound.
Churn them out and never tire
if to greatness you aspire!'

'Rot! Write satires bold and witty,
criticisms devoid of pity!'

'Why don't you your feelings vent
in manifestos vehement,
fraught with malice, vitriol,
and prejudice political?
Stick them up on buildings tall,
plaster them to every wall,
but don't sign them with your name
and you will escape the blame!'

'In hexameters compose!
Better them than flaccid prose!'

'Write of heroes of the past,
lines heroic loud reciting,
boldly slaying dragons vast
and performing deeds exciting.
Paragons of manliness,
they save maidens in distress!'

'No! Of death and devastation write,
morbid readers to delight!
Vampire bats and hounds of hell
are the themes that really sell!'

Finally, when the self-opinionated old tomes had harangued the Yarnspinner puppet into a state of total bewilderment – it was merely staggering around and uttering histrionic 'Oh!'s and 'Ah!'s – another curtain rose, enlarging the panorama of the dripstone cave. Into view came more stalagmites, more shelves filled with picturesquely mouldering volumes, and in the centre an outsize book that appeared to consist entirely of metal! It was standing on end, had a silver cover with gold and brass fittings and ornamentation, and glittered in the artificial lighting like the entrance to a treasure chamber. On the cover, where the title would normally have been inscribed, was a golden frame enclosing a curtain of beaten copper. It resembled the proscenium of a puppet theatre.

'Goldenbeard's *Book Trap!*'* I gasped. It really did look the way I'd described it, except that this one was the size of a coffin!

' I ignore that dogeared advice'

the metal book suddenly commanded in a robotic voice.

' The classics will far from suffice
to guide you. Better come with me
and you will many marvels see!
I am the future, no decay
will ever eat my flesh away.
Time' s insignificant to me,
I ' ll live for all eternity!'

While he was speaking, parts of his ornamentation began to revolve and became enmeshed with each other, ticking like parts of a clockwork motor.

---

*See *The City of Dreaming Books*, p. 173 ff. (Tr.)

' Decay? To me that word's unknown,
my heart is harder than a stone
Maggots and insects from me flee,
of bookworms I am wholly free
You want these caverns to forsake?
I will you to the exit take
The route to freedom I can show,
so climb aboard me and let's go'

'Don't listen to that book of steel!'

the old books protested in unison.

**'It cannot love or pity feel!
It has no soul, no mind, no heart!
Ignore its urgings to depart!
It only wants to do you ill
and bend you to its evil will!'**

But the big book overrode these admonitions in a metallic voice:

' Those warnings are a waste of breath.
They'll only lead you to your death.
I am your guide, so come away
and marvel at my puppet play.
See the puppets, how they dance,
how they fight with sword and lance!
Hark to the music, feast your ears
on strains that come from heavenly spheres...'

Seductive, silvery bell notes rang out, playing a tune that reminded me once again of one of Evubeth van Goldwine's immortal melodies, in this case his famous piano piece in A minor dedicated to a girl with a charming name. The copper curtain rose to reveal some Bookhunters made of silver, like the two-dimensional puppets of a shadow theatre. They proceeded to dance and thrust at each other with their spears. At the same time, the cover of the huge book opened and the Yarnspinner puppet climbed inside like the unresisting victim of a fairground hypnotist.

Stop, stop, that wasn't what happened – you know that only too well, my friends! I neither climbed into a gigantic book nor did it address me or swallow me up. Goldenbeard's *Book Trap*, which I discovered in the Labyrinth, was made of precious metals and emitted mysterious music, admittedly, but it was of average size. It activated a complicated mechanism that set off a veritable avalanche of books and sluiced me straight into the rubbish dump of Unholm. However, the way in which the whole incident had been presented onstage – as a fight between good Zamonian literature and the cunning traps set by the Bookhunters – was naturally far more interesting from the dramatic standpoint, so I accepted it with amusement.

Scarcely had the cover closed over the puppet when the book descended into the ground and the stage went dark. The sound effects technicians must have used every available drum and thunder sheet to create the cacophony of rumbling and banging and rattling that ensued. But what was the matter with my chair? I suddenly had the utmost difficulty in keeping my seat, it was juddering around so violently.

'Is this an earthquake?' I exclaimed in dismay.

'It's all included in the price of the ticket,' Inazia told me with a grin. She was being thrown around like me. 'It gives you quite a shock the first time. The whole theatre is one big machine. Just wait, though. This is only the start, my friend!'

Now I understood: every member of the audience was intended to experience in person my slither through the catacombs' dark digestive system, which was why the ingenious theatre machinery was shaking all the seats. What an elaborate set-up! One or two theatregoers screamed, but before any real panic could break out among the children in the audience, the frenetic music and the rumbling and thundering and shaking ceased. It grew lighter, the biggest curtain rose with a swishing sound and we were confronted by a sea. A stormy sea composed entirely of mouldering books.

'The rubbish dump of Unholm,' I whispered. Yes, dear readers, it was just as I remembered it: a frozen sea of old, mouldering paper, billows and troughs of book dust with foaming crests of tattered leather. And in the midst of it, with a dark void overhead: myself, now a tiny puppet once more. The audience had hardly absorbed this impressive spectacle when another menacing sound was heard. At first no more than a dull but gradually swelling roar, it seemed to be rising inexorably from the bottom of the sea of books. And then, from the midst of the rubbish dump, something gigantic emerged: the huge bookworm, the subterranean ruler of Unholm! In an explosion of book dust and fragments of paper, the massive body broke surface like a whale. With a bestial roar, it reared up until, within a moment or two, its head brushed the ceiling of the theatre. But it, too, was a puppet suspended on invisible ropes and operated by internal machinery. I had no idea how this was done, nor – at that moment did I want to know. Gaping at the upper extremity of the monstrous bookworm was a fleshy, circular mouth armed with whole clusters of yellow teeth as long and sharp as sabres. Magnify a plump maggot a thousandfold, my friends, and furnish it with the poisonous fangs of a hundred snakes and the warts of a thousand toads, and you'll get a rough idea of the gigantic creature that was now looming over the audience. It remained poised like that – for an eternity, it seemed – as though waiting for the right moment to hurl itself at the auditorium and crush and devour its occupants. The whole theatre was filled with a pestilential stench of putrefaction.

The puppet that represented me in this infernal scene was lost from my view in billowing dust. However, another curtain rose beside this stage to reveal an enlarged detail of the same scene – a simple but highly effective theatrical device! There, a considerably larger Yarnspinner could be seen in close-up, desperately struggling through a sea of rubbish from which frightful denizens of the catacombs were emerging. I squirmed in my seat and drew my cloak more tightly around me.

Let us be honest, dear friends: any reasonably sane individual is scared of creepy-crawlies, no? Only anteaters, entomologists and totally insensitive lumberjacks are unafraid of creatures with more than four legs. When the outsize bloodsuckers infesting the rubbish dump of Unholm awoke and crawled out of the literary detritus with their groping antennae, scrabbling legs and lashing probosces – when their glossy black chitinous armour, clattering pincers and iridescent, faceted eyes came into view – pandemonium broke out in the theatre even though they were really just puppets. Children wept, mothers soothed their frightened offspring, and adult males squealed and climbed on their seats. I saw raw-boned Turnipheads quit the auditorium in tears! Meanwhile, my puppet bravely continued to fight his way through hordes of outsize beetles, spiders, millipedes and earwigs. I could feel sweat oozing from every pore of my body. That was just how it had been. I even saw the gigantic, white-haired spider that had haunted my nightmares ever since.

'This is the part where I always look away,' Inazia confessed, covering her eyes with her spindly fingers. 'Tell me when it's over.'

Personally, I devoted my full attention to the horrific scene. At its mercy but avid at the same time, I followed it with my eyes, ears and nose, utterly overwhelmed by the sight and my own memories. The music had now attained a wholly independent quality free from any form of plagiarism. It was like the background music to a nightmare created by the dreaming brain of a brilliant musician exempt from all the usual laws of composition. I heard harmonies and dissonances every note of which captured the essence of the horror but lent it a fascination that rendered it bearable. Frisson after frisson ran down my spine, but in an agreeable and wonderful way. It was the same as in my childhood, when my godfather Dancelot used to read me bedtime stories. Although tightly swathed in my bedclothes, I would shiver like a patient with fever when Dancelot, in his booming bass voice, read me tales of monsters and hair-raising feats of heroism. As I gradually drifted from the world of wakefulness into the world of dreams, I began to spin out what I'd heard, further and further, and continue it in my dreams. To me, that state is the epitome of my childhood, the early seed from which my literary activities grew. I was reminded of some lines from a poem by Perla la Gadeon:

All that we see or seem
is but a dream within a dream.

That was just how I felt at this moment: like a ghostly visitor inside my own head. Like a dreamer in a dream witnessing his worst nightmares. How often since then, during the little sleep still granted me, had I already been haunted by the frightful memory of that sea of books in Unholm? It was as if the whole theatre had been transformed into a monstrous version of my skull, into which the audience could see as if peering into a bell jar. I shared the feverish excitement of the little puppet wading through the loathsome rubbish, even though I knew the story had a happy ending. But, like a dreamer, I'd forgotten that this was a dream. Yes, it all had enthralled me so much, I'd forgotten that *I myself was the figure on the stage!*

The harassed audience emitted a collective sound of relief – a mixture of gasps and sighs – when the Yarnspinner puppet finally reached terra firma on the edge of the stage. With an ear-splitting roar, the gigantic bookworm reared up once more, then collapsed with a crash reminiscent of a mammoth tree being felled. Boom! Dense clouds of book dust billowed into the air and the clicking, crepitating insects vanished into the gloom.

It was a relief when the curtain fell and the music died away. There was no applause this time. Nonsensically, I patted my cloak as if it were infested with cockroaches.

'It's over,' I said, genuinely relieved.

'Not bad for a puppet theatre, eh?' the Uggly said with a grin. She also brushed some non-existent insects off her clothing.

'No,' I replied in a daze, 'that was . . . not bad at all.'

For a while I sat there without moving and devoted scant attention to the scene that followed. Less than dramatic, it showed Yarnspinner bemoaning his fate in song. That the next two major episodes in my book had simply been cut may have been attributable to the intensity of the previous scene. If you don't want to play to an empty house, you can't afford to give the audience too much horror all at once. At all events, my encounters with Hunk Hoggno and the many-legged Spinxxxes* weren't shown onstage, and I can't say I missed them. Instead, Yarnspinner came upon a mysterious trail of slips of paper that glowed magically in the dark and led him ever deeper into the Labyrinth until – yes, dear friends, I can't put it any other way – there was a sudden smell of Booklings!

Of that there could be no doubt. Booklings smell quite unmistakable. I could distinguish a Bookling from a hundred other creatures by its body odour alone. It smells a little like mushrooms after an autumnal shower. A little like freshly dubbined boots. Like rosemary, but only very faintly. Like ancient paper too, of course, but positively overpoweringly of bitter almonds. Yes, of bitter almonds, that appetising aroma often imparted to marzipan and sweet pastries. Bitter almonds are not, of course, native to the catacombs because they need sunlight in order to grow. But there exists in nearly all parts of the catacombs a phosphorescent fungus which, although an excellent provider of subdued lighting, is extremely hazardous to health. Its

---

*See *The City of Dreaming Books,* p. 186 ff. (Tr.).

smell bears a remarkable resemblance to that of bitter almonds. If one eats it, however, it proves to be sadly indigestible. As soon as it reaches the stomach, the fungus proceeds to devour its host, whether rat, Bookhunter or Spinxxx, from the inside outwards. This makes it one of the most feared denizens of the catacombs. The aroma of bitter almonds that we inhabitants of Overworld find so appetising indicates to most creatures in the Labyrinth that the fungus is dangerous and causes them, in obedience to the instinct for self-preservation, to give it a wide berth. How the Booklings contrive to smell of this fungus is still unexplained. Is it a natural component of their body odour, or do they use a perfume obtained from it by chemical means? The only certainty is that this olfactory mimicry is an effective protection against being eaten. Whether or not it would really be dangerous to devour a Bookling is a subject still in need of scientific clarification.

So the Puppetocircus Maximus smelt of Booklings beyond doubt! Only a few moments later, whole hordes of those legendary, one-eyed residents of the catacombs thronged the stage. Or rather, the stages, for all the curtains had risen in order to provide an adequate representation of the new scene: the Leather Grotto and its immediate vicinity. Here was the subterranean home of the Booklings at last! I had been waiting on tenterhooks to see this set, and my hopes were not dashed. There were caves of the most diverse kinds, large and small, some displaying stalactites, others shimmering crystals. Some were festively illuminated by candles, others by the multicoloured light of phosphorescent plants. One cave was lit by the red glow from a pool of lava. And all this one saw at a glance, spread out across the various stages. There were books wherever one looked, piled high or in lopsided, worm-eaten bookcases, in stacks large and small, in barrels and chests, on handcarts and in baskets. The floor was strewn with manuscripts and the stalactites sprouting from the roofs of the caves were papered with book jackets. And milling around every-where were Booklings of every shape, colour and size that this most remarkable of subterranean species is capable of adopting.

Well, before I become overly sentimental, dear friends, I will somewhat condense my synopsis of the play – inevitably so, because although my encounter with the Booklings took some time and was portrayed onstage with the greatest attention to detail, it contributed no more to the plot, from the purely dramaturgical aspect, than the corresponding chapter in my book. The ensuing scenes were islands of calm in a surging sea, oases of comfort in a storm-lashed desert, balm to the theatregoers' troubled souls. They were a relaxing series of delightful, comical ballet and choral numbers, all accompanied by wonderful, foot-tapping music. The children in the audience, as well as those adults who had remained children at heart, laughed and

crowed and applauded more exuberantly than ever before. They had
forgotten the recent horrific incidents as quickly as I myself had. This
was entertainment in the best sense: it helped one to forget one's fear.

Some of the Booklings were played by marionettes on strings
manipulated from above, but others were glove or stick puppets
whose operators worked from behind pieces of scenery or bookcases.
It was puppet theatre in its most original and transparent form, and
very charming to watch. One saw the strings and sticks that moved
the puppets, but – and this was the art! – one immediately forgot
them. Never before had I seen such subtle puppetry, and never had
glove puppets seemed so alive and amusing to me. The puppeteers

had to be the theatre's top-notch personnel – indeed, the finest of their profession. The puppets themselves, although of simple design, were miniature masterpieces of precision engineering. Their necks moved as naturally as if they possessed real spinal columns. Their eyes rolled in a wholly convincing manner, their eyelids opened and closed at natural intervals. It was only a few moments before I forgot they were puppets altogether. What contributed to this were their excellently imitated voices, for if there was one thing I did know, dear friends, it was how Booklings spoke! I am one of the few initiates to have actually heard their voices. They all have a slightly throaty, husky way of speaking, but they enunciate clearly. Frogs whose voices are breaking might sound like that if croaking weren't their only form of articulation. At all events, those voices sounded so familiar, they immediately took me back to my time in the Leather Grotto. Whoever was responsible for this production possessed a knowledge of the catacombs and their inhabitants that was in no way inferior to my own.

'They're like the meerkats in the zoo,' Inazia said softly.

'Eh?' I said.

'The meerkats,' she repeated. 'In the zoo. You always feel you'd like to feed the things and take them home with you.'

I was briefly thrown by the thought that Inazia actually went to the zoo to feed the meerkats there, instead of to the park to poison the pigeons. But I soon turned my attention to the stage again. The funny little creatures were restlessly bustling around the set, toting books, arranging them on shelves and reciting poetry or prose. They climbed around on the book machine, a gigantic prop that filled the biggest stage. There, whole shelves of books were gliding to and fro and up and down, constantly loaded and unloaded by the Booklings. In smaller caves, they self-importantly operated printing presses or tended tattered old tomes like terminally ill patients in their book infirmary. They polished huge crystals and wielded pickaxes in a diamond mine. You didn't know where to look, there was so much going on. And they sang and danced meanwhile! Yes, all the Bookling scenes were staged like one big, intoxicating dance routine, like a series of spirited waltzes composed – if my ears didn't deceive me – by Elemi Deufelwalt. Boom-ta-ta, boom-ta-ta . . . It was an incessant circling and turning and pirouetting, a single, intoxicating, rotating tribute to literature and life itself. There was an Orming* waltz, a waltz of the crystals, a waltz of the diamonds. Boom-ta-ta, boom-ta-ta . . . My leg twitched involuntarily in waltz time – I simply couldn't help it. Curtains rose and fell ever faster, scenes swiftly changed in time to the music. Coloured lights flared up and died, phosphorescent jellyfish and fungi danced in the dark – it was a feast for the eyes and ears. We saw a pas de deux performed by two Booklings composed entirely of diamonds that dissected the candlelight and torchlight into a hundred slivers and projected them on to the walls of the theatre. I had never before seen such sentimental but captivating puppetry. And it culminated in the most glorious of all waltzes, that masterpiece dedicated by Jonas Nussrath to a beautiful blue river. The Uggly beside me was swaying in time to it and so were the theatregoers below us. As for me, dear friends, I dissolved into nostalgic ecstasy! It was almost as if I had re-encountered the Booklings in the flesh.

I was just wondering if they would dare to interrupt this exuberant number by showing Colophonius Regenschein's tragic deathbed scene when I suddenly heard shouts and the clatter of weapons, and smelt a stench of pitch! The Booklings milled around in confusion.

The waltz ended abruptly, savage drumbeats rang out and the music took on a strident, positively hysterical note. Were those the martial rhythms of the overture to Flar Froc's alarming opera with its medieval choruses? Yes! Flames shot up and licked the sides of the stage. The stench became infernal: a mixture of smoke, sulphur and –

---

*Orming: rarely performed ritual with which the Booklings receive an outsider into their community if they choose to do so. See *The City of Dreaming Books*, p. 222 ff. (Tr.)

yes, wasn't that blood I smelt too? And then they converged from all directions: Bookhunters, dozens of them! Life-size marionettes, they were lowered from above and came striding on to the stage from the wings, swinging their battleaxes. Many more – not puppets but actors in costumes – even came running down the aisles with blazing torches. Children were not the only occupants of the stalls to scream in terror.

For one panic-stricken moment I thought the Bookhunters had *really* returned and would take over the theatre! Their armour of bones, insect shells and rusty metal, their terrifying masks and weapons – all were just as I remembered them. One Bookhunter wearing a death's-head mask actually burst into our box and aimed his crossbow at me, only to disappear, roaring with laughter, and leave me unscathed. I almost fainted, but Inazia laid a soothing hand on my arm.

'It's all part of the show,' she said.

'Really?' I gasped. 'And my heart attack? Is that also part of the show?'

Then darkness suddenly fell once more. Every light and flame was extinguished. The music ceased. The Booklings uttered a few more shrill screams, the Bookhunters' cruel laughter gradually died away until total silence fell. Even the appalling smells emitted by the scent organ had dissipated.

The King of
the Shadows

At first I genuinely thought I'd had a heart attack. High overhead, I saw coloured lights in a pall of utter darkness. Was this the legendary light you're said to see when you're dying? I hadn't imagined it would be so colourful. But then the curious light show descended. A dimly illuminated framework composed of thin rails and curved struts, it overarched the whole auditorium.

'What's that?' I asked apprehensively. My nerves were strained to breaking point.

'Don't you recognise it?' Inazia replied. She tittered. 'You described it in detail yourself. It's the Bookway.'

The what? Oh yes, now I remembered: it was the Rusty Gnomes' Bookway. That structure up there was supposed to be a model of it, of course: an extremely downsized representation of the miles-long railway that had transported consignments of books through the catacombs in days gone by. I had travelled on it personally and perforce during my escape from the Bookhunters and the Leather Grotto. My memories of it were far from pleasant, for I never came closer to death than I did on that wild ride.

I could already hear and see the little wheeled toboggan that came squeaking along the rails with me, in the form of a tiny puppet, aboard it. Incredible! They'd been bold enough to show this breakneck chase! The toboggan steadily gained speed until it was racing along the track, its wheels screeching and spewing sparks, right above the heads of the audience. The sparks struck by the iron wheels flew off in a wide arc and rained down on the theatregoers' heads. The fascination I felt for this extraordinary theatrical reproduction of a chapter in my book that really defied such treatment was great, but not as great as the delight it inspired in younger members of the audience. A regular commotion broke out in the auditorium. Children jumped to their feet, pointed upwards, craned their necks, clapped their hands. Music struck up again and with a vengeance! The well-known upbeat overture by Ossigichio Ronani, which always put me in mind of wildly galloping horses, it went quite well with my breakneck progress! I had completely forgotten that the Booklings scene in which I witnessed Colophonius Regenschein's death had simply been omitted. No matter! On with the action!

And then came a rustle of wings as some gigantic, fluttering, primeval birds swooped down on the track. These were the blood-thirsty Harpyrs, which had been pursuing me. Played by ingenious marionettes with huge leather wings and controlled from above by wires, they looked no less intimidating than they had in reality. Implacably, they chased the screeching, spark-spewing toboggan through the darkness and slashed at it with their sharp beaks. Then came an abrupt change of music that made the headlong pursuit more menacing still: it was the notorious *Ride of the Harpyrs* by Wanrich Drager.

One of the Harpyrs managed to cling to the toboggan and launch a fierce attack on the Yarnspinner puppet with its beak. I empathised with the puppet to such an extent that I lashed out at the terrible bird with both arms, causing Inazia to laugh hoarsely. But the production went one better! The curtain over a smaller stage rose with a whisper and I saw, to cries of delight from the audience, part of the scenery in close-up. In principle, this was the same trick as the one used in the rubbish dump of Unholm: Yarnspinner clung to the speeding toboggan, his cloak fluttering wildly in the headwind, while the Harpyr behind him, now a truly enormous puppet, crawled towards our hero with slashing beak and talons! We could hear the whistle of the wind – even smell the huge bird's noisome breath. The Murkholmer scent organist was manipulating his stops in ecstasy. I noticed out of the corner of my eye that sundry worried parents were leaving the auditorium with their sobbing children. Then, at the height of all this commotion, came a sudden bang! A crash! The lights abruptly went out and the music ceased. All that could now be heard was fluttering and a violent rush of air. My fall from the Bookway and my ensuing flight with the Harpyr, to which I had clung in desperation, had to be supplied by the theatregoers' imagination.

Then silence again.

Darkness.

A sulphurous smell.

Darkness.

A bubbling sound.

Darkness.

A hiss.

At last a dim red glow became visible at the foot of the stage, growing gradually brighter. Out of the darkness loomed a massive wall built of strangely shaped grey bricks, blind windows and a colossal façade that seemed to go up and up for ever. And then came . . . a disappointment! For me, at least.

Let me put it this way, dear friends: even the best theatre is incapable of imitating true immensity. For what we were shown was a set of Shadowhall Castle, that legendary place in the heart of the catacombs where the Harpyr had eventually set me down: the Shadow King's subterranean place of exile, where my fate was to take a drastic turn. Loath as I am to criticise them harshly, the stage designers had definitely found the external architecture of Shadowhall Castle too much for them – understandably so! If anyone is entitled to judge, it is I, for I saw Shadowhall Castle with my own eyes. Its sick geometry, which seemed to pour scorn on every law of nature, and the sheer size of that insanity-turned-to-stone in the bowels of the catacombs – these could not be satisfactorily reproduced within the ramped confines of a stage. It was a sheer impossibility! Given their limitations, however, the artists of the Puppetocircus Maximus had conjured a remarkable achievement out of their totally insoluble task with the aid of artificial lighting and sound effects, music and smells. The set must have stunned everyone in the auditorium (except me). Its designers had cleverly opted for a section of the castle's façade: the gate constructed of fossilised books through which Yarnspinner now entered it by way of a bridge. One couldn't actually see the molten lava boiling beneath this, just its red reflection on the masonry, but one could hear and smell it volcanically bubbling away. The scent organ diffused an infernal stench of sulphur that would have been sufficient for any scene of Hell.

Another curtain and another change of scene. We now saw Yarnspinner – this time as a marionette – roaming around inside the castle. The way the interior had been represented, with its converging and diverging walls and ceaselessly rising and falling floors, was a masterpiece of set-building and stage machinery. The exterior set was forgotten; I was back in Shadowhall Castle once more! How could anyone but me have known what it looked like? How could they have guessed what millions of petrified, lichen-covered books smelt like? Yet everything was utterly realistic. This was exactly how the place had looked and smelt! There was a sound like massive millstones grinding together as walls converged, stairways appeared out of nowhere and ceilings floated down like flying carpets, luring Yarnspinner's wandering figure ever deeper into the architectural labyrinth. I had once more forgotten that the figure onstage was meant to be *me*, so complete was the spell cast over me – and every member of the hushed audience – by the *mise en scène*.

The play then took a new turn. After the cheerful musical numbers in Bookholm, the almost buffoonish numbers performed by the singing books, the horrific scenes in the rubbish dump of Unholm, the Booklings' rapturous ballets and the breathtaking chase on the Rusty Gnomes' Bookway, a solemn and entirely different note was struck. Things now became *serious*, my friends! Even as Yarnspinner entered the castle, we heard the *Shadowy Scherzo* from Valther Musag's 7th Symphony – music that makes you think you see silhouettes on walls before they actually appear. Every sound disintegrated into hundreds of echoes that flitted through the auditorium like bats that had lost their way. Underlying everything was a sustained rumble like that of an awakening volcano that might erupt at any moment. Faint, ghostly voices whispered here and there like harbingers of some mental illness. My sojourn in that petrified magic castle was arranged like a collage, like sets dovetailed together at random: a brilliant but seemingly arbitrary series of scenes in which chronological order, time itself, dramatic structure and logic had ceased to play any part. And that was just how I had felt at the time! Time and space were dimensions that obeyed different laws in Shadowhall or were simply of no importance. They say that gravity steadily diminishes the closer you get to the centre of the earth. Perhaps it's just the same with time.

Well, at all events, chronology played a subordinate role in the play's dramatic structure. I was accompanied onstage by the Weeping Shadows, whose acquaintance I actually made much later. Although they were at first glance very simply portrayed by actors draped in grey veils, they could climb walls with surprising ease, wander across ceilings upside down and pass through masonry or emerge from it. Whatever the ingenious tricks employed to achieve such an effect, these scenes made my scales stand on end! The Animatomes – the live books – were also ubiquitous from the start, although I didn't make their acquaintance until much later and in extremely dramatic circumstances. *Made of leather and paper* – there couldn't be a more accurate description of the alarming multiplicity of creatures that crawled and scuttled around the stage, fluttered along the grey passages and strutted across the walls on long, spidery legs, casting even longer shadows. The Animatomes were so convincingly portrayed that the audience became as uneasy as if the auditorium had been invaded by a horde of rats or Kackertratts! Their persistent rustling and whispering and squeaking was another thing that didn't exactly inspire confidence.

This was an almost abstract theatre of mood and atmosphere. The plot had virtually ceased to matter. Melancholy, grief, pain, despair, fear – those were themes in Shadowhall Castle, only loosely conjoined by the logic or illogicality of a nightmare. Disturbing music by Smygort Messodusk and Stavko Shmiritoditch accompanied the oppressive scenes in the meandering passages. One alarmingly beautiful set followed another, but after a longish succession of such sombre impressions and moods the audience, especially its younger members, became noticeably restive, and I myself began to wonder impatiently where the Shadow King had got to. Where the devil was the secret protagonist of this play? Where was the lord and master of this ghostly castle?

Then, however, the walls parted once more and we finally saw the throne room of Shadowhall Castle – one of the most amazing sets in a play that was far from devoid of them! It was a simple but audacious edifice composed of geometrical blocks, like a ballroom-sized cave produced by tectonic displacements. Yes, this was how one imagined the secret heart of the catacombs might look: grey blocks of granite and huge beams of white crystal heaped up together like the trunks of felled trees, and dancing behind them the flames of an enormous open fire. That was all, but it was overwhelming in its simplicity. Accompanying this monument to solitude were the strident strains of Gynasok Strivir's famous and notorious firebird ballet suite, like music issuing from a burning madhouse. For there he was at last: the Shadow King!

Or rather, there he wasn't, for all one could see of him were shadows flickering over the walls so fast and so wildly, it was impossible to tell if they were made by real dancers or puppets. I clung to the parapet and leant over it so as not to miss anything. The real Shadow King would have to show himself some time. But then came another disappointment: no huge and impressive marionette, no splendid costume made of ancient papyri sewn together and worn by a ballet virtuoso in a brilliant mask – no, nothing of the kind. No tangible protagonist's presence. Just shadows, shapes and silhouettes, both now and in the ensuing scenes. When Yarnspinner and Homuncolossus were onstage together, the most one saw of the latter was an adumbration. When Yarnspinner and he were dining together at a massive table, the sinister monarch was hidden in a shadowy part of the stage and all one heard was his commanding voice – which, I must admit, sounded most impressive. When they were walking along the passages together, all one saw of the castellan was his immense shadow gliding along the walls. When Homuncolossus delivered his gloomy monologues he sat deeply ensconced and almost invisible in the recesses of his vast throne, with only his eyes glowing in the darkness. It was all very artistically and ingeniously staged, admittedly, but one couldn't help feeling a touch of disappointment that the principal character was never actually seen.

'What is all this?' I ended by demanding impatiently, almost indignantly. 'Where's the puppet that plays the Shadow King?'

'It's the best puppet in the play,' Inazia retorted, 'don't you get it?'

'No,' I said, 'I honestly don't.'

'They haven't shown him in the form of a puppet out of *respect*!' she hissed. 'You have to create him yourself.' She tapped her head with a spindly finger. 'In your imagination.'

I turned back to the stage and reluctantly watched Yarnspinner, who seemed to be conversing with thin air. 'But that makes me look as if I'm, well . . . insane,' I protested in a low voice. 'As if the Shadow King exists only in my head.'

'It's *Invisible Theatre*,' Inazia whispered, giving me a look that verged on fanaticism.

'Invisible Theatre?' I repeated stupidly.

'The very latest form of Puppetism! It doesn't matter what the Invisible Theatre shows onstage,' she whispered. 'What matters far more is what it does inside your head.' She put a finger to her lips and pointed to the stage.

I obeyed her unspoken injunction and redevoted myself to what was happening there. Against my will, I watched Yarnspinner conversing with the invisible Shadow King, but I defiantly refused – on principle! – to take part in this stupid experiment on the audience. What a shame! Everything had gone so well hitherto, and now they were ruining the vital denouement with pseudo-artistic tricks. Invisible Theatre? Nonsense! I started fidgeting in my seat again.

But then, my dear friends, something happened quite despite me. The more fiercely I fought against picturing an imaginary Shadow King on the stage, the more vividly he took shape in my head. It was like my insomnia: the more stubbornly I try to convince myself I'm tired, the more active my brain becomes, but the more I fear I *won't* be able to sleep, the sooner I nod off. The harder I tried to suppress my powers of imagination, the more overpowering they became. At first I saw the Shadow King only as a jagged silhouette in the dim light – a shape as nebulous as a ghost. But when my resistance diminished still further, he took on more solidity. I saw his tattered paper robes, his majestic head and sparkling eyes, the jagged outline of his sad crown – even, although I didn't use my opera glasses at all, the tiny, cryptic runes on his papyrus skin. At some point he was simply there – indelibly imprinted on my mind's eye.

The dialogue was a considerable help to me. It was like good music, which one readily follows without giving much thought to the harmonies of which it's composed. Great stage monologues possess a rhythm and melody that often move the audience more than their content – one has only to think of the plays by Aleisha Wimpersleake. You don't recognise the true quality of such texts if you merely read them; you have to hear them spoken, because they often owe more to music than to literature. Although I had some memorable conversations with the Shadow King in reality, our dialogues were never as elegant and musical as these, even in my book. The author of these lines possessed a quite exceptional ear for the spoken word, for how it works when divorced from paper and printer's ink: as pure sound. I was electrified! I wanted to be able to write like that too! I had already tacitly accepted that I'd exhausted my resources and reached the end of the literary road, but this was something new. It was a young art I might yet learn. Puppetism, a synthesis of the arts to which I could contribute something with my own abilities! It was exciting!

Only now did I fully grasp the radical nature of this artistic device. *Invisible Theatre* – of course! It would have ruined the production if they'd tried to portray the Shadow King with the aid of something as banal as a puppet, no matter how well-designed. As I have already said: true magnitude cannot be shown onstage, any more than superhuman strength demonstrated, genuine beauty simulated or natural savagery imitated. To that extent, any attempt to represent the Shadow King by technical means would have been doomed to fail from the start. It would have been like having a wild werewolf played by an actor in wolf costume – simply ludicrous! The only solution was to leave it entirely to the audience's imagination, a brilliant dramatic device to be employed only by someone who had total faith in his own abilities and didn't give a damn for sceptics. The act of a genius! This invisible puppet turned every member of the audience into a talented Puppetist, and that was what finally convinced me that the person behind the Puppetocircus Maximus must be a very great artist in *every* field: a jack of all trades who blindly obeyed his instincts and usually hit the target. I looked around because I suddenly felt that someone was watching me – someone hidden in the wings and looking out at us all like a puppeteer observing his marionettes. I couldn't help laughing at this paranoid notion – so loudly that the Uggly gave me a sidelong look of reproof. I pulled myself together and concentrated on what was happening onstage.

Of all the scenes set in Shadowhall Castle, the one I liked best was the one in which the Shadow King recounted his own story. For this, the director had fallen back on one of the simplest but most effective theatrical devices: the shadow play. Back-projected on the walls of the throne room were big planes of different colours – red, yellow, blue –

on which cut-out figures and scenery were moved around while the Shadow King was speaking. These were sometimes living creatures, sometimes buildings or landscapes, but also flames and rivers, birds in flight, scudding clouds, rushing rivers and windswept seas of grass, imaginary figures, picturesque dream personnel and whole spirit worlds. This was the way in which the play depicted the Shadow King's life and ideas, his childhood, his development into a writer and also, of course, the terrible part of his story in which Pfistomel Smyke and Claudio Harpstick transformed him into a creature made of paper and banished him to the catacombs.

Despite the magnificently detailed treatment of the Shadowhall Castle scenes, however, it did not escape me that, here too, my book had been drastically abridged. My fight with the Animatomes had been cut, for example, and so had my visit to the Library of the Orm. Why, I couldn't say, nor could I tell why the chapter with the giant in the castle's cellar had been left out. Perhaps there had been a reluctance to spoil the elegiac mood of the foregoing scenes by introducing another change of location and scenery and further rapid twists and turns in the plot. But the authors of the stage play may possibly have felt, like some readers of my book, that the episode with the giant was imaginary – that it was a flight of fancy and a figment of my overexerted brain. I do, however, have the utmost sympathy with that point of view, for in hindsight I myself often wonder if I actually underwent those experiences or only dreamt them.

Instead, my departure from the castle followed in short order. The Shadow King's exit from his subterranean place of exile in my humble company was celebrated on a grand theatrical scale with the use of countless puppets, brilliant lighting effects produced by hundred of candles, and musical backing from the famous intermezzo by Gipnatio Sacrem, which I have never been able to hear since without tears coming into my eyes.

The Shadow King's reconquest of the Leather Grotto, which

actually entailed the merciless slaughter of the Bookhunters and was an implacably brutal and bloodthirsty act of revenge, had wisely been presented as another shadow play. This lent the whole thing an artistic touch and made it acceptable even to the children in the audience. One Bookhunter after another could be seen sinking to the ground, felled by the infuriated Shadow King. Indeed, we even saw blood spurt and severed heads roll, but not in all the unappetising detail this scene would have called for if played by three-dimensional puppets. Presented thus, these terrible events seemed no more genuine than a bad dream.

As you know, dear friends, this ghastly episode marked the real end of my visit to Netherworld. The story ends with me ascending to the surface in the Shadow King's company. I saw the Booklings hypnotise the surviving Bookhunters into killing one another. I also saw the Shadow King execute Claudio Harpstick with a blow of his paper hand, only to set fire to himself and, once thoroughly ablaze, drive Pfistomel Smyke down into the catacombs of Bookholm. You know all this only too well, so I've no need to give you a more detailed account of these sad and horrific scenes, even though they were among the most memorable of the entire play. In view of this, I shall spare myself the task of describing them.

Let me, therefore, conclude my account of the Puppetocircus Maximus by describing the final set. It was a model of the *City of Dreaming Books* so extensive and detailed that it filled the largest of the stages. Even before the first flames appeared, a whiff of smoke foretold what was about to happen. Then little tongues of flame rose above the roofs here and there. The smell of smoke grew stronger, becoming so pungent, acrid and alarming that many of the audience looked around apprehensively for the emergency exits. And we heard, at first only faintly, the first notes of the fire tocsin. At the same time, Perla la Gadeon's well-known poem was declaimed by a powerful, resonant bass voice that seemed to come from all directions at once:

'Hear the loud Bookholmian bells —
brazen bells!
What a tale of terror, now, their turbulency tells!
In the startled ear of night
how they screamed out their affright!
Too much horrified to speak,
they can only shriek, shriek . . .'

The fires burning in the city onstage became still bigger and more alarming, and sent thin columns of smoke rising to the roof of the theatre. One heard distant screams and crackling flames, glass shattering and the crash of buildings as they collapsed. The flames spread like blood welling from an open wound and raced along the streets and alleyways. The tolling of the tocsin grew more insistent. A commotion broke out in the audience, many of whom began to sob, so convincingly was the disaster being reproduced in miniature. I clung to the parapet of our box, once more fighting back my tears. Several members of the audience were already rising from their seats. The doors of the auditorium opened and they streamed out, not in panic but as quickly as they could under the supervision of solicitous members of the theatre staff. I couldn't bring myself to leave, although Inazia was already standing beside the door of our box. I found the panorama of the burning city simultaneously heart-breaking and fascinating. It was, in a dismayingly authentic way, the same sight that had presented itself to my gaze when I had escaped from the city and turned for a last look. A voice rang out from above. It was doubtless meant to be my own, for it was reciting words from the description of this event that had appeared in my book:

'The Dreaming Books had awakened. Miles-high columns of black smoke were rising into the heavens fraught with paper transformed into weightless ash: the residue of incinerated thoughts. Swirling within them were myriad sparks, every one a fiery word ascending ever higher to dance with the stars. The rustle of the countless awakening books reminded me sadly of the rustling

286

laughter of the Shadow King. He, too, was ascending in the biggest, most terrible conflagration Bookholm had ever undergone.'

That was just how I felt at this moment. I was as stirred and saddened as I had been then. But I also felt absurdly alive and greedy for all that was to come: as highly charged as if I'd been connected to an alchemical battery! It was only a stage play performed by puppets, but I had felt I was reliving my own past!

I remained standing beside the parapet for a while, being embarrassed to weep in front of the Uggly. Not until my tears finally ceased to flow did I tear my eyes away from the sight of the burning city and plunge into the throng of theatregoers making for the exit.

'That was a bit more than I'd bargained for,' I said to Inazia when we were outside at last, standing in the forecourt of the theatre with members of the audience streaming past us, chattering excitedly. It was the biggest possible understatement I could think of at that moment. 'I'd give anything to meet the people who staged it.'

'Really?' said the Uggly, favouring me with one of her hideous smiles. 'What if I were to introduce you to the person who bears artistic responsibility for the whole production? The director of the Puppetocircus Maximus himself?'

'You could do that?' I asked in astonishment.

'Well . . .' she drawled with ill-concealed pride. 'It might be arranged. After all, I'm one of the patrons of this wonderful theatre. Look down.'

Inazia pointed to the ground between us. I noticed only then that the theatre forecourt we were standing on was paved with thousands of red and white stones laid alternately, and that they all had names carved on them. I looked more closely at the stone she had indicated.

There were two names on it:

Inazia Anazazi and *Ahmed ben Kibitzer*.

Puppetism
for Beginners

From the following day onwards and for quite a time thereafter, I was treated to some free and informative tours of modern Bookholm on which Inazia Anazazi the Uggly acted as my guide, theatre critic and expert on Puppetism. I rented some quiet rooms in a small boarding house, frequented mainly by writers, where I could not only get a peaceful night's sleep but also do some work occasionally. Whenever her shop's opening times permitted, or mostly at night, I accompanied Inazia on strolls through the various city districts and thus became acquainted with the new sights, theatres and, on occasion, restaurants and coffee houses. We must have looked an extremely odd couple: a Lindworm with his face forever hidden by a cowl, arm in arm with a tall, gaunt Uggly. We were usually deep in conversation, but I tended to supply the cues while Inazia spouted an endless stream of information about our special subject.

'When Bookholm had been burnt to the ground,' began the first of her series of lectures, 'many of its inhabitants were utterly destitute. Their houses, their shops and all their possessions had gone up in smoke. There are many ways of starting again from scratch, and putting on puppet plays was a very popular one. For two reasons.'

She inhaled deeply as though intending to tell me the rest of the story in a single breath.

'One reason was that a puppet theatre, and even the puppets for it, could be very easily fabricated out of the ruins of the gutted city. Nail a few charred planks together and there's your stage. Sew some scraps

288

of cloth together and there's your cast. Sew two buttons on a sock: the principal character. A leafy branch in the background: an enchanted forest. The other reason was the immense demand for entertainment after the disaster, not only from children but from adults hard at work on the city's reconstruction. Seated around their campfires at night – many of them still didn't have a roof over their heads, don't forget – they were eager to exchange their hardships for the world of the imagination. Readers and extempore poets, ballad singers and little puppet theatres – all took these traditional forms of communication to a higher level. Now, people could not only hear stories but see them enacted as well. They roasted potatoes in the fire, rejoicing in their survival, and the puppet theatres played to audiences of clamouring children. For many people that was a good end to a hard day. A lot of them still look back on those times with pleasure.'

We paused beside the remains of a huge, charred oak tree standing in the centre of a small square. I could still remember when, two centuries earlier, this ancient tree and its countless branches were in sap and had been one of Bookholm's most vibrant sights. Now it was a horrible black skeleton serving only as a surface for billstickers. The leaves it now bore were made of paper and advertised a wide variety of services or cultural events.

'Look,' the Uggly told me. 'Half those posters are to do with Puppetism.'

We slowly circled the huge, dead tree to enable me to read the posters and announcements:

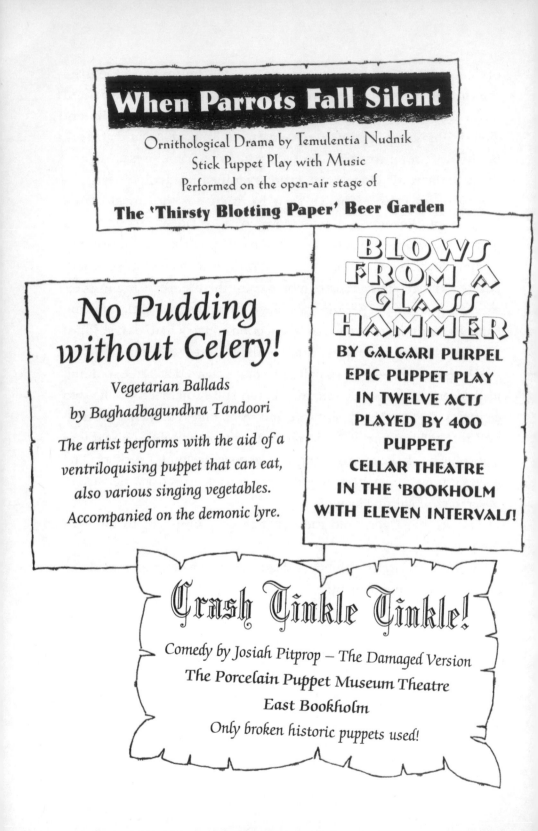

When Parrots Fall Silent

Ornithological Drama by Temulentia Nudnik
Stick Puppet Play with Music
Performed on the open-air stage of

The 'Thirsty Blotting Paper' Beer Garden

No Pudding without Celery!

Vegetarian Ballads
by Baghadbagundhra Tandoori

The artist performs with the aid of a
ventriloquising puppet that can eat,
also various singing vegetables.
Accompanied on the demonic lyre.

BLOWS FROM A GLASS HAMMER

BY GALGARI PURPEL
EPIC PUPPET PLAY
IN TWELVE ACTS
PLAYED BY 400
PUPPETS
CELLAR THEATRE
IN THE 'BOOKHOLM
WITH ELEVEN INTERVALS!

Crash Tinkle Tinkle!

Comedy by Josiah Pitprop – The Damaged Version
The Porcelain Puppet Museum Theatre
East Bookholm
Only broken historic puppets used!

POTATO PUPPET PLAY
FOR SMALL CHILDREN
by Finocchio di Geffetto
We LIKE your children to scream!
Entrance free, buffet not included.
'Horrorhouse' Family Hotel

Crocodìle!
Crocodìle!

'You must also read the small print,' Inazia prompted me.

I enlisted the help of my monocle in order to decipher the smaller notices.

ONE LOOK SAYS MORE THAN A THOUSAND WORDS
Three-day course on making mechanical eyes
Monday to Wednesday at the 'Bookhunter Inn'

The Carved Smile
A quick course on making puppets' heads
out of wood, plaster or rubber at
Greenmilk Pottery on Fairies' Pond Please
bring your own tools!

Drama on a Silken Thread
A marionette's life.
Autobiographical lecture by Danglio Donglio
(winner of Bookholm's 'Golden Limb-Dangler'
Award, president of the Marionettists' Guild)
In the City Hall Rotunda

Puppets' Skeletal Structure and Comparative Anatomy A five-part course

with Professor
Articulo Bone
Lecture Room 5b
Bookholm University
Small groups
by arrangement only

Prophecies based on broken puppets
Your broken puppet isn't the end, it's your future!
Qualified Uggly Ugnuzia Uggnozzi reads
split seams, sawdust and wood shavings
Daily from midday to midnight / No. 7 Uggly Lane

I found one poster particularly amusing:

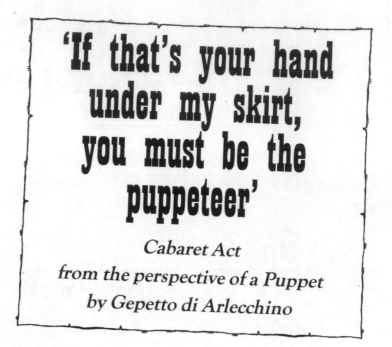

'If that's your hand under my skirt, you must be the puppeteer'

Cabaret Act
from the perspective of a Puppet
by Gepetto di Arlecchino

Another slip of paper bore nothing but two mysterious hand-written sentences:

Looking for yourself?
If so, you may find yourself
at the Invisible Theatre . . .

Yet another was less cryptic:

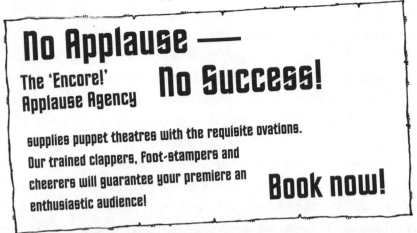

No Applause —
The 'Encore!'
Applause Agency
No Success!

supplies puppet theatres with the requisite ovations.
Our trained clappers, foot-stampers and
cheerers will guarantee your premiere an
enthusiastic audience!

Book now!

And so on and so forth . . . Hundreds of these notices, either pasted one on top of the other or nailed to the trunk, formed the dead tree's new bark. One day it would be completely encased in them. I was particularly struck by two things. First, that the titles of the plays advertised were rather unusual for a puppet theatre: *The Dead Art of Folding Cylinders*, *Malevolent Bananas*, *The Iron Eyebrow*, or *When Chairs Weep*, to name but a few. They weren't fairy-tale or mythical material and few of the productions were expressly directed at children. They were adapted from works of contemporary literature: novels, dramas and stories by modern authors like Arngrim Berserker, Juhanna Pignozzi, Petro Polognese, Count Pallaprat di Bigotto, Yury Yurk, Gwatkin de Latouche, Lapoleon Lonocle, Audrian van Eckenschreck and Hyppolitus Knotz – in other words, modern authors who had originally aimed their work at an adult readership in book form. Why was I so disturbed by the thought that so much contemporary literature was being adapted for the puppet theatre? The second thing that struck me about these notices was that nearly all the performances took place at timber-time.*

---

*Late evening, when it was an old Bookholmian custom to light a log fire and read aloud from books. Local bookshops sometimes used such readings for promotional purposes. See *The City of Dreaming Books*, p. 109 ff. (Tr.)

'Good heavens,' I exclaimed, 'what happened to good old timber-time? Are books ever read aloud in the old-fashioned way, or are they all automatically adapted into puppet plays?'

'Oh, timber-time!' the Uggly said in a dismissive tone. She looked at me pityingly. 'Timber-time? That's only for hay-wagon tourists these days!' She was alluding to one aspect of Bookholm tourism in which provincial visitors were hauled into the city on big hay wagons normally used for bringing in the hay harvest.

'There still are some good professional readers, of course,' she went on, 'but their performances are so overcrowded, you can hardly hear a word for the chattering of the audience. Besides, master readers play for safety. They almost always read from the popular stuff everyone knows. Your books, for instance.' She glared at me reproachfully.

'In that case,' I said quickly, to change the subject, 'do highbrow audiences go mainly to puppet theatres for their evening's entertainment?'

Inazia nodded. 'You can say that again. And to some extent, you're not entirely blameless for that.'

'I'm not?'

'Well, no. You may not have lit the fire that destroyed this city, but you did, so to speak, bring the torch that lit it out of the catacombs in company with the Shadow King. Puppetism arose from the ashes of old Bookholm. To that extent—'

'To that extent *I'm* to blame for everything yet again?' I laughed. 'Utter nonsense! You can pin a lot of things on me, but not the fact that timber-time is dying out and there's a puppet theatre on every street corner. *I'm* not responsible for that!'

The Uggly smiled. 'But that art form could never have attained its present greatness if the city hadn't been destroyed. It's a beautiful bloom that sprang from disaster. You can stick that feather in your cap with a clear conscience, my friend.'

To be honest, I was far from displeased by this idea. Optimus Yarnspinner, the spark that ignited a new art form, the father of

Puppetism! Why not? Speaking with all due modesty, I had already made a certain contribution to Zamonian culture, but I'd never created a new artistic discipline before. Inazia's bold assertion might possibly contain a grain of truth . . . An exciting idea began to germinate within me.

'I want to learn everything there is to know about Puppetism,' I demanded. 'Everything! I've missed out on so much since the old days.'

'Everything?' Inazia sighed. 'Pah! Do you know what that means? Have you any idea how much accumulated knowledge there is? How long it would take?'

'I don't care,' I said. 'I've plenty of time.'

She gave me a long look. 'You never know,' she said eventually, taking my arm again. 'Very well, though, I'll tell you all I can. You asked for it, and you'll regret it.' Then she laughed in the dismaying way in which only Ugglies can laugh.

Maestro Corodiak

During the next few weeks, my friends, I discovered how accurate Inazia's prediction had been. I learned far more about Puppetism than I really wanted. But isn't that the only sensible way of learning? Stuffing yourself with more than you can digest? Sucking up information like a thirsty sponge? Filling up with data like a camel of the desert hydrating itself for a long journey? It's the only way of finding out what you really need – what will lodge in the convolutions of your brain like intellectual, ideological fat and form the inexhaustible reservoir that will sustain you for a lifetime. Any serious course of study is an orgy, an information-gathering bacchanal. Most of it you subsequently forget like anyone who has indulged to excess. What matters is what sticks in the mind – except that you never know in advance what it will be. So in with it! I've never thought much of strictly organised and methodical study. You can't arrange a library in alphabetical order until you've collected one.

Yes, I wanted to learn! At a relatively advanced age for a Lindworm I became an avid student of Puppetism, and to that end the Uggly mercilessly dragged me along every street and through every district in the city. She showed me every gaming room, every cellar theatre, every bookshop specialising in Puppetism, every little museum of curiosities, every factory and every shop that had any connection with that novel art. We roamed the backyards of Slengvort, where there were workshops producing almost every part of a puppet's anatomy: wig-makers, eye mechanics, wood carvers for kinetic lips, beard and plait braiders, workshops for mechanical hands and mobile ceramic faces, carpenters' shops that produced wooden limbs on a lathe. There were studios redolent of turpentine that specialised in the elaborate painting of puppets. Other artists concentrated on scenery and posters. There was a cloud-painting studio, prettily named *Cumulus*, which would paint you any theatrical sky you chose. There were also smithies that turned out perfect little metal joints, sewing rooms for tiny costumes, factories producing miniature tableware and articles in daily use, a rope works producing puppet strings only, and several dwarfs' joineries specialising in miniature furniture. In one of Slengvort's side streets there was even a tattooist whose ink-laden needles decorated puppets in an unrivalled manner.

We visited a shop that traded in the Doodleton Musical Puppets I'd seen at the Puppetocircus Maximus: walking basses, dancing violins, flying trumpets, eyelash-batting clarinets, and drums and xylophones that played themselves with spindly metal arms and tiny fingers. The proprietor, a talkative Frogling with a gurgling voice, proudly told us about an opera of his own composition that dealt with the historically attested musical war between the *Grailsundian Frogling Polka* and the *Florinthian St Vitus's Dance*. We fled from his premises before he could start to yodel us some of it.

In antiquarian bookshops we rummaged around in handwritten scripts for hitherto unperformed puppet plays. There were thousands of these, for nearly every other waiter and bookseller's apprentice strove to render his lot more lucrative by writing them. In cellars and attics I discovered a multitude of unused or forgotten puppets such as I would never have imagined in my wildest dreams. They ranged from the tiniest of flea circus marionettes, which were adequately visible only through a magnifying glass, to whole armies of tattered puppet supernumeraries and huge, colourful book-dragons the length of a whole street but made of featherweight balsa wood. These were stored in interconnecting vaulted cellars, where they collected dust while waiting to be borne through the streets during the annual puppet carnival.

I stood marvelling in a crowded shop that specialised in butterfly marionettes. Thousands of wonderful *Lepidoptera zamoniae*, which I initially mistook for hand-painted paper puppets, were suspended from strings or mounted on thin sticks, adorning the shelves and walls in such profusion that the sheer wealth of colours made one's eyes ache. When the proprietress, who reeked of wild garlic and was an Uggly like Inazia, informed us that they were all *real* butterflies, individually mummified and mounted, it gave me the creeps. Even her assurances that the creatures died a peaceful, natural death and had been reverently embalmed by the Uggly herself failed to appease me altogether. This Uggly-owned business made an almost more sinister impression on me than a shop named *The Witching Hour*, which we visited shortly afterwards, although that one positively aimed to give its customers the creeps! As its name betrayed, it specialised in puppet actors that played demons, ghosts and similar imaginary, otherworldly creatures. Dangling from its ceiling were greenish victims of drowning with bulging eyes; ghostly, skeletal figures swathed in cobwebs that glowed by day as well as in the dark; headless bodies and bodyless heads; transparent, nebulous figures made of glass and crystal; dancing will-o'-the-wisps; and every imaginable kind of shadowy creature whose appearance on the stage of a puppet theatre was calculated to provoke gooseflesh and childish screams. Inazia, who was clearly a regular customer, acquired a shrunken head reputed to weep when the clock struck midnight. I never asked if it worked, nor did I want to know!

Housed in one backyard basement was a workshop specialising in the manufacture of puppets related in various ways to books – a very special type of Bookholmian Puppetism. Here we found marionettes similar to some of the protagonists I'd seen at the Puppetocircus Maximus, for instance, talking puppets composed of piles of books or dangerous Animatomes complete with eyes, legs, mandibles and venomous stings, though in this case they were hanging motionless on strings. There were also the talkative classical volumes that had spoken in rhyme onstage in the scene involving Goldenbeard's book trap, but here they were mutely arrayed on a shelf.

The knowledgeable proprietor, a gaunt Druid with a green beard reaching to his waist, explained that many of these figures had been operated as glove puppets or marionettes in the traditional manner, whereas others were extremely complicated products of precision engineering which, when wound up, could speak or even sing in mechanical voices. That was also how the versifying classics in the book trap scene had worked! They were really disguised clockwork machines.

The patient proprietor took a key and wound up one of the mechanical books, which resembled a miniature building from the Zamonian Late Middle Ages. Scarcely had he done so when its lilting, metallic voice proceeded to recite a quatrain in Old High Zamonian:

'Ye river quickly floweth.
Who careth where it goeth?
Ye cow it loudly loweth.
Wherefore? Nobody knoweth.'

'Those are the earliest verses on record,' the Druid explained, wrinkling his brow. 'They're by Eggfrith Strongitharm. Not everyone's taste, to be honest. No idea why anyone would want to listen to such stuff these days.' He thoughtfully stroked his green beard. 'It's dormant stock, so you can have it for a special price. Maybe it would make a nice present for an Old Zamoniologist.'

Inazia off-handedly brushed this suggestion aside and pointed to another mechanical book on the shelf. Its leather cover was very skilfully and lavishly tooled with elaborate ornamentation and adorned with gold leaf.

'What's that one?' she asked.

Without a word, the proprietor took another key and wound the book up. It proceeded to lecture its listeners in a slightly supercilious tone of voice:

'Know then thyself, presume not books to ban;
write as thou wilt, write only as one can,
with too much knowledge for the sceptic side,
and too much weakness for the stoic's pride.
Wield well thy pen, nor ever be deterred;
across Zamonia let thy voice be heard.
Brave poet, write, and send thy verses wings,
so ev'ry heart of ev'ry listener sings.'

'Delightful!' Inazia exclaimed. 'And, if I'm not mistaken, by . . . by Pandrex Opeela, right? A regrettably well-nigh forgotten representative of Zamonian Late Barococco.'

I cast a puzzled sidelong glance at the Uggly, whose knowledge of such un-Ugglian poetry rather surprised me.

'You're right,' replied the Druid. 'That puppet contains all of Opeela's poetic works. It depends how many times you turn the key. If you do it correctly – an instructional leaflet is included – it recites a different poem every time. The mechanism inside these puppets is very intricate. More complex than any form of clockwork.'

'I'd patent it if I were you,' I observed. 'They're mechanical works of art.'

'That isn't up to us,' he replied, shaking his head. 'We don't really know how these puppets work, to be honest. We get the plans from the Puppetocircus Maximus and follow them meticulously, screw for screw and spring for spring. Sooner or later you imagine you could build such things yourself, but that's a big mistake! Every time we tried to construct our own puppets along the same lines, they turned out to be defective. They simply talked nonsense or offended our customers by hurling obscenities at them. Either that, or they started screaming and smoking, and eventually fell to pieces. Maestro Corodiak is a genius and genius is inimitable.' His voice trembled with awe.

'Maestro Corodiak?' I said. I couldn't recall having heard the name before.

'He's the artistic director of the Puppetocircus Maximus,' said the Druid. 'But for him, this entire district would be out of work. Would you like to buy a talking-book puppet? Advance orders only, though. The waiting time at present is six months.'

'No thanks,' I said. 'Don't think me discourteous, but I still read books myself. I prefer the old-fashioned kind. The silent ones.'

The puppet-maker laughed politely and we left the shop.

'Maestro Corodiak,' I said when we were outside. 'Didn't you promise to introduce me to the director of the Puppetocircus? Is that his name?'

'Yes,' Inazia replied. 'I've been trying to fix an appointment for days, but Corodiak is a very busy person. It's far from easy to obtain an audience with him.'

An 'audience' with the director of a puppet theatre? I couldn't help laughing. It was really remarkable, the status Puppetists enjoyed in this city. People paid court to them as if they were royalty! That thought brought me up short, dear friends. Could it be envy whose gentle but insidious pang I felt?

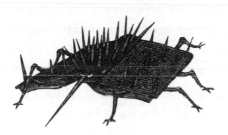

Puppetism for
Advanced Students

On our excursions we usually ate at the small, inexpensive eating houses in Slengvort, the district where most of the creative artists and craftsmen of the Puppetocircus Maximus lived, together with many other Puppetists. Almost as surreptitiously as secret agents, we eavesdropped on their artistic discussions and technical shop talk, and held informative conversations with one puppet-maker or another – although, dear friends, it wasn't so easy to make social contacts with an Uggly in tow! I had long become inured to Inazia's herbal perfumes, but most people preferred to sit at least one table away from us.

The one name that cropped up again and again was that of Maestro Corodiak. This had steadily whetted my curiosity about that mysterious personage and filled me with profound respect. Maestro Corodiak . . . I was forever having to write his name in the notebook I always carried during my study of Puppetism, filling it with facts, technical terms and snippets of dialogue:

'But Maestro Corodiak said . . .' 'Maestro Corodiak would never have accepted such a botched job . . .' 'They say that Corodiak is recently displaying a strong retrograde tendency towards Marionettism . . .' 'It's rumoured that Corodiak means to stage the whole of Wimpersleake's works . . .' 'Maestro Corodiak would have thrown such a crude eye mechanism back in your face . . .' 'A play in seven acts under Corodiak's direction would be quite unthinkable . . .'

Corodiak here, Corodiak there, Corodiak everywhere – it was like that all the time. I might have entered a strange land ruled by a wise old king to whom everyone looked up in reverence. The further I accompanied Inazia into the labyrinthine and multifaceted realm of Bookholmian Puppetism, the more I relaxed. I almost forgot that not far beneath my feet was the beginning of a dark and dangerous world that extended into the depths for miles; a world that had once been my long-time prison – nearly my grave. That memory scarcely troubled me now. I could at last enjoy the new, Overworldly Bookholm as if it were a traveller's normal destination, a pleasant holiday resort or spa. I had not long arrived in the city, after all. Puppetism itself was a kind of labyrinth, but a bright, colourful maze filled with diversions and entertainments, humour and culture. In this world, the greatest danger consisted in turning up late for a first night.

For we went to the theatre regularly, of course – on occasion as many as three times a day! We went to puppet theatres, needless to say, but we didn't immediately go back to the Puppetocircus Maximus. The city had such an abundance of smaller theatres, they were hardly less numerous than its restaurants and bookshops. Almost one street in three boasted a puppet theatre, not that it was always recognisable as such from the outside. It would sometimes be hidden behind a beer garden, in the cellar of a tavern, on the roof of a bookshop, or in a carpenter's shed. Right at the beginning we went to one whose only form of seating comprised five wobbly milking stools, yet it was, Inazia assured me, one of the most rewarding and enchanting in the whole of Bookholm.

The length of a play was no measure of its quality, either. Going to the theatre three or more times a day was quite possible, when one considers that no limits were set on the duration of a puppet play in Bookholm. There were performances that lasted an entire day or even a week, but there were also some, aimed at impatient tourist audiences, that could be over in ten minutes. These didn't necessarily leave one feeling cheated; it all depended on the quality of what was on offer, and this, my friends, even in cases where the play was very short, could be extraordinarily high. I still have particularly pleasant memories of the play presented at the aforementioned theatre with five milking stools.

It lasted for barely seven minutes, but *what* minutes! All that appeared onstage in the course of that performance was a blown and painted hen's egg, but I couldn't help laughing so persistently, even hours afterwards, that my midriff ached for days on end.

There were also plays that seemed to last an eternity. The only muscles that ached after I'd seen one of those were the muscles required for sitting still. I never counted how many worthless puppet plays I had to endure in order to get to the ones that were really worth seeing. Like me, and although she claimed to possess the power of divination, Inazia could never tell in advance whether a new play would be of the quality we were looking for. She was considerably more knowledgeable than I, of course. She knew the names, merits, shortcomings, weaknesses and strengths of many producers, authors, puppeteers, and property masters. Although this made it easier for us to choose, it didn't completely insure us against let-downs and disappointments. Puppetry was like any art: *There are a hundred potboilers for every masterpiece*, as my godfather Dancelot used to say in his avuncular way. Crackbrained directorial ideas, misshapen puppets, slipshod scripts, inappropriate music, ill-painted scenery – the things that could ruin a puppet play were many, various and unforeseeable. Often there wasn't even a poster that might have made us think twice. We would simply go on the strength of a leaflet handed us in the street or the confidential whisper of a waiter who steered us in the direction of some dive of a theatre which, according to him, staged the most illicit and shocking puppet plays in the whole of Zamonia. We were fearless, though. There was *nothing* we wouldn't sample!

In the course of my studies, as I've already mentioned, I always carried a small notebook in which I made brief entries relating to things or events that struck me as noteworthy enough for subsequent inclusion in my book. In order to impart a few pieces of advice to future students or spare them bitter disappointment, I shall here publish excerpts from my *Notes on Puppetism*, as I called them. They are chosen quite at random and adhere to no form of chronological order:

Stage shows devoid of intervals and exceeding three hours in length are an imposition not to be sat through or uncomplainingly tolerated. On the contrary, I consider it a form of moral courage to walk out of such performances protesting loudly. Those responsible have neglected to bear in mind that one cannot lay a stage play aside like a bad novel and go for a recuperative walk. There are limits to anyone's physical endurance! Besides, ANY room occupied by more than ten people should be aired at least once an hour.

* * *

One's mental and nervous stamina is also limited! Plays for the puppet theatre should not deal with problems of higher mathematics or folk music competitions in the Impic Alps, let alone singing Megaspiders! Three titles for my personal BLACK LIST:
'MR PUNCH IN THE LAND OF DIFFERENTIAL EQUATIONS'
'THE ACCORDION WAR' and
'THE BLACK WIDOW'S WEDDING'

* * *

These *Notes on Puppetism* form a chapter of the novel that gave me quite a headache when I came to translate it (see also my Postscript). I found myself compelled to drastically abridge this *Yarnspinnerish digression*, but it is not absolutely essential to one's comprehension of the plot, even in its present form, so the reader in a hurry may safely skip it. (Tr.)

Let us look facts in the face: in future, I would do better to steer well clear of HEAVYWEIGHT PHILOSOPHICAL PUPPETISM! I consider it extremely questionable to attempt to represent philosophical ideas on a puppet theatre's stage by dramatic means. Some things simply don't belong together, and among those, in my opinion, are epistemology and marionettes! A puppet playing Manu Kantimel's ZAMONIAN IMPERATIVE looks simply absurd and isn't, as I myself can attest, a protagonist with whom one can empathise. It's especially boring to the children in the audience and positively asks to be booed.

* * *

You have to keep your eyes open and look upwards if you want to get anything out of BOOKHOLMIAN AERIAL PUPPETISM. Other prerequisites include windy to stormy weather conditions (but no rain!). Aerial Puppetists prefer to stage their plays above spacious squares or outside the city gates, where they have more scope for manoeuvre than in narrow streets. This art is practised mainly by fleet-footed dwarfs who fly their puppets in the air like kites.

When cavorting in the heavens, fancifully painted protagonists made of flimsy paper and thin silk or gauze alternate with streamers inscribed with lines of dialogue – an extremely artistic spectacle whose aerial athleticism is at least as worth seeing as the plays themselves. One marvels at black storm gods in huge top hats; at colourful flying fish; at fantastic, circling birds and fairy-tale dragons made of fluttering scraps of silk and controlled from below like upside-down marionettes; at wildly dancing spirits of the air and storm demons fitted with flutes and flageolets that can, as the wind rises, produce a cacophonous, ear-splitting crescendo such as one has never heard before. The nimble dwarfs even send whole landscapes into the air! I saw rivers composed of blue and green strips of silk with flying fish leaping in them; sand dunes made of brown and yellow bandages with caravans traversing them; cloud castles of inflated white silk pillows; seas of paper waves that roared as authentically as the ocean itself! I've spent half a day watching the dwarfs as they raced to and fro, staging a succession of plays based mainly on ancient sagas and fairy tales.

Another advantage of Aerial Puppetism is that it costs the spectator nothing. The artistes are paid by the municipal authorities and tips are curtly refused. Well, they do have the biggest stage in the world – the sky – at their disposal and they don't have to pay rent for it.

* * *

Another candidate for my personal BLACK LIST: Puppetism with a medical background. A hypochondriac like me finds it almost unbearable to spend several hours watching puppets dressed as doctors talking shop in Zebraskan dialect about ear, nose and throat operations as they excise a screaming patient puppet's eardrum. The writer of this play, the title of which I flatly refuse to commit to paper, should confine himself to his principal profession, which is probably that of a

Zebraskan ear, nose and throat specialist (or sadist).

* * *

A unique attraction: THE MICROSCOPIC THEATRE OF THE ABSENT TEENIES in Arlis Worcell Street! A genuine sensation, but visible only to the well-equipped eye. Although you have to stand in line for hours in order (finally and for a small fee) to spend five minutes marvelling at the attraction through one of ten colossal magnifying glasses, it's well worthwhile. What you then see is a futuristic-looking city that bears the apt name MICROPIA – apt mainly because the whole place is about as big as a medium-sized pumpkin. It was allegedly imported from another planet reputed to be equally small. The minimetropolis, which is displayed in a glass bottle, is (allegedly) inhabited by tiny extraterrestrials who are (again allegedly) invisible but go about their daily business – allegedly, mark you! You don't see them, therefore, but you can spot some minute, futuristic-looking vehicles driving swiftly around the streets. You can even make out others, which resemble metal cigars, flying around the curiously tall, pointed buildings. Miniature circular doors and windows open and close as if by magic, smoke and coloured fumes issue from grotesquely distorted chimneys and stovepipes, and you can even hear a hum of traffic and little, piping voices all talking at once in a foreign tongue, together with noises of every kind and outlandish music. It's quite enchanting!

Of course, this is all just a well-made piece of theatrical trickery aimed at tourists, and the glass bottle containing the miniature city is really no more than another triumph of Puppetism – this time in the field of stage design for flea circuses and theatres on the smallest scale. All the same, be sure to see it! A Puppetistic theatre should NEVER be judged by its size.

* * *

The so-called THEATRE OF THE STARS, which is situated a few streets further on, can only be branded a blatant swindle. Latching on to the

Microscopic Theatre with the parasitic effrontery of a leech, it offers its customers – for a wholly unjustified fee – the opportunity to peer at the night sky through a lousy telescope during the hours of darkness. The criminals who run this theatre have summarily proclaimed the whole of the universe to be their stage and the heavenly bodies therein to be cosmic puppets – a particularly dirty trick that actually took ME in. I even doubt there were any lenses in the confounded telescope. Hard to say, because the sky was heavily overcast.

***

I have a very high regard for the work of Zank Frakfa and admire his services to literature, even though they have led to the fact that certain unpleasant matters better not mentioned are nowadays referred to as Frakfaesque;* for instance, income-tax returns or what happens if you fill them out incorrectly. When I attended the puppet theatre adaptation of one of Frakfa's best

---

*Purely by the by, should a similar honour ever be bestowed on yours truly, I'd like to suggest that the appropriate adjective be 'Yarnspinneresque'. Many thanks in advance from the author!

stories, however, I found it hard to identify with the principal character, a giant cockroach with manic-depressive tendencies. This applied particularly to the scene in which the protagonist's father pelts him with apples until his chitinous armour splinters. Frightful! Who wants to see such a thing in a puppet theatre? Not even a cockroach, probably.

* * *

Underwater Puppetism – a whole chapter in itself! I'm jotting this down in an inn, shortly after attending (with Inazia) a performance at the AQUANAUTICAL AMPHITHEATRE in Colophon Lane. Incredible! The circular aquarium is situated in the centre of a covered amphitheatre whose uppermost tiers of seats (the best) afford a view of the whole thing. It's the biggest theatrical aquarium in Zamonia, the Uggly informed me. There would be room enough in it for a whale! Even the stage tank at the Florinthian opera house, which I've seen with my own eyes, is only half as big, though that one is used by professional balletic swimmers, whereas here they are puppets.

Puppets underwater! What enchanting nonsense! What business do puppets have in a destructive element like water, especially those fitted with extremely sensitive mechanisms consisting mainly of wood and metal, in other words, materials that easily swell up or rust? And yet the puppets I saw in the AQUANAUTICAL AMPHITHEATRE looked as if water were their natural element! They really deserve a technical designation of their own. Divopets? Swimmonettes?

(NB Must write a letter to the editor of the ZAMONIAN DICTIONARY!)

All one saw at the beginning of the show were a few little luminous bubbles, pale yellow eggs that scarcely moved, just drifted gently to and fro. Then they started to twitch nervously, to dilate and expand, seemingly in all directions, until they eventually burst with a loud plop. Then there were twice as many eggs as before! These likewise burst in their turn, and so on and so forth until the whole basin was a mass of luminous eggs. They milled around wildly, here and there converging into groups and forming shoals. The water turned red and bubbled up, then subsided, and where the shoals of eggs had been one now saw simple life forms floating: algae, sponges, molluscs, primitive jellyfish.

Aha, I thought, didactic Puppetism illustrating the origins of life in the ocean with the aid of trick puppets. Very pretty and instructive – the sort of thing biology teachers take whole classes of schoolchildren to see. But it was much more imaginative than that. The water changed colour again and again – green, yellow, blue, pink, violet – and every time it cleared, new and higher marine fauna took shape. Jellyfish and molluscs turned into agnathous fish and nautilus cephalopods, trilobites and sea scorpions, and the latter gave way to ever more complex creatures such as phosphorescent fish that glided through the water like coloured lanterns. Looking closely, one could make out puppeteers in camouflaged costumes operating their complicated marionettes from among the floating seaweed or behind banks of coral. This they did by hand or with wires and strings – and without air, for they were also underwater and had to hold their breath. With every transformation, the puppets became more and more bizarre – and, one has to say, more scientifically incorrect. I saw sea creatures I'd never seen or heard of before: jellyfish with faces like cats, sharks with bony armour, crabs with sucker-studded tentacles, octopuses with claws, huge sea horses resembling unicorns. The submarine fauna became more diverse and fantastic with every change of lighting and colour, until pale green water sprites with cute, doll-like faces and piscine bodies rose to the surface of the tank and gasped for air. Corpulent mermen swam around, chuckling and slapping their bellies. Thin, almost transparent marine hobgoblins appeared, giggling, out of the mist. I realised only now that this was a representation of the genesis of the whole of Zamonian marine mythology: the creatures that appeared by degrees included Serpentoids and Marsh Moomies, Pond Demons and Poseidans, Jelly Ghosts and Unxes, Frog Princes and Melusines, Mudwitches and Mist Sirens, Coralliforms and Kelp Kobolds, Sea Demons and Lagoon Lubbers, Gill Goblins and

Riverlings, Tide Tots, Mermanikins, and Spume Sprites. Together, they formed the cast for an epic journey through the underwater world, the leading role being played by Mundine, a childish marine elf whose name was also the title of the play. Inazia confided to me that Mundine was played by a puppet carved entirely out of sea foam.

We saw a ballet performed by transparent jellyfish skilfully made of blown glass with coloured liquids pulsating inside them. A gigantic octopus of luminous rubber was simultaneously controlled by eight puppeteers, one to each tentacle. Sea spiders the size of truckles of cheese and made of genuine coral strutted around submarine volcanoes, singing in liquid voices. A three-headed sea serpent conversed with itself. The audience went wild when a whole shoal of flying fish with golden scales leapt out of the aquarium and circled the auditorium above their heads. Where technical mastery was concerned, this form of puppetry was little inferior, artistically speaking, to that of the Puppetocircus Maximus. (I'm breaking off here – too excited by such an incredible spectacle! Need a drink and some talk now. More on the subject later.)

***

Political or social concerns belong in a petition; their right to be aired in a puppet theatre is at least debatable. I, too, consider that the lousy wages paid to Hoggling members of Bookholm's Horse-Dung Shovellers Union are a political hot potato and deserving of public condemnation. However, the sight of dung-shovelling Hoggling puppets reading out wage scales to each other onstage may even be counterproductive to the elimination of social grievances – especially when real, malodorous horse dung is used as a prop! I left the theatre with a burning desire to coerce the Hogglings into exploitative wage contracts and then make their lives a misery by subjecting them to intolerable hours of work. That can't have been the purpose of the play!

***

319

The expressive capabilities of the so-called head marionettes of the MIMISTIC THEATRE are so subtle that you have to watch them closely through opera glasses throughout the performance if you don't want to miss anything. The MIMISTIC THEATRE's head marionettes are made up of countless movable components – lips, eyebrows, cheeks, eyeballs, eyelids, eyelashes, folds of skin, warts, strands of hair and so on, which are operated by as many strings. A great art mastered by very few puppeteers.

There are usually no more than two characters onstage, and all you can see of them are the head and upper body because they're almost invariably seated at tables or concealed from the chest down by some other means. Their faces are forever in motion, but in such a focused and imperceptible way that you have to take the utmost care not to miss the highlights of a performance, which often consist in some diminutive but all-important detail. The greatest importance is also attached to the play scripts, which can only, so Inazia says, be written by the finest authors in the city. Usually consisting of longish monologues or polished dialogue of extreme density and emotionalism, they require just as much attention as the brilliant puppetry. The strain is such that I usually leave the MIMISTIC THEATRE bathed in perspiration although I've hardly moved a muscle during the performance. I once developed such severe cramp that I had to lean on Inazia on the way out.

To quote one example based on personal experience: A puppet so wrinkled that it resembled a centenarian Root Gnome confessed to another puppet that it had committed a murder, allegedly quite against its will. For nearly half an hour it described its motives and the unfortunate circumstances that had fatefully and inexorably led to the crime. And all the while one could see every possible emotion reflected in its face: grief, fear, rage, joy, disappointment, ecstasy, resignation. Until, in the end, while it was describing the murder, a single tear trickled down its cheek. At that moment, every member of the audience sobbed aloud – me included!

* * *

Aerial Puppetism isn't the only form of entertainment that doesn't hurt one's pocket. The so-called NOCTURNAL MARKET is a sort of public advertising show for Puppetism held almost nightly in the square where the GRAVEYARD OF FORGOTTEN WRITERS used to be. In good weather one can not only buy little snacks from stalls and enjoy them by the dramatic light of torches, but watch talented young puppeteers, puppet-makers, musicians, poets, singers, etc. trying out their first attempts on the public free of charge (though modest donations are always welcome). Standing on little wooden stages or simply in the street, they show off home-made puppets, read dialogues or monologues and debate with the public. The NOCTURNAL MARKET is also frequented by numerous agents, talent scouts and theatre people in search of new staff or fresh ideas. A lot of artistic experimentation goes on there. At its best, therefore, the market has some exciting and trailblazing experiences to offer; at its worst, a load of half-baked nonsense. For all that, a stroll around the NOCTURNAL MARKET can often be more entertaining than a visit to a regular

322

theatre, and because of the late hour the subjects and humour cultivated there are often daringly satirical and aimed at an adult audience. Anyone with an open mind can admire true innovations in the field of Puppetism at first hand and take part in heated discussions, or at least listen to them with amusement. I spend many a sleepless night at the market and linger there until dawn, tirelessly filling my notebook.

Here is a poem. It was recited by a young poet and puppeteer named Alcolis von Frin, who smelt faintly of cheap liquor but could have a great future ahead of him if he gets a grip on his high-proof problem. Delivered by his puppet, which resembled him down to his poetically long and dishevelled hair, his 'Critic's Tongue' poem certainly chimed with my innermost thoughts on the subject:

'In unslaked lime and molten lead,
in sewage from a river bed,
in urine from a mare in heat,
in sour milk from a witch's teat,
in snake venom and old wives' spit,
in bathwater and mongrels' shit,

all authors say, in that foul brew
a critic's tongue deserves to stew.

In slime that oozes from a frog,
in slaver from a rabid dog,
in rancid oil and, worse than this,
in bucketfuls of monkeys' piss,
in horses' snot and camel dung,
in fluid from a dead toad wrung,
all authors say, in that foul brew
a critic's tongue deserves to stew.'

* * *

Dwarfs are very big in Bookholmian Puppetism
– I simply couldn't resist that laboured joke,
but it's a statement of fact. At least two-thirds
of all the city's puppeteers and puppet-makers
are of small stature, a circumstance they seek
to disguise by wearing tall caps and high
heels. Because of their build, dwarfs are
excellently suited to concealing themselves
behind a minimum of scenery and slipping
into little one-piece bodysuits. Their tiny
hands and fingers are a great advantage when

it comes to making puppets and their high-pitched, piping voices often go well with puppet characters – which are quite often dwarfs in any case, ha ha!

Dwarfs are also well-represented among authors, probably because of their above-average intelligence and creativity, which are, however, of a very special kind. As a general rule, it's easy to laugh AT dwarfs but difficult to laugh WITH them. There are several purely dwarf theatres in Bookholm, but I can only (after a few personal experiments) advise non-dwarfs against going to them. Anyone of normal build will find it hard to make a dignified entrance through a dwarf theatre's door and sit on its tiny seats. Moreover, the scripts and content of the plays presented can serve to intensify one's sense of being wholly out of place and unwelcome. Like Ugglies, dwarfs have a very peculiar sense of humour and artistic ideals of their very own. To them, for example, everything big is funny on principle. In a dwarf theatre, the mere mention of a giant or a skyscraper, a tower or a barn door, can evoke prolonged laughter.

By contrast, things that are very small are taken fanatically seriously. Objects which we sometimes find amusing, like tall top hats, pointed caps or high-heeled shoes, are regarded by dwarfs with quasi-religious reverence, and laughing in the wrong place at a dwarf theatre can result in your being immediately barred from the premises – as I myself discovered. We creatures of normal stature like to reach for the stars in our imagination and dream of other planets, whereas many dwarf plays deal with journeys into the Microcosmos, a world where everything is far smaller even than dwarfs themselves. I discovered only later that MICROPIA, the ABSENT TEENIES' miniature city, was created and run by dwarfs. I could have figured that out for myself!

* * *

On mature consideration, I must also advise against patronising Bookholm's BLOOD THEATRES, even though these are extremely popular and can sometimes be well worth a visit. Only sometimes, mark you, because in hindsight

their disadvantages definitely predominate and I
believe that Puppetism would be no whit the poorer
without these corpse-strewn aberrations. I must
at once absolve Inazia from having had anything
to do with my visiting a BLOOD THEATRE,
because I more and more often roamed the city
on my own and had strayed into one of those
dubious establishments on my own initiative.
Indeed, the Uggly had urgently advised me not
to enter one. They were idiot fodder, she told me,
but I was eager to find out for myself, so I yielded
to the allure of a long queue of theatregoers and
the bombastic posters outside ('Countless brave
knights slaughter each other without mercy!
Historic armour! Genuine explosions! A hundred
gallons of artificial blood per performance! Free
peanuts!'). I had no idea what to expect. Well, if
you've a fancy for glittering gold and silver
armour, and dying knights warbling about a
hero's death, you certainly get your money's
worth. BLOOD THEATRES devote themselves
to historical themes based on actual conflicts
such as the BATTLE OF NURN FOREST or
the Florinthian dynasty's FIFTY-YEAR
DESERT WAR. This does, admittedly, involve

a considerable technical and artistic outlay,
and call for specially constructed puppets,
skilful pyrotechnical effects and impressive
scenery. Heads must roll and limbs be hacked
off. Intestines and other innards spill out.
Characters scream as they burn to death onstage,
are skewered by spears or blown to bits – all in
the most shockingly realistic manner possible.
And, these being BLOOD THEATRES, blood
must naturally flow – whole torrents of it.
They use a special kind of artificial blood, which
is also sprayed liberally over the audience, but
after the performance it miraculously disappears
from their clothes of its own accord. The plot, as
may well be imagined, plays a subordinate role.
A play normally begins with some potentate or
dictator declaring war on some other potentate or
dictator in thoroughly insensitive language,
and then they go at each other hammer and
tongs, usually to the accompaniment of martial
music. Spurting blood, clashing blades, screams
of mortal agony, thunderous cannonades – no
demand for dialogue. The latter occurs only in
the numerous monologues by characters at
death's door, which are usually sung. Why

anyone should break into song when he's dying, even in a theatre, is something that escapes me and always arouses my amusement or annoyance. Mind you, this can be quite entertaining the first time, because the martial effects are truly amazing. After all, where else can you see a puppet being decapitated by a cannon ball and staggering around the stage for minutes afterwards with a fountain of blood spurting from its neck? Once the first act ended the next time I went, however, I started to pay far more attention to the audience than to what was happening onstage – and with growing distaste, because their enthusiasm soon gave me the creeps. Those people seemed to have come to the theatre filled with a desire to refight the BATTLE OF NURN FOREST or burn down some villages and cut off as many of their inhabitants' heads as possible. After the performance they drowned their disappointment at the sad impossibility of fulfilling that ambition in one of the neighbouring inns, all of which bore names like 'The Armageddon Arms' or 'The Home for Heroes'. Combined with the soul-destroying blaring and

329

drumming of the march music, the uproar and yelling onstage soon gave me a headache.

Around the exits of these theatres, I was perturbed to note, lurked recruiting agents and tricksters enlisting personnel for mercenary armies. I saw some knuckleheaded individuals who, after attending a BLOOD THEATRE play, willingly signed cut-throat contracts sentencing them to employment as cannon fodder! I couldn't help fearing that I might be hit over the head in some alleyway near one of these theatres, destined to wake up the next day as an oarsman in a war galley bound for a sea battle! In future I shall give such establishments a wide berth.

* * *

Far more entertaining, though in an entirely different way, are the little theatres devoted to ANTI-MARTIAL PUPPETISM, all of which are situated in the vicinity of the BLOOD THEATRES so as to oppose them with the idea of non-violent puppetry. One can't really claim that their productions even approximate to the technical standards attained by the BLOOD THEATRES' battle scenes, far from it. On the other hand, admission is free, the music played is considerably more relaxing and the audiences are far more congenial. Nor do their plays display any real dramatic structure. All that usually appears onstage are two or three simple, hinged-jaw puppets in the form of harmless creatures like hares, tortoises, deer, or doves. These volubly expatiate on non-violence or belt out anti-war songs to guitar accompaniment. You don't go there to follow what's happening onstage so much as to look for people to talk to, play chess, or take part in the platform debates. Deserving of special mention are the cups of tea on offer and the biscuits that are handed around. Despite their rather strong, resinous taste, both possess qualities that take some time to develop. However, you should limit your consumption to ONE cup of tea and ONE biscuit unless you want to spend the whole night rolling around on your hotel bed in paroxysms of laughter over some stupid joke you'll have forgotten by the next morning.

* * *

CULINARY PUPPETISM. Although this sounds quite delicious at first hearing, closer acquaintanceship reveals it to be among the most unappetising aberrations of the new art form I've ever come across. It involves staging puppet plays in big marquees at the same time as the audience is served a meal comprising many courses. At the same time, be it noted, not during the intervals. I found that just as tasteless as the unspeakable BLOOD THEATRES. Those who fill their stomachs simultaneously empty their brains. I felt sleepy after one course, nor was my concentration aided by the clatter and tinkle of cutlery and crockery, the audience's lip-smacking and belching (and worse!), and the constant comings and goings of the waiters and wine waiters. The puppetry was uninspired and mechanical because the players secretly knew that the audience was more interested in its broccoli-on-the-side than in their art. In my opinion, it's as tactless and disrespectful to eat a meal during a cultural function as to perform a play during a meal.

* * *

UGGSISTENTIALIST PUPPETISM. One ought to go to one or two plays of this genre in order to be able to pronounce on it. More would be unnecessary or even injurious to one's mental health, so be warned!

Needless to say, the Ugglies had also discovered puppetry in Bookholm and developed an offshoot of it. Being under Inazia's strict supervision, I was occasionally – and regrettably – obliged to sample its curious efflorescences. Although the shrewd antiquarian bookseller had excellent taste in other respects, when it came to applied Puppetism, I fear I must in this instance charge her with a form of professional blindness specific to Ugglies. This compelled me to spend many an excruciating hour sighing and groaning in cramped little underground theatres; more precisely, root-infested holes in the ground teeming with the millipedes and earthworms that Ugglies favour for their theatrical performances. It should be said that, although they certainly have a sense of humour, the latter is so peculiar, it's fully comprehensible to Ugglies alone. They possess what I would term an 'elliptical view of the world'. This begins by leaving the viewer far behind and then, like a boomerang, returns to its source in a wide arc. It's connected with the Ugglies' talent for prophecy and has ideological consequences, which will be examined more closely at a later stage.

The most popular puppet play in the Uggsistentialist canon is entitled 'Waiting for Yogibeard' and was written by a talented Ugglian playwright named Beula Smeckett, who enjoys the highest esteem in Ugglian circles. It tells how two Ugglies sit beneath a leafless tree and do nothing but wait for a third Uggly who never shows up. The theme of the play may be despair at the futility of existence, but wouldn't it be possible to handle the subject in a somewhat more entertaining and less redundant way? And to be honest, hasn't this outlook on the world become a bit long in the tooth these days – if a world outlook can be said to have teeth? Do I really have to spend a whole evening sitting on an infuriatingly hard root-wood seat in order to arrive at that conclusion? It's possible that at the time of its premiere (around a century ago, as Inazia informed me with a touch of pride) the play

possessed a certain philosophical potency, but
isn't it also possible that this has dissipated over
the years? However, the other theatregoers seemed
to have quite a different opinion of 'Waiting
for Yogibeard'. They were royally entertained
and clapped and laughed at every third line of
the dialogue, some of which they could repeat
by heart in unison with the speaker. I should,
however, add that the audience (twelve in number)
consisted entirely of Ugglies.

***

Lest I create the wrong impression, though, I must stress that, at the time I studied it in Bookholm, Puppetism was in its absolute heyday. I mention the poor examples only in order to convey that such a study demands a certain amount of patience and self-sacrifice, and that those who undertake it must also put up with mediocrity and tedium. But doesn't that apply to every art form?

As I'm sure you've guessed by now, my quick-witted brothers and sisters in spirit, I was evolving a plan to write a book about Puppetism. One such as didn't yet exist. There already existed whole stacks of specialised works on the subject, but they all dealt with individual aspects of it. None of them took an overall view. I proposed to fill that gap with the kind of book I'd never written before. Nor had anyone else. Just as my new red scales had lent me an almost new outward appearance (I had well-nigh stopped moulting), so I intended to reinvent myself artistically. Here in Bookholm, where I had once become a writer, I planned to become one again.

A Biblionaut
in Three Acts

When my study of Puppetism was already far advanced, it so happened that I got into conversation with a Biblionaut. I had often encountered those weird individuals, who bore such a perturbing resemblance to Bookhunters, on my daily explorations of the streets and alleyways, antiquarian bookshops and markets, and also when attending cultural functions. However, it would never have occurred to me to speak with one of them! I have no wish to gloss over any part of that curious conversation, nor will I deny that it had its sinister and alarming aspects. I must admit, though, that I didn't find it at all unpleasant, in fact, in retrospect it even struck me as informative, let's say. Anyway, it fundamentally changed my view of Biblionauts.

In the course of my studies I went to one of those awful medieval dramas in which puppet knights clad in shining armour warbled doggerel about heroism and patriotism, then slaughtered each other to spectacular effect. I'm referring to a Blood Theatre play, as can well be imagined. Inexhaustible fountains of artificial blood were gushing, the din of battle was ear-splitting and the background music was utterly inappropriate. All these things were tolerable only in the interests of my research into Puppetism. The one redeeming feature was that the seat beside me had remained unoccupied, which gave me more elbow room.

The first act had been in violent progress for quite a while, and a fair-haired knight with blood spurting from several wounds was hymning the beauty of a hero's death, when my next-door neighbour

made a belated appearance and claimed his seat. He was, I was utterly horrified to note, a Biblionaut!

I had an urge to jump up with a scream and dash outside, vaulting over all the intervening rows of seats.

For a Bookhunter, however, his mask and outfit were comparatively unperturbing and unintimidating. He wore an ankle-length hooded cloak of gnarled, dark-brown leather. His cowl, which was raised, concealed neither a demonic gargoyle nor a stylised insect's head, just a face mask with grilles for the eyes and mouth. This lent him an almost elegant and athletic appearance, like a fencer's mask. His only warlike attributes were his gloves, which had iron spikes riveted into them, and the spurs on his boots. I couldn't see any weapon, but that he probably kept hidden under his cloak.

Something prevented me from making a run for it. I simply remained seated, paralysed by a mixture of fear, fascination and good manners. The Biblionaut was equally well-mannered. I'm bound to admit that I've seldom sat next to anyone at a cultural function who knew how to behave so impeccably. He didn't talk during the performance, either to me or to his other immediate neighbour. He had no nervous tics like jiggling his knees or drumming his fingers, he didn't pick his nose, shuffle his feet, or produce a bag of nuts and noisily crunch them. He was, quite simply, the ideal theatregoer. He remained sitting exactly as he had sat down, and when I say exactly, I mean it! The Biblionaut didn't budge an inch throughout the first act, but remained glued to his seat. The only sounds I detected coming from his direction were an occasional buzz or hum, but those were probably made by the flies circling us in the gloom.

His behaviour was so impeccable, it struck me as almost bizarre. I kept watching out of the corner of my eye to see if I could catch him moving, but he didn't stir. Not a muscle! Only when the first act ended did he rather stiffly move his arms and hands, and join in the applause. He clapped precisely six times, then lowered his arms, turned his head slowly in my direction and said:

'Coming here almost gives me a bad conscience, the plays are always so bloodthirsty, but I find this theatre simply magnificent. There isn't another in Bookholm that attaches so much importance to historical accuracy where armour is concerned.'

He spoke in a quiet, almost diffident voice. It had a monotonous, unmodulated quality, but was not disagreeable. I was speechless. This Biblionaut not only had perfect manners but seemed to possess a certain measure of intelligence.

'However,' he went on, 'I strongly disapprove of the use of Heljaph Belcanon's immortal piece in D major as background music for the battle scenes. A musical faux pas like that is almost more barbarous than the massacre itself.'

'Y-you're . . . r-right,' I heard myself say haltingly.

'I am, aren't I?' said the Biblionaut. 'It's as tasteless as the march music they used for the burial scene. But then, if one wants to hear some really appropriate background music, one should go to the Puppetocircus Maximus, shouldn't one? Have you seen the Yarnspinner adaptation? A dream, I tell you! A genuine Puppetist masterpiece! The musical arrangements are phenomenal.'

Now would have been my perfect opportunity to escape. The interval had come. I could have stood up and excused myself, pleading a call of nature, and surreptitiously sneaked out of the theatre. It was now or never!

'I have had that pleasure,' I blurted out instead, and remained seated.

'Then you know what I'm talking about,' said the masked stranger. 'The first time I heard Gipnatio Sacrem's intermezzo accompanying the king's departure from Shadowhall Castle, tears came to my eyes! Tears! And they have done every time since. I've already seen the play five times. Fantastic! Do you know Yarnspinner's book?'

'Er . . . no . . . ' I lied.

'Lucky devil! Then you can still read it *for the first time*! How I envy you!'

For a moment I thought the Biblionaut had recognised me and was playing a sarcastic game, but he went on:

'It always sounds a bit blinkered when someone says they have a favourite book, but in this case I simply can't deny it: I know of no better book about Bookholm, period, and there it is. I've read it again and again! Get hold of a copy, you won't regret it.'

That was that, dear friends! Instantly disarmed, I melted like butter on a hotplate. He could have told me that he kept severed heads stacked in his wardrobe or quaffed Booklings' blood in the catacombs, and I'd still have found him likeable. I loved this masked stranger – I yearned to fling my arms round his neck! He had read a book of mine. Several times, what was more, and he thought it wonderful! Could there be any greater proof of his intelligence and discrimination? Hardly! He had earned himself carte blanche from me – freedom to do anything! As far as I was concerned, he was welcome to pursue a sideline as a serial murderer or an executioner; it wouldn't have diminished my liking for him.

'You're . . . a Bookhunter?' I asked stupidly, meaning to make at least some contribution to the conversation. *Bookhunter?* Now I'd put my foot in it! What an idiot!

'We prefer the professional designation *Biblionaut*,' he replied in measured tones. 'It may sound a trifle pompous, I grant you, but ask yourself this: Aren't we literally afloat on an ocean of books down below? But we aren't like the barbarous old-time Bookhunters, who were lawless and immoral, oh no! We resemble peaceful mariners and fishermen peacefully competing under strict juridical rules. We may cut a competitor's net adrift from time to time, but never his throat. That's a mark of progress, isn't it?' He laughed softly.

'Please forgive me,' I said. I was about to make a fitting apology, but he cut me short by raising a leather-gauntleted hand.

'Simply picture Bookholm as a city beside the sea with a prosperous harbour full of boats that go out every day. But instead of fish and crustaceans we catch books and manuscripts in our nets. And instead of selling marine fauna to markets and restaurants, we convert antiquarian books into money in bookshops and libraries. I think Biblionautics is a good description of what we do.'

I nodded submissively.

'I know it's a naively romantic metaphor,' he said with a shrug, 'but it's one of the things you need down there, or you'll go insane. A simple dream you can dream again and again without having to think too much. I often dream of the sea when I'm making my way through the catacombs – of being on the high seas and seeing a horizon I'll never reach. Of clouds and blue sky. A touch of marine romanticism keeps me going.' He gave another gentle laugh behind his mask. 'Though there's nothing in the least romantic about what we do in the catacombs. It's a science. A very dangerous science. Being a Biblionaut is the toughest job in the world, you know.'

'Do you employ Colophonius Regenschein's methods to get your bearings?' I asked, anxious to display some knowledge of the subject.

The Biblionaut turned his masked face in my direction and remained silent for a while – a perturbing sight.

'Yes . . . and no,' he replied slowly. 'Yes, because Biblionautics would be inconceivable without Colophonius Regenschein and his writings. You can compose a fugue without being able to read music, but you can't paint a body well unless you know your anatomy and you can't erect a building unless you've a grasp of statics. Regenschein's book contains the seeds of all that Biblionauts do today. We can now discover the location of a valuable book with the aid of a few old documents, a slide rule, a syllabic septant, and a vertical compass, but that is possible only because Regenschein provided us with the basic methods. He supplied the alphabet with which we now spell Biblionautics.'

I was dumbfounded for a moment, but less by his well-chosen words and the intelligence and courtesy with which he spoke than because of a thoroughly odd and inexplicable sensation that had suddenly come over me: I couldn't shake off the feeling that I was *personally acquainted* with the person speaking behind that mask!

'Yes and no,' he went on. 'No, because Regenschein is, of course, completely out of date today.' He gave another laugh. 'His book abounds in errors. *The Catacombs of Bookholm* is teeming with mistaken conclusions and fanciful theories. It's almost like the oneirocritical writings of Dr Fidemus Grund.* Regenschein and Grund are founders of entire scientific disciplines. Geniuses both, oh yes, but read them today and you can't stop laughing. That's the fate of all pioneers. They're confronted by so much that's new, they just can't afford to use reliable scientific methods. You mustn't look left or right when you conquer new terrain, you must blindly forge on straight ahead. That doesn't detract from their achievements, though. Don't misunderstand me, but the wheel of history has turned since Regenschein's death. If you ask a Biblionaut of today whether he takes his cue from Colophonius Regenschein, it's like asking a writer if he can read.'

I strove to calm down. My feeling that I knew this masked stranger was nonsensical, of course. There was probably something about his voice that reminded me of some acquaintance – a similar way of speaking or choice of words. Either that, or it was simply a cerebral reflex. If you talk to someone who hides his face, you try to find some something familiar.

'Please permit someone who hasn't been to Bookholm for a long time to ask another naive question,' I replied. 'How did the Biblionauts come to appear on the scene? You didn't simply spring up overnight, surely – or is that a professional secret?'

'Not at all, but in order to answer that I must go back a bit further, if you'll allow me.' He opened his cloak for the first time, probably because he was feeling too warm. I now saw that he was indeed

---

*Dr Fidemus Grund: celebrated Zamonian psychoanalyst and founder of night-mareology. His most important work: *Nocturnal Unease,* Caput & Co., Grailsund. (Tr.)

carrying a weapon, namely, an elegant sword with an intricately chased hilt. Now that the lights were up, I saw that his cloak consisted of old leather book covers sewn together like the wallpaper in the Leather Grotto! Perhaps he'd got the idea from my book.

'The old-time Bookhunters,' he went on, 'were entirely driven by two simple motive forces: self-interest and greed. That was pretty much the extent of their motivation. To a Bookhunter, nothing existed but himself and the hostile world that stood between him and his quarry. Do you know the famous Rule No. 3 from *The Way of the Bookhunter* by Rongkong Koma? It reads: *Anything alive can be killed. Anything dead can be eaten.*'

I nodded. 'I'm familiar with it, I fear.'

The masked figure sighed.

'But Biblionauts don't kill in order to eat, nor are they cannibals like Rongkong Koma. We do occasionally kill to avoid being killed ourselves, but in general only largish, ill-intentioned insects or rats with poisonous fangs.'

'I've heard it said that Biblionauts have a code of conduct.'

'Quite so. We subscribe to a social contract, believe it or not. It's true we're also loners and recluses – that's an occupational disease of ours – but we see the full picture, the social community. We pay our dues and taxes, we conform to the rules. We don't smuggle valuable books out of the catacombs the way the old-time Bookhunters used to. True, we bring them to the surface – that's our profession – but we do so for all the world to see, without evading any laws. In the long term, any other way of conducting business would wreck the whole of the antiquarian book market. Only fools hawk rare books on the black market for a quick profit. The old-time Bookhunters were brainless usurpers who scoured and looted one territory after another, leaving behind nothing but scorched earth. It's a blessing they've gone, because they would have wrought total destruction in the end. We Biblionauts want to preserve the catacomb system, not despoil it. It's smarter to milk a cow than eat it. You don't have to be exceptionally intelligent to recognise that. Every farmer understands it.'

'When did the Biblionaut community come into being?' I asked, somewhat emboldened now. 'Was there an actual occasion? A date?'

The masked stranger shook his head. 'It's impossible to say, exactly. We were originally a group of adventurers and bibliophiles, collectors and antiquarians – of eccentrics, if you like. We founded an association and held regular meetings in Bookholm. You know the sort of thing: lectures and technical discussions, election of a chairman, approval of the accounts and so on – we resembled a rabbit breeders' association to begin with.' He uttered another of his low laughs, mingled with which I suddenly thought I heard the ticking of a clock. Or was it his leather cloak creaking? The sound ceased when he went on.

'And then we organised our first communal excursions into the catacombs and did a bit of rummaging for old books armed with torches and clubs. It was all just for fun at first. We used to spend the evenings together in taverns after those forays and there came a time when someone raised some fascinating questions: What if Bookhunters reappeared? How would the public react? What effect would it have on Biblionism, which was just developing in the city? What would the modern Bookhunter look like? How differently would he behave? And so on.'

The Biblionaut opened his cloak still wider and I saw that sewn to the lining were numerous pockets containing small books. In a manner of speaking, he went around with a secret library on his person – a library that also served him as armour. Very ingenious!

'Well, we all agreed that modern Bookhunters mustn't resemble the old ones in appearance. They were killers and criminals, not role models worthy of imitation. On the other hand, if they possessed some essential feature that wasn't really wrong but had later been regrettably perverted, why shouldn't we give it some more thought and make it better than it ever had been? What would be reprehensible about that?

The Bookhunter is a wonderfully romantic figure, after all. A bit like those knights on the stage, don't you think? Somewhat bone-headed, alas, but marvellous to look at. Armour exerts a strange fascination, doesn't it?'

The stage was still being scrubbed clean of artificial blood in preparation for the next act. It struck me only now that our conversation was more interesting than anything this theatre had to offer.

'Well,' the Biblionaut went on, 'the new Bookhunters definitely had to wear sinister armour and masks for their own protection and to deter enemies, but those costumes had to be completely redesigned. So we studied old depictions of Bookhunters and, in the process, came across another analogy with seafaring. Every Bookhunter wore an individual uniform, though that is really a contradiction in terms, because how can something uniform be individual? No Bookhunter resembled any other, yet he was immediately recognisable as one from his appearance. In that respect, Bookhunters resembled pirates! No pirate resembles any other, each being armed and attired in an original way, but you always know he's a pirate.'

'But pirates aren't exactly peaceful seamen and fishermen,' I ventured to object, since the masked stranger had broached this comparison himself.

'True! True, I'm afraid, but being a pirate wasn't originally a reprehensible activity. On the contrary! To begin with, most pirates were innocent seamen compelled by injustice, meagre pay, intolerable sanitary conditions and brutal oppression to make use of their last resort, mutiny, and were then unable to escape their enforced outlawry. Once a pirate, always a pirate until he ends up swinging from the yardarm, right? Well, one can't make a direct comparison between pirates and Bookhunters, far less Biblionauts, but those occupational groups are not dissimilar in some respects and not only outwardly. Their love of adventure, for example. Or their courageous braving of the elements in order to traverse unfathomable depths and their desire to lay hands on legendary treasures. Why shouldn't one revive such a fine, romantic idea? Why not reinvent, ennoble and perfect it? Rid it of all its negative elements? What's wrong with that?'

At a loss, I shrugged my shoulders.

'What we still needed were two things: an icon and a vade mecum. We found our icon in the person of Colophonius Regenschein and our vade mecum in his book *The Catacombs of Bookholm*. That is and remains our guide, the Biblionauts' great instruction manual. Even though the methods it prescribes seem rather antiquated today, Regenschein's concept and ethics remain exemplary for all time. And unsurpassable! You can't improve on the two-times table, but you can develop it into higher mathematics. Colophonius Regenschein was the first Bookhunter – and the best, too.'

A bell rang to indicate that the interval was over and the Biblionaut adopted precisely the same position as before. He uttered not a single word throughout the next act, nor – I swear this on the ashes of my godfather Dancelot, dear friends – did he move a muscle. All I caught occasionally was the faint hum of the invisible insect.

When the second act ended and the next interval came, he turned to me again and picked up the thread of our conversation exactly where he had left it, just as if nothing had happened in the interim and this although some hundred knights had stertorously breathed their last on the stage and buckets of artificial blood had flowed.

'Today, the world of the Biblionauts is almost as Colophonius Regenschein pictured it in his idealistic imaginings,' the masked stranger said in his soft voice. 'A belated development, but not *too* late.'

'In that case,' I rejoined, anxious to keep the conversation going, 'the catacombs can't be as dangerous as they used to be?'

The Biblionaut gave me another long look, and there was a touch of pity in his voice when he replied. 'You've never been down there, have you?'

That came of asking stupid questions to which I knew the answer! I found it quite hard not to reply nonchalantly: 'You bet I have! Probably far deeper and for a longer time than you, my friend! I went to Shadowhall Castle and met the Shadow King in person when you were still wetting your nappies, Mask-Face!' Instead, I said humbly, 'No, never.'

'Not as . . . *dangerous*?' This time the Biblionaut echoed my words in a sarcastic drawl. 'The catacombs? Well, I'd say it depends on your definition of the word. Do you consider it dangerous to move around in a world where lack of oxygen may send you to sleep at any moment, possibly never to wake up. Do you consider huge caverns full of creatures with long tentacles dangerous? Eh? Do you apply the word "dangerous" to streams of lava that can incinerate you in an instant, like a sheet of paper? Or how about gases that can demolish whole tiers of tunnels if a single spark ignites them? Passages that fill up with sudden influxes of water and mud? Unheralded tectonic displacements? Unquenchable fires? All-consuming flames that have roamed the catacombs like restless spirits for the past two hundred years? Is *that* dangerous enough for you?'

I decided that it might be better to say nothing at all and wait for the Biblionaut to calm down.

'That unfathomable world has become considerably more unpredictable since the last great fire in Bookholm, you realise that? Never before has a fire on the surface penetrated so deep into the Labyrinth. Never before have so many supporting columns been eroded by fire or burnt away entirely. In parts, what remains down there is no more stable than a house of cards built on quicksand. The noises – the everlasting creaks and groans – are so terrifying, there are occasions when I wouldn't dare remove a book from a bookcase, even if it appeared ten times on the *Golden List*! I'd be afraid it would bring everything crashing down.'

That one sentence made it even clearer to me than the whole of his preceding lecture that he really did belong to a new generation of Bookhunters. None of the old breed would ever have admitted to being scared of anything. A Biblionaut considered it unwise and stupid *not* to be scared.

'It often happens that some immense old library telescopes like an accordion from one moment to the next because a sudden vacuum has developed somewhere. Passages in which you were standing upright a second ago can all at once cave in on you – without any warning. Being buried alive is one of the worst ways to die, wouldn't you say, but down there you have to be prepared for it at any, literally any, moment! Why the Bookhunters of yore made life a misery for each other on top of everything else is something that defies a modern Biblionaut's comprehension.'

I suddenly thought of an argument that could put a little dent in the idealistic picture the masked stranger had just painted of himself. It was rather risky of me to broach the subject because I didn't know how he would react to a sceptical question, but I had the bit between my teeth. He made a civilised impression and we were in the middle of a crowd of people. What could go wrong?

'Is it true', I said slowly, in an outwardly casual tone of voice, 'that Biblionauts still deal in literary relics? I mean, in the severed limbs or mummified organs of dead authors?'

He gave me yet another long look and I braced myself in readiness for a fierce verbal onslaught or even a challenge to a duel. But all he said, very softly, was, 'You've touched on an unpleasant subject there, my friend. I'll try to explain, so listen. A lot of people complain about the steadily rising prices of books on the *Golden List,* don't they? But those prices are simply relative to the increased dangers prevailing in the Labyrinth. How much is a life worth and how many lives have been hazarded by most of the antiquarian treasures we bring to the surface? One? Two? Three? I've retrieved many valuable books from the hands of skeletons. I'm sure you've grasped that I'm talking about the immense risks our profession entails and thus about the need to do an occasional deal for which our own lives *don't* have to hang by a thread. We may be crazy, but we aren't insane. Ultimately, we're business people.'

That sounded disarmingly honest, but how much credence could I put in someone who wore a mask?

'Those hands and ears and hearts and noses pickled in alcohol – all that morbid stuff is already there, you know. I can't help that. We Biblionauts didn't do it. We didn't murder any authors or desecrate graves or dissect dead poets into marketable chunks. We didn't encase Dölerich Hirnfiedler's brain in quartz; it was the old-time Bookhunters and other criminals, the body-snatchers and grave-robbers. Besides, most relics don't even stem from those illegal sources, but from writers' estates! These days, a lot of artists leave their bodies to be embalmed by their heirs – and, consequently, sold by the piece! That isn't legally prohibited. Many posthumously discovered authors make more money out of their dead bodies than all their books brought in during their lifetime! On its own, the hand Zank Frakfa wrote with has made ten thousand times what he earned from all his writings when alive. It's a complicated subject, therefore, both legally and ethically.' The Biblionaut gestured as if shooing away the still invisible fly that continued to buzz around us.

'So these relics are now on the market and it isn't illegal to trade in them. Antiquarian booksellers go mad for them. A signed first edition of a novel by Balono de Zacher is a fine thing in itself. But display that book in your window with the mummified hand that wrote it reposing on its cover or alongside the brain that conceived it, preserved in alcohol! What collector could resist such a treasure? Demand regulates supply. Look at it this way: it's like the silver horns of the Great Forest tricorn. It's sad that those animals became extinct, purely because their horns used to be sought after for superstitious reasons, but the horns still exist and are more valuable than ever before. If I acquire one today, I can rest assured that no tricorn was killed on my account. My conscience remains unsullied! I won't bring the poor beast back to life if I *don't* buy it, so why shouldn't I trade in it?'

He shrugged his shoulders.

'You see no difference between an animal's horn and the writing hand of . . . Aleisha Wimpersleake, let's say?' I asked.

He thought for a moment. 'Honestly? No. In both cases it's a piece of dead tissue. There's nothing special about it. Anyone who bought it I would consider sick, but for quite different reasons. He could have purchased something more meaningful for the same money or done some good with it, but he preferred to acquire a mummified hand of no practical or social value. *That* I find reprehensible. So, would I buy it? Never! But I'd certainly sell it. A few inanimate bones change hands instead of lying in a grave. Who gives a damn?'

'And if it were your own hand?'

The Biblionaut looked up.

'Well, I wouldn't care so long as it wasn't cut off while I was still alive. But that's a hypothetical question. Biblionauts don't attain a sufficient degree of celebrity for their limbs to become sought-after commodities.' I could have sworn he was grinning under his mask.

The bell for the third act rang and we turned our attention to the stage again. The play had altogether ceased to interest me. I couldn't wait for the puppets to finish slaughtering one another and enable us to continue our conversation. When the time finally came, we politely joined in the applause and went on chatting in our seats while the other theatregoers streamed towards the exit.

'Thank you for our talk,' said the Biblionaut. 'Please excuse the fact that it was rather one-sided. I held forth at such inordinate length, but you know, that always happens when I'm up here for a few days. I then feel a overpowering urge to talk. We Biblionauts observe a code that restricts communication to a minimum when our paths cross in the catacombs. Each of us being engaged on a mission of his own, no agreements, alliances or groups should come into being – that's the underlying sense of it. Only in cases of extreme emergency or sickness do we make contact and assist one another, but at other times . . . To cite one last analogy with seafaring: when two Biblionauts encounter each other in the catacombs, they resemble two ships on a foggy night. We take care not to collide and drift past each other without really meeting. We only *sense* the other's presence. We may hear breathing or a rustling sound in the darkness – and then we're alone once more. That's why I tend to bubble over with sociability when I spend time on the surface. Don't hold it against a lonely Biblionaut if he's subjected you to more verbiage than Yarnspinner does in his novels.'

I gave a start – imperceptibly, I hoped.

'Don't mention it,' I rejoined quickly. 'It was a privilege to learn so much about the ethos of Biblionautics. I have a different idea of it now, believe me.'

'Then my speechifying has been to some purpose.' The masked stranger chuckled. 'Shall I tell you what Biblionauts *really* dream of?'

'Please do!'

'Well, we'd like all parts of the catacombs to become habitable some day. *All* parts, down to their very last twist and turn. And by "habitable" we mean transformed into a normal habitat accessible to all without exception. Even a child should be able to play safely down there, miles below us, unsupervised and free from fear or danger. That sounds a high-flown, fanciful aim, I know. It won't be fulfilled in our lifetime, of course, but you have to set the bar high if you want to excel at the high jump. Just imagine what a unique city Bookholm could then become: a community like a majestic old tree with roots extending deep into the earth, not just a few subterranean levels accessible by means of shafts, as they are now. Oh no, that's just the start. I'm talking about the whole Labyrinth.'

'That really is a beautiful dream,' I said cautiously.

'It's utopian as yet, but it's feasible. All we have to do is bring light into the darkness. Have you ever held up a burning torch in a cellar infested with rats and vermin? The whole unsavoury bunch make off of their own accord. Life below ground isn't an unnatural condition, just a largely unknown and unseen one. A vast amount of all organic life takes place below the surface. None of what we do up here would be possible without subterranean life. Just think of books. Books are made of paper, paper comes from wood, wood comes from trees, trees grow in soil, and soil is fertile only when ploughed up and manured by living creatures. Not only trees but most plants conceal the bulk of themselves below ground. A root can survive without blossoms, but never a blossom without roots. We use only a small fraction of the habitat granted us and only because we have an irrational fear of the dark. Bookholm could become the most exciting city in Zamonia, if only we colonised it vertically as well as horizontally.'

There it was again, that curious sensation! Why did this masked stranger seem so familiar to me? Was it his voice? His choice of words? His gestures? His enthusiasm? Who did he remind me of? Or was it just a sense of déjà vu? An overreaction on the part of my brain, fuelled by my multifarious experiences in recent days and evoked by the present situation? That wouldn't be surprising. My last few days had been more eventful than a whole year spent in Lindworm Castle. After all, I was chatting with a Bookhunter!

'Imagine a subterranean Bookholm,' the Biblionaut said eagerly. 'One in which the few buildings up here represent only the tip of the iceberg. Ten, twenty, or even a hundred times as much of the city lies below the surface as above it. And don't think of it as a dark, sinister place, oh no! Not a dark Labyrinth fraught with shadows and dangers, but a series of festively illuminated caverns. Candlelit halls and passageways. Flights of steps, covered squares, whole boulevards ablaze with light! If we wish, we can make it brighter down there than up here on a rainy day, using specially bred luminous algae, phosphorescent fungi and jellyfish, and old and new technologies of which we still have no conception. Sunlight can be directed into the earth's interior by means of mirrors, did you know that? I've seen crystals the size of trees down there which give off light like hundred-branched chandeliers, colonies of luminous, multicoloured sponges that illuminate whole cave systems. Streams of lava can be channelled and used as sources of light and heat – the Rusty Gnomes did that.'

Well I never, the Rusty Gnomes! The Biblionaut was reviving memories I'd long thought buried in oblivion. I was almost as infected by his sudden enthusiasm as he was himself. Unfortunately, I couldn't tell him that I'd seen similar phenomena with my own eyes. I had been in the Crystal Forest and ridden the Bookway, which glowed in the dark. Why did those memories suddenly seem so much less frightening than before? Why were they unexpectedly making me feel nostalgic?

'We expend vast amounts of energy in erecting tall buildings that tower into the air,' said the Biblionaut, 'and can collapse in the slightest earthquake or tornado. We build towns beside the sea or big rivers, where they can be destroyed by spring tides or floods – we even build towns on the slopes of dormant volcanoes or in deserts, where they're parched by the pitiless sun. We nonsensically scale mountain peaks on which the air is too thin to breathe. Nobody questions that, but when we suggest building a city down into the earth, where it's protected from the elements, from cold and heat, frost and rain, hail and lightning, wind and weather, people say we're mad. The ground is the best shelter of all. Many animals know and take advantage of that, but we ignore it. It was different once upon a time. The early inhabitants of the Labyrinth must have known things we've forgotten. There used to be flourishing civilisations down there, highly developed cultures and urban life – and they still exist today. Think of the Booklings! They lead a sheltered and highly civilised existence in the catacombs. They're said to be incredibly old, in fact, they're even rumoured to be immortal! Read Yarnspinner's book. The Leather Grotto makes an ideal habitat for civilised creatures.'

It was all I could do not to grin. The Booklings, yet! I would never have believed that a Bookhunter, of all people, could make me feel nostalgic for the catacombs, but it was true. I was on the verge of throwing back my cowl and revealing my identity.

'The Rusty Gnomes – they're a subject in themselves,' the Biblionaut pursued eagerly. 'Their hitherto unresearched technologies and literature could be an inexhaustible aid to opening up the catacombs, for they were in advance of us in many ways. By mathematically calculating the advantages of gradients and declivities, ups and downs, they were able to traverse the catacombs at a speed of which we up here can only dream. We could renovate the Bookway and turn it back into the ingenious transport system it used to be. I've seen some extremely complex technical structures down there: elevators, flywheels, gigantic chain hoists. Rusty and dilapidated, but only apparently devoid of purpose. If we ever deciphered those mechanical ruins – which is only a question of time – we could probably reconquer Netherworld far more rapidly than we now hope and dream. We're like children who live on top of a brimming treasure chamber and don't dare open it because they think an evil spirit dwells within. We must bring more light into the catacombs, then the evil spirits will flee them like rats and vermin.'

There was no stopping the Biblionaut now. I had no need to interpolate any more questions; he grew more and more rhapsodic. I seemed to hear him crackle like a charged alchemical battery, but it was probably just his cloak rustling. 'The ancient civilisations that made their home down there,' he lectured on, raising a forefinger, 'were well aware that it afforded the ideal conditions in which to establish large-scale libraries. No injurious sunlight! Low humidity! *That's* why Bookholm is still the epicentre of Zamonian literature and the entire book trade. We are still profiting from that forgotten faith in Netherworld and its age-old treasures. And we haven't even scratched the surface of the resources offered us by that dark world down there! There are metals to be mined of which no alchemist knows. Golden coal that burns for ever. Oil that runs up walls and whispers. Black diamonds the size of houses. The Rusty Gnomes are said to have mined vast quantities of Zamonium down there. And we still know nothing about the fauna. Nothing at all! We can't even guess what can be evolved by a biology that doesn't have to squander its energy on shielding itself from sunlight. I wouldn't even talk about some of the creatures I've seen down there for fear of being declared insane.'

The masked stranger laid a hand on my arm.

'Believe me, we Biblionauts are far more aware than anyone else of the dangers lurking in the catacombs. That's our profession. But we also try to gain a rational understanding of those threats and explain them, not exaggerate and magnify them. Enlightenment, that's one of our tasks. We don't concoct old wives' tales about Book Dragons and "Fearsome" Booklings, as the old-time Book-hunters did. You don't solve problems by embellishing them with horror stories. Most people don't venture into the catacombs because their fears are greater than the actual dangers that exist down there. That's the Bookhunters' destructive legacy and we're still having to combat it!'

One of the stagehands engaged in clearing up bumped into some scenery, which fell over with a crash. The Biblionaut seemed suddenly to awaken from a trance. He released my arm and straightened up.

'Heavens!' he said. 'I've been talking nineteen to the dozen. Where are my manners?'

The auditorium was deserted save for us and the stagehands getting ready for the next performance. We got to our feet at last.

'Please forgive a lonely Biblionaut, but perhaps I can offer you a little compensation. You're clearly interested, not only in puppet theatre, but in conditions in the catacombs, so perhaps I'll take the liberty of giving you a tip. I know of no institution in Bookholm that could teach you more about both subjects – in the most exceptional manner. Here . . .' He handed me a small card, which I accepted with thanks. Then he gave me a little bow, wished me a pleasant stay, and went out.

Staring after him, I couldn't help feeling yet again that I'd already met him at some stage in my life. I tried to shake off the sensation by examining the card he'd given me. It was blank, so I thought I must be looking at the wrong side. I turned it over, but the other side was equally blank. He'd given me a piece of white card, nothing more. Was it a joke? A mistake? A Biblionaut's sense of humour? Puzzled, I put it in my pocket and left the theatre too. The daylight outside was dazzling.

Puppetism of
Absolute Perfection

When I wasn't out and about with Inazia or going to the theatre on my own, I often went to the *Kraken's Tentacle*. This was one of Bookholmian Puppetism's most important institutions – the first and still the best emporium for puppet-makers and puppeteers, producers and property masters, because it stocked simply everything that was regularly required by those and related professions. It was at once a warehouse, a workshop, a coffee house, a rendezvous, a first-aid post for injured puppets, an assembly point for striking puppeteers, an authors' debating society, a university, a museum and a library. Like many of the city's theatres, it was open around the clock. The staff consisted of a dozen Midgard dwarfs. Though usually overworked and ill-tempered, they were not only very informative when it came to questions about Puppetism, but positively omniscient, each in his different field.

The huge establishment, which comprised three floors, smelt of coffee and rubber, machine oil and glue, wet paint and turpentine, and was permanently filled with the sounds of hammering, sawing, conversation, oaths and laughter. There were marionette strings of all gauges on the roll, arms and legs moulded in a wide variety of materials, thousands of puppets' eyes, blanks for wooden heads, paints and brushes, ready-made costumes, sacks of wood wool, sheets of canvas in all sizes, black all-over bodysuits for puppeteers, ready-made ventriloquist's puppets, cut-out silhouettes for shadow theatres, powdered magnesium for rubbing on hands, buckets of plaster, lumps of clay in damp cloths, stacks of slabs of plasticine, thunder sheets for sound effects technicians, ushers' uniforms, reference books of all kinds, curtain material, preprinted posters – everything, in fact, that a stage artiste could require. Even boxes for sawing in half with girls inside and the saws to go with them.

The Uggly had strongly recommended the *Kraken's Tentacle* to me on the grounds that its book section stocked the best and most comprehensive collection of technical literature on Puppetism. You could spend hours lounging around there, reading books on your feet without having to buy them. Also on offer – free of charge, what's more – was fresh coffee, theatre folk's principal form of sustenance. While rummaging among the books or leafing through them, I was able to observe many a notable incident, and overhear and make a note of dialogue that could be useful to my studies. I eavesdropped on puppeteers loudly arguing about how puppets should be operated, why marionettes were preferable to stick puppets (or vice versa) and what type of wood was essential for their manufacture. On the stairs between the floors there were heated debates over the content, style and stagecraft of current productions. Ventriloquists tried out new puppets among the shelves, vocalists and puppeteers practised their synchronous acts together. There was always something going on, even in the small hours. Two long-armed puppeteers almost came to blows over whether or not puppets' joints should be lubricated. One of them said you shouldn't inflict squeaks on the audience, whereas the other complained that oil made your hands slippery. Their altercation became so deafening, they were ejected from the premises and continued their argument in the street. All I heard after that was the sound of slaps being exchanged. Although I'm not in favour of physical violence, I must confess that this scene not only amused me but actually justified my studies. I had completely forgotten that it was possible to pursue a profession with such passion that it put one's health in jeopardy. How far removed from that was my own elitist pen-pushing in Lindworm Castle!

The library of the *Kraken's Tentacle* extended over two floors of the huge building and was really remarkably well stocked. It included not only modern technical literature but also a unique store of antiquarian books on subjects such as puppet-making, dramaturgy, lighting, stage technique, scene painting and many other theatrical arts ranging from make-up to sound effects and conjuring. Does that sound like fascinating reading? No. Was it an adventure in reading nonetheless? Definitely so! Why? Well, I was wholly uninterested in whether or not puppets' joints should be lubricated with machine oil, or how to bake a puppet's china head, or how to light a scene perfectly with candles and mirrors. I had no desire to become a puppeteer or a scene painter. But if one patiently assembled the history of Bookholmian Puppetism out of all those separate components, a saga of positively epic dimensions took shape: a magnificent mosaic composed of fascinating elements and scenes, with countless protagonists and myriad anecdotes. And a history of modern Bookholm into the bargain! In short, a read that was equal, if not vastly superior, to many a great novel. And I include my own in that statement!

I had found the material for my book! More than that, I had scratched a vein of gold, struck oil, opened a treasure chamber, broached an inexhaustible reservoir that was plain for all to see but had never been exploited by anyone as I proposed to exploit it. And for me, writing non-fiction was an entirely new departure. I would never have dreamt of trying to succeed at that genre, never! Non-fiction was really just for academics and experts on Old Zamonian sitting in dusty records offices, poring over ancient reference books, deciphering hieroglyphs and scanning papyri through magnifying glasses. I had never given such things a thought until now, but the history of Puppetism was turning out to be a combination of thriller, comedy, encyclopaedia, drama and art history – an immense surprise packet.

So I spent a lot of time at the *Kraken's Tentacle*, fishing one book after another out of the shelves, more or less at random, and reading or dipping into it until it ceased to interest me any longer. I would then move on to the next, sometimes simply because it was the next in line on the shelf. It might be in the middle of a popular puppet-maker's biography, or in the introduction to a book on the manufacture of miniature costumes, that I discovered the next fragment of my mosaic. A little chapter here, a footnote there, a woodcut there and a bibliographical reference elsewhere. My notebook was steadily filling up. Sometimes the whole of an appallingly boring book would contain just one single sentence that struck me as useful, but it, in its turn, could open up entirely new side caves in my treasure chamber. Reading other people's books, a pastime I'd almost abandoned, being so preoccupied with my own work, was an adventure that now captivated me as much as it had in my earliest youth. Reading, reading, just reading and forgetting about one's own miserable existence! I'd completely forgotten what a blissful state that could be. Fortunately, the *Kraken's Tentacle* was always so busy that a cowled Lindworm standing around in the library and leafing through one book after another attracted no attention. Besides, I'd made it a habit at the end of each visit to buy a few of the books that seemed most useful to me and take them back to the hotel. If the staff noticed me at all, therefore, they thought of me at most as a regular paying customer.

What books did I read? *From Rag Doll to Micromechanical Marionette, Planar Puppetism Versus Three-Dimensionality in the Theatrical History of Bookholm, Adventures in Rubber-Moulding, Uggsistentialist Drama Before and After Beula Smeckett* – I doubt there could be any titles more off-putting to a normal readership, yet those were some of the books most in demand at the *Kraken's Tentacle*, and I devoured them all.

From its beginnings in the makeshift puppet theatres beside the devastated city's nightly campfires to the Puppetocircus Maximus and its many competitors in modern Bookholm, Puppetism had a colourful process of development behind it full of bold innovations, fanciful abstractions, artistic aberrations, creative ventures, and advances and backward steps of all kinds. It was, so to speak, a cultural history of Zamonia in miniature, all reduced to the confines of the city and the circle of Puppetist initiates. This additionally lent the subject a theatrical element, namely, a stage that was visible at a glance. The players? A few hundred theatre folk, a few thousand puppets and countless theatregoers. Magnificent material drawn from real life, my friends! So let me at least try to acquaint you with it in condensed form, just as I myself absorbed it: like an industrious but aimless bee that is tempted by this or that beautiful bloom and eventually bears its store of pollen home.

There were shelves full of instructions for the manufacture of puppets out of wood, paper, metal, glass, rubber, straw, or wire. These I was soon done with because I only skimmed them. There is hardly a material from which puppets cannot be made or with which they cannot be decorated, filled, or stabilised. Shells, paper, beads, paste, china, wood wool, shavings, wax, grass, sand, coal, gold, silver, even genuine diamonds – all have been used. Then I got out works on the manufacture of complicated eye mechanisms and articulated skeletons of wood and metal, books on clockwork puppets and the manufacture of giant marionettes. Indigestible fare, those purely technical instructions – I scarcely understood them, to be honest, but I did my level best, for those were arts in themselves. Many practitioners competed at them, each after his own manner and each with his own effect on Puppetism's stylistic development – and, thus, on those who determined its content. All this was important, so I couldn't skip anything for lack of interest or ignore it out of mental laziness, often though I was tempted to do so. I remember groaning so loudly while reading a book on glass-blown puppets that one of the sales assistants, a dwarf, asked me if I had heart trouble.

I was relieved, therefore, when I could finally turn to the art and history sections of the library in the *Kraken's Tentacle*. At last! It contained some genuinely exciting stuff, and that was when I really began to browse. No matter how ingenious their exterior and intricate their mechanical innards, what use would puppets be if the scripts of the plays in which they performed were no good – if the content, the ideas, the dialogue, the artistic intentions were of no account? They would then be no more than expensive walking cadavers, good to look at but devoid of true animation. What mattered most to me was that part of Puppetism which originated in the heads of playwrights. Only when brilliant dialogue, plot and characterisation were combined with supreme achievements on the part of stage designers, puppeteers, musicians and costumiers – only when a puppet became *slengvo,* as the puppeteers called it – did they give birth to those masterpieces whose secrets I was endeavouring to fathom.

For a start, I learned that Puppetism must not be conceived of as a single, purposefully growing plant – not as a big tree or shrub with numerous branches, oh no, but as a whole, multifarious rain forest in which *everything* grew in different directions, and in which new growths were forever being promoted by mutual pollination and fertilisation – and, of course, by the never-ending fight for survival. All attempts by the authorities to curtail and tame it by means of laws, regulations or censorship had failed over the years. Experimental theatres had been banned and closed, only to reopen somewhere in the underground and attain cult status with the public. If you want a work of art to be a lasting success, you have only to get it strictly prohibited; that had always been the best method. Plays were placed on the black list, but they continued to be performed in secret and developed into modern classics. To flog the botanical metaphor a trifle harder: Puppetism reminded me of the neglected garden behind my godfather Dancelot's house, which was always abandoned to the wind and weather. 'One doesn't go into a garden to work,' Dancelot used to say, 'but to enjoy it. For goodness' sake don't hoe it! There's nothing more beautiful in the spring than weeds.'

Yes, like a garden whose gardener had died, Puppetism embraced a gallimaufry of styles in countless variations. Far from coexisting peacefully, however, they competed fiercely, at least in the early years, for this young art form certainly wasn't a tame affair. On the contrary.

In order to understand the conflicts that smouldered inside Puppetism, one must first learn to distinguish between the champions of various styles and their motives. In the beginning there were only the *Marionettists,* who categorically condemned the practice of touching a puppet with the hands during a performance, and the exponents of *Manual Puppetism,* who joined with the *Stick Puppetists* in categorically rejecting the use of strings. That was the extent of the controversy in those days, but it sufficed to provoke lively arguments. The Marionettists declared that a puppet could be operated with little expenditure of effort by using gravity for one's own purposes, whereas a Manual Puppetist had to fight the force of gravity, which constantly tugged at his arms. A Marionettist could perform for hours without growing tired, whereas Manual Puppetists had to rest after a few minutes. The Manual Puppetists argued that a marionette moved so unnaturally that it sometimes looked positively idiotic, bumping into scenery or getting its strings entangled. When walking it only floated along, waggling its legs. 'A marionette moves like a mouse that's been grabbed by the scruff of the neck and held in the air,' one popular stick puppeteer remarked scornfully. 'It's undignified.' The Marionettists retorted that hand puppets didn't even have legs.

As if that were not enough of an issue, Puppetism continued to splinter more and more in the next few years. The first to join the three basic styles was *Planar Puppetism,* which refused to sanction any but two-dimensional puppets, and only in the non-colours black, white and grey. This style was soon opposed by the so-called *Expressionist Puppetists,* who made three-dimensional puppets on principle and painted them in gaudy colours. They spent most of the time onstage shouting at each other, weeping, or declaiming high-flown emotional speeches. What developed in opposition to this was *Naturalistic Puppetism,* which cherished a positively fanatical devotion to realism and accepted only ultra-realistic puppets that recited thoroughly prosaic dialogue. This meant that puppets had to conform exactly, in shape, colour and size, to the life forms they represented, a requirement that led for the first time to a perceptible increase in the size of the stages in Bookholm's puppet theatres. In response to this, students at the Bookholm Academy of Art evolved *Abstract Puppetism*, which grotesquely exaggerated and caricatured puppets' faces and anatomy, producing hunchbacked figures of fun with huge noses, crooked teeth and lips like bolsters. These amused the public immensely and drew big audiences. They, in turn, gave birth to the *Unreal Puppetists*, who ventured a few steps further. Their puppets and scenery almost defied description, because the 'Uns', as those radical artists were popularly known, rejected reality as such: trees grew out of the sky, buildings stood upside down, lamp-posts went walking. Their scripts were just as out of this world, and their first nights regularly ended in uproar and pandemonium. After the 'Uns' the dam broke, so to speak, and almost anything became possible.

The so-called *Cubetists* dissected their naked puppets into geometrical shapes that were only loosely connected by joints and seemed to obey none of the laws of perspective or anatomy. Some of them possessed only one eye or had lips adhering to their foreheads. The Cubetists' scenery, too, did nothing for one's spatial orientation and could induce seasickness if looked at for any length of time. *Gagaistic Puppetism* deliberately set out to be meaningless, as well as humorous in an absurd way. This aim found expression mainly in rather silly dialogue that really belonged on the walls of a school toilet. The puppets, which were quite often sausages, empty suits, flying hats, or exotic fruit, did things that were wholly preposterous but got a lot of laughs. By contrast, the strictly formal puppets of the *Doll's House Group* resembled the talking furniture in a Zebraskan tax inspector's office, and their plays, which read like instructions for putting them together, had titles like *The Secrets of Double-Entry Bookkeeping* or *No Rebates Given without a Rubber Stamp*. *Delicatist Puppetism* favoured fragile china puppets, painted in delicate pastel shades, that spent most of their time onstage complaining of depression or unrequited love amid scenery depicting water-lily pools or oleander bushes. The antithesis to that was *Brutalist Puppetism*, whose wooden puppets, which were rough-hewn with axes and painted in garish, brilliantly slapdash colours, delivered speeches couched in earthy language while thunderstorms raged in the background. *Micropuppetist* plays were rooted in the flea circus and could only be watched through powerful opera glasses, whereas *Macropuppetism* was dominated in the main by megalomaniacally inclined producers for whom no puppet could be big enough. Their plays had consequently to be performed in the open air and outside the city gates, where the gigantic marionettes were moved around by cranes. Every performance was genuinely spectacular and each character required a dozen puppeteers to operate it.

'All that can hang by a thread is a puppet.' Such was the implacable maxim embodied in the first paragraph of the so-called *Radical Puppetist Manifesto*. The result was that, in Radical Puppetist theatres for the next few years, largely naked wooden puppets strutted across bare stages devoid of scenery and the audience had to bring their own lighting (in the form of candles). Exactly when *Barococco Puppetism* came into being cannot be determined at this stage, but it was a definite declaration of war on the purist ethos of Radical Puppetism. Not only the puppets but also the costumes and scenery of this stylistic tendency were designed with an almost absurdly over-elaborate attention to detail and a performance could last for several days – indeed, weeks. The puppets' sometimes towering perukes were a trademark of Barococco, and their popularity attained such heights that similar artificial coiffures were even worn by first-night audiences.

Futuristic Puppetism was imported by immigrants from the notorious industrial metropolis of Ironville, who brought their unnerving cultural assets with them. Their puppets bore an unpleasant resemblance to the *Copper Killers* or warlike mechanical toys. The soulless impression created by their appearance extended to the productions themselves. The sets of Futurist plays looked like ruined munitions factories eroded by acid rain, and the plots usually involved hard-hearted arms manufacturers decreeing increases in output, wage cuts and mass redundancies. It was grim stuff. I read a few of the scripts, and they made me shudder! Most normal theatregoers shunned these plays, and no wonder, but the expatriates from Ironville loved them because they reminded them of home, especially when the suicidal protagonists ended by drowning themselves in a river of mercury, singing the while.

I have already given a detailed description of the distantly related *Blood Theatre,* with its collective heroic suicides, which has sadly survived to the present day. It is only for completeness' sake that I include it in my list of theatrical aberrations. Also numbered among them must be *Mummy Marionettism,* in which genuine embalmed bodies from the graveyard city of Dullsgard were used as life-sized puppets. That the mummies were genuine escaped notice until, during one performance, the fragile bandages around them burst and a collection of brown bones came clattering down on the horrified audience. Nine Ugglies in the front row fainted and five Bluddum grave-robbers were expelled from the city. Another variety of this genre was *Taxidermic Puppetism,* which employed stuffed animals in a similar way, this time to the horror of animal lovers. For once, the Bookholm authorities stepped in and promptly shut the theatre down because they could count on widespread public support.

Compared to the sinister products and practices of Bookemism, however, these were only a few absurd offshoots that soon withered or were cut off in their prime. The Bookemists, by contrast, system-atically and unconscionably used Puppetism for their own political and propaganda purposes from the outset, at least for as long as they remained in power. That is one of the darkest chapters in this history, partly because it involved the use of *Leyden Manikins* as puppets.

Those alchemically produced artificial creatures, which could only survive in flasks of nutrient fluid, were removed from their containers by the Bookemists before a show, then masked, made up, costumed and made to perform tricks onstage. The result was that most of them died of exhaustion soon after appearing.

These practices did not come to light until the Bookholmers rose in revolt against the Bookemists. Beneath one Bookemistic theatre they found a vast storeroom filled with flasks containing Leyden Manikins that had been especially created and bred for this purpose. The sight must have been heart-rending, the stench nauseating. Most of the manikins had died a miserable death in their containers and were already half decayed. Also found were a number of broken and empty flasks in which dregs of nutrient fluid remained, which suggested that some of the alchemical creatures had managed to escape into the catacombs, where they would quickly have expired for lack of nourishment.

Dumb Puppetism, Glass Puppetism, Black Magic Puppetism, White Magic Puppetism, Syncopated Drumming Puppetism, Bookholmian Dialectal Puppetism, Magnetopuppetism, Zebraskan Expressive Dance Puppetism, Philosophical Profundopuppetism, Demonistic Horrificopuppetism, Vegetarian Organopuppetism, Antipuppetist Puppetism – one 'ism' followed hard on the heels of another, and it would be too much of a good and bad thing to list and describe every one. At times, the pavement on almost every street corner in Bookholm was occupied by a little rabbit hutch of a theatre, which claimed to represent a new and exciting offshoot of the art form. Strollers went for walks with marionettes that caricatured their own faces and wore scaled-down versions of their clothing. Ventriloquism became a positive craze, beggars used beggar puppets to ask for handouts, and people took dog and cat puppets for walks in preference to live domestic pets.

Puppet theatres had catered at first for exclusively youthful audiences. Either they derived their material from Zamonia's store of classical fairy tales, epics and sagas, or the playwrights aimed their plots and dialogue straight at childish hearts, featuring the maximum possible number of talking animals, enchanting elves, or dwarfs with magical powers, plus at least one dragon per performance. At some stage, however, the playwrights began to wonder more and more why the adults who sat beside their children during these performances, looking as if they were serving a prison sentence, should not have some fun themselves. This was how more and more ambitious elements came to be woven – indeed, smuggled – into plots, with the gratifying result that more and more people went to the theatre and the performances turned into regular family get-togethers at which far more laughter and applause rang out than before. Now that adult audiences had been tapped into in this way, their attendance became a major financial consideration, for Puppetism was steadily gaining commercial importance in Bookholm. Pioneering managements ventured to put on purely adult plays at which children were merely tolerated or from which they were actually excluded. Plays became more serious, conflict-laden and complicated, their vocabulary richer, their characters more multifaceted and believable. Playwrights began to comb contemporary literature for suitable material and found it. Although *Lemon Breath*, *The Frozen Beard*, *When the Wind Weeps* or *A Ship of Waves* are hardly titles calculated to lure pleasure-seeking people into theatres, performances were sold out. Stages became larger. This created new problems, because the bigger a theatre, the harder it was for people sitting at the back to grasp what was happening on the stage. Not only did puppets and sets have to be bigger, but voices and sounds had to be louder, music more resonant, and special effects more convincing. Bookholmian puppet theatre probably lost its amateur status the first time dialogue was spoken behind the scenes through megaphones. These funnels of wood or metal magnified the sound of voices by a means that only fairground quacks had employed hitherto. Someone hit on the idea of getting two actors to deliver particularly striking monologues in unison and the dual monologue was invented! The same thing was tried with four actors not long afterwards and audiences were delighted with the wrap-around effect.

Mechanical cut-outs, live marionettes, steam puppets, Underwater Puppetism – innovation followed innovation in quick succession. Many disorientated puppeteers sought refuge from this bewildering diversification of their art form by establishing sectarian groups. This brought into being regular clans recognisable by their uniform clothing or hairstyle. Some of these groups even imitated the movements and characteristics typical of their puppets. The Marionettists walked in a loose-limbed, gangling, deliberately casual way, whereas stick puppeteers moved rather stiffly and jerkily, and made big, sweeping gestures. They gave their groups names like 'The Wooden Rascals', 'The Bookholm Blockheads', or 'The Slengvort Shadows' and had the emblems of their associations tattooed on their arms. When two of these hostile tribes had an alcoholic encounter in a tavern, ructions and smashed furniture could result. Competition between the two biggest Puppetist groups, the Marionettists and the Manual Puppetists, which had smouldered from the first, culminated in tragedy when an initially verbal dispute between a Marionettist producer and a Manual Puppeteer developed into a vicious brawl in the course of which a beer mug stove in the Marionettist's skull and ended his life. That this incident did not lead to a free-for-all, or even to a Puppetist civil war, was probably attributable solely to the fact that a so-called Gloomberg Mountains thunderstorm was raging over Bookholm that night. A natural disaster such as occurred only every few centuries, it kept the whole city in suspense until dawn. Hailstones the size of cannon balls fell, half a dozen ferocious tornados danced through the streets, ripping the roofs off buildings, and a sustained bombardment of thunderbolts set a paper factory and several antiquarian bookshops ablaze.

Storms clear the air, they say, and the sciences teach us that all diversity eventually strives to return to unity. Puppetism was no different in that respect. At all events, that memorable day marked the young art form's temporary and inglorious apogee. Passions perceptibly cooled thereafter and everyone entered calmer waters. What crucial regulatory role the Puppetocircus Maximus and its impresario, Maestro Corodiak, played in the reorganisation that followed was another chapter in the rich cultural history of Bookholmian Puppetism. I had still to get to grips with the subject, but I was eager to learn more about it.

When looking through a book on stage tricks during one of my study periods in the *Kraken's Tentacle*, I lingered over a chapter headed 'Magic Writing'. This referred to messages that could, as though conjured up by magic, appear before the eyes of the audience during a performance – a trick favoured by stage magicians in particular. One of the most popular methods was not only simple but very old: all you needed was lemon juice and heat. You held a sheet of paper inscribed in invisible lemon-juice ink near a candle flame, and *voilà*: the writing became visible.

On reading this, I suddenly became very excited. I rummaged in my pockets. Did I still have the Biblionaut's blank card? I found it, hurried over to a candelabrum and held it over a flame.

The brownish writing soon appeared:

If you want to see the Invisible Theatre, you must use your intelligence as well as your eyes.

That was all. I had to laugh. Lemon juice as ink – a well-known schoolchild's trick for producing cribs, but ingenious and effective! When the secret message appeared on the card, it was almost as if the writer had whispered the words in my ear. Images appeared before my mind's eye, together with smells, sounds and brief flashes of memory relating to my childhood: my classroom in Lindworm Castle;

the smell of a freshly cleaned slate; the merciless ringing of the school bell and the laughter of my classmates. I was so fascinated by this primitive magic that I forgot to take the card away from the candle before it went up in flames in my hand.

'It doesn't matter what the Invisible Theatre does onstage,' the Uggly had told me at the Puppetocircus Maximus. 'What matters far more is what it does inside your head.'

Startled, I let the burning scrap of card fall to the floor, where it turned into a flake of grey ash. A hand descended on my shoulder. I spun round like a shoplifter caught in the act.

Inazia was standing behind me, grinning.

'I thought I'd find you here,' she said. 'I've some good news for you. I finally managed to get you an audience with Maestro Corodiak. Midday tomorrow. Unless you're otherwise engaged?'

Corodiak's Web

Entering the Puppetocircus Maximus by way of the rear exit rather than through the front entrance was quite a different experience. You almost forgot it was the same building. It was like approaching some wonderfully painted scenery from behind and seeing only the nailed-together battens and the dirty side of the canvas. Overflowing dustbins, mountains of sacks of rubbish and bulky wooden crates stood everywhere. There wasn't just one back door into the vast building, there were at least a dozen, so I was completely disorientated at first as I stood among all the crates and sacks, chests and handcarts, pieces of scenery and scurrying stagehands, tenors practising their scales and puppeteers warming up.

I accosted a dwarf hurrying past with an armful of puppets. 'Excuse me,' I said. 'Where do I find . . . er . . . Maestro Corodiak?'

The diminutive puppeteer laughed derisively without stopping. 'In your dreams!' he called and disappeared down a passage.

'But I've got . . . an audience . . .' I added half-heartedly. I stood there for a moment, flummoxed, then simply trailed after him through the doorway that had swallowed him up. Unlike the spacious foyer at the front of the theatre, the backstage areas were dark, cramped and bewildering. Narrow passages and low ceilings instead of a big lobby, storerooms, meagre lighting provided by oil lamps, locked doors, junk and disorder wherever I looked. And unfriendly people who treated me like a caterpillar that had strayed into an anthill.

'Out of the way, Fatso!' they called.

'Don't just stand there, move it!'

'Get lost!'

'Stand aside, you idiot!'

'Wake up, you dozy fool!'

'Gangway, Hoody!'

'Goddamned tourists!' I was treated to those and other similarly encouraging remarks before I was jostled and elbowed aside or a piece of scenery came crashing down on my head. At last I discovered a flight of stairs with three signs above it. One read *Costumes and Scenery*, the others *Workshops* and *Management*. This at least might be the way to Corodiak. Afraid of being summarily ejected, I didn't dare ask any more stupid questions of those rude fellows and simply set off up the stairs.

Why was I so nervous? I didn't even know who Maestro Corodiak really was. Was he a gnome? A giant? A frail old puppeteer? An overworked theatre manager? An antipathetic type? A charmer? A tartar? I had no idea. All I wanted was to ask him a few harmless questions for my research. It wasn't a job interview or a police interrogation and I had no other kind of unpleasantness to fear, so why couldn't I rid myself of the feeling that I was on my way to a trial at which I would be the accused? In recent weeks I had too often heard the name Corodiak uttered in low voices trembling with awe not to feel uncomfortable about meeting the person who bore that name, but was that reason enough to make my knees tremble as I climbed the creaking wooden stairs? If our conversation followed a satisfactory course, I had decided to reveal my identity and congratulate him on his successful adaptation of my book, but that was no good reason for my heart to be pounding this way!

I came to an upper floor on which the rooms were considerably more spacious. For whatever reason, there was no one else to be seen. I wandered through a huge room in which hundreds if not thousands of puppets' costumes were stored. They were suspended from floor to ceiling on metal rails that could be lowered on ropes. The place smelt of mothballs and lavender. No staff were around because a performance was in progress, so I was at liberty to reconnoitre the adjacent room, which was also used for storage purposes. This was where painted scenery was kept. Whole landscapes and townscapes were propped or stacked against the walls. I strolled past sand dunes, arctic wastes and a seashore at sunset, past temples with golden roofs, jungles and mountains, grey castle walls and dark, stormy skies, until I came to the next room.

This had to be one of those referred to by the sign as 'Workshops'. Everything there was made of pale wood: the walls and the creaking parquet floor, the six quadrangular columns supporting the lofty ceiling and also the crossbeams below it. The place distantly resembled a country barn; all that was missing was some hay and a donkey. Like the rest of the Puppetocircus Maximus, it had no natural lighting but was brightly lit by oil lamps standing on the shelves. This room harboured no secrets; anyone who entered it was meant to take it in at a glance and find whatever he was looking for. Hanging on the walls were hammers, pliers and hand drills, screwdrivers and planes, knives and chisels, angle irons and rules, folding bones and pestles, stencils of numerous shapes, ropes and tackle, leather straps and wire nooses. Complete vices hung from strong hooks, axes and two-handed saws dangled from the ceiling. Tubs were neatly stacked, one inside another, hempen ropes were coiled as meticulously and exemplarily as on any sailing ship in the Zamonian navy. Stored in wooden cabinets were screws, nuts, rivets and nails of every size, likewise bolts, eyelets, hooks and even cogwheels, all clearly visible through little glass windows in the drawers and doors, and neatly labelled. Buckets of paint, oil in wicker-covered bottles, pitchers of turpentine, barrels of horsehair. Even the smells in this room – linseed oil, turpentine, varnish, petroleum, dubbin, glue – created the impression that they, too, had been neatly arranged and stacked on top of each other. They gave me a bad conscience, because I always felt ashamed when I came into contact with sound craftsmanship. This, of course, is partly because I myself have two left paws and am all thumbs, being quite incapable of driving a nail in straight. But the room inspired me with respect for another reason as well. I realised that it was far from being just a storeroom and workshop; it was a Puppetist museum, a precious collection of important artefacts. That tool there wasn't just a common-or-garden hammer. It was a hammer belonging to the Puppetocircus Maximus – one that Maestro Corodiak himself might have wielded! He might have used it to drive nails into the scenery for *The City of Dreaming Books*! As for that thing there, it wasn't just any old tackle-block, oh no! It might be *the* tackle-block used for punctually lowering the Bloxxberg backdrop in countless performances of Fontheweg's *Weisenstein*. And those scissors there! They might be the historic scissors used for tailoring King Carbuncle's costume in *King Carbuncle and the Drowning of Thursday*. Yes, every tool in this room, every nail and eyelet, had a story – even if that story had still to be written. I slunk across the hallowed hall feeling more and more overawed, and was highly relieved when I reached the other side and entered a passage.

From there I could see a wooden archway leading to the next sizeable room. The curved beam surmounting the arch, as I saw when I hesitantly approached it, was covered with mezzo-relievo carvings of scenes from Zamonian literary works that had, as I knew from my research, been successfully adapted for the Puppetocircus Maximus:

The cannibal scene from Felino Deeda's classic novel in which one of the two principal characters bears the name Wednesday, and beneath it an ornate **C**.

The tattooed harpoonist from Vermel Hellamin's novel *Whalebone*, and behind it an ornamental **O**.

The sinister Ugglies' Sabbath scene from Wimpersleake's *Thambec*, followed by an **R**.

The shipwrecked sailors on their raft from Perla la Gadeon's adventure novel, then another **O**.

Zimom and Trax, the two pranksters from Helmub Wischl's immortal children's story in verse, and behind it a **D**.

The young heroine falling down a rabbit hole in Arlis Worcell's fairy tale, followed by an **I**.

The one-eyed ship's cook from Trebor Sulio Vessenton's pirate tale, then an **A**.

The terrifying tiger from Plairdy Kurding's grand exotic fable, baring its teeth. And, last of all, a **K**.

I came to a halt. This, as the carved letters unmistakably indicated, was Maestro **Corodiak**'s sanctuary. Or his workshop, his office, or whatever else the legendary director of the Puppetocircus Maximus might choose to call his control centre. Although there was no door in the archway, I found it impossible to cross this magic threshold. Not even a foot-thick iron door could have constituted a greater barrier than my diffidence, so I lingered there irresolutely, at a loss. I couldn't even knock! However, this was an undignified state of affairs in the long run, so I eventually summoned up all my courage and cautiously peered round the corner.

The room was unilluminated but not entirely in darkness. There were no candles or lamps, but the glow from the oil lamps in the passage was sufficient to dispel a little of the gloom. I could make out some massive wooden tables, several workbenches equipped with vices, wall cabinets and tools. Hanging on the bare brick walls were marionettes and stick puppets of all kinds. Many were lying or seated on the tables and one was wedged in a vice. Others had split open, lacked heads, or were still unfinished. One particularly large puppet resembling a gigantic worm was leaning upright against a bench. So this, beyond doubt, was Maestro Corodiak's centre of activity.

I breathed a sigh of relief because the room was obviously unoccupied. This enabled me to relax somewhat. I had turned up for the appointment on time, so I could afford to wait here with a clear conscience until Corodiak put in a belated appearance. Meanwhile, I could nose around a little.

There was no *No Admittance!* sign or anything of the kind to be seen. I ventured inside.

And was immediately brought up short because my head had encountered some obstruction! What was it? A wire, a string, a rope? It was, in fact, a thin string tautly suspended across the archway at head height. Screwing up my eyes, I now perceived that the whole room seemed to be divided up into segments like an irregular mesh. Straining my eyes still more, I grasped that the workshop was criss-crossed by lengths of string and cord running this way and that. Somewhere, something gave a creak.

I had already seen some sensationally impressive rooms in my life, for instance Pfistomel Smyke's book laboratory or his gigantic subterranean library, the Booklings' Leather Grotto or the Shadow King's throne room. At first sight this modest room could not, of course, hold a candle to them; even the meticulously arranged tool storeroom I'd been in moments ago had made a deeper impression on me. But what of this mesh of strings that filled the whole room like a three-dimensional spider's web? The threads and strings attached to the walls, ceiling joists and drawer handles were alarmingly suggestive of an inexplicable 'installation' created by some mentally deranged artist. Or, in an even more disquieting way, of a cage. Who or what dwelt here? How could anyone mess up a room so nonsensically? I could not have taken another step without tripping over a string or having to duck, so I remained where I was, more at a loss than ever. Should I simply leave? Bewildered, I scanned my surroundings for some indication of what to do. And then, all at once, my scales stood on end!

Is there anything more frightening than a thing you think is inanimate but *suddenly comes to life*? This is exactly what happened in the case of the big puppet leaning against the workbench. At first it merely twitched and quivered a little, but then it detached itself entirely from the workbench and straightened up. Good heavens, it wasn't a puppet at all but a living creature! It resembled a huge worm or a fat, monstrous snake with a blanket draped over it and a cap on its head. And it now turned, *very* slowly, in my direction.

My scales bristled in a way that was new in my experience. In that one moment I probably sloughed off more of my old scales than I had in all the last few weeks put together! Something equally horrible had happened to me only once. That was when, as a child, I found a supposedly dead grasshopper in a drawer and it suddenly leapt out in my face. That experience inflicted a lasting trauma and haunted my dreams for a long time. But I wasn't a child any more and something supposedly dead that suddenly comes to life isn't fundamentally sinister unless one believes in the supernatural, which I do not. So I strove to remain calm, at least outwardly. No easy task, for the creature moved like a spider bestirring itself when a victim has become lodged in its web. A thoroughly apt comparison, when one considers that I had just run into one of the threads in that curious entanglement. Those slow, positively majestic movements were infused with a leisurely arrogance peculiar only to a creature utterly confident of its physical superiority. My thoughts were in a whirl. Could it be a puppet after all – a puppet suspended from one of those countless strings? And could this whole mysterious room be a stage set into which I'd strayed? But the solution to this mystery, dear friends, surpassed my wildest imaginings, for it embraced three superlatives:

Number one: its *most surprising* feature was that I knew the person currently turning in my direction. I knew who he was, I knew his name and I'd encountered him more than once.

Number two: the *most dismaying* feature was not only that the person in question had been dead for over two hundred years, but that I'd actually seen his skeleton and touched it.

Number three: the *most shocking* feature was that he was a member of the Smyke family, for he was Hagob Salbandian, Pfistomel Smyke's uncle, an artist by profession and the lamentable victim of a perfidious murder plot. Yes, I had actually seen his desiccated cadaver *twice* in the

Labyrinth and I knew what he had looked like during his lifetime from a large oil painting in Pfistomel's possession. All that differed from the Hagob Salbandian in that portrait was that the creature turning to look at me possessed no eyes, just two dark, empty eye sockets. You can be sure of one thing, dear brothers and sisters in spirit: if there had ever been a moment in my life at which I genuinely lost faith in everything including my own sanity, it was then.

Family Ties

Might this sinister apparition be a puppet after all and was Corodiak's workshop just a stage set? After all, I was in that part of the Puppetocircus Maximus devoted to backstage technology. There were strings suspended everywhere whose purpose had so far eluded me. Another potential explanation was that I had overslept from sheer exhaustion and was really still lying in my hotel bed, entangled in the sheets in the throes of a confused dream from which I would soon wake up. In view of my recent exertions and sleepless nights, that was entirely possible. Alternatively, all my current experiences might be a belated hangover from my visit to the Fumoir. Why not? I had heard that the hallucinations induced by certain herbal drugs could periodically recur without warning, days or even weeks after the event. The research into Puppetism I had undertaken with such excessive zeal was certainly not conducive to good health. So was I merely ill? Drugged? Could it all be a feverish dream?

'Oh, so sorry, I must have nodded off,' the eyeless creature suddenly said politely in a high-pitched, almost sing-song voice. 'It keeps on happening to me lately. We're soon premiering a new play, so I've been working night and day.' Puppet or not, it was undoubtedly an example of that rare species of so-called Shark Grubs to which the Smyke family also belonged. This was apparent mainly from the fourteen little arms it was now extending in all directions. It briefly contracted its vermiform body, then stretched and gave a hearty yawn.

'I assume, since you seem to have collided with my web, that you aren't a member of staff,' it went on. 'My name is Corodiak Smyke, I'm the manager of this theatre. Did we have an appointment?'

This was Maestro Corodiak? I was still in shock. Had he really just admitted, without being asked, to membership of the Smyke family? Why would he have done so if he were really Hagob Salbandian – which, according to all the findings of science and the prevailing laws of Zamonian physics and biology, was totally impossible? No, this was no feverish dream or drug-induced delirium. I had quite simply gone mad.

'Oh,' I said. Then, after a few moments' desperate cogitation that seemed to me to last for years, I finally remembered the pseudonym which the Uggly and I had concocted for me.

'My name is, er . . . Septimus Syllabub. Inazia the Uggly was kind enough to arrange this appointment – I mean, audience. I'm by way of being a student of Puppetism. That's to say, I'm planning to write a book about it.' Never had I felt so relieved at having uttered two or three coherent sentences without stumbling.

'An *audience*?' Corodiak sounded amused. 'Is that what people are calling an appointment with me these days?' He chuckled almost inaudibly. 'I'm embarrassed. This personality cult of mine has been getting out of hand lately. Let's call it an appointment and leave it at that.' He groped in the air with several of his rudimentary arms, then fastened on one of the cords and clung to it. For a moment he remained like that, breathing heavily and obviously mustering his strength. At last he proceeded to haul his larval body along it in my direction, one little hand over another. I noticed only now that he was wearing a richly embroidered cloak and a guild cap such as I had often seen in Puppetist circles.

That was the whole secret! The web was his system of orientation, his only mainstay in a sightless world. It was neither a vicious megaspider's death trap nor the demented work of a lunatic; it was merely an ingenious form of guidance for the blind. I now grasped why the strings and cords were of very different gauges and knotted in numerous places: it was to enable him to distinguish them easily and know at once where he was. The web instantly lost its sinister effect on me. I had as much need to be afraid of it as of a crutch, a wheelchair or an ear trumpet; it was just a disabled person's aid. What an idiot! I suddenly felt guilty for having been so suspicious and paranoid.

'I'm sure you've been wondering about this peculiar web of mine,' Corodiak said as he crawled on. 'No, it isn't for hanging up washing, nor is it a form of knot writing. It simply enables me to find my way around the workshop. I like to work on several projects at the same time. I construct a puppet here, repair another there and tinker with an eye mechanism between times. Or do the accounts at my desk, deal with my correspondence, and make notes. Then I go back to moulding, polishing or screwing. I simply have to be doing something all the time, and my attention span is roughly on a par with that of a nervous child. I'm always in such a rush, I devised this primitive guidance system in order to locate my various workplaces, tools or drawers.' His little hands having reached a knot in the web, he switched to another string with practised ease. Gradually, hand over hand, he continued to move in my direction.

'You've no idea how much easier it makes my life,' he went on. 'I'd like to criss-cross the whole world with strings like these, but I can't do that, of course, so I spend most of my time in this workshop.' He waved several little hands in the air. 'Not that I'm complaining. Most of the world's misfortunes stem from the fact that people can't stay where they belong and I belong here. This room is the head of the Puppetocircus Maximus and I'm the brain.'

If this was a feverish dream after all, it was as detailed and convincing as any dream could be. I could more and more clearly see Corodiak's face and the dark eye sockets in it. No, this was no puppet!

Although high-pitched, his voice had a pleasant timbre. I was filled with the sort of fear and ecstasy a mouse might feel when cornered by a snake. Could I move my legs if I wanted to? I didn't know. I was simply rooted to the spot.

'Of course,' Corodiak went on, 'this room is also a kind of prison, but without such captivity I couldn't have made the theatre what it is today. The cage of strings helps me to concentrate on essentials. It may sound a bit incongruous for a blind person to say so, but I can oversee things best from here.'

Although the Maestro seemed to be very talkative, even without any encouragement from me, I thought it appropriate to embark on my interview if I didn't want simply to stand around like a fool, gawping at him. I still felt I was in a trance.

'You, er, make all these puppets yourself?' I asked.

He paused for a moment, then took a little crocodile glove puppet from a workbench, dusted it off and fitted it over one of his hands. 'No,' he replied, 'that would be impossible, but I think I may claim to have designed most of them. I always make the important prototypes myself. That much self-praise is permissible!' He laughed and worked the crocodile's jaws up and down a few times. 'I don't hide my light under a bushel, but without my many talented assistants I'd be as helpless as they would without me. I strike the sparks, but fetching the kindling and getting the fire going is up to those with better eyes and stronger arms than mine. The theatre functions like a beehive. Nothing would work without the queen, but she would be completely helpless without her industrious courtiers – she would inevitably starve to death. The Puppetocircus Maximus is a collective enterprise. I could have called it the Circus Corodiak, but I preferred an all-embracing name.'

Having trickled some linseed oil into the crocodile's wooden jaws, he clattered them together in an amusing way that betrayed his skill as a puppeteer, then laid it aside and recommenced his laborious progress. He reminded me of a gorgeously plumaged parrot in a gilded cage that keeps sidling from one end of his perch to the other and chattering because it has nothing else to do. Ought I to fear him or pity him? I still didn't know. He took hold of one of the knotted strings and headed purposefully in my direction, feeling his way along the workbenches and chests of drawers. I got out my notebook so as to convey a professional impression, then remembered that he couldn't see.

'Perhaps we should simply begin at the beginning,' I said in the self-important tones of a journalist. 'How did you get into Puppetism? What brought you to Bookholm?'

Corodiak straightened a few tools on a workbench as he shuffled past it, swept some wood shavings to the floor and deposited a lead weight on top of a stack of papers. His restless hands seemed to have a life of their own. Their perpetual quest for employment captured my attention. That was all right with me; it meant I didn't have to stare into his empty eye sockets.

'Well,' he began, 'I don't know how well-informed you are about the history of Bookholm. And about the Smyke family's involvement with it.'

'I, er, know very little about the latter,' I lied brazenly.

As he shuffled onwards, Corodiak picked up a small lump of modelling clay and used four deft little hands to knead it into a small head that vaguely resembled his own. 'Well,' he said, 'you may possibly have heard about my evil nephew Pfistomel. The black sheep of the family. Every child in Bookholm knows his name and his story.' He carefully put the little modelled head down.

'Of course,' I replied. Had he called Pfistomel his *nephew*? This confirmed that he really was Hagob Salbandian. But that was quite impossible, damn it, even though he did bear a purely outward resemblance to popular notions of a zombie. And why did he call himself 'Corodiak'? None of it made any sense. I strove to seem unimpressed and look calm, but I was becoming more and more bewildered. I felt like shouting, 'I'm Optimus Yarnspinner, and I saw your confounded corpse in the catacombs! How do you explain *that*, Maestro?' Instead, just for something to do, I scrawled some meaningless doodles in my notebook.

'So you've heard of Pfistomel,' he muttered as his nimble little hands switched to another string and he made a minor change of course in my direction. 'But you probably don't know the name Hagob Salbandian.'

I thought it best not to reply, nor did he wait for my response in any case.

'Well, it's a rather complicated aspect of the Smyke family history – one that few people care about today. Very few people are interested in anything that happened earlier than yesterday – it's just how things are. To cut a very long story short, it's like this: Hagob was my brother, whom Pfistomel murdered in a cruel and underhanded manner from the basest of motives: avaricious legacy-hunting. That's all I wish to say on the subject. Read more about it in the municipal records if you wish! It was a disgusting business – it sullied the name Smyke for ever, and I'd prefer not to dwell on it. It doesn't have the slightest thing to do with Puppetism, or with me either. Hagob Salbandian Smyke was my twin brother, to be precise. We were as alike as two peas in a pod, to employ a hackneyed old simile. Even our talents were similar. We were both endowed with manual dexterity.' He raised a few of his hands and waggled them.

Twins! Well I never! A simple biological defect, a harmless genetic curiosity, and I'd once more leapt to the conclusion that I was going mad! My hypochondria was assuming such alarming proportions, I told myself I ought to consult a psychiatrist some time. Well, well! Although I wasn't exactly ecstatic – the shock of meeting a Smyke in the flesh after all those years was still too traumatic – I did feel rather relieved under the circumstances. So Hagob and Corodiak were identical twins! That naturally explained a lot of things.

'When I heard from our family lawyers – I was living in Florinth at the time – that my brother Hagob and Pfistomel were both missing, presumed dead, I couldn't have cared less. The members of my family had gone their separate ways at an early stage – the Smykes always do, being devoid of sentimentality. Our family ties are very loose: the birthday cake was not invented for the Smykes, if I may put it that way. Our family feelings become aroused only when there's something to inherit. Which wasn't so in this case. Hagob's property in Bookholm had been reduced to ashes and any of it that might have survived would be claimed by the Zamonian authorities, so I continued to keep my distance from the city as before. Many years went by, enabling a veil to be gradually drawn over those unpleasant events. That I ultimately went to Bookholm after all had nothing whatever to do with my family ties, only the desire cherished by nearly all educated Zamonians to pay at least one visit to this fascinating city during their lifetime. For I was, when I still had my eyes, a positively fanatical reader, a bookworm of the worst sort. My own family history had hitherto deterred me from exploring Bookholm because I feared that a Smyke would be promptly tarred and feathered if he ever showed his face here. But time is a great healer, isn't it?'

The closer Corodiak got to me, the more nervous I became. How did one maintain eye contact with a person who possessed no eyes? Better to keep looking at his hands! He picked up a tiny puppet costume and a needle and thread, sewed on a button at lightning speed, and hung the costume neatly on a hook. And he never stopped talking for a moment.

'At first, when I finally ventured into Bookholm, I either never mentioned my family name at all or simply, if there was no alternative, made up a false one. In a sense, Puppetism had already passed its heyday by that time. And its lowest ebb too, for it was shortly after the disastrous tavern brawl in which one puppeteer had killed another. You know the story? No matter. At all events, you'd think it was the worst possible time to develop a love of Puppetism, but any student of the stock market also knows that a slump is often the best time to invest in an industry. There was plenty of work to be had, anyway. Theatres weren't exactly being besieged by the public, but they couldn't simply close down just because there was a lull in demand. It was no wonder that someone with fourteen arms found employment with ease. I moved into a small apartment in Slengvort, asked around, and before long theatres were employing me nearly every day and in many different capacities. Puppet-maker, costumier, puppeteer – I turned my nose up at nothing. I possess manual dexterity, as I told you.'

Corodiak was now halfway across the room. He paused again and casually ran his fingers over a half-finished puppet clamped in a vice. Taking a piece of emery paper, he polished it a little.

'After a year I had not only gained wide experience of Puppetism but developed quite muscular arms. And saved a small sum with which I intended to set up on my own.' Corodiak put the emery paper down and shuffled onwards without interrupting his flow of words. 'Don't go thinking that I had a better perception of the historical situation than anyone else – that I had a flash of inspiration or a trailblazing vision of Puppetism, or anything like that. Nonsense!' He laughed. 'That's how many exponents of Puppetism interpret it today in hindsight, but I'm afraid it wasn't as simple or brilliant as that. Oh no, it was mainly hard work that did it. Quite simply, I instinctively did what had to be done without being able to give it much thought. That's how the best things often come about, believe me. For a nominal price – for as good as nothing – I acquired a small puppet theatre that had just gone bankrupt and made desperate efforts to get it back in business. In so doing, I conformed to a very simple principle: I employed only the best people: the most skilful puppeteers, the most creative directors, the most talented playwrights, the most imaginative stage designers and so on.

Only the very best. At the time, that was far from difficult because, although there were plenty of talented Puppetists in Bookholm, the art form itself was stagnating. As I said, it all happened without much planning or forethought, but I gave Puppetism exactly what it had lacked hitherto: inner cohesion. I assembled the mosaic. I fitted the jigsaw puzzle together. I screwed the puppet's limbs together, that was all. It was immaterial to me whether someone was a stick puppeteer or a marionettist, or whether he subscribed to Brutalism or Delicatism. The sole criterion was ability. It didn't matter a damn to me if puppeteers or puppets of differing Puppetist persuasions appeared onstage together. One puppet had strings and another didn't, but so what? They all served the interests of the production, that was the main thing. You wouldn't believe the resistance this provoked. I had to break strikes and stop puppeteers from coming to blows. On many first nights we had to employ bouncers to prevent theatregoers from smashing up their seats. If any of this was to my credit, it was because I didn't let it get me down and won through, for my initially aimless fight for survival had developed into a regular strategy. One grows with experience. Shark Grubs have soft bodies but hard heads. We made it from the ocean bed to the Zamonian cultural scene; our evolutionary history says a lot about our ability to succeed. I wanted diversity – eclecticism, if you like. And what do you know? Audiences were just as indifferent to whether a stick puppet acted alongside a marionette, or whether a Naturalistic puppet danced onstage with a Cubetist – as long as the result was *interesting*! Because that was my basic requirement, my everlasting question: "Yes, that's a very fine puppet with a fantastic eye mechanism, but is it *interesting*? Yes, that's a good play with an important social message, but is it *interesting*? Yes, that dialogue is perfectly polished, but is it *interesting*?"'

Corodiak tidied some pencil sketches lying on a table. Seeing him run his little hands over the wafer-thin pencil lines, I realised that he could 'see' them with his fingers.

'As far as I was concerned,' he went on, 'anything that aroused an audience's interest was permissible. Suspense, humour, fantasy, technical precision and meticulous craftsmanship, caustic satire, improvisation, emotional profundity – they weren't mutually exclusive. All of them at once was best! Shrewd theatregoers – and they're what matters – don't like categories. They abhor boundaries and limitations, and they don't like seeing their expectations fulfilled on the stage or the results of statistical surveys. Those are wishful thinking on the part of lazy-minded, uncreative Puppetists! Good audiences like a challenge, that's my motto! And that's what I gave them. *Corodiak* became a trademark in Bookholm. Why go to a traditional play when you can see a Corodiak production? Why settle for mediocrity when you can get the best for the same money? People would sooner go to the same Corodiak play three times than see three poor ones.'

Whenever I tried to ask a question, the Maestro's narrative flow forestalled me. It may have been a rehearsed speech which he felt impelled to deliver like an experienced tourist guide, but that didn't diminish my interest in it.

'I was soon in a position to buy up more and more theatres, and I ran them all in accordance with the same standards of quality. By this time my membership of the Smyke family was a secret no longer – I'd had to put my real name to too many official documents – but I found to my surprise that no one was particularly interested any more. And after all, I was Hagob Salbandian's twin brother, not Pfistomel's. I belonged to the reputable side of the Smyke family. We aren't all evil, you know.'

Corodiak was so near me now, he no longer had to raise his voice. I could see every blemish on his skin. How old was he? What had happened to his eyes? And what had those eyes seen before he came to Bookholm? Those were only some of the questions I dared not ask.

'And then the mayor of Bookholm personally suggested that I build the Puppetocircus Maximus,' he said. 'With loans at a favourable rate of interest, tax reliefs, no building regulations and so on. I didn't hesitate for a moment, as you can imagine.'

'Of course. Did you design the building yourself?' I asked.

'Yes,' he replied with a smile. 'It was a crazy idea, really, constructing a solid stone building in the shape of a tent. To carry out such a plan despite my own misgivings demanded nerves of steel I no longer possess. Still, everyone has come to terms with the design since. Even I have!' He laughed. 'The theatre has become a Bookholm landmark.'

His hands had suddenly come to rest. He had let go of the web and folded them on his chest. Corodiak was now immediately in front of me, only a body's width away.

'I subordinated everything to the Puppetocircus Maximus,' he said, very softly now, 'even my own state of health. Do you know what I consider to be the best thing that can happen to you? That an idea you have becomes bigger than you yourself thought it was. In my case it was this theatre. It attained dimensions – dimensions in every respect – of which I never even dreamed.' He paused for a moment and cleared his throat.

'The building was still unfinished when the trouble with my eyes began. The doctors told me they'd never come across anything of the kind before. Some of them still contend to this day that it's a disease from the Labyrinth – a tiny parasite, invisible even through a microscope, that feeds on eyes! It allegedly exists only in the deepest depths of the catacombs. Well, I've never been in the catacombs at all, far less the deepest ones, and it doesn't matter anyway, because the disease is incurable. My eyes simply disappeared and there was no remedy. The strangest thing was, I felt no pain at all. My sight was rather blurred for quite a while, but then . . .' Corodiak broke off. He leant against a workbench, breathing heavily.

I felt rather queasy for a moment. I only hoped that the frightful parasite had disappeared like Corodiak's eyes and wasn't infectious. I dearly wished he wouldn't enlarge on this subject.

'When I finally accepted the fact that I would lose my eyesight,' he continued, 'no matter how many faith healers and quacks I allowed to tinker with me, I threw myself into my work as never before. I sketched the designs for so many puppets, mechanisms and stage effects, we still haven't managed to make them all or try them out and we'll subsist on them for a long time to come.'

Corodiak pointed to the big stacks of paper that were lying around in various places. Some of the drawings were pinned to the walls, which were plastered with structural diagrams, columns of figures and small sketches.

'When the Puppetocircus Maximus gave its first premiere I was already completely blind. I attended it in total darkness, but believe me, I saw everything that happened onstage. In here.' Corodiak tapped his forehead with one of his tiny fingers.

'I had not only speeded up the construction of the scent organ with all my might, but designed and developed a mechanical orchestra capable of performing the entire repertoire of classical Zamonian music, plus some of my own compositions as well. I had engaged the best sound effects technicians, the most talented playwrights, and the most resonant singers and speakers. I also engaged Murkholmian organists famed for their virtuosity and trained them myself to get the most out of the scent organ. I wanted to create a theatre in which it didn't matter if one was sighted or not. And, in a desperate frenzy of inspiration, I developed things that far exceeded the theatre's requirements. Thanks to my experiments and my research into Puppetism, I evolved all the ideas that eventually gave birth to the Invisible Theatre.' Corodiak grinned. 'I assume that's why you're here, isn't it? You're one of these journalists who want to winkle the tricks of the trade out of me, am I right?' He laughed and I couldn't tell if he'd meant the question seriously or not.

'The Invisible Theatre is an idea of yours?' I asked in surprise. 'I didn't know that, really not. And no, I'm not a journalist. I'm a . . . er, scholar working on my own behalf.' My real name almost slipped out, but I just managed to restrain myself. I could for the first time hear noises on the floor below us.

'A scholar working on your own behalf, I see.' Corodiak drawled the words. 'Very well, I believe you. Not that it matters in any case. The secrets of the Invisible Theatre can't be elicited by journalistic means. You'd need to bring up heavier artillery than that. Yes, this new form of Puppetism was initially a by-product of my work on the Puppetocircus Maximus, so to speak. Only a hobby at first, it then became a passion – an obsession. Today I'm convinced that the Invisible Theatre will one day become far bigger than the Puppetocircus Maximus. Its consummation, the art of theatre in its purest form, divorced from and superior to the material world.'

There was nothing fanatical about his words, though they may convey that impression when written down. What he said sounded quite axiomatic, and his serene self-confidence impressed me more than any fiery oration.

'The Invisible Theatre is still in its infancy, but believe me, it will one day render all this puppetry, this monstrous ballet, this whole Puppetocircus Maximus, completely redundant! At first it worked for me alone and continued to do so for a long time, at least in this theatre. It was only when staging the Yarnspinner play that I ventured to try it out on a big audience and leave a puppet – that of the Shadow King – solely to their imagination. With overwhelming success, I might add! But the real Invisible Theatre takes place somewhere quite else, before a hand-picked audience. And I can promise you one thing: we're considerably more experimental there – positively revolutionary, in fact. We've ventured into areas of Puppetism which other people wouldn't dare even to dream of.'

This bold assertion electrified me. 'Really?' I exclaimed. 'Can one see it somewhere?'

'Well, *see* isn't perhaps the right term.' Corodiak laughed. 'But yes, one can *experience* it.'

It was all I could do not to beg him for an opportunity to do so. But who was I to ask that? I wondered again whether to reveal my identity, but something held me back. It was a trump card I preferred not to play yet.

'You'd like to attend an Invisible Theatre performance?' he asked.

'You're joking! Of course I would.'

'No problem,' he said casually. 'I'll invite you. When would suit you? Tomorrow, perhaps? Otherwise, the next one is in three weeks' time. Performances are rare and given at irregular intervals.'

I was completely dumbfounded. 'Er . . . yes! Tomorrow would be fine. Yes, tomorrow!'

'Good,' he said, 'I'll give you an invitation.' He went over to a chest of drawers. The din from downstairs grew louder. People were shouting and laughing. I could even hear singing. It was a theatrical performance in itself to watch Corodiak remove the invitation from a drawer – a plain white card, it passed through each of his fourteen little hands as he undulated towards me – and present it to me as deftly as a conjurer.

'That's your admission to the Invisible Theatre. It's non-transferable, mind. You must go yourself or the invitation lapses.'

I examined both sides of the card. They were blank.

'Yes,' said Corodiak, 'that's the kind of humour we incorporate in our little advertisements. There is something written on it, but in invisible ink. No matter which member of the Invisible Theatre staff you show it to, he'll understand. One more thing: even if you're gnawed by curiosity, please resist the temptation to render the message on it visible. Wait until you're at the performance. Will you promise a blind person that? It's very important, because it'll greatly enhance the pleasure you derive from the Invisible Theatre.'

'Of course,' I assured him. 'You have my word. I can't thank you enough.'

'Don't mention it. The Invisible Theatre has no commercial aims and makes no charge for admission. Just be at the entrance to the *Kraken's Tentacle* at nine a.m. tomorrow on the dot. You know that establishment?'

'Yes, I know it well.'

'Then be there! A carriage from the Invisible Theatre will collect you.' Corodiak raised his head. 'You hear that?'

'You mean that noise downstairs?'

'Yes. There'll be no more peace and quiet from now on. The morning show is over and here come the fans. They come bearing bouquets and so on, because they think it's obligatory at a theatre. Still, success brings obligations with it. Fortunately, my disability absolves me from having to meet the public's wishes too often and they usually leave me in peace. Even the most primitive societies cherish a natural respect for the blind, did you know that?'

What I didn't know was whether that should be construed as a tactful hint that I'd overstayed my welcome. I interpreted it as such, however, and didn't take it amiss because my own reserves of energy were exhausted. It had been a long conversation, and I needed to digest it.

Behind me, the floor seemed to be filling up with people. I could hear laughter and footsteps. Before long I would again be standing around in the way, jostled by ill-tempered dwarfs or enthusiastic fans, so I preferred to take my leave rather than be thrown out. For a moment I struggled with the temptation to reveal my identity after all. The conversation had passed off very pleasantly and it would have been fun to give Corodiak a surprise in my turn, but I lacked the courage. Besides, perhaps we would meet again. My legs were feeling weak and trembly.

'Many thanks for a very informative conversation,' was all I said.

'Be there on time for the carriage,' Corodiak warned me. 'Don't forget, no allowances are made for passengers who turn up late, and you won't get another invitation.' Then he turned and made his way back into his spider's web of a domain.

'Actually,' he added, 'my species is excellently suited to blindness. Our tactile sense is our most acute sense of all, perhaps because of our numerous fingers.' He paused and turned his head in my direction once more. 'But sometimes, especially when total silence reigns, I wish I had my eyes again, because that's when even I get scared of my puppets. I hear noises, you know. A creak here, a rustle there. And sometimes I even believe they're whispering and giggling together. I've invested so much time and effort in animating my puppets, I sometimes think I've succeeded too well.' He laughed softly.

That was when I grasped it for the first time: *the whole workshop was Corodiak*. The web of strings was his optic nerve, the tools and vices were extensions of his arms. The plans and sketches were an extension of his brain, the puppets and mechanisms the fulfilment of his dreams and ideas – of his nightmares too, perhaps. Only because of his self-imposed exile could the Puppetocircus Maximus continue to exist and only in this solitary dungeon could the blind monarch, Corodiak Smyke, survive. If he were removed from this room, he would inevitably perish like a spider without its web. Even though I still didn't know the exact nature of his part in creating the Invisible Theatre, and although I had just learned some remarkable things about the Puppetocircus Maximus and my admiration for the Maestro and his creations was undimmed, I didn't envy him any more. The price he'd had to pay for his genius was too high and no applause in the world could compensate for it. It was sad to see him making his way back, hand over hand, along his strings and into the depths of his workshop, where he instantly relapsed into the immobility in which I'd found him.

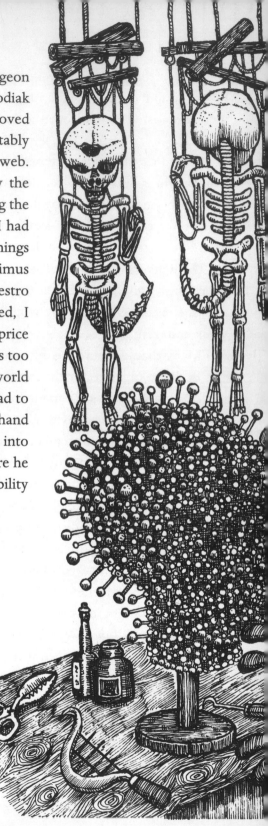

The Invisible
Theatre

I tried to see Inazia the same day, to tell her about my meeting with Corodiak, but her shop was shut and she didn't respond when I knocked. I tried twice again that evening, but with equally little success. What was unusual was that she'd left no message for me pinned to her door, as she usually did, so I had dinner on my own and then spent a sleepless night. My thoughts were in too much of a whirl. How could I sleep peacefully *after* an appointment with Maestro Corodiak and *before* a performance at the Invisible Theatre? It was quite impossible!

The next morning I turned up an hour too early for my rendezvous at the *Kraken's Tentacle*, where the carriage was to pick me up. Not knowing how long this outing would last, still less where it would take me, I did what I did before any lengthy excursion and came armed with a shoulder bag containing a bag of biscuits and a bottle of water. I also packed the *Bloody Book*, which I was still carrying around with the intention of getting rid of it at last. It occurred to me that I could have given it to Corodiak, who had something of a legal claim to it, since it was part of Pfistomel Smyke's inheritance. I decided to give the matter more thought.

At the *Kraken's Tentacle* I passed the remaining time in the book section of the ever-open establishment and drank a cup of coffee, but I was far too nervous to read. When I at last heard the clatter of hoofs and horses neighing, I went out into the misty morning.

If what was standing on the damp cobblestones outside the

Kraken's Tentacle, hissing and steaming like an outsize field kitchen, really was a carriage, I'd never seen its like before. Its unusual shape was vaguely reminiscent of the architecture of the Ironvillean buildings found here and there in Bookholm, which created the unpleasant impression that they'd been built according to plans drawn up by a war ministry. This vehicle outside the *Kraken's Tentacle* evoked similar martial associations and was really a miniature fortress on wheels. The passenger accommodation resembled a castle keep complete with loopholes instead of windows and a drawbridge instead of a door. Every part of it including the wheels appeared to consist of black iron. Paving stones could have been hurled at it for hours without inflicting so much as a scratch.

The driver was a Bookhunter – your pardon, dear friends, I mean a Biblionaut. I'll get into the habit some time, I promise! At all events, his iron armour made him look like a screwed-on component of the carriage. Even the horses were encased from nostrils to tail in defensive chain mail. Steaming and bubbling on the roof of the bizarre vehicle was an alchemistic-looking contraption whose function I dared not imagine. A stylised eye and two theatrical masks above the door were the only decorative accessories that indicated it might actually be the Invisible Theatre's carriage, but what really perturbed me was the thought that, if a vehicle looked like this, the place it was bound for defied the imagination. Not without fear and foreboding, I went over to it.

With a shrill squeal, the door was lowered on jangling chains, making the carriage look even more like a castle. Whistling sounds from the alchemistic apparatus on the roof aroused my fears that the whole caboodle was about to explode with a bang. On top of that, bleating laughter was issuing from the interior of the passenger cabin. Not even in my wildest dreams had I seen a less reassuring form of transport! The Biblionaut on the box turned his horned iron mask in my direction and gestured brusquely with his whip – presumably an invitation to climb aboard. It's still not too late to make a run for it, I thought half-heartedly, but I got in notwithstanding. You get just one invitation to the Invisible Theatre, Corodiak had told me. It occurred to me only now what a different interpretation one could put on that statement.

Three other passengers were already seated inside. Before I could examine them more closely in the gloomy cabin, the door jangled shut behind me. I heard the driver crack his whip and a strident blast on a steam whistle. Then the carriage set off so abruptly that I was thrown around on my seat like a sack of potatoes.

'Good heavens,' I said half jokingly as I adjusted the folds of my cloak. 'Anyone would think we were going into battle.'

'That's not so wide of the mark,' said a reedy voice beside me. 'At least, the area we have to cross could well be described as a kind of war zone.'

Someone turned up the wick of an oil lamp and I could at last see who my travelling companions were. They were three in number and I knew them all. That's to say, I had encountered them all in the last few days. They were:

The Murkholmian organist from the Puppetocircus Maximus. Wearing a black suit and hat, he was sitting right beside me and holding the oil lamp on high.

The green-bearded Druid from the shop I had visited with Inazia, the one that sold intricate mechanical book puppets. He was sitting immediately opposite me.

The ugly and unsympathetic dwarf I had encountered on my arrival in Bookholm. He was seated diagonally across from me and glaring belligerently.

I promptly pulled my cowl down lower over my face. 'What do you mean, a war zone?' I asked the Murkholmer beside me uneasily. 'I thought this carriage was bound for the Invisible Theatre.'

'So it is,' he replied rather superciliously. 'I'm your host and guide for this performance. May I see your invitation?'

I felt in my pockets, fished out Corodiak's invitation and handed it to him. The Murkholmer turned the blank card over in his whitish, wormlike fingers. 'But there's nothing on it,' he said in a surprised tone of voice.

'What?' I said in alarm. 'Maestro Corodiak said you would know . . .'

The Murkholmer raised his hand. 'Only joking. Welcome to the Invisible Theatre,' he said with a smile and handed the card back. The other passengers laughed.

'*This* is the Invisible Theatre?' I asked in astonishment, pocketing the nonsensical card once more. 'This carriage here?'

'It's only one component of it,' our guide whispered mysteriously, 'but you may consider the Invisible Theatre open. Everything that happens from now on is part of the performance.'

'I know this fellow!' the dwarf exclaimed above the noise of our progress. In motion, the carriage sounded like a whole army on the march. 'He looks familiar to me somehow.'

I pulled my cowl down a trifle lower and behaved as if I hadn't heard him. 'Please tell me a little more about the war zone,' I asked the Murkholmer. 'What do you mean?'

'Well, we'll soon be crossing the Darkman Sector. Or the Toxic Zone, as the Bookholmers also call it. The gutted heart of the city. The no-man's-land. Didn't you know?'

The Toxic Zone? No-Man's-Land? The Uggly had mentioned it. An area even more inhospitable than the environs of the Magmass, that was all she'd said, so I wasn't particularly eager to become acquainted with that part of Bookholm.

'Please enlighten me,' I asked the black-clad Murkholmer. 'I'm not from Bookholm.'

'I recognise this fat slob!' crowed the ugly dwarf from across the way. 'It'll come back to me in a minute!'

'The Darkman Sector', the Murkholmer pontificated like a tourist guide trotting out his spiel, 'covers the whole of the area formerly occupied by Darkman Street. That was a street of spiral conformation in historic Bookholm and once inhabited mainly by Bookemists. It was the oldest part of the city and the location of Bookholm's most exclusive antiquarian bookshops. Also resident there was the legendary Pfistomel Smyke, who—'

'You don't say,' I broke in impatiently. 'That's in every guidebook. Please get to the point!' I made no secret of the fact that I couldn't abide Murkholmers. Disguising one's instinctive aversions is only a waste of precious time.

'Darkman Street,' he persisted, 'burned more fiercely than any other part of Bookholm. That was because of the chemicals and alchemical substances stored in the cellars of the ancient buildings, as well as the extensive libraries and stocks of old paper. The Darkman Sector was still burning a full year after the fires had subsided elsewhere. The conflagration ate deeper into the ground than anywhere else in the city. That was where the catastrophe had begun and that was where it ended. It's the only district in Bookholm that has never been rebuilt or restored.'

The carriage was filled with a sirenlike wail from the roof. It pierced me to the marrow.

'That was the signal that we're over the border and into the sector,' the Murkholmer explained. 'It also keeps the animals away.'

'The animals?' I said. 'What animals?'

The green-bearded Druid uttered a bark of amusement.

'The animals of the Toxic Zone,' the Murkholmer replied. 'Please don't ask me their correct scientific names – not even the zoologists at Bookholm University could tell you those. No research has yet been conducted into the flora and fauna of this district, and for sound reasons.'

'There are wild animals here?' I asked nervously. 'In the middle of the city?'

'We aren't really in the city now,' said the Murkholmer. 'The Darkman Sector is a no-man's-land. Legally speaking, it's wilderness – a lawless area. A blank space on the map in the middle of Bookholm.

An urban curiosity. Nothing lives here apart from mutating insects and other unappetising creatures.'

I eyed our guide suspiciously. 'You're pulling my leg,' I said. 'I've never heard tell of anything like that.'

'Then you should read the new guidebook you claim to know so well,' the Murkholmer said tartly. 'The Toxic Zone isn't promoted as a tourist attraction, but it isn't a secret either. People usually give it a wide berth – they don't talk about it. It isn't a pleasant subject.'

There was a muffled crash as if something had struck the underside of the carriage, followed by some fierce squeaks and screeches such as I'd never heard before. Then came another blast on the steam whistle and peace returned.

'Animals!' said the green-bearded Druid. He relapsed into silence as if that explained everything to everyone's satisfaction.

'What sort of animals are they?' I asked rather shrilly. 'Can they get into the carriage?' Involuntarily, I lifted my feet off the floor.

'No,' the Murkholmer said calmly. 'Why do you think it's armour-plated? Only Biblionauts in armour venture outside here. The alchemical filters in their helmets protect them from the toxic fumes. They work like our filter installation on the roof.'

'You mean the air outside is toxic?' I asked and held my breath for a moment. I was already regretting having got out of bed at all. What on earth had I let myself in for?

'It isn't half as bad as it used to be, but even today I wouldn't advise anyone to spend too long in this sector, with or without a respirator. Do you suffer from allergies? From asthma? That could even prove fatal. It just depends how strong your immune system is. Sometimes it's just a cough that refuses to clear up for years, but sometimes it's a cerebral fever that prevents you from sleeping properly for evermore. Chronic oozing rashes, hepatic fistulas, temporary blindness, loss of eyelashes – everyone reacts differently to the Toxic Zone. I know someone who—'

'All right, all right!' I exclaimed, raising my paws. 'I get the picture.'

The Murkholmer smiled. 'Just stay inside the carriage with the door shut, then nothing can happen.'

I made every effort to remain calm, but the hostile atmosphere in the carriage wasn't exactly an aid to composure. I had an urge to kick open the door and run off, screaming. There was another strident whistle from the roof and the bumps and bangs ceased again. All that could be heard was the carriage rumbling along and we sat for a while in brooding silence.

Just a minute! An outrageous thought had occurred to me. Surreptitiously, I looked around and studied the faces of the other passengers from beneath my cowl. Weren't they grinning covertly and weren't they far too calm, given the prevailing circumstances? Were they genuine passengers at all?

'You may consider the Invisible Theatre open,' the Murkholmer had said. 'Everything that happens from now on is part of the performance.'

Exactly! Could all this be no more than *theatre*, and of the simplest kind? Had the carriage budged even an inch from the spot since I got in? All it needed was a few stout fellows from the *Kraken's Tentacle* to rock the vehicle a bit and hit it with sticks. All my fears had hitherto been aroused by noises from outside. Squeaks and screeches and jolting, nothing more. *What matters is what the Invisible Theatre does inside your head!* Wasn't that what Inazia had told me the other day?

I had an audacious idea.

'I'd be quite interested to see what it looks like outside,' I said as casually as I could, putting my paw to the bolt that secured the shutter over the loophole beside me.

'Don't touch that!' the Murkholmer said sharply. 'It's prohibited and dangerous.'

'Oh, sure,' I retorted. 'And I know why.'

I promptly unbolted the shutter, pushed it aside, and peered out through the narrow slit.

'No, don't!' I heard the Murkholmer call, but it was too late.

The paved road we were rumbling along was flanked by the sparse remains of what had once been a vibrant city district. Its blackened ruins resembled a forest consumed by fire, so little of it remained – little more than charred timbers and mounds of rubble. The sun, which was just rising, bathed everything in an orange glow, which created the illusion that the Great Conflagration of Bookholm was still burning. What additionally contributed to this impression was a smell of charcoal, which was still remarkably pungent after so many years. The skeletons of the old buildings were overgrown with vegetation I had never seen before. Violet moss was growing almost everywhere and blood-red climbing plants were winding themselves around fragments of half-timbering. Whole meadows of transparent-looking weeds were proliferating between the ruins. This was Darkman Street beyond a doubt, for I recognised the worn old paving stones I'd trodden an eternity ago. The sight made me go hot and cold by turns. No, the carriage was no longer standing outside the *Kraken's Tentacle*, assuredly not! We were deep inside the Toxic Zone. Something black and glossy that looked like a cross between a gigantic stag beetle and a trilobite came crawling out of a crevice in the rubble. It was about the size of an adult cat. Having taken a short run, the monstrous creature hurled itself at the carriage with all its might. Bang! More beetles appeared in the charred ruins, croaking like belligerent ravens. The Biblionaut cracked his whip and there was another strident blast from the steam whistle. An acrid stench came wafting through the loophole and into the carriage. I instinctively shrank back.

'Close the goddamned shutter, you idiot!' cried the dwarf. 'Do you want to kill us all?' But I was too overwhelmed by the spectacle outside to raise a paw. The Murkholmer thrust me aside and secured the shutter.

'Are you crazy?' he shouted at me. 'I expressly warned you! I'm responsible for my passengers, kindly remember that!'

Not altogether without reason, I was feeling like a fool. Guiltily, I subsided on to my seat.

'I'm sorry,' I said humbly. 'I had no idea . . .'

'No, you didn't!' croaked the dwarf. 'I know who you are, Fatso!'

'Perhaps you'll believe me now,' the Murkholmer said peevishly. 'The whole district, the rocks, the subsoil, the ground water – everything's saturated with toxic Bookemistic substances. Barrels of alchemical liquids burst and drained away in the Great Conflagration. Chemicals of the most obscure provenance mingled and were boiled and vaporised by the flames. It was an uncontrolled alchemical experiment on an unprecedented scale. Nobody knows what this ground beneath us has absorbed and accumulated, or what it may yet do to us. No wonder everyone prefers to keep quiet about it. There are creatures here today that never existed before the fire, either in Bookholm or anywhere else. They survive only here in the Toxic Zone, on this alchemically fertilised soil. Which is a blessing. As soon as they try to leave the sector, they die. Hairy frogs, yards-long worms with legs, rats with poisonous barbs in their tails – no scientist is eager to come here and research these new fauna and flora. Nobody wants to die attempting to categorise or catalogue them.'

I glanced at the shutter to reassure myself that the Murkholmer had fastened it securely.

'Preliminary attempts were naturally made to research the creatures,' he went on. 'And to exterminate them. People tried to plough up and level the whole area, but it wasn't long before they developed hitherto unknown diseases and ailments – multicoloured rashes, hallucinations, incurable nervous diseases – and some of them even died. Immediately after the Great Conflagration the inhabitants of Bookholm were so hungry, they gathered mushrooms in the Toxic Zone. Not a good idea! I'll spare you the details. Suffice it to say that mushroom-picking has been prohibited ever since, not only in the

Toxic Zone but throughout Bookholm. Try ordering mushroom risotto in a restaurant here. It's impossible.'

'Where are we going?' I asked, to change the subject.

'We're making for the Pfistomel Shaft,' the Murkholmer replied as if it were the most natural thing in the world. 'That's our destination.'

'The . . . Pfistomel Shaft?' My voice almost broke. 'You mean there's a Bookholm Shaft named after that criminal?'

'Of course not. Not officially, at least. That shaft doesn't have name – it's the only one that has remained unnamed, but that was a mistake on the part of the municipal authorities. I suppose they thought it deserved a special form of reverence because it's the entrance to the Labyrinth where the fire first started. And since it's situated precisely where Pfistomel Smyke's house once stood—'

'Just a minute!' I broke in excitedly. 'You mean we're heading for the spot where Pfistomel's house used to be and there's a Bookholm Shaft there now? An entrance to the catacombs? Is that what you're telling me?'

'Yes. It's common knowledge, actually, so why do I need to explain everything to you? People christened it that for want of an official name. You can also call it the No-Man's-Land Shaft if you want.'

This was incredible! I had, of my own free will, got into a carriage that was taking me to the spot whence I'd ended up in the catacombs! It was the very last place I wanted to be.

'Turn round!' I demanded on impulse. 'Turn this carriage round and drive back at once! I want to get out.'

'Out of the question,' the Murkholmer said coldly.

'Are you mad, Fatso?' cried the dwarf. 'You aren't the only person in here.'

The green-bearded Druid just looked at me pityingly.

'Driver!' I called loudly, rapping on the ceiling with my cane. 'Stop! We must turn back!'

The carriage promptly pulled up.

'There,' I said, feeling relieved. 'I'm sorry, but I can't possibly accompany you to your, er, No-Man's-Land Shaft. It's not on for . . . well, very personal reasons. Sorry to have to have to spoil your party, but I wasn't fully informed about it. I'll naturally meet any expense incurred. Please instruct your driver to turn round.' I was determined to wring the impudent dwarf's neck if he made another snide remark.

'It's no use,' said the Murkholmer. 'We're already there.'

'There?' I asked stupidly. 'Where?'

'At the Pfistomel Shaft. Our destination.'

The door opened with a loud creak and a rattle of chains.

'Don't worry,' the Murkholmer said soothingly, 'one can breathe here without a respirator. Right beside the shaft the fire raged so fiercely that all the chemicals were vaporised without trace. The air still smells rather acrid, but the incidence of noxious fumes is zero, it's been scientifically measured. Please get out, gentlemen!'

'Out the way, Fatso!' the dwarf demanded, pushing past me.

I was stunned. For a moment I continued to sit there as if paralysed, but then I got out too. What else could I do?

The sight that met my eyes as I left the carriage by way of the door-cum-drawbridge was so breathtaking that I desisted from any further protests for the time being. The carriage was standing on blackened soil from which ruins jutted here and there like the charred bones of huge birds. We were on the edge of a pit some 300 feet in diameter: the Pfistomel Shaft.

'The biggest entrance to the Bookholm Labyrinth,' the Murkholmer said proudly, as if he had excavated it himself. 'And the least often used.'

'Incredible!' said the dwarf. 'I've always wanted to see this.'

My knees were almost buckling, but I pulled myself together and turned in desperation to the Biblionaut, who was still sitting on the box.

'Driver!' I called as peremptorily as I could. 'Please take me back to the city, I'm afraid I can't attend this function! You can name your own fare.'

The Biblionaut didn't utter a sound. He didn't even turn his head in my direction. To be precise, he didn't move at all.

With a groan, the Druid climbed up on the box beside the Biblionaut and did something to him, not that I could see what it was. All I heard was some metallic creaking and grating, clicking and clanking sounds. Then the Biblionaut suddenly moved his head, laid his whip aside and climbed down from the box followed by the Druid. Ignoring me completely, he proceeded to tether the horses to a charred beam.

'What did you do to the Biblionaut?' I asked the Druid suspiciously.

'Oh,' he said in an amiable tone, 'the poor fellow had a problem with his armour. I loosened the hinges a bit and lubricated his joints.'

'What's it to you, Fatso?' said the dwarf. 'You ask a lot of silly questions. I think I've remembered where I know you from.'

'Really?' I said. It was a matter of some indifference to me if he'd finally recalled that I'd trampled on him once. He could accuse me of cruelty to dwarfs in front of everyone, for all I cared. I wasn't going to forge any lifelong friendships in present company, that was for sure.

'You were at that performance of *The City of Dreaming Books*,' he spat at me. 'At the Puppetocircus Maximus. You were sitting in a box with that crazy Uggly, right? I saw you! Got a permanent box, eh, Fatso? I suppose you think that makes you a cut above the rest of us in the stalls, who have to crane our necks?'

'Guilty as charged,' I admitted.

I had no wish to argue with a dwarf under present circumstances. Perhaps he would leave me in peace now.

'I knew it!' the little creature cried triumphantly. 'I know you, Fatso.'

'Well,' the Murkholmer exclaimed in a genial voice, 'we're here. Let's go down into the Invisible Theatre.'

'Down?' I gasped. 'What do you mean, *down*?'

'Why, into the catacombs,' he said casually.

'What? You mean to go down into the catacombs? From here?' I hoped I'd misheard.

'Over there is a flight of steps leading down into the shaft,' our guide explained. 'It's a bit makeshift because so few interested parties come here, but it's quite safe, the Biblionauts constructed it. It's only a few steps down, we won't be going very deep.'

No, I hadn't misheard. He was in earnest.

'Out of the question!' I cried. My voice had taken on a note of hysteria.

The Murkholmer sighed. He came over to me and lowered his voice.

'Listen,' he said, 'we've long experience of visitors who suffer from panic attacks. Every Invisible Theatre performance takes place in an unusual location, that's inevitable, but I can assure you it'll be perfectly safe. We've spared no expense – we've even hired an experienced Biblionaut to protect us. He's really quite redundant, though, because there's no danger where we're going, Maestro Corodiak stakes his reputation on that.'

'I don't care,' I said stubbornly. 'I'm not entering the Labyrinth, not in a million years. It's out of the question. If you won't drive me back I'll stay here beside the carriage and wait until the performance is over.'

'I can't permit that,' said the Murkholmer. 'I couldn't take the responsibility. If we leave you alone up here, you'll have no protection from the animals.'

'The animals?' I said. 'What about them?'

'It won't take long for the animals in the Toxic Zone to pick up your scent and converge on this spot. Why do you think the horses are wearing full body armour?'

'What's up?' the dwarf called impatiently. 'Is Fatso making difficulties? When are we getting going?'

The Murkholmer came still closer. 'Let me tell you something,' he said in a low voice. 'I know a bit more about your fears than you think. Inazia the Uggly told us you were terribly scared of the catacombs.'

I was surprised 'You know Inazia? You spoke with her?'

He smiled. 'Who do you think got you this invitation? Attending an Invisible Theatre performance is an honour. Even established Puppetists would give their eye-teeth for an invitation. The Druid has worked for the Puppetocircus Maximus for many years and this is his very first chance to attend although he's been on the waiting list for ages. You've been in Bookholm for only a few days, yet you're privileged to be here. You don't seem to realise what a rare opportunity you'd be missing. I know people who would pay a fortune to be in your shoes, but the Invisible Theatre can't be bought.'

'I don't care,' I repeated mulishly. 'I'm not going down into the catacombs.'

'I'll tell you something else,' the Murkholmer whispered. 'You can kill two birds with one stone: not only watch an Invisible Theatre production but conquer one of your direst fears. I know about your nightmares. Free yourself from them for ever! Enter the catacombs, but do so in the safest and most innocuous way imaginable: under professional guidance and the personal protection of an experienced Biblionaut. I'll wager you'll feel reborn afterwards. I feel sure the Uggly had an ulterior motive when she wangled this invitation for you. Don't be a spoilsport!'

'What is it now?' called the dwarf. 'We're waiting!'

Dear friends, I was definitely suffering from an acute attack of *excitrepidation* – if you recall the term I coined at the beginning of my journey for a state of suppressed adventurousness. The old, spent, risk-averse, safety- and comfort-loving side of my brain urgently advised me to dig my heels in. But the other, artistic side, revitalised by my love of travel and my studies, urged me to comply with the Murkholmer's suggestion. For how could I write a book about Puppetism – how could I rediscover the artist in myself – if I passed up

417

such a pioneering artistic innovation because of some irrational phobia? How could I explain that to Inazia, who had probably moved heaven and earth to obtain me this unique opportunity?

'Very well,' I said resolutely. 'I'll come.'

The Murkholmer looked relieved. 'Let's go!' he called to the others and we made for the edge of the shaft.

The Labyrinth
of Dreaming Books

It may sound odd, but the Pfistomel Shaft reminded me of Ojahnn Golgo van Fontheweg's birthplace. On one of my travels, when I set out to visit that historic place of pilgrimage dear to lovers of classical Zamonian literature, it turned out to have burned down a short while before, with the result that all I found there was a deserted, blackened site, a few crumbling walls and a bronze plaque. I then spent an interesting hour conjuring the house out of thin air and imagining what it might have looked like when little Golgo ran up and down the stairs or wrote his earliest poems. I regarded it as a lesson on the meaning of transience. How can any writer speculate on eternal fame if even the birthplaces of our greatest classical writers aren't fireproof?

Now, as I stared into the yawning pit, the biggest shaft in Bookholm, down which our bizarre little party would descend into the catacombs and the Invisible Theatre, I cudgelled my powers of imagination once more. I tried to picture how I had once on this very spot, where now there was only an enormous hole, accompanied Pfistomel Smyke down his cellar steps and into the Labyrinth; and how, many days and adventures later, I had found my way out again with the Shadow King, whose friendship I had sadly lost when he set fire to himself in Smyke's laboratory. But I found it impossible. Instead, I started to weep like a little child! Big tears trickled down my ageing cheeks. I tried to convince myself it was just nerves, but it wasn't: I was mourning the passage of time, which runs away from us all, leaving nothing behind but fading mental images.

Yet I had every reason to be clear-headed and dry-eyed! To describe the rickety wooden steps leading down the side of the shaft as 'makeshift' was a disgraceful understatement of their condition. As for 'safe', only the Biblionauts who had constructed them could have thought them that, but then *they* were used to fighting beetles the size of cats and venomous albino rats, and they described their medieval armour as 'working clothes'. The Biblionaut who preceded us down the timber framework didn't have to steel himself to progress from step to step, whereas for me every step was an effort of the will! Nor did the fact that it was a sunlit morning, when everything was clearly visible, help to mitigate my acrophobia. I would probably have preferred to go down there by night, when I would have been unable to see every detail of the abyss below us as clearly as I could in daylight. The shaft, which was inversely conical in shape, tapered sharply towards the bottom and was at least 300 feet deep. Its walls, being jet-black all over, effectively heightened the feeling that I was looking down into an all-consuming void, a rotating maelstrom. Smaller shafts branched off it here and there, and the ash-grey scrub sprouting from their entrances was a measure of how little work had been done over the years to this shaft in the midst of a contaminated no-man's-land. There were no wooden platforms or reinforcements, no hand rails or stable ironwork steps, and no giggling tourists descending with miner's lamps, picnic baskets and safety ropes. There was nothing here but the Biblionauts' hastily constructed steps, which certainly weren't up to tourist standards. The alarming thing about this crude wooden structure was not so much its lack of stability as the fact that, when looking down, one could see between the steps as if through the ribcage of a skeleton. Birds flew past us, screeching derisively. I made several attempts to ask how many steps there were, but the gusts of wind that swirled around the shaft like playful dust devils tore the question from my lips every time and hurled it into the air. They also kept shaking our flight of steps, which creaked and groaned like an old, timber-framed roof in a storm.

For all these reasons, I was positively delighted when we finally – I myself could hardly believe it – entered the catacombs through a disappointingly small entrance in the wall. Perhaps I was simply relieved to be back on terra firma, but I had also, more or less willingly, set foot in the *Labyrinth of Dreaming Books*! My exhilaration was undiminished even when the loathsome dwarf, who was walking ahead of me, turned round with a grin and said mockingly, 'Well, Fatso, still wetting your knickers?'

Reluctant though I was to admit it to myself, the Murkholmer had actually been right: I did feel proud of my own courage. My mood was almost euphoric. I had looked a long-standing fear in the face. I had returned to the catacombs and survived, by heaven! I had neither had a heart attack nor lost my reason. Whether or not this meant that I had genuinely overcome my fear was another matter, but at least I had taken the plunge!

But it was only a fire-blackened tunnel we had traversed so far, dark and deserted as a chimney flue. There were no ancient libraries here, no worm-eaten shelves or disintegrating books, nor was there anything else that might have reminded me of my former journey into Netherworld. There was nothing here at all. The interior of a blast furnace would probably have looked much the same.

The Biblionaut beckoned to us without a word and we followed him into the next tunnel that branched off. Here we left the last of the daylight behind us, which rather dampened my initial euphoria, but our Murkholmian tourist guide lit his oil lamp and spoke a few soothing words that were doubtless directed mainly at me. 'We're now in what is probably the safest part of the catacombs,' he said. 'The exit is only a few yards off and these tunnels were completely decontaminated by the ferocious fires that raged through them. There are neither plants nor animals here – not even any microscopic life forms. It's almost like walking through the cannula of a sterilised hypodermic syringe. The walls are composed of rock-hard coal yards thick and completely stable. Not even the entrances to the most-frequented Bookholm Shafts meet this safety standard. Please follow me, we'll soon be there.'

So saying, he took over the lead and shepherded us along some more low, narrow passages that displayed no noticeable difference from their predecessors. At last he came to a halt halfway along one of these dark tunnels and said, 'We've come here because we need to prevent any daylight from reaching us. That is the Invisible Theatre's most important prerequisite. And now, we should like you all to gain an impression of what it's like to be in the catacombs without any form of artificial lighting.'

Before I had really grasped his meaning, he extinguished his oil lamp and plunged us in darkness.

Utter darkness, dear friends!

It was darkness such as I hadn't experienced since my first sojourn in the catacombs. Even when you go to bed and blow out the candle, you're accustomed to seeing at least a hint of reflected light from somewhere, aren't you? The glow of a street light or moonlight coming through a crack in the curtains. A sliver of light from under a door. Something you can *see*.

But there was nothing here but absolute darkness.

'Hee-hee!' the dwarf cackled inanely, but there was a hint of fear even in that little laugh. Everyone is afraid of the dark. Why? Because it's a reminder of death.

The Murkholmer's voice rang out in the gloom, this time with greater solemnity. 'Esteemed members of the audience, I bid you welcome to the Invisible Theatre on behalf of Maestro Corodiak. We wish you all an entertaining time.'

I was speechless at his effrontery, but I had to admit that Maestro Corodiak clearly had a sense of humour. It was indeed a bold move to confront the audience with total darkness – and thus with what he himself saw – right at the start of the performance! It was a clever intro, because things could only get better thereafter. Even the faintest glimmer of light would come as a relief.

But nothing of the kind happened. No ray of light, no flaring match. No candle flame. The darkness persisted, as did the graveyard hush. Even the cheeky dwarf remained silent. Nobody cleared his throat, nobody coughed, nobody shuffled his feet. Not even a creak from the Biblionaut's armour could be heard. We remained like that for a considerable time, which soon struck me as inordinately long.

I found it surprising, even rather amusing, that I seemed to lose patience more quickly in the dark than in the light. *That's enough!* I thought. This wasn't such a good idea after all! But I would sooner have bitten off my tongue than be the first to break the silence, because I fully realised that a contest had long been in progress: a silent contest between the dwarf, the bearded Druid and myself to see which of us would be the first to give way to his fear and beg for a light or lose his nerve in some other way. That alone could explain why my two companions were preserving such a stubborn silence and that alone was why I was doing so too. Indeed, I even strove not to make any loud noises. In an ordinary theatre I would probably have booed a theatrical artifice of this kind, but there was more at stake here. I wanted to teach the disrespectful dwarf which of us three was a veteran of the catacombs. Puerile and pig-headed of me though it was, I was determined to hold out. I had endured worse things in the Labyrinth of Dreaming Books than a bit of Invisible Theatre in the dark and I knew what a nerve-fraying effect on the mind these subterranean conditions could exert – in the case of a novice, after a very short time. I felt convinced that the little runt would be the first of us to fly into a panic, because I credited the taciturn Druid with more phlegm.

But I'm bound to admit, dear friends, that defiance failed to dispel my own fears. Far from it. There's nothing relaxing about standing around in the catacombs in total darkness, especially when you have personal experience of the perils lurking there.

Sterilised or not, this tunnel was part of a cave system that teemed with all kinds of dangerous, aggressive and poisonous or otherwise menacing organisms. To that extent, my veteran's status might not be the trump card I'd originally thought. It was, above all, the silence I felt in a positively palpable way, like a damp mist creeping into my ears. I'd experienced the ghostly hush of the catacombs before, but it had been of a different nature. Then, sounds could clearly be heard because I was close beneath Bookholm, whose muffled acoustic emanations had come to my ears, but here there was no inhabited city above us any more, just a deserted no-man's-land.

The mist creeping into my ears became steadily more intrusive – it positively pulsated in my auditory canals. It wasn't mist, though, but my own blood pumped by my ever more anxiously beating heart. I concentrated on it so hard that I eventually started to hear noises in the dark that couldn't exist. I heard paper rustle as if the pages of a book were being hurriedly turned, although, as far as I could recall, there were no books or documents in this tunnel. I heard a faint whistle, a scraping sound, then the heavy breathing of some very big creature. Now I even heard ponderous footsteps! They were approaching me, slinking around me. Indeed, I thought I even felt something leaning over my shoulder. Whispering in my ear!

It was pure imagination, of course – my overwrought nerves were to blame. But my heartbeat steadily accelerated and I started to sweat profusely. What had the Uggly told me? *It doesn't matter what the Invisible Theatre shows onstage. What matters far more is what it does inside your head.* For the first time, I truly grasped what she'd meant.

The Shadow King has returned – that sentence in the enduringly mysterious letter that had lured me into making this trip came back to me and began, fuelled by my morbid imagination, to take on a life of its own. I almost thought I could hear the Shadow King's rustling laughter! It was at once terrifying and magnificent. What was happening here resembled what I had experienced at the Puppetocircus Maximus, but in a highly concentrated and far purer form: the Shadow King's figure was taking shape in my mind's eye. Nothing more was necessary. No scenery, no theatrical tricks, no additional puppets, no music, no scent organ; just my own creative imagination, which was being stimulated in a way I hadn't experienced for a long time. I couldn't see him properly yet, but I could already hear him. And feel him! So this was Invisible Theatre: seeing the catacombs through Corodiak's dead eyes. I was simultaneously perturbed and delighted, and I wanted to make myself heard – to applaud and express my approval – for I had long forgotten about the stupid contest. But I found it impossible to move my hands. My body was paralysed, whereas my brain was positively consumed with ecstasy. Lighting up before my mind's eye were things I had never seen before. Events I had never witnessed. Subterranean places I had never visited. Persons and creatures completely unfamiliar to me. And all these alternated wildly with the whirling letters and billowing sentences that flooded my brain. I looked along endless passages and tunnels filled with a pulsating glow. I sank into bottomless pits almost weightlessly, as if I were myself a puppet lowered on strings. I saw a lofty hall of dark grey granite with torrents of incandescent lava thundering into it, a black river filled with decaying books that swirled, gurgling, into an abyss. And I myself was drifting down that river on a raft! Again and again I saw Biblionauts in their terrifying masks and armour. One of them, who wore a bronze helmet in the shape of a boar's head, appeared to me several times. I saw the Biblionaut in the fencing mask. An avenue of books the size of houses. I saw Booklings! Whole hordes of them, more than had appeared onstage at the Puppetocircus Maximus and in all shapes and colours. A creature as white as milk with four spindly legs and a frightful head resembling the a bird's skull. What did these images want with me?

But the visions answered no questions, they only posed riddles and filled my brain unceasingly. A power that seemed at once familiar and strange to me, and which I'd thought for years I had lost like my own childhood, was whirling those images around in my brain to such an extent that I thought I was losing my mind, or at least my balance. Where did I know that feeling from? To complete my bewilderment, I now heard the voice of the Shadow King! I heard it as close and clearly and truly as if he were standing beside me in the flesh and whispering in my ear. *'Yes, you can sense it, the Orm!'* he said in his dark, rustling voice. *'These are the moments when ideas for whole novels rain down on you in seconds. It can rip the brain from your head and reinsert it the other way round! Can you sense it, the Orm?'*

I knew those words, for he had said them to me once before, a long time ago. In my nonsensical fear, I had failed to understand that it was the Orm that was once more surging through me at last! It was the themes, figures and scenes of a whole book that were raining down on me! It was a novel that was taking shape in my head!

And then, quite suddenly, it was over. The fear, the sounds and images, the intoxication of the Orm – all left me in a flash and darkness returned. I noticed only now that I was bathed in sweat and breathing as heavily as if I were recovering from some great physical exertion.

It was some time before my heart slowed down a little. I listened. Had all these things really just happened? If so, why were the others so quiet? Had they undergone the same experience? Or something similar? Or nothing at all? I couldn't imagine why the gabby dwarf was keeping his mouth shut for so long. Hard as I tried, I couldn't even hear anyone breathing.

'Hello?' I called timidly.

No answer.

'Hello?' I whispered again.

Enough of this! After all, I had everything I needed with me. Why else had I been carrying it around the whole time? I felt in my cloak and found a candle and a box of matches. Quickly, I struck a match and lit the candle. There! Then I held it up.

I wasn't overly surprised to find myself alone. The Murkholmer, the dwarf, the Biblionaut, the bearded Druid – all had disappeared. I was more concerned to know how to behave in this situation without seeming ridiculous, for I felt quite sure that this was a test and that the others were watching me. At last I thought of Maestro Corodiak's invitation.

Wait until you're at the performance. Will you promise a blind person that? Corodiak had asked me. *It's very important, because it'll greatly enhance the pleasure you derive from the Invisible Theatre!*

I had kept my promise, but now the time had come to decipher his message – if there was one. I felt in my cloak again. And then, dear brothers and sisters in spirit, when I eventually found the card, I was suddenly overcome with the greatest unease. With a trembling paw I held the little card over the dancing candle flame until the pale yellow secret writing appeared. There was only one sentence on the invitation: It read:

This is where the story begins.

Translator's Postscript

And here my translation ends. Only my translation, though, because Yarnspinner's story in the Labyrinth of Dreaming Books naturally continues.

Much to my regret, I have been compelled to divide the novel into two books because of its length and complexity. This is mainly to do with the massive cuts I have once more had to make – an almost invariable task in the case of Yarnspinner's often absurdly long-winded prose works. In the present volume this applied principally to the *Notes on Puppetism*, which I had to abridge by all of 400 pages, or the book would have been impossible to read with any pleasure.

In the second part, on which I am currently hard at work, the situation is even worse. This embodies a pseudoscientific text which Yarnspinner entitled *The Secret Life of the Booklings* and runs to 700 pages. Unreadable! Reducing this colossal Yarnspinnerish divagation to a tolerable length – without falsifying the book – is costing me considerably more time and effort than I had anticipated. At this point I should immodestly like to draw attention to my dual function as translator and illustrator, which entails an expenditure of effort that is often underestimated.

When I realised that the novel, were it to appear in a single volume, would not be ready by the contractual deadline, I had no choice but to warn the publisher. His reaction was unexpectedly fierce – indeed, positively unsympathetic – and he threatened me with legal proceedings. I had not only to admit that my assessment of the project had been at fault, but to come up with an alternative solution.

Hence my idea of making a virtue of necessity and turning one book into two. This would kill two birds with one stone: for one thing, I would have the requisite time in which to produce a conscientious translation of the second part (and illustrate it!); for another, readers would have the pleasure of reading a new Zamonia novel by Yarnspinner as soon as ever possible.

I am aware that my translation breaks off at a point at which my readers would, I believe, have liked to read on. But isn't this better than if they were glad they had finished the book? Granted, they are temporarily left with a series of burning and unanswered questions. Can Yarnspinner once more escape unaided from the Labyrinth, or is he already in too far? What is the Invisible Theatre all about? Is our hero merely the victim of a harmless practical joke, or are quite different forces and intentions at work behind the scenes? Why did Corodiak give him that card? Is the blind Puppetist playing him false? Where has the Uggly got to and what is her role in the whole affair? Last but not least, what is the significance of Yarnspinner's visions of Biblionauts, Booklings and unfamiliar scenes, persons and creatures during his visitation by the Orm? Were they a preview of what awaits him in the Labyrinth, or just a literary delirium?

If the answers to these questions are taking somewhat longer than I originally anticipated, I apologise. The blame is all mine, not Optimus Yarnspinner's. I should therefore like at this point to go down on my knees, metaphorically speaking, and solicit a little patience. All I can do in the interim is to assure my gentle readers that their patience will be rewarded. For, as Yarnspinner has already promised, the true story really begins here. Everything hitherto has been just a prelude.

Walter Moers